Ecliptic Kingdoms
Wild Youth

Marianne Clayton

ISBN: 9781099380136

DEDICATION

To Andrew James M. Wherever you are in the universe now, I'll find you.

CONTENTS

ACKNOWLEDGMENTS

This book would never have been written without the friendship, love and support of Christian P. and Chris G., as well as the inspiration, advice and feedback of Susanne D.

CHAPTER ONE
"THE SWORD AND THE STONER"

The walls around the city were high, made of long wooden planks, and existed primarily to keep the wild things of the forest - including forest folk - out. Tomorrow, however, was the Reaper's Cotillion, a day for celebrating (and selling) the annual harvest's bounty. To that end, outsiders, even forest folk, were allowed within the city's gates for the day, providing they had a ticket.

A large clearing between the forest line and the city wall was scattered with bonfires and a few tents, illuminated well by seven bright moons. By mid-morning, one more moon would peak around the horizon. The tiny Reaper was mythologized as the Lord of Death. It was he who watched over the crops, and it was said to be his scythe that felled the crops, although there were quite a few farmers in attendance whose calloused hands and aching backs would attest otherwise.

A long line of tourists and forest folk stretched out from the wall's gate, snaking all the way to the edge of the gargantuan trees. Most were dressed in some sort of costume, as the festival tradition called for. "How many in your party?" muttered a disinterested young soldier as he verified the tickets of those in the queue. "That's five counting the baby, then? Very well, move along."

The soldier's interest suddenly piqued as he came upon the last occupant of the line, a young blonde woman whose stunning gown and mask resembled a dragon, with shiny, green sequins mimicking scales. "Well, aren't you a pretty sight?" the soldier asked. “What’s your name, Little Miss?”

The young woman gave a coy smile and asked in return, “Are you flirting with me?”

“I wouldn’t pass on the opportunity, love,” the soldier replied. “But I do need your name to verify your ticket.”

“Darra,” the young woman named herself, as she stroked the soldier’s cheek with a gloved hand. The soldier stiffened and reddened with arousal. “But that’s the problem, you see,” she continued. “I haven’t exactly got a ticket.”

The soldier smiled and admired Darra’s masked face for just a moment longer, then removed her hand from his cheek. “Sorry, love, but I can’t let you in without a ticket.” Darra leaned in closer and placed her hand on the soldier’s chest.

“But it’s already so late,” she purred. “No one will notice.”

“I - I could get whipped, or even stripped of my rank,” the soldier said. “I’m sorry.”

“Perhaps a stripping and a whipping are exactly what you need,” Darra said. “Is there nothing I could do to harden your resolve?” she asked, dropping her hand from his chest to grasp his thigh. The soldier gasped and grabbed Darra by the shoulders. He moved in to kiss her, but she held a single finger up to his lips to stop him.

“Not here, with all those eyes on us,” she said, indicating a group of soldiers near the gates. “My sister’s waiting in the forest,” Darra said, inclining her head toward the tree line and the dark of the forest beyond. She pulled away from the soldier playfully and beckoned him to follow her. “Come, soldier boy,” she teased. “We’ll show you our secret charms in the woods, before you... show us your wood.”

The soldier licked his lips and moaned softly as Darra whirled away and made for the trees. “Ooh, you talk like a dirty poem,” he groaned, before rushing after her. He fought his way through the thick forest growth, following the sounds of her ahead of him. “Dragon girl, where’d you go?” he asked in an excited whisper. He peered through a dense weave of branches and found Darra in a small clearing, lit by a tiny lantern. The soldier drew his sword and hacked his way through the branches, stepping into the clearing with a palpable machismo. “There you are, Little Miss,” he said cockily.

"Here I am," Darra answered invitingly. A tall, slim figure in a mask and shawl resembling a lion appeared out of the darkness, stepping between Darra and the soldier.

"This is the sister, then?" the soldier asked. The lion looked away demurely, smiled at Darra, and then swung around and punched the soldier, who collapsed to his knees in a daze. "Your s-sister's mean," the stunned soldier stuttered. The lion kicked the soldier in the head with a heavy boot, and the young man collapsed into unconsciousness.

"What did you do that for?" Darra asked. The lion removed his mask, revealing a scowl on his fine-featured, young-looking face, brows furrowed above brown, almond-shaped eyes, and the pointed ears that would betray him as half-elven to anyone who glimpsed them.

"Not sister – father. Aleksey, pleased to meet you," he greeted the unconscious man. "And I'm not mean. I am simply vigilant." Darra grabbed Aleksey by the shoulders and spun him around to face her.

"Dad!" Darra almost yelled, "I said, why'd you do that?"

Aleksey put his hands on her shoulders. "Sweetie, that was part of the plan," he said soothingly before he stooped to rifle through the soldier's pockets, finally bringing out a set of keys. He jingled them triumphantly at Darra. "Lure a soldier back here, steal his key to the servant's passage, sneak into the city. Remember?"

"You know what I mean," Darra said impatiently. "He was down! We could've just tied him up."

"He had his sword drawn, honey," the half-elf said defensively. "And anyway, I saw the way he was pawing at you back there. I couldn't risk it."

"His 'pawing at me' was also part of the plan, remember?" Darra asked.

"Well... He didn't have to enjoy it so much," Aleksey said.

"See, this is exactly why I don't have a boyfriend!" Darra said. "You always overreact whenever a boy pays me any attention!" Aleksey drew a rope from underneath his shawl and moved to tie the soldier's hands.

"Don't have a boyfriend?" Aleksey repeated without looking up at his daughter. "What are you talking about, honey? He's in the royal guard. He's the enemy." The soldier coughed, spit up a little blood, and groaned as he began to regain consciousness. "Aha, there! See? He's fine!" Aleksey continued. "And maybe I wouldn't 'overreact' so often if you were a little more obedient."

Darra moved in and pushed her father out of the way, then began tying the knots on the soldier's bonds herself. She cocked an eyebrow at her father and said, "I followed your every instruction!"

"Are you sure about that, my little lamb?" Aleksey asked. "Because I recall stating very clearly that the gown you are currently wearing is far too revealing for a girl of fifteen!"

Suddenly seeming very lucid, the soldier squeaked, "Fifteen!?"

Darra sighed and reached into her pocket. She pulled out a handkerchief and stuffed the soldier's mouth with it. Ignoring his protests, she said meekly, "Sixteen by next summer..." The soldier rolled his eyes. Darra shrugged an apology and then spun around to face her father. "And that's something you ought to keep in mind!" she said. "At sixteen, children are considered adults in half the kingdoms, free to leave their parents if they wish!"

"Then I suppose I'll have to make sure we don't travel through any of those places, now, won't I?" Aleksey responded with a wicked, patronizing sneer. Darra shook her fists in the air in frustration and stormed off. "Darra, honey, wait!" her father yelled after her. "I didn't mean—" he started, but she had already disappeared into the forest. Aleksey picked up the soldier's sword and glared down at the man's swollen, bloody face. "Well, thank you very much for that nonsense!" he spat at the bound and gagged man. "I swear, teenagers! Am I right?" Aleksey waved away a bewildered reaction from the soldier and rushed after Darra, hurling the man's sword into the darkness as he went.

Inside the city walls, a mass of people milled about frenetically. They played games of chance and shopped and ate ferociously, and they enjoyed a variety of entertainments. From a fire-eater to a dance troupe to a pair of brown dogs doing tricks for treats, each had the crowd cheering, laughing and drinking in the shady streets. Under cover of the many large verandas or shaded by stylish parasols, they avoided the too-bright sun at all costs, even in their current revelry. So when a witchy old forest woman wandered into the blazing sunlight with no protection, people took notice of her.

"Eons ago, Ona, the earth goddess, married Arol, the sun god," the old woman began, as a small crowd started to form around her. "Ona, a dutiful wife, bore her husband dozens of children, the many-sided moons. But Arol was not so faithful. He soon took other lovers. Out of jealousy, Ona drifted as close to Arol as she dared. Arol's fiery passion brought new life to Ona. The forests and beasts of Ona thrived, even as her people suffered. New cities were built in the cool shadows of Ona's beloved children. The twelve kingdoms of man found salvation in math, science, and cold calculations. But the cities were not safe haven for all. Ona's magic was shunned. Those who held to the ways of magic were driven from the very cities they had helped to build, along with the poorest citizens. The magical races of Ona welcomed those forsaken by the cities. But the power-mad rulers of the kingdoms of man were determined to destroy all traces of Ona's magic. For decades, brutal wars raged in the forests surrounding the kingdoms of man. But eventually, the magical races withdrew to build their own kingdoms, until nothing remained in the forests but the beasts, and the Tribes of the Tree People."

A couple and their young son glared at the old woman from behind. The husband said, "We ought to close the city to these lunatics, not open the gates wide to any vagabond who manages to beg enough for a ticket to Cotillion."

"I swear, they get louder and dirtier by the year!" his wife replied.

"Now the heavens declare another great change is coming to Ona!" the witchy woman continued. The couple's son picked up a rock and hurled it at the old woman's back. She spun around and caught the stone in her hand. Intoning a few syllables, her eyes glowed magenta, and she crushed the rock to dust in her fist. "Such shall be the fate of the kingdoms of man, should they not heed nature's warning," the old woman said.

The couple recoiled in fear as their son let out a pitiful shriek. His mother screamed, "Call the constable! She's a witch!" The crowd around the old woman quickly scattered. A moment later a citizen rounded a corner with a few soldiers in tow and pointed at the old woman. She merely smiled as the soldiers drew their swords.

Darra and her father sat across from each other in a shadowy booth inside *Eliza Dell's*. The inn and tavern was bustling even more than usual today, as the patroness of the establishment herself was due to take the stage any moment. Aleksey's ears were hidden by his thick black hair, which he wore longer on top for just this purpose. A serving girl brought them a plate of seasoned, roasted potatoes, along with bread, two kinds of cheese and two glasses of blended fruit juice. Aleksey thanked her profusely and tipped her generously. He flinched slightly when a trio of soldiers sauntered in, but he relaxed as soon as they removed their sword belts and settled in to watch the show.

Suddenly a wild cheer went up from the crowd, as Eliza Dell and her band took center stage. Eliza stationed herself between a harpsichord and a piano, while her band took up their instruments alongside of her. The first song had a driving rhythm and, like most of Eliza's works, a seemingly otherworldly composition. The breathtaking performance left Aleksey and most of the audience transfixed. Darra saw the glossy look wash over her father's face and rolled her eyes. "It's a ridiculous double-standard, you know," she said.

"What's that, dear?" Aleksey asked without breaking his concentration from Eliza.

"We hardly ever stay in one place long enough for me to make any friends, let alone a boyfriend," Darra continued.

"Darra, you have friends. And frankly, you're far too young for–"

"And yet, somehow, we find ourselves in one of Eliza Dell's taverns a half dozen times a year, on the very nights when Eliza herself is performing," Darra said.

"I enjoy her music," Aleksey said defensively.

"You enjoy all of her, especially her ample bosom."

"There's no need to be crude, honey," Aleksey said, but he was smiling. "Eliza and I are old friends."

"You are definitely old, Dad," Darra said with her sweetest smile. "But if you think I haven't figured out what's going on between you two, you're also senile."

Aleksey chortled like the schoolboy his elven youthfulness made him resemble, then asked, "What gave us away?"

"You mean besides the fact that you sneak off for hours alone together every chance you get, then return reeking of her perfume?" Darra asked.

"Ah, lilac, lavender, peach blossoms," Aleksey sighed, then wafted the air toward his face, as if inhaling the scent from memory.

"It's not fair!" Darra said. "You get to live a full life: travel, adventure, romance."

"You've seen every major city in the kingdoms," Aleksey replied.

"From tavern windows and the balconies of rented rooms!" Darra countered. "I get stuck being the bait and doing the laundry and keeping your meals warm, but I'm old enough to be of real help to you now!"

"My work is dangerous," Aleksey said. "I couldn't live with myself if you got hurt."

"But I've been training harder than ever!" Darra said. "I know how to fight, and you said yourself that I'm the best you've ever seen with a crossbow."

Aleksey locked eyes with his daughter for a tense second. "Fine," Aleksey capitulated. "After I finish my work here, you can—"

"No," Darra interrupted again. "Not after. I want to come with you tonight."

"Tonight's heist is the biggest job I've taken in years! This map is supposed to show the way to a literal hoard of treasure. Which means more security, more soldiers, more danger—"

"And all the more reason to let me help you!"

"I'm sorry, sweetie, but I just can't risk it," Aleksey said. "When you're older, you'll understand."

Darra shoved her drink away and stood up indignantly. "When I'm older! That's all I ever hear from you. But I am older, Dad! I'm not like you. I won't look twenty when I'm nearly eighty!"

"Darra, lower your voice!" Aleksey commanded with a harsh whisper.

"You'll see me turn into an old maid before you let me have any freedom - or any fun!" Darra said before walking away in a huff. Aleksey sighed, took a long swig of his drink, and resumed ogling Eliza.

After Eliza bowed and left the stage, Aleksey met her in her dressing room. Their affectionate embrace was followed by several minutes of kissing and groping each other's excited bodies. Aleksey pulled away slightly, and Eliza pouted playfully at the disconnection. "What's wrong, lover?" she asked in her thick, throaty, exotic accent. "Have you grown tired of me after all these years?"

"Impossible!" Aleksey assured her. "It's just... Darra. She's mad at me. She says I'm too protective, too coddling. She wants to start dating."

Eliza merely shrugged ambiguously in response.

"What?" Aleksey asked. "You agree with her?"

"She's not a child anymore, Leks. Sweet candies and pretty dolls won't satisfy a woman's needs."

"Are you saying I should just let her strut around with whatever lecherous men catch her attention?" Aleksey asked incredulously.

"I'm saying you should try to see it from her side," Eliza said. "I was only a little older than Darra when I began travelling the kingdoms with my band. And I was no stranger to lecherous men, yourself chief among them."

"It was a different time. You grew up fast," Aleksey said.

"Everyone grows up fast in the eyes of a man who never ages!" Eliza said. Her statement was underscored by the image of the two of them together in the mirror; she was thirty years his junior, but she looked thirty years older. "My point is I learned what I wanted out of life by experiencing it. Darra's never had that chance."

"It's... complicated. You know the circumstances of her birth," Aleksey said.

"Is that what you're really worried about?" Eliza asked. "You always said you'd tell her the truth when she came of age."

"Yes," Aleksey said. "But I meant *old* age."

"Aleksey... Maybe it's time you—"

"Time!" Aleksey cut her off. "By the many moons, I'm late! Sorry, love, but we'll have to pick this up later. I've another lady waiting for me, and she is much more frightening and much less forgiving than you." Aleksey kissed Eliza goodbye and rushed off. Eliza sighed, her disappointment evident as she watched him disappear out the door.

Meanwhile, inside an imposing, well-guarded statehouse in the city center, Ramla, the witchy woman, sat with her arms folded on the floor of her cell, her head down. Two soldiers stood guard outside.

Seeming bored, one soldier said, "She don't do much, huh? For a witch, I mean. Just sits there."

"What'd you think she'd do?" his companion asked. "Pull a rabbit from between her legs?"

"You just hear horror stories about witches, is all," the first soldier replied.

The soldier banged his sword against the bars of Ramla's cell and shouted, "Hey, witch! Show us some of that magic you gypsies is famous for!" Ramla simply ignored him. Growing impatient, he banged his sword on the bars a second time. "Hey! I said, show us a trick!" he yelled. Ramla lifted her head and met the soldier's gaze coolly. "You know, my great uncle was killed by a tree gypsy during the Forest Wars," the soldier said with a note of menace in his voice. "He bled out for days," he continued, as he waved his sword at Ramla threateningly. "It's only fair I should spill a little witch blood in his honor, now, isn't it?" He drew a ring of keys from his belt and flipped through them until he found the key to the cell. The soldier put the key up to the lock, but before he could open it, a knife appeared at his throat.

Holding the knife and standing directly behind him was a gruff, battle-worn warrior who spoke stiffly into the soldier's ear. "Tell me, did I give you the order to spill the witch's blood, or to see to her confinement?"

"Commandant Burke!" the soldier said, pounding his fist over his heart in the compulsory salute. "I–I'm sorry, sir, I–" the soldier stammered.

"I asked you a simple question," Commandant Burke said, pressing the knife against the flesh of the soldier's neck for emphasis. "Please answer it directly. What were your orders?" the older man asked.

"To - to see to the witch's confinement, sir. I'm sorry, sir," the soldier said.

"Don't be sorry," the commandant said. "Be obedient, or you'll be banging on these bars from the other side!" The commandant removed his knife and released the soldier. Burke then turned to the second guard, who had been cowering quietly in the corner ever since he entered the hall. "And you! See that all of my orders are carried out precisely, or you'll be in there with him."

"Yes, sir!" the second soldier said without hesitation. As the commandant turned to leave, both soldiers again saluted the man they so clearly feared.

Commandant Burke made his way through the halls of the statehouse to a meeting chamber and entered. The room was scattered with noblemen and court advisors, many of whom clustered around Prince Trosclair DuVerres, a composed, stately, effeminate teen with curly, bright red and golden blonde hair that everyone said resembled fire. Burke made his way to the young prince.

"My apologies, Prince DuVerres," the commandant began. "But the discipline of the soldiers stationed in these border cities is... questionable."

"Your apology is appreciated, but unnecessary, Commandant Burke," Prince Trosclair said. "We have the utmost faith in your ability to maintain order in the ranks." Suddenly dropping his formal tone, Trosclair asked excitedly, "Were you seeing to the witch?"

"Yes, Your Grace," Commandant Burke answered. "She was promoting prophecies in the city square. Some witnesses even claimed they saw her working some sort of magic."

Milian, a slight, nerdy advisor, stepped forward meekly. "Has Duke DuVerres been informed of the witch's crimes?" he asked. "As Regent, he will wish to render his verdict immediately, so that she may be executed before the festivities begin tomorrow."

"Absolutely!" an older nobleman said. "I would hear no end of complaints from my wife, should the smoke from the witch's pyre linger on one of her best gowns."

"Unfortunately, that particular tragedy may be unavoidable," Trosclair said sympathetically. "Our uncle is unable to attend to his duties as regent at the present time, as he is currently occupied with... other affairs."

At that very moment, Duke DuVerres was indeed indisposed; more specifically, he was gagged and bound to a bed in the statehouse's royal suites. A young woman, scantily clad in thigh-high black leather boots and a harness, straddled him. She slapped a small riding crop against her palm, and the duke shuddered with desire.

Aleksey arrived at the statehouse through the back alleys of the city, which were largely empty, save for a scattered handful of vagrant alcoholics. He walked in a wide circle around the building, watching the guards to learn their routine. When he finally made his first move, the half-elf merely removed the reins from a horse and smacked it on its rump. The animal bolted, galloping directly past a set of statehouse guards. One stupefied soldier asked, "Is that one of ours?" As the men rushed after the loose animal, Aleksey sprinted to the statehouse wall and swung a rope with a grappling hook up into a third story window ledge. He pulled back the slack of the line slowly, until it was secure enough to hold his weight, and began expertly scaling the wall. He crawled through the window and made his way down the corridors toward the tiny holding cells with the ease of someone who had studied the buildings layout all the night before. He peeked around a corner and saw the guards outside Ramla's cell.

Reaching into a pouch on his belt, he pulled out a cone of incense. Aleksey lifted a candle from a nearby sconce and lit the cone, covering his mouth with his sleeve, and placed it on the floor before backing away. The smoke drifted toward the soldiers, who unknowingly inhaled it. Within a minute, the soldiers grew visibly tired, eventually slouching against the wall and onto the floor, deep in sleep. Aleksey approached a sleeping soldier and pulled his keys from his belt. He unlocked Ramla's cell and swung the door wide open.

"You're late," she said without a trace of humor or forgiveness.

"You're surly," Aleksey replied. "Even more so than usual, Ramla - especially since I'm here to rescue you. Did you find out where they're keeping this wondrous map?"

Ramla pointed one bony finger down a hallway. "One floor down," she said. "The second door on the left leads to a library."

"You're sure it's in there?" Aleksey asked.

"Four guards were posted outside the door when they led

me through the halls," she said. "Do you believe the good Duke DuVerres places such a high value on his fairy tales?"

"Not likely," Aleksey said. "I heard he only learned to read well enough to gloat when he recognizes his own name. Wait, did you say four guards?" Aleksey asked, looking down the hallway nervously. When he got no reply, he turned to find Ramla had vanished. "Tree gypsies!" he said under his breath.

Aleksey made his way down to the library and was pleased to find only two guards outside the door. "Tree folk are not known for their math skills," he whispered to himself. He drew out another cone of incense, and within minutes he was stepping over the sleeping guards to enter the library. Aleksey gasped in shock as he saw a ridiculously long, broad sword with a golden, bejeweled hilt and ornate carvings sitting on display on a rack on a table. He stepped forward and lifted the sword with both hands reverently, feeling the heft of the weapon. "Well, this is better than any map!" he said. "And less trouble to procure than I was told it would be."

Suddenly a chain flew around the half-elf's throat from behind. He was dragged backwards, off his feet. Dropping the sword, he sputtered and choked as he struggled to breathe. Aleksey's fingers clawed at the chain, but he was unable to pull it loose from the grip of the particularly muscular soldier holding it.

Commandant Burke strode in haughtily, trailed by another young soldier. "Ennio," The commandant said, nodding his head toward the sword and then the table. The young soldier immediately retrieved the weapon and placed it back on its display rack.

Aleksey was now fighting to remain conscious. The muscular soldier released the chain just enough to allow Aleksey one sharp intake of air, and then he tightened it once more, as Commandant Burke removed a single gauntlet. Burke punched Aleksey several times, until Aleksey spit up a smatter of bloody saliva.

"Now, then," the commandant began. "I suppose I don't have to ask you why you're here. Clearly, you came to steal the DragonSword. But I do have some other questions for you, and if you value what remains of your pretty young face, boy, you'll satisfy me with your answers. We took great pains to make sure no one knew in advance that the royal entourage would even be at this backwater border city's little Cotillion, let alone that our real presence here was related to that artifact. So my first question is, how did you even know about the sword?"

Aleksey answered Burke's piercing gaze with a bloody smirk. "A little fairy told me. What do you want with a DragonSword?"

Burke smacked Aleksey in the face with his gauntleted hand. Aleksey began chuckling. "I assume that means I... failed to satisfy you?"

Burke smiled evilly, and then struck Aleksey twice more. "I will not be laughed at, boy!" the old man growled. "If the loss of your pretty face is not of consequence to you, perhaps cutting off your balls would be?"

Seemingly frightened, Aleksey squeaked out, "Y-you wanna... cut off my balls? That's - that's so—" Aleksey dropped his frightened façade and said, "Queer. Like fully, fully queer. I mean, you keep saying how pretty my face is, and now you're getting all excited talking about my, uh, "jewel pouch," as the kids are calling it these days." Commandant Burke kneed Aleksey in the stomach and then hammered down on his back with an elbow. Aleksey dropped to one knee, his head down, as more blood and spit dripped to the floor. "Hey, I get it, man," Aleksey continued. "I wasn't, you know, judging. I have lots of friends that are queer. Including the fairy I mentioned. I was just thinking, you know, maybe you don't realize how you sound? Like it's a repression thing, or self-hatred or something?"

This time Commandant Burke kept his composure. He replaced his gauntlet and turned to Ennio. "So be it. Cut off his - what did he call it? His 'jewel pouch'?"

Ennio drew his sword and crossed to Aleksey. Aleksey jerked down on the chain around his neck, pulling the muscular soldier down with him just as Ennio jabbed his blade outward. The muscular soldier took the point of the blade in the shoulder. Aleksey spun a leg around Ennio's ankles, sweeping him off his feet, then pulled the chain away from the muscular soldier and leapt back up. Burke drew his knife. In a flash of motion, Aleksey snapped the chain and yanked the weapon from Burke's hand. The half-elf snapped the chain again, this time wrapping it around Burke's neck and pulling the man to his knees.

"Now that I think about it, you're probably not really queer," Aleksey said. "The queer folk I know have to be clever to get by in the Kingdoms. Most have become very adept at playing on the misconceptions of others. If you were queer, you would've known I was holding back. I literally had to bite my own tongue just so you'd think you were actually hurting me."

Rising behind Aleksey, Ennio pushed his sword into the side of Aleksey's neck, drawing blood. "Is this actually hurting you?" Ennio asked threateningly.

Reluctantly, Aleksey dropped the chain. Commandant Burke gasped, then sputtered, "K-Kill him!"

Suddenly, a taut cord snapped with a loud *thwang!* A crossbow bolt scraped across Ennio's hand, and he dropped his sword and yelped in pain. Aleksey and his attackers looked to the doorway as Darra entered, another bolt already loaded. She aimed her crossbow at the back of the commandant's head. "Told you I could help," she said. "Did you get the map?"

Aleksey grabbed the DragonSword and smiled. "Better," he said as he and Darra backed out of the room steadily, their weapons still trained on the men inside. Once outside, Aleksey slammed the library door shut with enough force to jam it, and he and his daughter sprinted away.

Aleksey headed back toward the window he'd come in through. But when he came to the turning point in the corridors, Darra stopped him by grabbing his arm and whispered, "This way!"

Darra pulled Aleksey into a shadowy nook and led him to a closer window, where she had affixed his grappling hook and rope. "We can't go down here!" Aleksey said. "There's a sentry below this window."

Darra climbed out the window and looked down nonchalantly. "Hmm. I don't see anybody," she said innocently as she began to descend. Down the hall, Aleksey's half-elven hearing alerted him to new soldiers that would arrive shortly. He looked out the window, saw there was indeed no guard, and began to follow Darra down the rope. Within moments, Darra and Aleksey hit the street and sprinted into the darkness of the city's back alleys.

"And just how did you know the guard was gone?" Aleksey asked as they ran.

"I may have promised to meet him in a certain dark alley right about now," Darra said.

This time it was Aleksey who grabbed his daughter by the

arm to stop her. "So you're telling me you deliberately disobeyed me, you sexually propositioned a soldier in the royal guard without me there to protect you, and you let him get a clear look at your face?" he asked. "Do you have any idea how insanely dangerous and stupid it was to do all of that?"

"Yes. But it also worked..." Darra shrugged. "Are you really, really mad at me?"

"Yes," Aleksey answered. "But I'm... trying not to be." Darra hugged her father tightly before they resumed their flight.

Back at the statehouse, Commandant Burke had pulled the grappling hook out of its lodging -- with more effort than he hoped he showed in front of his men -- and then he glared out the window. Burke turned his attention to the hook itself, and a look of puzzlement covered his face. Ennio rushed up behind him.

"They made their escape here," Burke said. "There was supposed to be a sentry at this wall. I want to know why he isn't down there. If the boy and girl didn't kill him, I might." Commandant Burke then handed the grappling hook to Ennio. "Take this to the Scientific Advisory Council," Burke continued. "This alloy is... unknown to me. The metallurgists will want to determine its composition. Ennio seemed to hesitate, so Burke asked, "Is there something else, Ennio?"

"I'm not sure, sir." Ennio answered. "This was found smoldering a few yards away from the unconscious soldiers." Ennio handed a half-burnt cone of incense to the commandant. Burke sniffed it, grimacing.

"Hmm. How intriguing..." Burke said. "Yes, take that to the Council as well. Perhaps it has something to do with how the boy got into the library."

"I'm sorry, sir, I wasn't clear," Ennio said. "This was found near two *other* unconscious soldiers, outside the cell the witch was in."

"Was in?" Commandant Burke asked. "Are you saying the witch is gone?"

"Yes, sir," Ennio answered.

"By the hairy balls of the old gods!" Burke swore, stomping off in an angry flurry.

"He really does mention other men's balls quite a lot,"

Ennio said under his breath as he watched him go.

Darra and Aleksey emerged from the back alleys with the sword hidden under the half-elf's cloak. They made their way back to *Eliza Dell's Inn* and bypassed the tavern, heading straight up the stairs toward their room. Halfway up the stairs, Aleksey quickly scanned the first floor for Eliza. He spied her at the bar, talking with a man he didn't recognize.

"You go on up to the room, sweetie," Aleksey instructed. "I'm going to... say goodnight to Eliza."

"Uh-huh," Darra said, raising an eyebrow suggestively. "Give her my love."

She took the cloak-wrapped sword from Aleksey and marveled at its wieldiness. "This thing is surprisingly lightweight for how huge it is. It's almost as big as me."

"We'll examine it later," Aleksey said, his attention torn between seeing his daughter off and keeping an eye on Eliza. "Just get it to the room and lock the door behind you. I'll be up in a minute."

Darra made her way up to their room, unlocked the door, entered - and cried out as someone emerged from the shadows behind her.

A few minutes later, the man speaking with Eliza departed, and she left the bar. She passed the dimly lit V.I.P. booth, which boasted a curtain for privacy, but was not at all startled when someone grabbed her by the arm and pulled her into the booth.

"Hello, lover," Aleksey greeted her.

"You're back," Eliza stated flatly. "Good. I need to tell you something."

"If you're going to confess to flirting with that other man, save your breath," Aleksey said, gently mocking. "You've made me no promises of fidelity. And frankly, I couldn't care less that you were caressing his puny little arm with no muscles, plus his hair is stupid."

"It's flattering that you care enough to act jealous," Eliza said. "But he's just a friend, a chef travelling with the DuVerres' royal entourage. And I wasn't 'caressing' him."

"Good, because I wasn't 'acting' jealous," Aleksey said,

grinning. He leaned in to kiss Eliza but was gently rebuffed.

"He mentioned that the guards have been put on alert after a theft at the statehouse," Eliza said, concern evident in her quiet tone.

"Did he, now?" Aleksey asked. "How fortunate for me that most of your friends are nosy gossips working closely with people of some authority. Did he mention the dashing young thief who stole away into the night?"

"He did," Eliza said, refusing to match the jaunty, nonchalant tone Aleksey had perfected. "He also said an order has been issued to close, lock and guard all the gates and passages out of the city, effective immediately, and that a door-to-door search for the thief and his accomplices will begin shortly."

A hint of panic flashed across Aleksey's face.

"I'm a respected businesswoman, Aleksey," Eliza continued. "If you're found hiding out under my roof, I'll be ruined."

"We'll leave immediately. The sewer—"

"Is flooded and clogged from the city's many visitors," Eliza interrupted. "There is, however, a steam train for the nobles and wealthier merchants, departing within the hour." Eliza handed Aleksey several tickets. "The seats are reserved under my name; the boys in my band are listed as my guests. I'll report the tickets stolen as soon as you're gone," she said.

"But you're Eliza Dell. Everyone knows you—" Aleksey began, before being cut off again by the lovely chanteuse.

"They know my name, my songs and my voice," Eliza said. "Not everyone has seen my face. And besides, the train is departing directly from the Moonlit Masquerade. If you don't draw attention to yourselves, you should be able to board without incident. I'll have the proper attire sent to your room."

Eliza stood up to leave, but Aleksey caught her hand, holding her back a little longer. "When can we meet again?" he asked, without waiting for an answer. "I've considered travelling to—"

Eliza pulled her hand out of his reluctantly. "I've also been considering things, Leks," she said. "We can't afford any more midnight rendezvouses. Too many people may have already seen us together."

"Oh. Of course. We'll take some time away, then, and in a couple of months—"

"It's just too dangerous," Eliza said. "Whatever you've stolen has whipped house DuVerres into a frenzy. Maybe in a few years—"

"A few years?" Aleksey balked. "Liza, are you... Are you breaking up with me?"

Eliza merely met his gaze with a look of pity.

"Now that was just painful to watch," Kaleb, a swarthy, short young man in tribal robes, said to Darra as they walked down the crowded festival midway together. "Why would anyone allow themselves to get dumped like that?" Kaleb asked, indicating a young woman climbing out of an icy cold dunk tank. "She must be so cold!"

"It's a rite of passage for city couples," Darra said. "A boy dunks a girl in freezing water, and then they have an excuse to hold each other close all night long. It's kind of romantic, don't you think?"

"I think you city girls have a strange sense of what 'romance' means," Kaleb replied. "If a man tried that with a woman from my tribe, they'd find him hanging from a tree limb." The pair passed a man juggling flaming pins, and Kaleb seemed to remember something. "Hey, wanna see something cool?" he asked. He reached into a pocket and pulled out a pipe, then snapped his fingers; a tiny flame appeared at the tip of his index finger.

"Are you mad?!" Darra exclaimed as she covered Kaleb's pipe with both hands. She then blew out his finger flame and hid the pipe inside her cloak. "Obviously, your Gram's been teaching you the tricks of the tribe, and I am impressed. But using even a tiny bit of magic can get you executed in the kingdoms!"

"I-I didn't know," Kaleb stammered. "I was just—"

"You are such a sheltered yokel!" Darra teased. "Wait. Is this your first time in a real city? Like, ever?" she asked.

"Uh, no!" Kaleb said. "Of course not! I'll have you know, I ran away to the capital city of this very kingdom last spring, and I got almost all the way over the wall! But then Gram caught up to me, and I've been grounded ever since. This is the first time I've been allowed out of her sight in months."

Darra grabbed Kaleb's arm as they strolled down the street. "Well, you're here now!" Darra said happily. "I'll teach you how to blend in and catch you up on the laws of the kingdoms, so you don't get in any trouble. For instance, that particular smoking herb in your pipe is also illegal here."

"Illegal? But it - it's medicinal. And it grows from the ground. How can something that grows from the ground be illegal?"

"They just say it is, and it is," Darra answered. "You can get in a lot of trouble if you're caught buying or selling it."

"Buying or selling it?" Kaleb asked. "But it grows from the ground!" he repeated. "That'd be like trying to buy or sell food."

"Your Gram really has been sheltering you," Darra said. "How is she?"

"She's good. She's been quieter since she brought me back to the tribe. More intense, I guess," Kaleb said.

"Wow," Darra said. "A *more* intense Ramla the Ominous, Chief of the United Tribes of the Tree People? Scary."

Back at Eliza Dell's, Aleksey entered his rooms and said over his shoulder, "You can come out from the shadows, Ramla. I have to get changed, and I haven't got a lot of time."

Ramla stepped into the light while still examining the DragonSword, which was taller than she was. "This is an object of skilled craftsmanship and great power," she said. "You did well to remove it from the possession of ignorant men."

"Yeah, well, it better get me a large box of gold bars, because I have a daughter who buys skirts and shoes as often as other people buy bread," Aleksey said.

"You cannot sell an ancient DragonSword!" Ramla exclaimed. "It is priceless!"

"Yes, I suppose an actual DragonSword would be priceless," Aleksey conceded. "But this one isn't real. And I was led to believe -- by a nasty, lying, haggard, old woman strongly resembling you -- that I was after a map to a hoard of treasure, not some fake relic."

"The sword is clearly old, and forged by Elven hands, not human," Ramla said. "Why do you believe it is not real?" she asked.

"Well, for one thing, merely holding a DragonSword is supposed to imbue an elf with mythic strength and vitality," Aleksey answered. "All I feel when I hold that thing is cold metal."

"Perhaps that is due to the jewels missing from the sword's hilt," Ramla suggested, showing the twin empty spaces in the hilt from which the largest jewels had clearly been removed. A dozen smaller jewels remained embedded in the hilt on each side. "Jewels were often imbued with strong magic in the old days,' Ramla explained.

"Damn!" Aleksey cursed. "That'll bring down the price."

"Or, perhaps your human heritage prevents you from feeling the sword's effect," Ramla said.

"It wouldn't be the first time my dual nature was a liability," Aleksey said with a sigh. "Where is my daughter, by the way? I told her to stay in the room."

"I sent her to the Cotillion," Ramla said.

"Damn it, Ramla!" Aleksey cursed again. "It's not safe for Darra to be out in the city alone."

"Kaleb is with her."

"Kaleb?" Aleksey asked, his worry still evident on his face. "That doesn't sound much safer. I adore your grandson, Ramla, but the boy is trusting to a fault, and he smokes far too much daydreamer's herb to be of any help if they run into trouble."

"You have not seen Kaleb in almost two years," Ramla said. "Trust me, you'll much prefer him when he's had his medicine... But tell me, why is this city suddenly so unsafe for your daughter? You seem more fearful than I can remember ever seeing you."

"It's nothing. I just..." the half-elf trailed off. "I made a powerful enemy tonight. That's all."

"Oh, good," Ramla said. "I was worried it was because the royal house of DuVerres is here, and Darra is their long-lost princess."

Aleksey's face lost all its color as he stared at Ramla, slack-jawed.

"Clearly Darra knows nothing of her true birthright," Ramla continued. "But I am curious, does the young prince know his sister is still alive?"

"How do *you* know?" Aleksey countered. "I've kept that secret between myself and exactly one other person for the last fifteen years!"

"When the people of my tribe reach old age, the forest has a way of whispering to us," Ramla answered vaguely. "I have learned many of life's secrets in recent months, including this one. That is why I am here. I need your help."

"With what?" Aleksey asked.

"With Kaleb," Ramla replied. "He is becoming a man, and he is going through some very difficult... changes. He needs guidance."

"Are you asking me to talk to your grandson about, uh, girls and boys and, you know -- doing it?" Aleksey asked awkwardly.

"Ha!" Ramla laughed. "As if I would ask a man who shies away from even the word 'sex' to educate a boy of the tribe! Unfortunately, the situation with Kaleb is more serious than that. He may have a very special destiny, one which would bring with it certain dangers if he were to stay with the tribe." Aleksey cocked his head curiously. "I cannot tell you everything. Not now, anyway. But it is enough to know that Kaleb can no longer stay with the tribe and remain safe. He is no longer content with life in the tribe, anyway. But he is not ready to be on his own."

"Okay... But I'm an outlaw," Aleksey said. "And you know about Darra's... situation. How is Kaleb any safer travelling with us?"

"You cling to the shadows and prize anonymity, and you are always moving," Ramla explained. "This has protected your daughter's secret her whole life. Also, you do not entirely lack certain important life skills and forms of cleverness."

"Aww. That's kind of a sweet thing to say, Ramla," Aleksey said.

"My grandson would benefit from learning from you," Ramla said. "But I also know that, if it became necessary, you would defend his life with yours. I do not trust outsiders easily, Aleksey. But your decades of friendship have earned it. Will you do this for me?"

A knock sounded at the door. Aleksey opened it to find an employee of the inn, carrying fancy formal wear. "Pardon my intrusion," the man said. "Ms. Eliza asked me to bring you these, and to ask if there is anything else you require before your departure?"

Aleksey took the clothing and considered for just a moment. "Actually, yes," Aleksey answered the man. "I'll need one more outfit for the Masquerade - but smaller, cut for a slim teenage boy. And if it's not too much trouble, I'd also love to get a bassoon."

"A... bassoon, sir?" the man asked hesitantly.

"With a carrying case, please," Aleksey instructed.

As Aleksey donned a black and white tuxedo, mask and cape, Ramla pointed out intricate markings on the DragonSword. He then removed the bassoon and its padding from its case, replacing it with the sword. Ramla departed, and Aleksey followed quickly behind her. Still, the old woman was lost in the tavern crowd before Aleksey was out his own door. Aleksey took the stairs slowly, admiring Eliza and her band. She sang a song that was a favorite from her latest recording, and he caught her eyes in a silent goodbye. As several armed soldiers entered the tavern through the far door, Aleksey broke eye-contact with the woman he loved, pulled down his mask, and departed.

The half-elf eventually caught up to Darra and Kaleb, pulling them out of line at a concessioner selling iced lemonade. Leading them into a deserted alley, the half-elf stood guard as Darra and Kaleb changed into the achromatic formal costumes Eliza had provided for them.

The trio then made their way to a large marble pavilion, which was playing Eliza's latest recording on a large phonograph. Darra, Aleksey and Kaleb mounted the steps of the pavilion and found a swirling sea of people in black and white formal wear, masks and veils, all perfectly executing an intricate ballroom dance. A middle-aged nun rushed out of the crowd and slammed into Darra, spilling a satchel of gold coins.

"My apologies, Sister," Darra said as she helped her gather the small fortune. "I had no idea your line of work was so lucrative," she continued with a smile. "Perhaps I ought to take the vows myself. Tell me, would you take offense if I asked to try on your veil?"

"Sadly, if you haven't the calling for it, I fear you would find my vocation rather tedious and confining," the nun said.

"Tedious and confining? Sounds pretty much like my life right now," Darra said, eying her father, who merely rolled his eyes. "I'm Darra."

The nun shook Darra's hand and said, "Lilith. Very nice to meet you."

Holding out a handful of coins for the older woman, Darra asked, "Which god do you serve?"

"Valeska," Lilith replied, accepting the coins. "Goddess of Love, Beauty, Health and Vitality. Do you follow The Faith?"

Darra shrugged and said, "Not really. But I like all the myths and holidays and stuff. I've never actually been to a service, though; my father always says church is for boring people."

"No offense, but it sounds like your father is prejudiced," Lilith said.

"Oh, he is," Darra said, a wide grin on her face. "But that's just because he's very, very old."

Lilith leaned in sympathetically and asked, "Is he... touched in the head?"

"Everyone who meets him thinks so," Darra said.

"Or maybe he just prefers the company of sinners," Aleksey said, no longer able to hold his tongue.

Lilith chuckled and covered her mouth with her hand demurely. "Yes, well, that could very well be the case," she said. "Thank you for your help," she said to Darra before she walked away, smiling.

Back at the statehouse, Duke DuVerres waved to his shy dominatrix as he shut the door to his bedchamber. He turned to face Commandant Burke and Milian. "Now, then," he began, irritated. "What matter is so urgent as to require my being dragged from that sweet young child's arms? Hmm?"

Milian looked to a still-fuming Burke timidly. Burke nodded, indicating that Milian should begin. "My Lord, an unfortunate, unforeseen circumstance has arisen in regard to the, um... special project," the advisor began. "Earlier tonight, this building was targeted by a pair of thieves. Professionals, by the look of it, well-trained and well-armed. They took the sword."

"They took the– The entirety of the project's success depends upon that blade!" the Duke shouted. He turned to Burke. "How in all hells did you manage to let this happen?"

Burke bristled a little at the duke's berating, but otherwise kept his composure. "The guard was fully tripled tonight, My Lord Duke," Commandant Burke assured him. "We were simply unprepared for the possibility that anyone other than the three of us knew the real reason for our being here. And as the Lord Advisor mentioned, the thieves were well-prepared. We believe they were aided by a witch."

"A witch?" the duke asked, alarmed. "Inside the city?"

"We believe so, My Lord," Milian confirmed. "A substance used in the execution of the theft was analyzed, and I am told that it displays the expected properties of the fabled powder referred to as 'sleepsmoke'."

"Sleepsmoke, eh?" the duke repeated. "We've been after a sample of that for years. Will the apothecaries be able to derive its formula from the sample?"

"With enough time, they believe it to be possible, My Lord," Milian answered.

"Imagine subduing whole cities with the smoke from a single bonfire!" Duke DuVerres said. "Time may yet squeeze a small victory out of this night's failures after all." He turned once more to Commandant Burke. "No thanks to you! Did you know that when I told the Council I wanted to place you in charge of the royal guard, they warned me against it?"

"I did not, My Lord," Burke answered, squirming under the criticism.

"They pointed to studies showing that a younger, more virile man would inspire the guard to greater diligence," the Duke said. "I ignored the Council's wisdom, and I have been burdened by your incompetence ever since. You will find these thieves, and you will bring me back the DragonSword, along with their heads. Or I will have your own. Now get out of my sight!"

Burke bowed stiffly, suppressing his wounded pride, and quickly exited.

The duke sat and reached for a bottle in the center of his desk. Milian snatched the bottle away and poured the older man a whiskey. "Your mother raised you well, Milian," the duke said. "You're one of the few men I know who still observes proper etiquette. The commandant could watch me pouring my own drinks all night and never think to offer a hand."

"It's his noble birth, sir," Milian said. "He takes his position for granted. But we Advisors never lose the memories of having earned our titles through hard work and faithful service."

"You're probably right," the duke agreed. "Perhaps when I'm the king, and not merely regent, I'll do away with the nobility altogether. Or at least the ones I don't like."

Milian smiled serenely at the duke's violent proposal. A knock sounded from the outer door. A moment later, Ennio entered, flanked by two more soldiers. All three saluted the duke formally.

"Please stand to receive Prince Trosclair Alyssandro BenMichael Stavros DuVerres, the fourth of his noble name, he who is called 'the Fair and Noble' and 'Tomorrow's Gift,' sole heir to the Kingdom of DuVerres, rightful ruler of the citizens of DuVerres, in justice for eternity may he reign," Ennio said.

The duke stood reluctantly, clearly annoyed by the exhaustive formality, and Trosclair finally entered. "Be at ease," the young prince said.

The soldiers relaxed their formal stance, and the duke sat back down. "Welcome, Your Grace," the duke said to his nephew. "To what do I owe the honor of your visit at this late hour?"

Trosclair nodded almost imperceptibly toward the duke and greeted him with a simple, "Uncle." He then turned to Milian and said, "It was actually you we were seeking out, Lord Advisor."

"Oh?" Milian said. "How may I be of service, Your Grace?"

"We overheard a rumor that the witch escaped?" Trosclair asked.

"Yes, Your Grace," Milian said.

"It's nothing to concern yourself with, Trosc," Duke DuVerres said.

"We were also informed of an order for heightened security around both ourselves and certain security checkpoints throughout the city," Trosclair continued, unabated. "This has, of course, frightened some of the more squeamish lords and ladies of our entourage. Needless to say, this seems to clearly be a matter we should most definitely concern ourselves with."

"The good duke was only trying to spare you any worry over a minor matter, Your Grace," Milian said. "I can give you a full report of the incident, and you'll see that there's no reason—"

"Fine, but give us the report later," the prince said. "We are already late for another formal engagement, which is a habit considered terribly tacky when found in the future king." Turning back to the duke, Trosclair said, "Uncle, you really ought to get used to keeping us in the loop about these happenings. We should probably understand the workings of our kingdom before our coronation this summer, don't you think?" Trosclair then turned and walked out of the room without waiting for a reply. Ennio and the two soldiers followed quickly behind him.

The duke swallowed a gulp of whiskey as their footsteps faded. "That boy grows more patronizing with each hour of his life!" he spat bitterly. "He's been perfecting that little routine for months, parading around and reminding me in a half dozen different ways that he's to take the throne soon... To think I used to bounce him on my knee! That arrogant little twit has no idea what he's got coming to him, does he, Milian?"

"Indeed," Milian agreed readily. "My Lord, before I withdraw, I should relay one more significant detail of tonight's events, which I thought best to keep from the young prince, and perhaps even from Commandant Burke. One of the tools used in the thieves' escape is composed of an alloy known to have originated in the elvish kingdom."

"The elves?" the duke asked, and Milian nodded. "There hasn't been an elf sighted in the kingdoms for a generation. You were right to keep this from Burke. He would urge the nobles toward a costly, pointless crusade if he thought the elves might return."

The door to the duke's bedchamber opened just enough for his companion to poke her head out. "My Lord?" she asked timidly. "Are you planning on returning to bed? I'm cold."

"I'll be in momentarily to warm you, girl," the duke assured her with a wide smile. "But close the door for now. We men are discussing confidential matters of the kingdom." The young girl blushed and did as instructed. "The one saving grace of the border cities is the opportunity they offer to meet young women like her," the duke said, sighing.

"I'm glad she's pleased you, My Lord," Milian said, while topping off the duke's drink.

"More than pleased," the duke said, growing wistful. "To take an innocent girl like that, who's never known a whiff of power or authority of any kind, and put a whip in her hand... It changes them, Milian. You can see it in their eyes. The innocence melts away, and something ferocious is left in its place. It's like watching a lion cub take down its first gazelle, or a dragon hatch from its shell. I find it absolutely titillating. It is a true miracle, and one of the few experiences in life I hold holy." The duke took a long swig of his whiskey. "But this one seems the chatty type. And a man of my station cannot appear weaker than a woman, even for a moment of pleasure. I'm going to dress and take a brief walk in the courtyard, Milian. When I return, I expect her to be gone."

"Of course, My Lord," Milian said.

"And tell her— Tell her that it was no fault in her, but one within me, which has led to our parting," the duke said. "Give it to her gently, my friend, and use discretion. There is, after all, a happy time being had outside these walls -- a mood which would surely spoil upon the discovery of that dear, sweet child's corpse."

Milian nodded his understanding, bowed his head slightly, and took his leave. Duke DuVerres took another long swallow, staring blankly ahead at nothing in particular.

Kaleb, Darra and Aleksey pulled their masks on and entered the pavilion. Aleksey spotted a line of people waiting to board the steam train as it idled at a raised platform. "They're loading passengers from the far side," Aleksey said. "We'll have to join the dance to reach it. This should be fun." Aleksey held a silk-gloved hand out elegantly toward Darra. "Do you remember the steps, dear?" he asked.

"I wanted to be a dancer from age seven to eleven. Of course, I remember!" she said jubilantly.

"I don't know this dance," Kaleb fretted.

"It's easy," Darra encouraged. "It's just a standard *cantratta*, with an added kick, swing, spin or dip on every other third-count."

Kaleb grew visibly more embarrassed. "What I meant to say is, I don't know any dance," he said. "In the tribes, we just move around however we want and try not to hit each other."

"Not to worry," Aleksey said, patting Kaleb on the back. "You can carry the luggage. It fits with our cover story better, anyway. Every popular band in the kingdoms has a young person or two toadying around behind them."

Aleksey and Darra loaded Kaleb up with their own bags and the bassoon case. Aleksey took Darra's hand and they began swaying, entering the dance with clockwork precision. Kaleb followed along behind them, clumsily dodging flailing limbs and lurching torsos. On one of the choreographed kicks, a man's boot nearly hit his face.

"Oh, yes, this is definitely fun," the tribal lad mumbled

under his breath as Darra and Aleksey whirled and twirled expertly ahead of him. The trio made it nearly half-way across the floor before a noblewoman tripped on Kaleb's case. "I'm so sorry!" he blurted out. "I didn't see you." The dancers nearby cleared a small area but kept dancing. Kaleb stooped, offering the noblewoman his hand, and her annoyance yielded to flattery. After she was back on her feet, Kaleb was jerked backwards roughly.

"You clumsy little oaf!" a large, angry man spat. "How dare you touch my wife!"

"I was just helping her back to her feet!" Kaleb said defensively.

"There's no need to cause a scene, dear," the noblewoman said. "It was an accident, and this handsome young man was merely being polite."

"Where I was raised, being polite meant keeping the hands of young men away from the bodies of other men's wives!" her husband replied, shaking Kaleb by the shoulders.

The man reared back to punch Kaleb. Aleksey moved swiftly, catching the man's wrist. Darra pulled Kaleb away. The husband swung a second fist that Aleksey dodged easily, and he countered with a blow of his own that laid the man out. The crowd gasped, and Darra shot her father an annoyed look.

"He swung first!" Aleksey said defensively. "It was a reflex!"

"Can't even get through one stupid dance," Darra said.

A few soldiers near the door began moving toward the commotion on the dance floor.

"Well, we're in it," Aleksey said. "Only one way out now." Aleksey offered Darra his hand again; she rolled her eyes and took it. Father and daughter rejoined the dance, but this time their kicks and leaps and swings collided with other dancers intentionally. They relied on the blurry speed of the dance, as well as the fact that everyone was wearing masks and similar clothing, to help camouflage their actions. A formal, black-and-white brawl soon erupted on the dance floor behind them as they went along. Aleksey and Darra slipped out of the melee before it could escalate into a full-on riot. Darra grabbed Kaleb's arm and dragged him toward the platform. The trio quickly climbed the steps to the ticket booth as the fight spread throughout the pavilion.

Unaware of the violence due to a partition and the loud

phonograph playing nearby, the usher held out his hand, palm up expectantly. "Tickets?" he prompted.

"Oh, right!" Aleksey said. He dug into his pockets and pulled out the tickets. He handed them to Darra, who gave them to the usher. The man perused them and then glanced up at Darra excitedly.

"Very good, Ms. Dell," the usher said. "It is an honor to meet a performer of your renown."

Darra contorted her posture into an imitation of Eliza's sexy, exotic demeanor, and she mimicked her accent as best she could. "Yes, I am her. I mean, I am me. I am Eliza Dell," she said.

Aleksey aimed an unimpressed look at his daughter as the usher merely nodded.

"Kind sir," Darra continued. "My band and I have been playing all day, and I am very weary. Will we be able to board the train directly?"

"Of course, Ms. Dell!" the usher said. "I'll just need to announce you," he said, as he drew back a curtain to reveal Prince Trosclair formally greeting people before they boarded the train. Darra was momentarily startled when the usher pulled her forward, face-to-face with the prince.

"Ms. Eliza Dell, I present to you His Grace, Prince Trosclair DuVerres the Fourth, in justice for eternity may he reign!" the usher said.

Aleksey barely stifled his alarm when Trosclair took Darra's gloved hand and lifted it to his lips for an elegant, formal kiss.

"Ms. Eliza Dell," Trosclair greeted her. "We are honored to make your acquaintance. We have long been a fan of your work."

"How... flattering." Darra managed in a slightly better accent.

"Truly, we await each successive recording of your remarkable music with breath that is baited," Trosclair said. "Your songs seem eons ahead of the times, or plucked from another world entirely."

"You are too kind, Your Grace," Darra said.

Darra's worried gaze flitted toward Aleksey only briefly, but Trosclair still picked up on her discomfort, though not the reason for it. The prince dropped his regal tone and said, "You must forgive my formality, Ms. Dell. I am capable of making casual conversation. But proper etiquette is my only defense against the tediousness of court life."

"Oh! How... refreshing," Darra said.

"Your Grace," the usher said at a signal from the first car. "The engineer has issued a call for departure."

"Of course," Trosclair said. "Allow me to say, Ms. Dell, you are every bit as beautiful as your music is magical. If you're ever near the capital, I do hope you'll consider playing at the palace."

"I would enjoy nothing more!" Darra lied enthusiastically.

Trosclair bowed politely to Darra, and she responded with a formal curtsey, blushing behind her mask. The usher led the three of them past the prince, onto the train and to the door of their very own sleeping compartment. Once there, the three of them finally removed their masks.

"Did you see that?" Darra asked, freeing her pent-up excitement.

"Unfortunately, yes, I did," Aleksey said.

"Prince DuVerres not only fell for my impression of Eliza—"

"Which needs a lot of work," Aleksey interjected.

"He also called me beautiful!" She continued. "And he's probably met every noble girl in all the kingdoms. I guess I must have the bearing of a woman from a much higher station in life."

"Calm yourself, darling," Aleksey said. "Every man lucky enough to meet you thinks you're beautiful. What difference does the opinion of one silly boy make, no matter how highborn he is?"

"Oh, Dad! That's so cute!" Darra said. "It must have burned you up inside to hear the future king flirting with your little girl. But I am proud of you for staying silent about it, for the first time in... ever."

"Well, I was motivated just a tiny bit by all the armed guards," Aleksey admitted.

With two flat bellows from a loud horn, the train rolled away. As Trosclair watched the train disappear into the night, Ennio approached him with a piece of parchment in his hand.

"Is that the Lord Advisor's report?" Trosclair asked the young soldier.

"Not the full report, Your Grace," Ennio answered. "Just sketches of the intruders to pass around the guards, in case the thieves ever show up again."

Trosclair took the parchment from Ennio and examined it,

recognition and then worry covering his face.

"Oh, dear! Um..." Trosclair began. "It seems there may have been a slight– That is to say, in our haste, we might have inadvertently–" he stammered. The young prince then threw his hands up sheepishly and simply said, "Oops!"

Back on the train, the trio of fraudulent passengers had settled into their private compartment. Kaleb watched out the window as the train sped through the dark forest, while Darra reclined into her father's shoulder.

"Where are we going?" Kaleb asked.

"We'll disembark at daybreak, near Morning's Peak," Aleksey answered.

"Ooh, Morning's Peak!" Darra said. "You'll love it there, Kaleb. It's gorgeous, and a different type of city altogether."

"There are different types of cities?" Kaleb asked.

"Oh, sure," Darra confirmed. "Most are shadow cities, like the one we just left. But there are also snowbound cities, seaside cities -- those can seem a bit dreary, covered in clouds and raining all day. There are even a few underground cities. But if we travel through one of those, be prepared to eat a lot of potatoes."

"I like potatoes," Kaleb said.

"Basically any plot of land that manages to shut out the sun for a significant amount of time has had a city built on it," Darra continued. "But the mountain cities are my favorites. And Morning's Peak has a series of steamy waterfalls that are absolutely brilliant to bathe in, or–"

"Don't get too excited, Darra, dear," Aleksey advised. "I said we'll be getting off near Morning's Peak. We won't be entering the city proper," he said.

"Why not?" Darra asked plaintively.

Aleksey checked to make sure the door was locked, then opened the bassoon case and pulled out the DragonSword. "Because of this," he said, swinging the huge sword in slow motion as best he could in the cramped compartment.

"I thought you intended to sell it?" Darra asked, puzzled.

"That was my first thought," Aleksey confirmed. "But then Kaleb's Gram showed me these," he said, pointing to tiny etchings all over the blade.

"Is that—" Kaleb began to ask.

"The old speak, yes," the half-elf finished Kaleb's question by answering it. "The language of magic. Ramla said you've become quite the little scholar, and that you would be able to read it for us."

Kaleb examined the writing on the sword slowly and carefully. "Well, yeah," the boy said. "I mean, sort of. A lot of things written in the old speak are lost in translation. They just come out gibberish. But this looks like a—"

"A map!" Aleksey finished the young man's sentence once again, excited himself now. "Or directions, anyway, for navigating a maze of paths and tunnels running through the mountains. It seems your Gram was right to believe this could lead us to a hoard of treasure."

"Exactly how much treasure qualifies as a 'hoard'?" Darra asked.

"If this pans out, you'll have everything you could ever ask for," Aleksey promised. "We could even stop thieving altogether and look into purchasing a small plot of land to farm, or a house to rent in one of the smaller cities. Some place fitting for a girl your age to... live a fuller life."

Darra beamed up at her father. "A fuller life?" she asked. "Like with dates? Dates with boys?"

"Then again, the open road will always beckon to those of us with wandering spirits," Aleksey deflected.

Darra glared at her father playfully.

"But that's an argument for another night," the half-elf continued. "For now, let's just enjoy our rest. The elves have a saying: A new day always comes, but not until this one moves beyond midnight."

Duke DuVerres snored loudly, passed out in a puddle of whiskey, still clutching the bottle. An urgent knock woke him, and he cursed. The duke hauled himself up and made his way over to a mirror, where he made a futile attempt at straightening his robes and his hair. Finally he unlocked the door, and Milian rushed in.

"My Lord, I apologize," the Lord Advisor said. "But you were scheduled to wake hours ago! We must hurry, or you'll miss the eclipse altogether." Milian held up a complex orbital clock apparatus to indicate the time.

"Yes, yes! I am aware of how time works, Milian," the duke said. "But... would you mind pouring me a drink first? This is a dark morning, and one I do not wish to face soberly." Drawing a fresh bottle from a nearby cabinet, Milian poured a glass of whiskey as the duke lamented.

"You're lucky to have been born a peasant, Milian," the duke declared. "The burden of greatness weighs heavily on the soul of a man such as me... You understand that I do not regard the murder of mere children as some sort of trifle or amusement, don't you, Milian? You understand that my hand is forced into making these ghastly decisions?"

"I understand perfectly, My Lord," Milian assured him.

A little while later, the duke stood at a podium on a stage, flanked by nobles and members of the Council, including Milian, Commandant Burke, and the prince and his entourage.

"Citizens of the fine city of Shadowhaven, I address you on this day with great pride, but also with sad remembrances," the duke began. For all his lechery, the man was a gifted orator. "It was fifteen years ago that my brother, our last great king, and his beautiful bride, mother to our Fair and Noble Prince, were taken from us far too soon." Trosclair flinched slightly at the mention of his parents' deaths, though likely no one off-stage could tell. "But this is not a day for dwelling on the past," the duke said, "Today is a day during which we look forward, and upward." The duke pointed one hand at the sky as a moon began to eclipse the sun. "Today, Rebos the Reaper Moon passes over your fine city, in precise alignment with the last harvests of fall, symbolizing both great change, which may be difficult, and the promise of a new and better tomorrow." The duke then pointed to Trosclair. "Our young prince, my beloved nephew, has himself become a powerful symbol, as he has grown from infancy to manhood," he said. "No longer a child–"

The duke slumped forward onto the podium and then fell flat on his back, an arrow buried deep in his left eye socket. Gasps of shock and cries of all kinds sounded out throughout the stage and the square as both erupted into chaos. Ennio had to physically restrain Trosclair to keep him from running to his uncle's side. He then quickly led the boy off the stage, surrounded by soldiers.

In a clock tower overlooking the stage, Lilith knelt, set aside her longbow, and clasped her hands in prayer.

Meanwhile, in the mountains near Morning's Peak, Darra and Aleksey felt their way along a wall through a cavernous, dark tunnel. Kaleb followed behind them, using his finger-flame to read from the sword and also to light their path.

"Okay, so...," Kaleb began less than authoritatively. "So yeah, we need to turn right at the next passage... No, wait, that might say 'turn back,' not 'turn right.' But why would they want us to turn around and go back the way we just came? Unless it's some kind of trick, and we're really supposed to go forward? Or left?" Darra and Aleksey stopped to wait for Kaleb's next translated direction. Kaleb lifted his hand to his chin in a thoughtful pose and singed an eyebrow with his finger-flame. He squealed in fear and shook his finger until the flame went out. Darra laughed at Kaleb in the dark. A moment later, Kaleb snapped, and his finger-flame reappeared, brighter than before.

Darra screamed this time, jumping back from the large, scary, scaly head of a sleeping dragon now visible behind Kaleb.

A burst of steam spewed out of the Dragon's nostrils. Kaleb and Darra both screamed this time, and Aleksey clamped a hand over their mouths to silence them as he backed them up with small, slow steps.

"Stay as still as you can..." Aleksey whispered slowly. "Do not even breathe... Dragons see very poorly in the dark... But they still see better... than two gullible human children!" he said, before simultaneously yelling and goosing the teens, who both screamed yet again. Aleksey doubled over with laughter. "It's not real!" the half-elf said. "I saw it earlier, sweetie, but I didn't want to spoil it for you! It's just a carving, probably with a steam trap inside to make it 'breathe.' Oh, but you should've seen your faces!"

"I'm sure it was hilarious," Darra said. "I can only imagine the joy you must feel, knowing your only daughter was terrified. Say, I wonder if your sense of humor is somehow related to your lifelong bachelorhood?" Aleksey turned away from her jibe awkwardly. "Besides, Kaleb was way more scared than me," she added.

"Hey!" Kaleb said defensively. "Only because it sneezed on me!"

"Does this carving mean we're close to the treasure

chamber?" Aleksey asked Kaleb.

Kaleb held his finger-flame back down to the sword. "Um, hold on..." the teen stalled. "Uh-oh. I lost my place again. Okay, so we came in through the east middle corridor, right? We decided it was the east middle?"

"Kaleb, we've been wandering around in the dark for hours," Aleksey said impatiently. "Can you read that thing, or not?"

"Yes! Mostly," he assured him. "It's just - it's almost gibberish. It's like it's written in some sort of poetic verse, but the lines don't connect to each other in any meaningful way. And it doesn't even rhyme," Kaleb complained. "I mean, who wants to read a poem that doesn't rhyme? That's not poetry. That's just saying stuff."

"Well, can you make that flame of yours a little bigger?" Darra requested. "Maybe if we could see better, we'd be able to find our way. Or at least keep from swallowing more spiders."

Aleksey gagged, remembering the taste of a spider. Kaleb pulled out his pipe, lit it, and took a big puff. "Well, I can make it bigger, but... it gets kind of hard to control sometimes. I guess I could try." Kaleb exhaled a huge cloud of smoke. "I mean, it's not like there's a forest to burn down in here."

"You burned down a forest?" Aleksey asked, his eyebrows raised.

"No! Not a whole forest, anyway," Kaleb replied. "Just a teeny, tiny, little itty-bitty-bit of a few different forests."

"Uh-huh. Okay, then..." Aleksey said. "Hmm... If the directions to the treasure chamber start on this side of the blade, and they aren't making any sense," he said, flipping the sword over. "Can you start reading at the other end and work your way back to us?"

"Hey, yeah, that might work!" Kaleb said excitedly. "Like, start at the treasure and then..." he said, his voice trailing off when he caught a glimpse of the text. "Oh, no, sorry. It's still gibberish and not-rhyming poems. Unless..." Kaleb flipped the sword back to the first side, then started flipping it over and over every few seconds. "Okay, this is actually making sense. The writing flows from one side of the sword to the other, so you have to read both sides of the blade at the same time. I think... Yes! That's it!"

"What's 'it?' Did you figure out where the treasure chamber

is?" Aleksey asked.

"Oh. Uh, no, not yet," Kaleb said. "But now it rhymes!" The young man read confidently from the blade. "Okay, so now we turn 'back.' Aha! 'Turn back!' I knew it was a trick!"

At the statehouse in Shadowhaven, Prince Trosclair sat at the head of a large table, flanked on one side by Commandant Burke and the nobles, and on the other by Milian and the Council. Trosclair stared straight ahead as the men around him whispered or shouted their various opinions to one another. Finally, Trosclair rose from his seat, rapping loudly on the table to draw the group to silence.

"Gentlemen, please!" he called them to order. "We have heard and considered your arguments and proposals, and on three matters, we are resolved: One, that no new regent shall be named before our coronation. Two, that the Lord Advisor of the Science Advisory Council will assume the administrative duties of the kingdom until that time." Milian nodded gratefully to the prince, while Commandant Burke gritted his teeth. "And finally, that Commandant Burke's request shall be granted. A full brigade will be commissioned under his command," Trosclair said. At this, the commandant smiled graciously.

Trosclair lifted the sketch of Darra and Aleksey. "We agree that it is highly unlikely that the assault and impersonation directed at the royal entourage by these two last night and the duke's murder this morning are unrelated," the prince said. "These criminals must be brought to justice! Now, we will be hearing no more arguments and issuing no new decrees today. You are dismissed," Trosclair concluded, striding toward the door.

Ennio dropped in line behind him and began, "Please stand for the departure of Prince Trosclair Alyssandro—"

"For the sake of the heavens, Ennio, not now!" Trosclair cut him off sharply. Ennio flinched at the reprimand, hesitated just a moment, and then followed Trosclair out the door in silence.

A few moments later, Trosclair entered his bedchamber and shut the door. He crossed to the bed and fell down onto it face-first. A soft knock signaled Ennio's entrance.

"How are you faring, Your Grace?" Ennio asked politely.

"I understand the importance of keeping up appearances in

front of the others, Ennio," Trosclair said. "But we were friends long before you became my bodyguard. No more 'Your Grace' – at least not in the privacy of my own room."

"Of course," Ennio agreed. "I'm sorry."

"No, I am. I shouldn't have snapped at you."

"It's normal, in these circumstances," Ennio said.

"These circumstances of having the weight of an entire kingdom thrown over me, without any preparation or warning? Or these circumstances of having my uncle killed in front of me?" the young man asked. "He was a drunk, a lout, and an awful regent. And I'd heard rumors about other– Things too horrible to speak of, Ennio. But he was also the last family I had."

Ennio crossed to the bed and draped an arm around Trosclair's shoulder.

"I'll make you my new family, okay, Ennio?" Trosclair asked.

"Okay, kiddo," Ennio said. "Make me your new family."

Trosclair hugged the young soldier tightly. "I will," Trosclair said. "I'll decree it, then sign it, then seal it. Because I know I'll always have you." Ennio kissed Trosclair's forehead. "And I won't need anybody else," the prince said, as they eased down onto the bed together.

Milian waited in a secluded, private garden outside the statehouse. Lilith arrived precisely on time, neither a minute early nor late. Milian held open a box, showing the lady the gold bars stacked neatly inside.

"Twenty thousand credits worth of gold," he said. "That was a very precise shot; thank you for making sure he didn't suffer. Will you need anything else to complete your new assignment?"

Lilith took her payment and said simply, "No."

"Good," Milian said. "I don't want Commandant Burke breathing over my shoulder, so his new mission needs to be a long and fruitless one. I need these two eliminated as soon as possible." Milian handed over a sketch of Darra and Aleksey. The woman took a long look at it, stuffed it in her pocket and nodded her head in understanding.

As Darra, Aleksey and Kaleb worked their way through a

maze of dark tunnels, they finally came upon a bright glow in the distance. "Is that sunlight?" Darra asked.

"This must be it," Aleksey said. "You said the chamber would be lit in sunlight. You did it, Kaleb!" he said, slapping an enthusiastic hand on the tribal lad's back.

"Ow," Kaleb said, smiling.

They rounded the corner of the glowing chamber and were not disappointed by its contents. As they entered, they gaped at piles of gold and silver items of all kinds, chests and crates of coins and gold bars, and more jewels and finery than any merchant's inventory, scattered over several tables. "Wow," was all Kaleb could think to say.

"So this is how much a 'hoard' is," Darra said. "Dad, what are we going to do with all this? How will we even get it out of here?" she asked.

Aleksey started rummaging, searching for the most valuable and gaudy trinkets in the piles. "We'll have to come back with sacks and wheelbarrows, I guess," he answered. "Or maybe a cart. But for now, stuff your pockets and fill your satchels with as much as you can carry."

Darra and Kaleb obeyed and began rifling through the treasure. Darra came upon a beautiful gem-encrusted jewelry box. She opened it and found two large, loose gems with a soft pinkish tone. She admired the other contents of the box for a moment before putting it in her satchel, then stuffed the gems in her pocket and moved on.

"I'm eager to have a look around this side of the mountain," Aleksey said. "Maybe there's a path we can pull a cart up." Aleksey moved toward the ornately carved, arched passage that was letting in all the light.

"Wait! Stop!" Kaleb bellowed.

Aleksey froze. "Is there a spider on me?" he asked.

"What is it, Kay?" Darra asked.

Kaleb pointed to some squiggles and lines carved around the archway. "There's some sort of warning here..." he pointed out. "It says something about the DragonSword. Okay, yeah, it is a warning. It says we can't leave this chamber without the sword, or we will look death in the face... Or maybe it says we *must* leave this chamber without the sword, or we'll look death in the face," he equivocated.

Aleksey took the sword from him and continued toward the opening. "Dad, you can't!" Darra exclaimed. "You could die!"

"Honey, I have to!" Aleksey said. "If we leave the sword here, we'll never find our way back. Besides, someone had to have taken the sword from this chamber at some point," he reasoned.

"But for all we know, they died from doing it!" Darra said.

"Or from not doing it," Kaleb added.

Aleksey patted his daughter's shoulder reassuringly and stepped toward the exit threshold. He crossed outside, onto a large outcropping on the mountainside. Aleksey scanned, but saw and heard no sign of danger. He turned back to face Darra, relieved. "See? It was just a trick," he said. "I'm not 'looking death in the face' any more than the two of you."

A shadow fluttered over Aleksey from behind. Darra and Kaleb backed away, fear spreading across their faces.

"Dad!" Darra said urgently.

"You're finally going to have the life you deserve, sweetie!" Aleksey said.

"Dad!" Darra said again with even more urgency, but again, she was ignored.

"I know I haven't been a perfect father, but–"

"Dad!" Darra screamed. She pointed behind her father, who turned to see a large black dragon hovering over his shoulder. Darra tackled her father, pushing him out of harm's way just before the dragon spat a spear of flame at him. "This one looks real!" she said as they scrambled to their feet. Aleksey pushed his daughter behind him, lifting the DragonSword over his head threateningly.

"Get back in the cave, Darra!" Aleksey said. "You can't help me. Only a DragonSword can kill a dragon."

"But you said it was a fake– *ow*!" Darra flinched, reached into her pocket, and pulled out one of the large gems she'd stolen. It was now glowing bright red with heat.

The dragon swiped at Aleksey. The half-elf rolled underneath its talons, but still earned a bloody scrape across his back. Aleksey stood up and waved the sword high over his head again, and the dragon hovered backwards several yards.

"Hey!" Darra called, trying to draw the dragon's attention. "Stay away from my Dad!" she said, throwing the glowing gem at the winged beast. The gem smashed as it hit the dragon in the chest, exploding into a swirl of bright pink energy in the middle of the sky. A small, sleek space shuttle zipped out of the swirling energy; it crashed into the dragon, and both seemed to buckle. The shuttle and the dragon plummeted to the ground. One of the shuttle's wings flew off, right over Aleksey's head, knocking the DragonSword from his hand. The blade shattered into several large fragments.

Aleksey, Darra and Kaleb shuffled to the edge of the cliff and peered down at a pile of blood, bones and scaly flesh surrounding a hunk of bent metal and frayed, sparking wires. After a few seconds, a hatch on the shuttle opened with a pressurized hiss, and a lone figure stepped out of the wreckage, wearing a sleek, dark space suit. The figure removed his helmet, revealing the confused face of a handsome young pilot.

"Oh, hello," Darra said, thoroughly impressed.

The crew bustled around the command deck of the space station. Most were positioned at various screens, although several also attended Admiral Alyson Brandt, who paced the deck impatiently.

"Full diagnostic isn't in," an actuary said. "But we can confirm the shuttle is out of range. Admiral... We lost them."

"Damn it!" the admiral cursed. "I gave an order not to approach. Why the hell would they--"

"I'm showing a strange fluctuation within the anomaly just before the event," the actuary said. "Looks like the gravity spiked, pulling them inward."

"Admiral, the shuttle did beam out one last data stream before we lost it," a signal analyst said. "It's jumbled, but I'm analyzing it for any discernible patterns."

"Unscramble it," the admiral ordered. "We need to determine if the anomaly poses a threat."

"Unscrambling... Okay," the signal analyst said. "It's audio, from the shuttle's long-range scanner. Wait, this can't be right... It looks like music. But that would mean sentient life."

"Or another non-terrestrial bird species," the admiral said. "Or whale songs. Let's listen to it before you start beaming up little green spacemen."

The signal analyst tapped a few buttons on her pad, and the

tinny recording of Eliza Dell's music filled the air.

"Is that..." the admiral asked slowly and incredulously, "*Ziggy Stardust*?"

CHAPTER TWO
"WYRMHOLE"

"The attraction to the anomaly appears stronger than normal," Tarun intoned into his recorder, as he pulled the shuttle to a stop halfway between the anomaly and the space station. "Looks like the admiral's theory about proximity-based stimuli is sound," he said. "What's your read-out say?" Tarun received no immediate answer. "A.J.!" he said harshly.

His distracted co-pilot snapped out of his daydreaming. "Sorry," A.J. said, "I was just thinking."

"That's never a good sign," Tarun said.

"Do you believe in God?" A.J. asked.

Tarun rolled his eyes and sighed. "I'm Hindu. I believe in many gods," Tarun answered. "But if you think I'm gonna get into a theological discussion with you right now, you're crazy. We have a lot of work to do."

"Scanners will take ten, maybe fifteen minutes to complete their cycle," A.J. said. "That's an awful long time to fill with awkward silence."

"Fine," Tarun capitulated. "Why are you asking about God?"

"I was just thinking about this," A.J. said, indicating the anomaly ahead of them. It was relatively small, no larger than the shuttle, and from it emanated a subdued, pulsating pink glow. "It looks so... benign. Almost like a beating heart. You don't think it really destroyed those freighters, do you?"

"Admiral thinks it did, and that's good enough for me," Tarun replied.

"She's smart, but she's not infallible, you know," A.J. said.

"I know," Tarun said. "So what does the anomaly have to do with God?"

"It just seems so cruel to make something that beautiful so dangerous. If God made it," A.J. said, "Then we are talking about a creator with a very active sadistic streak."

"If God made it - and I'm talking about the one, big-G God here - then it's part of His design. It's supposed to serve a larger purpose," Tarun said.

"Tell that to the crews of those freighters," A.J. said.

The shuttle suddenly lurched forward violently, which brought both pilots' attention back to their consoles. Tarun pulled back on the steering column, which should have stalled the shuttle in its place, but another bumpy jolt kept them moving forward.

"Is that thing getting brighter?" A.J. asked, as the anomaly in front of them glowed with a new intensity. It began to grow as well, and its pulse quickened.

"I need more power to the reverse thrusters!" Tarun said, and A.J. turned the corresponding dial as far as it would go. The shuttle fought against, but could not compete with, the pull of the anomaly. Instead of falling backwards, the shuttle began veering from side to side, while steadily moving toward what had become a gaping, swirling pink maw in the black of space. The swaying movement was anything but gentle, and the pilots would have been thrown about, had they not been buckled into their seats. As they neared the anomaly, Tarun locked eyes with A.J. and said in a quiet voice, "I don't want to die." The shuttle was swallowed whole by the anomaly, which unceremoniously returned to its former, seemingly docile state.

The anomaly froze mid-pulse. Admiral Brandt stared long and hard at the holographic image. She gestured to the actuary on duty, Clayton, an older, portly man who immediately approached her with his tablet in hand. "Call the senior staff together," she instructed. "I need fresh eyes on this." Clayton saluted her and left to carry out her order. The admiral returned her attention to the holographic image of the anomaly. She pressed a button on her own tablet, and the image rewound. She paused it again just before the shuttle disappeared within the anomaly. "Where did you go?" she asked, expecting no reply.

Darra, Aleksey, and Kaleb watched as A.J. climbed down from the wreckage of the shuttle, which was still entangled with the mangled body of the dragon on the mountainside below. Darra stepped toward the edge of the cliff and yelled down a "Hello!" as she waved. A.J. waved a slow, confused hand back at her. Darra started to ask if he was okay, but Aleksey clamped a hand over her mouth and pulled her back toward the cave.

"Have you gone mad?" Aleksey asked Darra in a tone reserved for parents scolding children. "We know nothing about him. He could be dangerous. We need to get out of here," he said.

"He could be hurt," Darra said.

"That's not our problem," Aleksey said.

"But he saved us!" Darra said.

"His arrival was very timely, killing the dragon and all," Kaleb put in.

"So what would you have me do?" Aleksey asked. "Climb down to the wreckage of his... flying carriage and introduce ourselves?"

"Exactly," Darra said.

"The noise from that crash would've echoed for miles," Aleksey reasoned. "Anyone watching the skies in Morning's Peak may even have seen it. There will be people here soon to investigate. Before then, we need to collect our treasure and go."

The inside of the cave glimmered as the sun's last rays hit the obscenely large piles of gold, silver and jewels inside. Aleksey entered the cave, but as he passed the ornately carved threshold, the jewels on the broken DragonSword he was carrying began to glow.

The ground beneath Aleksey began to shake, and the roof of the cave began to crack and crumble. Aleksey leapt out of the mouth of the cave just as it began to collapse, in a move that no human could have duplicated. The half-elf landed on his stomach just clear of the larger falling rocks.

As the dust settled, Darra offered a hand to help her father to his feet.

"So much for that escape route," Kaleb said.

"And for the treasure inside," Aleksey added. "Damn it!"

"Not all of it," Kaleb said, showing off a satchel full of gold and jewels.

"Well done, Kaleb!" Aleksey said, and the swarthy fledgling mage beamed.

"I guess we're going down this way, then?" Darra asked with a sly smirk of triumph as she walked toward the edge of the cliff. She looked at her father expectantly. "Well, are you going to give me a hand down?" she asked. Aleksey looked down at the strange sight of the wreckage below. Scowling, he took a rope from his satchel and began tying it around the trunk of a tree, while his daughter smiled behind his back.

Farther down the mountainside, A.J. clambered down from the wreckage of his shuttle. He slipped on a bloody patch of metal and fell the last few feet to the ground. When he picked himself up, he was staring the dragon in its lifeless eye. The dumbfounded pilot shuddered.

"Where am I?" he asked in disbelief.

Prince Trosclair and his entourage had boarded a train that was now racing along the tracks, trailing black coal smoke. Every powerful family in the kingdom of DuVerres had tried to place a young personage in the prince's entourage, and most had succeeded. Therefore, the train car was packed tightly, with a few people even reduced to standing in the aisles. Of course, everyone had made room for Trosclair and his inner circle at the head of the car: Ennio, Trosclair's stalwart bodyguard, rarely left his side. Flanking the teenager on his other side was Armand DiPietro, whose father owned half the banks on the continent. Next came Alicia and Frederick Gagneux; distant relatives of the DuVerres royal line, they had been plucked from a life of farming at an early age and placed in the palace as Trosclair's childhood playmates. The trio remained close to this day. And finally, rounding out the group was Devon Bayu, a young playwright who developed his friendship with Trosclair through their shared love of the arts. Altogether, they were a handsome (and powerful) clique. Their tastes had governed court life ever since Trosclair became a young man. From the clothes people wore to the food they ate to the musicians and artists they patronized, everyone at the palace followed the example of these trendy young folk. Today, that meant donning black clothing with a single accent color to mourn Duke DuVerres, Trosclair's late uncle.

Alicia was wearing a somber black dress that fell to the floor, with a purple, gossamer scarf for her accent piece. "To honor the Duke's royal stature," she said, when Trosclair asked her about it.

Not to be outdone, Armand withdrew the red handkerchief from his pocket and declared solemnly, "For the spilt blood of his defeated enemies."

"Why did you choose blue?" Devon asked the prince, who was sporting a large, bird-shaped broach of that color.

"I don't know. It just seemed... peaceful," Trosclair answered. "I hope he's at peace."

"I'm sure the Reaper took him straight to the arms of the Undying Mother," Frederick said, meaning it quite literally. Stylish though he was, his provincial origin could still be gleaned from his strict adherence to The Faith, the religion of the old gods. Most of the court regarded The Faith as an antiquated institution whose primary function these days was charity, not theology. Still, Frederick's companions respected his beliefs enough not to snicker or make fun of his sincere sentiment.

Frederick's sister was a little bit wilder. Alicia withdrew a flask from her dress and raised it in a toast, saying, "To the good Duke. May his legacy be a prosperous kingdom." She took a short swig from the flask before handing it to Trosclair. The young prince hesitated just a moment before downing his own shot of what turned out to be vodka. The group passed the flask among themselves until it was empty and they were buzzed. Ennio alone refused to drink, his excuse being that he had to remain sharp while he was on duty.

The train rounded the last of the mountains, and the palace came into view in the distance. A sparkling jewel situated on the eastern edge of the kingdom's sprawling capital city, the palace had been built less than fifty years ago, after Trosclair's great-grandfather grew tired of living in a cold, crumbling castle. No expense had been spared in its construction; as the largest and most powerful kingdom on the continent, DuVerres had an image to uphold.

Trosclair looked out the window at the only home he had ever known and sighed his relief at returning. He imagined court life would be different now that his uncle was no longer Regent. He rubbed the edge of the window absentmindedly with one finger. Ennio placed his own hand over Trosclair's and asked, "Did you want the window opened, Your Grace?" The soldier's formal tone was betrayed by the intimate touch of his hand upon the prince's. Ennio's touch always brought a flush of color to Trosclair's cheeks, and a rush of excitement to his head - and other parts. Trosclair jerked his hand away, as if Ennio's touch burned him.

"No, thank you," he replied, feeling all eyes on him and hoping no one had read too much into the brief exchange. "Excuse me," Trosclair said, rising. "I need to use the little prince's room." The prince and his bodyguard made their way to the back of the train car and entered the lavatory. The window had been opened, and the air in the small room whipped and swirled around them. Ennio wrapped his arms around Trosclair and pulled him in close. "Never in the presence of others," Trosclair gently chided, and the soldier nodded his understanding.

Admiral Brandt and her senior staff sat in a comfortable conference room, re-watching the holographic images of the shuttle's disappearance inside the anomaly.

"Fascinating," Andre commented, as the images dissolved. "And the audio file the shuttle beamed back?" he prompted. Admiral Brandt pushed a few buttons on her tablet, and a snippet of the tinny recording of Eliza Dell's music filled the air. When it was over, the group was subdued into stunned silence.

"Any thoughts?" Admiral Brandt asked.

"Too many to process," Andre replied. "For starters, it looks like the anomaly is some kind of opening or portal. That is to say, the shuttle seems to have entered into it, as opposed to merely colliding with it."

"That was my take, too," the admiral said. "And that means the pilots may have survived contact. What does this tell us about the anomaly?"

"Well, if they entered into it, the anomaly could be some sort of wormhole, or even a rip in the fabric of space/time," Myra, the Chief Academic Officer, ventured. "We've also theorized that it could be a teleportational entry point, most likely created by alien technology. All we know for certain is that the shuttle is... elsewhere."

"And that, wherever it went, this music came from there," Andre added. "But the long-range audio scanners don't kick in unless the shuttle is in atmo."

"The shuttle could have been displaced into an existing atmosphere as easily as any place else, I suppose," Myra said.

"We're missing the significance of the music itself, though," Clayton put in. "It's Earth-originated."

"Are you suggesting that thing sent them all the way back to Earth Prime?" the admiral asked.

"More likely one of the colonies. After all, the simplest explanation, etc. ..." Clayton trailed off with a flourish of his wrist.

"No way," Andre said. "The sensors would have picked up countless signals from a colony, not just the one song."

"Okay, but we can conclude that the presence of the song – wherever the shuttle ended up – is another possible indication that our pilots could still be alive," Myra asserted.

"Because the song indicates a possible preexisting human presence in the... place the shuttle ended up," Admiral Brandt reasoned. "Thank god," she added. "Okay, people, let's move quickly. However bizarre it seems, this just became a search and rescue op."

Soon after, on the command deck, the admiral and her senior staff watched the anomaly in real time. In its resting state, it once again resembled a celestial heart softly beating; but the admiral could no longer look upon the anomaly with the naïve scientific curiosity with which she had approached it before. Now each pulse seemed to signal an ominous warning, like the *tick* of a time-bomb counting down to detonation.

"Any theories on the catalyst for the anomaly's behavior?" Admiral Brandt asked.

"If your theory about a proximity-based distortion of the gravity field is correct, it could have been the shuttle itself," Andre suggested.

"They got too close and just... set it off?" the admiral asked. Andre shook his head in the affirmative.

"But why this shuttle, this time?" Clayton asked. "Our other pilots have flown much, much closer without producing the same effect."

"We cannot assume the anomaly required any kind of catalyst to open – at least not one from this side," Myra cautioned.

"That's a possibility I won't consider for now," Admiral Brandt said. "Until proven otherwise, we're going to assume there is some way to manipulate the anomaly to our advantage."

"You're not seriously thinking about trying to open that thing back up, are you?" Andre asked. When the admiral equivocated with a slight shrug, he continued, "Admiral, we know next to nothing about the anomaly. I'm not sure agitating it is the wisest course of action. We are talking about forces potentially powerful enough to destroy this entire station, after all."

"Actually, if we're talking about the manipulation of space-time, we could be dealing with the destruction of much more than this vessel," Myra said. "What is the sound of a universe imploding?" she asked rhetorically as she straightened her glasses.

"We owe those boys a decent rescue attempt," the admiral argued. "This was supposed to be a simple training op. They were never supposed to be in this kind of danger."

"Exactly," Andre agreed. "So to put us all in that kind of danger is–"

"A risk we'll simply have to take," Admiral Brandt said with finality.

"Don't worry, Andre," Clayton consoled him, as the admiral walked away. "I've run the numbers, and our chances of destroying all of creation as we know it are less than two percent."

Andre smiled, choosing to believe the actuary was joking.

A.J. rounded a corner on the body of the dragon and let out a sharp squeal of surprise. Darra stood a few feet away, her crossbow pointed straight at his heart.

"That's close enough, for now," Darra said. "Are you hurt?" she asked.

"I'm fine." A.J. managed to reply. "But my co-pilot–" Darra tilted her head in confusion at the word. "My *friend* – hit his head in the crash. He's still in there."

Kaleb and Aleksey approached, the latter looking seriously annoyed to hear his daughter say, "We'll help you get him out."

"No, we won't," Aleksey said firmly.

"Dad!" Darra protested. "You're the one who's always saying we need to help those in need. His friend is hurt."

Turning to A.J., the half-elf said, "You just appeared out of thin air up there. You must be a sorcerer of some skill. I'm sure you'll be fine."

"A sorcerer? Like with magic?" A.J. laughed nervously. "Oh. You're serious. No, no! I'm not a sorcerer. I'm a pilot."

"I don't know what that means," Aleksey stated matter-of-factly.

"It means... I'm just a normal guy," A.J. said. "And I don't have a way to get my friend out of there without your help."

"Dad, please!" Darra begged. Her pleading eyes usually worked on Aleksey, and this was no exception.

"Fine," Aleksey said. "We'll help you get your friend clear of this mess." Aleksey turned to Darra and added, "But then we are leaving!"

A few minutes later, Aleksey and A.J. handed Tarun's unconscious body down to Darra and Kaleb, who laid him out on the ground.

"Do you think he'll be okay?' A.J. asked.

"Well, I'm no physician, but I've seen worse injuries," Aleksey replied. Tarun began to moan softly, as if in response. "See? It looks like he's coming around already."

"That's a good sign," Darra said, smiling at A.J. reassuringly.

"I forgot to ask your name," the pilot said. "I'm A.J."

"Darra."

Aleksey was quick to jump in before they could shake hands. "And I'm her father, Aleksey, and this young man is Kaleb."

"Father?" A.J. asked. "You don't look old enough to be her father."

"I moisturize," Aleksey deadpanned. "So now that the introductions are over, we really must be going."

"His friend isn't even on his feet yet," Darra said. "We are not just abandoning them here!" Darra crossed her arms and stared down her father, who eventually relented yet again. Tarun began to stir, and Kaleb dropped down to the young man's side.

"Don't try to move just yet," Kaleb instructed the injured

pilot. "Gram says head wounds can be tricky," he explained to the others as he pulled out his waterskin. "Here, drink this," he said, lifting the skin to Tarun's lips. Tarun drank deeply.

A.J. stepped forward. "Are you okay, Tarun?" he asked. "You gave me quite a scare."

Tarun locked eyes with A.J., spat up the water, and screamed, full-throated and full of true terror. He scrambled backwards and somehow found the strength to rise to his feet, never breaking eye contact with A.J., who was dumbfounded by his friend's behavior. "You're alive!" Tarun finally said in a breathy whisper.

"Yeah, I'm fine," A.J. replied. "A few bruises. But you know what they say about a landing you can walk away from."

"Does that mean... I'm alive, too?" Tarun asked, his eyes large and glossy as he surveyed his surroundings. "Is this world real?" He reached out a hand and touched Kaleb's robe disbelievingly.

"I know what you mean," A.J. said. "This world is too much. We crashed into a friggin' dragon, for Pete's sake!"

Tarun looked over the crash site, then chuckled before mumbling, "Pete's Dragon. High fantasy world. Sword and sorcery." He spied Kaleb's bag of gold and jewels. "Precious metals, precious... things... Objects of power!" he blurted out as if in excited discovery.

A.J. tilted his head in concern. "Are you sure you should be on your feet?" he asked. "It seems like you hit your head pretty hard."

Tarun ignored A.J. and continued rambling, "Power-over. Means tyrants. Human or... something else..."

"Is he alright?" Darra asked as Tarun kept spitting out fragments of sentences with no clear thread of meaning.

"I don't know," A.J. answered honestly. "He must have a concussion or something."

"Well, let's hope he can still walk," Aleksey said, his gaze aimed worriedly at a ridge a few thousand feet away. "Briskly," he added.

"What is it?" Kaleb asked.

"A company of soldiers just rounded the path from Morning's Peak," Aleksey answered, pointing. "They'll be here in less than ten minutes."

"I don't see anybody," A.J. said.

"You wouldn't. Dad's half-elven, so his senses are sharper than a human's," Darra explained.

"Darra Esmerelda Fabian!" Aleksey said, as he pulled his daughter aside. "We know nothing about these men! Some discretion would be appreciated, especially where it concerns *my* secrets! For all we know, they could be mercenaries, or spies, or bandits--"

"I don't think they're bandits, Dad," Darra said, rolling her eyes. "In fact, judging from their flying carriage and this strange armor, I don't think they're from around here at all." She reached out her hand and knocked on A.J.'s chest for emphasis. The sleek black spacesuit's material surprised her with its pliability, and she pressed a curious hand along the contours of the young pilot's torso. "Oh, wow," she said, as she suddenly drew her hand back. "That's not a chest plate, is it?"

"Nope. That's just my chest," A.J. said with a soft, nervous chuckle.

"Well it's very, um, shapely. I mean, it's shaped like a chest plate," Darra said, before turning to her father to hide her reddening cheeks. "You said something about running away now?" she asked him, a thin note of desperation in her voice.

"First attempt at physical contact with the anomaly initiated," Admiral Brandt intoned into her tablet as a shuttle slowly made its way toward the pulsating celestial sphere. Her senior officers and the entirety of the command deck crew monitored the approach apprehensively, watching for any sign that the anomaly was powering back up.

"We're approaching the approximate location of the previous shuttle before it was pulled into the anomaly. Be ready for anything," Andre warned the crew. A tense moment passed as the shuttle reached the threshold of its predecessor and came to a halt.

"Gravity is within our projected range and holding steady," said Gracie, a young signal analyst, as she took readings from her console.

"Damn it!" the admiral cursed.

"It looks like the anomaly isn't taking the bait," Myra said.

"Fine. We'll go in closer," Brandt said.

"How close are you planning to get?" Andre asked.

"If my theory is correct, the closer we get to that thing, the stronger its gravitational pull will become," the admiral said. "We'll stop and observe when the grav spikes."

"If the anomaly allows us to stop," Myra said.

Brandt spoke directly into her tablet again. "Med-ship One, move in to standby coordinates."

"Affirmative," a pilot said, her voice through the tablet as clear as if she was in the room. The Med-ship, about three times the size of the shuttle, zipped out from the space station's launch bay and followed the path of the smaller ship.

"Admiral, we're approaching a distance of a hundred kilometers. That's the closest our pilots have taken us," Gracie said.

"Shuttle One, report," Brandt prompted.

"The anomaly is behaving as predicted, Admiral," a man's voice returned. "Gravitational pull has increased with increased proximity, in accordance with the predicted model."

"Continue on, then," the admiral said.

"Affirmative," the pilot replied. The shuttle drew in closer and closer to the anomaly.

After a few seconds, Gracie said, "Grav's spiking! There's some fluctuation, but it's up at least seventeen percent."

"That's way too strong, too fast," Clayton said. "At that rate, it'll likely swallow the whole station within the hour!"

"Shuttle One, stall your approach immediately," Brandt ordered.

"I am unable to comply with that order, Admiral," the man's voice came again. "The anomaly's gravitational pull is overpowering the thrusters. The shuttle will come in contact with the anomaly in approximately thirty-two seconds, no matter what I do."

"Admiral, this is Med-ship One. Do we have orders to move in?"

"Negative," the admiral said. "Maintain your distance, but stay ready to make your move once contact occurs."

"Affirmative," the Med-ship's pilot replied once more.

The shuttle began pulling from side to side, just as its predecessor had, as it fought the pull of the anomaly in vain. This time, however, the anomaly didn't open up and swallow the craft; the vessel was merely crushed. The admiral visibly flinched as the crumpled remains of the small ship bounced off the anomaly and drifted aimlessly into open space. "Tell me that was worth something," she said.

Gracie shook her head in the negative. "I'm sorry, Admiral," she said. "There's no discernable evidence that the anomaly is powering up like it did before."

"It didn't work, then," Andre said.

"Don't sound so relieved," Admiral Brandt said. "That just means we have to try something else."

"Forgive my bluntness, but we've already lost two shuttles and three pilots, if you count the android you just sacrificed," Andre said. "This was supposed to be a simple recon mission, and I'd say we've determined rather conclusively that this anomaly does pose a danger to our shipping route. I think it's time we sent a beacon back to headquarters asking for clarification on any further mission parameters."

"Okay," the Admiral said, after a moment's consideration. "You get on that. But the rest of us will continue looking for a way to rescue our lost pilots while we wait for new orders."

"And that means another attempt at opening the anomaly?" Andre asked.

"Probably," Brandt answered. "But I have no idea what a second attempt would even look like,"

Myra smiled as she stared at a screen of statistics on her own tablet. "As it so happens," she said, "I may have a bead on that."

Trosclair and Ennio broke with tradition and entered the banquet hall ahead of the guests. Their reasons were two-fold: Ennio was averse to ceding his position at Trosclair's side to the advisor who would be announcing the guests, and Trosclair didn't want to shake hands with every single person as he made his way to the chair at the head of the table. By entering the hall first, Trosclair got away with merely smiling and nodding his greetings. When the introductions were over, thirteen nobles (each representing a major city of DuVerres) and all nine advisors of the Council had been seated. Two delegates from DuVerres' closest neighboring kingdoms had also already arrived. Trosclair expected to entertain many more such delegations as news spread across the continent that the Duke was dead.

Milian was seated immediately to Trosclair's right; the Nobles and remaining Councilmembers had seated themselves as close to the prince as they could, but inevitably, many were disappointed to be at the far end of the table, as the two foreigners had the honor of sitting to the prince's left. Genevieve San Laurient was Duchess of Rushrivers and cousin to the king of Vilmos, which bordered DuVerres to the northeast. She had been the first woman of that kingdom to inherit her title directly instead of through marriage, and she was regarded by many as something of a trailblazer. Acton Pryce of the Shadowshore could not rival his Vilmosi counterpart in pedigree, having been born a commoner. Nonetheless, he now ruled over the largest city in the kingdom of Laur. The relative importance of both guests attested to DuVerres' strength as a kingdom – and to the power that Trosclair would one day wield as its king.

The young prince rose and tapped the side of his wineglass with his knife, and the conversations around the table quieted as all eyes turned to him. "It is with great sadness that we welcome you all today. Our late uncle and regent, the Duke of Seventhstead, was an honorable man," Trosclair said, though he was unsure of the veracity of his own words. "Our kingdom is the lesser for the loss of him. But life must go on, and so we feast in his honor." He raised his glass in salute.

"In his honor!" came the bellowing response from the rest of the hall's occupants, and everyone drank.

The prince signaled, and several servants began bringing in the food on large silver platters. Trosclair settled back down into his chair. He squirmed as discreetly as he could in the large seat, not quite a throne, which had been occupied by his uncle at every formal meal until now. Trosclair hated that the chair's immensity made him look even smaller than he already was, and he made a mental note to have it replaced with something less ostentatious before the next meal.

"I trust the train from Vilmos was comfortable?" Milian asked the Duchess.

"Comfortable and, more importantly, on time," she answered with a polite smile.

"Have you seen the play *One Night in Nuru*?" Trosclair asked.

"Sadly, it hasn't yet come to Rushrivers," the Duchess said. "I've heard wonderful things about it, though."

"It's hilarious!" Trosclair said. "It concerns a baggage handler at a train station who mixes up the traveler's luggage, leading to much chaos and confusion. Our good friend is the playwright."

"Ah, how fortunate," Genevieve said. "Perhaps you can convince him to have his troupe travel through my city? I would gladly pay the artists' emolument for a night of cultured entertainment."

"We'll see what we can manage," Trosclair said. Turning to Acton, he asked, "And you, Lord Chancellor? Do you follow the theatre?"

"I must admit I do not," the man said. "Most of my waking hours are devoted to the duties of my office, and it leaves me little time for the arts. But I do patronize the temple of Kesari, goddess of the arts, and in turn, the clergy entertain the city's important visitors when I am unavailable. Music, dancing, comedy - the whole works. I'm told their improvisational actors are—"

"I'll not stand for this!" a noble shouted from halfway down the table, as he rose and threw his napkin down onto his plate. "We duel at dawn!" he said to a man sitting across from him looking equally upset.

"Fine!" the other noble readily agreed. "Short swords!"

Milian rose and addressed them both. "This is a solemn occasion. What is the cause of this outburst, Lord Ocran?"

"My deepest apologies, Your Grace," Lord Ocran said, eyeing Trosclair. "But honor forbids that I sit idly by while this thief mocks me!"

"He's the thief!" the other man blurted out, red-faced. "And with the gods to witness, tomorrow morning I'll gut him for it!"

"Lord Fallon, we cannot allow our noble cousins to slaughter each other every time there is a disagreement," Trosclair said.

"Well put," Milian said.

"There's no regent to settle this dispute. If we're not to duel, how would you have us proceed?" Lord Fallon asked Milian. "Would you hear the facts of the case?"

"I fear that's out of the scope of my administrative duties," Milian answered. "But perhaps His Grace could render the verdict."

Trosclair squirmed in his seat again. "But we have no experience in legal matters," he protested.

"Our two esteemed guests have no personal interest in this affair," Milian said. "If it will ease Your Grace's concerns and they've no objections, they can act as advisors in an informal tribunal."

"I've no other plans for my stay here," Genevieve said.

"It would be an honor to help guide the prince in these early days of his ascension," Acton agreed.

Milian looked to Trosclair for confirmation, and the prince nodded his acquiescence. "So it shall be," the young man said with mustered authority. "We'll hear the facts of the case on the morrow. Until then, we can assume there will be no more outbursts?" he asked as he fixed his gaze upon Lord Ocran and Lord Fallon. The former bowed deeply while the latter merely grunted. Lord Ocran reseated himself at the far end of the table, away from the occasional angry mumblings of his rival, and the banquet resumed. Only Ennio noticed the slight stiffening of Trosclair's posture throughout the remainder of the meal.

After several hours racing down the mountainside, Aleksey finally called the group to a halt in a small clearing. "The sun is setting," the half-elf observed. "We should make camp here for the night. Kaleb, you stay here and keep an eye on these two. Darra and I will gather some wood."

Darra sat her satchel at Kaleb's feet and followed her father back into the forest. When he was sure the others were out of earshot, Aleksey said, "I can tell you like this boy."

"I don't like him," Darra said. "I mean, I like him well enough, but I don't *like*-like him. We only just met. He is certainly interesting, though."

"And you find yourself attracted to him?" Aleksey asked.

"Dad, I'm not talking to you about this," Darra said as she stooped to pick up a fallen branch. "This is what girlfriends are for."

"I just wanted to make sure you have realistic expectations about him, honey. I heard most of your conversation, and I can tell you were right. He and his rambling companion are not from around here - which means they'll probably be going back to wherever they came from soon."

"I don't know," Darra said as she picked up another branch. "They aren't going anywhere in their flying carriage, obviously."

"I believe he called it a ship," Aleksey said.

"Well whatever it is, it's not in working condition. They may have to stick with us for a while." Darra paused as a puzzled look came across her face. "Why are you allowing that, anyway? You couldn't wait to get away from them before. Now we're making camp together. It's almost like you're... being reasonable."

"You haven't left me much choice! Now that they know so much about us, it's in our best interest to see them safely out of this kingdom. We can't have them telling people our whereabouts."

"This should be enough for first watch," Darra said, indicating the firewood in her arms. "Which I lay claim to!" she added as they started back toward the clearing.

A little while later, Aleksey handed out *aori,* a type of bread with a layer of cheese and vegetables baked into it, from his pack. Everyone ate except Tarun, who had succumbed to the rigor of the hike down the mountain and was sleeping soundly with his back up against a log. Kaleb arranged the firewood, raised his hand in a simple gesture, and intoned a few syllables in the old speak; a robust fire leapt into existence. A.J. flinched and caught his breath.

"How - how did you do that?" he asked Kaleb, with a look of wonder on his face.

"It's just a simple fire spell," the young man said, surprised at the pilot's reaction. "Let me guess: you're from a city that doesn't allow magic."

"Uh... something like that," A.J. replied.

"Where *do* you come from?" Darra asked.

"New Titan," A.J. said.

"Never heard of it," Aleksey said suspiciously. "And I've traveled to the farthest reaches of this world."

"That's just it," A.J. said, "I'm not from this world."

"What do you mean?" Darra asked.

"That portal back there – or whatever you want to call it – we were studying it. And then it swallowed our ship and brought us here," A.J. explained. "I don't know how or why. I was hoping maybe you could tell me something about it."

"I don't know much," Darra said. "I found a gem in the dragon's hoard; it must have been enchanted. I think that's what brought you here."

"That does make some sense," Aleksey put in. "Dragons are known to travel to distant realms."

"You're saying... magic brought us here?" A.J. asked. Darra shrugged and shook her head in the affirmative. The young pilot turned to Kaleb. "So can magic send us back?"

"A dragon's magic is powerful," the young mage said, pulling out his pipe. "Way more powerful than mine. Sorry."

"That's okay," A.J. said. "Truthfully, I don't want to leave until I've seen more of this world for myself anyway. It's all just so... fascinating! Like, how can you possibly speak English?"

"English?" Darra echoed. "You mean the common speak? Everyone speaks it. That's what makes it, you know, common."

Darra took the first watch, and A.J. was too excited to sleep, so he kept her company. The teens took turns being impressed by the details of each other's worlds, with only scattered interruptions from Kaleb and Aleksey, for several hours. A.J. tried to explain New Titan to Darra, but the concepts were so foreign to her, she was able to picture only a little of what he described. In turn, she told him stories about creatures and places he wouldn't have thought possible the day before. As they spoke to each other in excited whispers, neither Darra nor A.J. noticed that Tarun had woken up; he listened to their conversation intently as he lay there, feigning sleep long into the night.

Aleksey took the second shift, during the middle of the night, when the forest's nocturnal predators were most active. A few birds and a large jackrabbit came into the clearing but stayed far from the fire and the people sleeping around it. Aleksey busied himself arranging the pieces of the shattered DragonSword, which he laid out on the ground. When he had it assembled, he took a book from his pack and began copying the inscriptions on the blade. He completed his work on the first side, flipped the fragments of the sword over, and copied everything on the second. Finishing about two hours before sunrise, he put the pieces of the sword back into his pack, woke Kaleb, stretched out on the ground and closed his eyes.

Kaleb shook him awake a few hours later. "Aleksey!" the teen whispered. "They're gone!"

Aleksey blinked a few times as his eyes adjusted to the daylight and then surveyed the campsite. Darra was curled up on the other side of the dwindling fire, but there was no sign of the pilots. He frowned, knowing his daughter would be disappointed.

"And they took my satchel!" Kaleb added.

"Unholy Hells!" Aleksey said, rising, as Darra began to stir. "Honey, wake up."

The young woman rolled onto her back and shielded her face with a hand before aiming a squinted eye at her father. "What is it?" she asked, as her vision cleared and revealed his scowl.

"Have a look for yourself," he instructed.

Darra rubbed her eyes with both hands and looked around the camp. "They're gone?" she asked in a worried tone as she got to her feet.

"I'm afraid so," Aleksey said. "They've taken off with our treasure."

"And everything else I had in there!" Kaleb said.

"What else did you have in there?" Darra asked.

"Mostly clothes," Kaleb answered. "But they've also got my spellbook and some other... stuff. We have to go after them!"

"No," Aleksey said firmly. "You two should wait here. I'll follow their trail faster on my own. How did they manage to sneak away, anyway? You were supposed to be keeping watch."

"I was!" Kaleb said. "But after the sun rose, I went out to

scavenge a little breakfast."

"Did you find anything good?" Darra asked.

"Brushberries and almonds," the young man answered, pointing out the food in two mounds on his bedroll. "When I came back, they were gone."

A rustling of leaves and branches in the nearby trees alerted the adventurers to the approach of something large and lumbering. Aleksey picked up his short sword, and Kaleb drew a pair of throwing knives from a concealed pocket in his robes. "Be ready," Aleksey whispered to his daughter and the young mage. The rustling came to a pitch, and A.J. stumbled out into the clearing.

"Oh," Aleksey said. "It's just you. Where did you go?"

"I had to use the bathroom," he answered. "What's with the weapons?"

"Your friend stole my satchel," Kaleb said.

"That doesn't make any sense," A.J. protested. "Tarun was barely on his feet yesterday. And he's as lost in this world as I am. Why would he go out on his own?"

"I'll be sure to ask him when we catch up to him," Aleksey said, returning his sword to its sheath as Darra began gathering her things and Kaleb stomped out the fire.

A few minutes later, they were back in the thick of the forest, Aleksey leading the way. Kaleb followed the half-elf closely, while Darra and A.J. lingered several paces behind. Aleksey pretended to follow the trail of half-formed footprints and damaged vegetation, but he was really following his nose. His heightened olfactory sense had been useful on more than one occasion, but it was nonetheless a source of embarrassment for him. He felt like a bloodhound, more animal than human, when he honed in on another person's scent like this.

"Hey!" Kaleb exclaimed as they came upon a pile of clothes. The young man stooped to gather them up. Underneath the clothing, he found his spellbook, his bedroll, a few common magical accoutrements, and a large pouch of daydreamer's herb. Aleksey rummaged through his own pack and came out with a thin linen sack, which Kaleb filled with his belongings. "Why would your friend bother to dump this stuff?" the teen asked. "It's not very heavy."

"Who knows?" A.J. asked rhetorically. "I think he's... not right. It has to be his injury making him do this."

"I've never heard of a head wound turning someone into a thief," Aleksey said.

"He was sound of mind enough to sneak away when no one was watching, with our hard-earned fortune," Darra added. "That shows cunning. How well do you know this man?"

"He's my best friend," A.J. answered.

Aleksey titled his head and inhaled deeply, closing his eyes, and his expression soured.

"What is it, Dad?" Darra asked.

"Something's coming," he said, placing a finger over his lips to quiet the group. After a few seconds, they heard the unmistakable sounds of a forest creature approaching. "Quick!" Aleksey urged the others. "Up the trees!"

Kaleb followed Aleksey up a low-hanging branch as Darra and A.J. made their way to another tree. Before they could scramble up into it, an army of ants, each about the size of a human fist, swarmed the forest floor in front of them. A.J. cried out as a shaggy insectivore almost six feet tall and fully ten feet long poked its slender snout around a tree right in front of him. Darra grabbed the startled young man by the arm and backed him up several paces as the ants skittered away from the creature in all directions.

"It's an ant bear!" Aleksey called down from his perch. "Run!"

Trosclair, Genevieve and Acton sat behind a short table on a raised dais, with Lord Ocran and Lord Fallon at even smaller tables facing them. Ennio stood directly behind Trosclair, and Milian stood beside the young soldier, quietly observing.

"To begin, we will first hear the claims of Lord Ocran," the prince said.

"Thank you," Lord Ocran said, nodding politely. "As you know, Lord Fallon's city and my own share a common border. That border falls in the middle of a large valley, which both cities use to pasture our grazing herds. In the spring of this year, I went hunting. I was out several days. When I returned, my steward informed me that fifty head of cattle had gone missing, and that he had personally seen Lord Fallon's men leading them away. As a courtesy, I reached out to Lord Fallon, who claimed his newly swollen herd had been a gift from his liegeman, to celebrate the birth of his latest child."

Trosclair was surprised, as Lord Fallon was nearing seventy, but he successfully hid his shock at the old man's virility. "Congratulations on the newest addition to your family, Lord Fallon," the young prince said.

The old man waved the sentiment away. "It was only another girl, Your Grace," he said. "But that's not the end of the tale, now, is it, Cousin?"

"Certainly not!" Lord Ocran shot back. "After Lord Fallon proved immune to reasonable suggestions of recompense, I had my own men secure twenty-five head of cattle from his pastures."

"Why only twenty-five, if fifty had gone missing?" Acton asked.

"Our cities do most of their trading with each other," Lord Ocran said. "I thought a compromise would be the best way to keep the peace."

"And I'll say now what I said then," Lord Fallon said. "There is no honor in compromise! Why should I lose a single animal? It's his man's word against my own, and I am a Noble! Why must I pay for a servant's lies?"

"My steward is an honest and capable man," Lord Ocran asserted. "He is not mistaken."

"Have either of you any evidence to present to support your claims?" Genevieve asked.

"I have herd tallies and purchasing records going back several years, all in my steward's own hand," Lord Ocran answered, holding up a thick stack of papers.

"And I could produce the same," Lord Fallon said. "I've also the witness of the liegeman who gifted me the cattle."

"Is that everything, then?" Genevieve asked.

"Nothing further need be said!" Lord Fallon answered. Lord Ocran nodded his head in agreement.

Trosclair cleared his throat and stood. "Thank you for your testimonies. We will now consider this matter in private." Ennio crossed to the door and held it open for the Lords, who each bowed to Trosclair before departing.

"Well," Genevieve began, as Trosclair took his seat again. "Your position is a difficult one, Your Grace. In my view, neither side presented a clear preponderance of the facts."

"You would not side with either of them, then?" Trosclair asked.

"Unfortunately, that is not an option," Genevieve said. "A ruler cannot shirk their responsibility to sit in judgment, even when they have only intuition to go on. Who does your gut tell you is the more truthful of the two?"

Trosclair thought for a moment, then said, "Lord Ocran. Lord Fallon seemed oddly defensive."

"I thought so, too," Genevieve agreed.

"So you would advise me to side with Lord Ocran?" the teen asked, looking to Acton for confirmation.

"Not so fast," Acton cautioned. "There are other aspects to consider. Lord Ocran admitted that he stole from Fallon's herd. That's a crime, justified or not. And the old man was right about one thing: In the eyes of the law, a noble's word is worth more than a commoner's. And Lord Fallon's word is bolstered by that of his liegeman."

"But any liegeman can be pressured by their Lord into giving false testimony," Genevieve said.

"As can a servant," Acton countered politely. "And supporting documents can be forged."

"Lord Ocran was willing to compromise," Genevieve said. "Surely that counts for something?"

Acton merely shrugged. "I suppose that will be at His Grace's discretion." Trosclair shook his head slowly up and down, carefully considering all that he had heard.

Darra and A.J. raced through the trees, the ant bear close on their heels. "Why is it still chasing us?" the pilot asked.

"It must be male," Darra said. "They're very territorial." The pair came upon a small stream and had to change their course. They ran alongside the creek, their feet sinking several inches into the muddy bank with each footfall, until they came upon a small backwater. "In here!" Darra instructed, as she splashed into the shallows. "He won't follow us into the water!" she said, and A.J. hurried in behind her. They waded to the center, where the water settled just above their waists. The ant bear reached the backwater and sounded out his rage as he paced back and forth; the strange utterance was like the grunt of a pig mixed with the growl of a lion.

Aleksey and Kaleb heard the beast from their perch in the tree far away. Aleksey's paternal instinct was to rush toward the sound to make sure Darra was unharmed, but the ground was still covered by the colony of highly agitated ants. "Can you summon fire to clear us a path?" he asked Kaleb, who looked down at the ants uneasily.

"I could try," the young mage said, pushing up the sleeves of his robe. "But there are so many of them, I'd probably lose control and burn down the forest. I have a better idea." The teen pulled his spellbook out of the linen sack and began rifling through the pages. He found the page he was looking for and handed the book to Aleksey. "Hold this," he instructed the half-elf, as he read from a page labeled 'Predatory Nature.' Kaleb contorted his hands in a series of strange gestures, mimicking the illustrations on the page. He read a few syllables aloud in the old speak, then cupped his hands around his mouth and exhaled deeply. The sound that came forth was a perfect imitation of the ant bear, and the ants below scurried away as if the predator had returned.

"Very impressive spell," Aleksey said, handing the book back to Kaleb.

The teen stowed the volume back in his sack, beaming. "Thanks," he said. "But I'm pretty sure that was a mating call. We should probably leave before the real ant bear comes back to investigate."

"Good idea," Aleksey agreed, and the pair hopped down from the tree.

Darra and A.J. stood still and close together in the middle of the backwater as the ant bear paced along the bank. They both kept an eye on the animal while also sneaking glances at each other. A.J.'s knees suddenly buckled, and he grabbed Darra's hand so he wouldn't fall.

"Are you okay?" she asked as she helped steady him.

"Yeah. Yes. I'm fine," he stammered unconvincingly. "I—I think a big fish just grazed my thighs, but other than that, I'm fine."

"Good," Darra said, shivering from the chill of the mountain stream in autumn. She looked A.J. up and down. "Aren't you cold?" she asked.

"Nah. My suit's waterproof and temperature-controlled, so I'm actually... toasty." A.J. blushed as he locked eyes with the young woman for several seconds. He leaned toward her, and Darra was sure she was about to be kissed -- when through the trees echoed Kaleb's ant bear impression, commanding all their attention. The creature heard the call as well, and with a final grunt-growl, he turned away from the water and doubled back on his own trail.

"He's gone," Darra said when the animal was finally out of sight. A.J. realized he was still holding her hand, but he didn't let it go. Neither did she pull it away, he noticed with a smile, as she led him out of the water.

Admiral Brandt and her senior staff watched from above as the *Morningstar* was outfitted with its latest feature: a large, sophisticated cannon being secured to the ship's bow.

"Walk me through this again, please?" Andre asked.

"It's a simple theory," Myra said. "The vibrational frequency of the anomaly changed when it opened and swallowed the first shuttle, and it changed again when the second shuttle came in contact with it. It could be that vibrational frequency is the key to communicating with the anomaly. The vibratory cannon will facilitate that."

"But why risk our flagship on this experiment?" Andre asked.

"Had to," Brandt said. "The cannon's too big for a shuttle, and all our larger ships are out."

"But if we waited—"

"We can't wait," the admiral interrupted. "We already lost the night configuring the cannon. The pilots could be in danger."

"Admiral," Andre said, pulling her aside. "I mean no disrespect by this, but are you sure you're not letting your personal feelings influence your decisions?"

"*Hmph*! That is such a male thing to say," Myra muttered under her breath.

"Of course I am!" Brandt replied, as if she hadn't heard. "Feelings are a valid source of insight. But I'm not just doing this because A.J. was in that shuttle. I would do the same for you or any member of my crew whose life was in danger. This is the right call."

"I truly hope so," Andre said. "I'll assemble the *Morningstar*'s crew and get them briefed."

"Actually, I've already put out a call for volunteers. I do realize how dangerous this mission is, Andre," the admiral said. "That's why I'll be captaining the ship myself."

"Stifle your urge to argue," Myra advised Andre. "She's made up her mind."

"I have," Brandt confirmed. "And before you try and volunteer, I'm ordering you all to the Command Deck. No sense in risking the brain trust." Andre nodded his understanding, and the senior staff exited the platform.

About two hours later, they were watching from the command deck as the *Morningstar* zipped out of the station's largest launch bay. The ship maneuvered into position directly in line with the anomaly.

"*Morningstar* to command deck," the admiral's voice said through Andre's tablet. "We're in position. Firing up the vibe cannon now..." Several seconds passed, and then the admiral's voice came again. "Vibe cannon is fully charged and locked onto the anomaly. Discharging in three... two... one!" The cannon fired, and invisible waves of vibration shot out at the anomaly.

"Vibrational frequency of the anomaly is increasing," Gracie said.

"It's working!" came Brandt's excited voice as the anomaly's pulse quickened. "The anomaly appears to be powering up." The pink celestial sphere began to open up in its center, but before the admiral could get out an order to approach, the *Morningstar* began to shake violently.

"What's that?" the admiral asked, grabbing onto a rail.

"Some kind of backlash from the cannon," answered a woman at a console. "It's like the anomaly is redirecting the vibrational waves at us."

"Cease fire!" the admiral ordered. A man tapped on his tablet, and the cannon powered down. A few seconds later, the ship stopped shaking.

"Admiral, the anomaly looks to be returning to its resting state," the woman at the console said.

"Damn it!" the admiral cursed. "*Morningstar* to Command Deck. I'm aborting the mission. Prepare to receive us."

"Affirmative," Andre answered.

When Admiral Brandt returned to the station, she made her way toward her private quarters instead of the command deck. Andre anticipated this move and cornered her in the halls.

"That shouldn't have happened," she said.

"I know," he said. "You came very close."

"No, I mean it couldn't have happened," she continued. "Clayton ran hundreds of failure simulations, and not once did the vibrations redirect like that. It's a physical impossibility. It's almost like the anomaly was... defending itself."

"You think it has some sort of mind of its own?"

"Or it's been preconditioned to react in certain ways," she said. "*By* someone. I'm convinced now that this is not a naturally occurring phenomenon. Andre, I think it's alien in origin - and it's time we let headquarters know that."

"I'll prepare another beacon," he said.

"I'll be adding a couple of private messages to the bundle," she said. "It's time I notified the families." Andre nodded solemnly and departed. The admiral opened the door to her rooms and entered. She pressed a series of buttons on her tablet and placed it upright on the dresser, facing her. Her face was framed in the video image that appeared on-screen. She pressed another button and spoke directly into the camera. "Sis, it's me," she began. "I don't know how to say this, but I have some terrible news... about A.J. ..."

A.J. and the adventurers were back on Tarun's trail, having successfully avoided the ant bear on their second trip through his territory. The animal's large paw prints were everywhere, and Aleksey couldn't believe he had missed the tracks before. When he honed in on a particular elven perception, however, it was like the rest of the world fell away. Still, this time around, he was relying on both his eyes and his nose. Tarun's scent was strong in the air, and Aleksey drew his sword.

"He's close," the half-elf whispered.

"Is that really necessary?" A.J. asked, eyeing Aleksey's blade.

"Your friend is dangerous," Aleksey said.

"He's sick, that's all," A.J. said. "He isn't even armed."

"But he's smart," Aleksey replied. "He left those clothes where he knew we would find them, right on the ant bear's trail."

"You're saying that was a trap?" A.J. asked.

"Or he has the Goddess of Luck on his side," Aleksey said. A clap of distant thunder warned of impending rain. "Either way, I'm not taking any more chances with my daughter's life."

"You're gonna kill him?" the pilot asked worriedly.

"Not if I can help it," Aleksey said. "But if he poses a threat, I'll do what's necessary to stop him." The group came upon a large gully, about fifteen feet deep and thirty feet wide, and Aleksey held up a forbidding hand as he surveyed its walls. "See the marks where he scrambled up?" he said, pointing to the other side. "It looks like he fell several times, but he eventually made it."

"So we can probably make it, too," A.J. reasoned, starting down the gully.

"I wouldn't go down there," the half-elf cautioned, eying the other side.

"Why not?" the pilot asked.

"Because it's another trap," Darra answered for her father, as she loaded a bolt into her crossbow. "We go down there, and while we're struggling to get up the other side, your friend is free to crush our skulls in with rocks."

"I think you're being a bit paranoid," A.J. said. "Tarun's not capable of–" Before he could finish his thought, Tarun leapt down from a tree a few feet away and grabbed Kaleb from behind, pressing a sharpened stick to the young mage's throat.

"A.J., believe me when I say: You don't have a clue what I'm capable of!" Tarun said.

Trosclair called the feuding Lords back into the conference chamber, and both took up their places at the tables facing their prince.

"To begin, allow us to say that we are highly disappointed in both of you," Trosclair began. Lord Ocran squirmed under the criticism, and Lord Fallon scowled. "It is the duty of the nobility to set an example for the peasantry, and in this matter, both of you have shown unseemly amounts of stubbornness and pride. Lord Ocran, you admitted that you stole from Lord Fallon's herd." Lord Fallon grinned, sure of his victory, but his amusement did not last long. "And Lord Fallon, we find it highly probable that you are mistaken, and that the original fifty head of cattle did belong to Lord Ocran."

"Are you calling me a liar?" Lord Fallon bellowed.

"We have called you mistaken," Trosclair said. "And you will address me as 'Your Grace'!"

The old man looked like he was about to argue, but then he said, "Of course, Your Grace. My apologies."

"Unfortunately, neither of you has presented a strong enough case to rule in your favor," Trosclair continued. "And each of you feels he is owed twenty-five head of cattle. Therefore, you shall each have twenty-five head from the herds in our own pastures."

Lord Ocran smiled and said, "Your Grace honors us with his generosity."

"In return," Trosclair said, "You shall each contribute equally to the building of a fence between your respective pastures."

"A fine idea!" Lord Ocran readily agreed, but Lord Fallon seemed hesitant.

"Are you agreeable to these terms?" the prince asked the old man.

"Your Grace," he said, "The valley in which we pasture is large. To fence it would be an expensive endeavor."

"That is not our concern," Trosclair replied. "We have made our judgment, and we expect to be obeyed."

Lord Fallon held the prince's gaze for several seconds

before he said, "Yes, Your Grace." He bowed stiffly and left the room. Lord Ocran smiled at Trosclair, bowed, and followed the old man out.

Milian left his place at Ennio's side and crossed to the prince. "Very well done, Your Grace," the Lord Advisor said.

"Yes," Genevieve agreed. "You gave them both what they were asking for and found a way to make sure their feud did not escalate. It was a wise decision."

"But I didn't follow precedent," the prince said, looking to Acton.

"No," he said. "But perhaps you've set a new one. Laws change with rulers. I knew your uncle, and I can tell you with some certainty, this would not have been the decision he would have made. But I am sure he would be proud of you, regardless."

"Thank you," Trosclair said. "That means a lot."

"Tarun, let him go," A.J. said, taking a cautious step toward Kaleb and the mad pilot. "I don't know what you think you're doing, but–"

"What I'm doing?" Tarun asked incredulously. "I'm surviving! They were right, you know; this was a trap. Only you didn't fall for it. Now things are getting... messy."

"Okay. But you don't have to hurt anybody," A.J. said.

Tarun laughed, then said, "Shows what you know. Fish out of water! Can't swim; can't breathe."

"I don't think appealing to his reason is gonna work," Aleksey commented dryly.

"Oh, I'm very reasonable," Tarun said. "For instance, if you put your weapons down now, I won't kill your friend."

"Fine," Aleksey said, dropping his sword, and Darra knelt to place her crossbow on the ground. "Now release him."

"After I get a head-start," Tarun said, backing up with Kaleb in tow.

"Why are you doing this?" A.J. asked. "Just give them back

their gold, so we can find a way home."

"Home?" Tarun asked in a weak voice. "This is home now. I'd rather die than go back through that... thing."

"The anomaly?" A.J. asked.

"Yes!" Tarun said. "Yes, that's what we used to call it, before! I remember."

"Before what?" A.J. prompted.

"Before it sent us through hell," Tarun said quietly. "Or me, anyway. I can tell the trip was easy for you. You just blinked, and when you opened your eyes, you were here. But it was different for me."

"Different how?" A.J. asked.

"It was... longer," Tarun said. "I was in there for years, frozen inside my own body. Never eating, never sleeping - and never dying."

"Jesus," A.J. said.

"Eventually, I started dreaming. I walked in worlds I'd never been to, spoke to people - and creatures - I'd never met. But it was always in dreams, and when I woke up, I was always back in that shuttle, caught between infinity and nothingness."

"I'm... sorry," was all A.J. could think of to say.

"It's okay, now," Tarun replied. "I'm out of there. Back in my body. And this world is... workable. I mean, I know how it works. You do what you have to do to survive."

"And that means taking our gold?" Aleksey asked.

"Ha!" Tarun said. "Your gold? I'm pretty sure it belongs to someone else. Anyway, I've hidden it so you'll never find it, and if you—"

"Is that it?" Darra asked, pointing to a pile of leaves with a satchel strap protruding from it.

"Damn it!" Tarun cursed. Aleksey used Tarun's momentary distraction to make his move, grabbing the stick with both hands before the deranged pilot could plunge it into Kaleb's neck. Tarun let go of the improvised weapon and pushed Kaleb into Aleksey before darting toward the satchel. He slung the bag over his shoulder and disappeared into the trees. Darra and A.J. sprinted after him. Aleksey helped Kaleb to his feet, and then the two of them joined in the chase.

Tarun put his helmet on as he ran. When he hit the stream, he waded into the deepest part and submerged himself completely, then kept moving with the current.

When the half-elf caught up to his daughter and A.J., they were standing at the edge of the creek. Tarun was nowhere in sight.

"His tracks lead straight into the water. Can you tell which way he went?" Darra asked her father, who sniffed at the air.

"No," he finally replied. "It's like his scent just... ends."

"Then we'll split up," Darra suggested. "You and Kaleb search this side of the stream, and we'll take the other."

"Too risky," her father said, noting that she had chosen to go with A.J. "If he got one of us alone, who knows what he'd do." A light rain had begun to fall, and Aleksey looked to the darkening skies. "Besides, we don't need to chase after him. The thunderstorm and the forest will slow him down - if it doesn't kill him - and we'll pick up his trail when the weather clears. Right now, we need to find shelter, and I think I saw a spot that'll do."

Aleksey led the trio of teens back into the woods. They made their way to a tree with a large flat branch hanging down to the ground. Together with the tree trunk, it created a rudimentary barrier from the rain. The ground underneath the branch was even dry to the touch, and there was room enough for all four of them when they squeezed in tight. Aleksey and Kaleb left to gather firewood, and Darra laid out her bedroll and plopped down onto it. A.J. took the spot next to her.

"Is it always like this?" he asked.

"Is what always like what?" Darra asked.

"This world. Is it always so... exciting?"

"Exciting? We've been traipsing through the woods all day," she said. "If that's your definition of 'excitement,' I'd hate to see you bored."

"This is all second nature to you, isn't it?" he asked, looking deep into her eyes.

"Not everything," she said, returning his gaze. "Ouch," she said, as she shifted her weight and felt something pressing into the back of her thigh. She shifted again and put her hand in her pocket, closing it around the gem she still hadn't told anyone else about. She thought about telling A.J. the whole truth of the dragon's second bauble, but the words didn't come. Instead, she just smiled, and the pilot smiled back.

Up the mountain slope, at the crash site, the soldiers from Morning's Peak had returned with several hired hands. The men gathered the pieces of the shuttle that were light enough to carry and loaded them onto a large cart. Another man set up a tripod and camera and took several shots of the mangled ship and beast. One of the hired men even cut a tooth from the mouth of the dismembered dragon. When the rains started, they doubled back along the path to the mountain city.

None of the men were there to notice the dragon's tail twitching, or his one good eye opening, or the wondrous sight of his wounds beginning to magically heal.

CHAPTER THREE
"A WOMAN'S WORK"

Aleksey, Darra, A.J. and Kaleb had made it almost all the way up the mountain before the pilot pointed out the obvious: The trail they were following, that of his friend and co-pilot, Tarun, was leading back toward the site of their crash. They approached the wreckage cautiously, lest they fall for another of Tarun's traps. When they were still several hundred yards away, Aleksey squinted his eyes and honed his half-elven vision in on the crash site.

"Unholy Hells," he cursed. "It's gone."

"What?" A.J. asked in disbelief. "There's no way that shuttle was going anywhere!"

"Not your... ship," Aleksey said. "The dragon! It's not there anymore."

A few minutes later, they were examining the crash site up close.

"How is this possible?" Darra asked. "The dragon - it was ripped to pieces! You don't just get up and walk away from that."

"You or I don't. But I guess it's true: Only a DragonSword can kill a dragon. Besides, it didn't exactly walk," Aleksey said, examining a series of impressions in the ground. "See those claw marks? He dragged himself out from underneath your ship. Probably rested a few more hours over here in the shade, and judging from the blood in the dirt, he wasn't through healing. When he was able, he just... flew off."

"To where?" Kaleb asked. "And will it, you know... come

back?"

"I don't intend to find out. We came to find your friend," Aleksey said, turning to A.J. "His footprints lead that way, along the path to Morning's Peak."

"Are you sure?" A.J. asked. "There seem to be a lot of tracks around this area."

"Trust me, you and your partner's boots have a distinct pattern. It is unmistakable," Aleksey said. "So unless he switched shoes with someone, we're on the right track. We should try to catch up to him before he gets himself arrested - or worse. But before we get to town, there's something you have to do. And you're not going to like it."

"What do I have to do?" the pilot asked warily.

Darra laughed at A.J. when he emerged from the trees a few minutes later in Kaleb's clothing. The tribal teen was much shorter than the pilot, and Kaleb's pants came to a stop well above A.J.'s ankle-high boots. The bright colors of Kaleb's shirt did nothing for A.J.'s paler complexion either, but its bold pattern did distract from how tight it was, especially over his chest.

"I look ridiculous," A.J. complained. He lifted his arms slightly, and his shirt rose up to expose his bellybutton.

"We'll get you some proper clothes when we get into the city," Darra said, as she rifled through her satchel. She pulled out the jewelry box she'd taken from the dragon's hoard and handed it to her father. "How much do you think this'll get us?"

Aleksey surveyed the jewelry inside and smiled. "Probably four, maybe five hundred credits, if my haggling skills haven't atrophied," he said. "Not as much as Kaleb had in his bag, but still plenty to see us through, for now. Is this everything?"

Darra hesitated, then said, "Yep. That's everything."

When the quartet arrived at Morning's Peak, the first thing that caught A.J.'s eye was the city's sophisticated architecture. "Oh, wow," he said, taking it all in as they walked down a major street. "These structures are so... imposing. And big! How many stories is that?" he asked, pointing to the city's tallest structure, a temple with a high spire.

"You act like you've never seen a building before," Darra said.

"It's just, from the swords and... everything else, I expected something different," the pilot said.

"Different how?" Darra asked.

"I don't know," he said. "I guess I was expecting thatched roofs, or teepees, or something."

"We have plenty of those, too," Darra assured him. "In the villages. But Morning's Peak is a city proper. And you know what that means?" she practically sang the question.

"Oh, dear lord," Aleksey said, feigning worry. "That's the voice she uses when she's about to ask for money."

"Just enough for new shoes!" she said. "The ones I'm currently wearing are being held together mostly by mud. Please, Dad?" she asked, batting her eyelashes at him exaggeratedly.

"Fine," he said. "I'll locate a pawn broker and get some cash flowing; you two take our outworlder friend to *Shalah's* and find him some clothes that fit."

"You'll be back in time to pay?" Darra asked, as her father crossed the street.

"I always am!" he replied without looking back.

Darra led Kaleb and A.J. through the city blocks, until they were standing in front of a large brick building with several mannequins posed in its windows. The sign above the shop read: *Shalah's Fine Clothing*.

"I take it you've been here before?" A.J. asked as they entered the store.

"Oh, yeah," she said. "*Shalah's* designs are the best. She has a store in every major city in the kingdom. Dad claims he knew her before she got famous, but I think he's exaggerating." Darra crossed over to a table piled high with pants and began rifling through them. By the time Aleksey arrived, A.J. had been outfitted in all new clothing, including a smart leather vest that Darra had to plead with her father to buy. A.J. also got his own bedroll, and he and Kaleb left with new canvas satchels. After trying on several pairs, Darra finally picked out her new shoes – and the total for all this new gear was just under one hundred credits. Aleksey paid for the apparel with an impatience that was palpable, at least to his daughter.

"What is it, Dad?" she asked as soon as they left the shop.

"The pawn broker was the talkative type," he said, guiding the teens along the city streets. "It seems a number of men tried to sell him the wreckage of your ship yesterday. He didn't buy any of it, but he did recommend they ship the pieces to an interested party in Middlestead."

"The Free City?" Kaleb asked, and Aleksey nodded in the affirmative.

"But the fragments of my ship are useless," A.J. protested. "Why would anyone want to buy them?"

"There's a famous academy of the sciences in Middlestead," Darra explained. "They'd likely want to study such a marvel."

"Anyway, it looks like we'll be spending the remainder of our money on tickets," Aleksey said.

"To Middlestead?" Darra asked. "Why?"

"Because that's where the soldiers took the madman who showed up in strange armor claiming to have killed a dragon with his flying ship," Aleksey said.

"They took Tarun?" A.J. asked. "Why? Did he hurt someone?"

"Human society is often cruel to those deemed strange," Aleksey said. "And your friend is stranger than most. They probably assumed the buyer would want to speak to him."

"Did you get the name of the buyer?" Kaleb asked.

"No, but I got an address," Aleksey said, flashing a small slip of paper. "If we make the next train, we'll be there by morning." Aleksey led the three teens through the city streets, toward the train station. He bought their tickets for the next train to Middlestead, which was scheduled to depart in just over three hours, for sixty-two credits each. He decided that with the money he had left over, they should eat something, as all they'd had for two days was foraged nuts and fruit. He asked the friendly Station Attendant about local eateries and came away with the information he was looking for. He once again led the teens through the city streets, until they came upon a restaurant called *Uncle Abha's.*

Aleksey and the teens entered the small dining room and were greeted by a smiling hostess, who quickly seated them and asked simply, "Buffet?"

Kaleb beamed, and Aleksey nodded and said, "And four teas, please."

The four made their way to the back wall of the restaurant, where they were pleased to find a smorgasbord of vegetarian dishes.

"There's no meat," A.J. observed.

"Dad and I are vegetarians," Darra said.

"You get used to it," Kaleb said. They each made a plate for themselves, with Kaleb piling on so much that the hostess asked if he wanted a second platter, which he readily accepted.

"I like this part of city life," Kaleb said, as he sat down with his two plates of food before him and popped a piece of fried okra into his mouth.

"Well, eat up," Aleksey encouraged. "I don't know when we'll have the chance to splurge like this again. At least not until we get your pack back."

"I dunno, Dad," Darra said. "If soldiers took Tarun, wouldn't they keep the treasure for themselves? We may have to call this one a loss."

"The pawn broker didn't mention anything about the gold," he said, turning to A.J. "Which means your friend may have hidden it somewhere before he entered the city. We'll get it all back after we find him."

"And then what?" A.J. asked. "Tarun needs medical attention. Have you figured out a way to send us back home?"

"No," Aleksey said. "But when we recover Kaleb's pack, we'll share one-fourth of the profits with you. That ought to be enough money to hire an experienced sorcerer to return you and your friend to... wherever it is you come from."

Darra hid her frown behind her napkin and said, "Let's hope we find him soon, then."

The couple seated directly behind them got up to leave, and though their movements were a bit rushed, the four travelers did not notice. When the couple got to the city square, they stopped and stared at a piece of parchment posted in the middle of a large bulletin board. "I told you it was them!" the woman said, as she pointed at the sketches of Aleksey and Darra underneath the single word 'Wanted.'

Far away, in the kingdom of DuVerres' capital city, Trosclair was settled down at his own dinner. Joining him tonight were his usual cohorts, Armand, Alicia, Frederick and Devon. Ennio even ceded his watch over the young Prince to another soldier, so he could join them for the meal.

"I'm bored," Trosclair declared halfway through the meal.

"Devon, what were you saying about a new project?"

"Oh, it's nowhere near finished," the young playwright answered. "But I hope to have a new comedy by this summer."

"How wonderful!" Trosclair said. "Perhaps your troupe can perform it during my coronation festivities?"

"It would be an honor," Devon said.

"What's it about?" Alicia asked.

"Death," Devon replied.

"A comedy about death?" Armand asked. "You do choose the strangest themes."

"Go on," Alicia prodded. "Set the stage for us."

"Well, once upon a time, there was a gambler, a cleaner, and a puppeteer, all riding in the same carriage," Devon began. "The carriage overturns, and all three are killed instantly. When the Reaper arrives to collect their souls, the carriage driver is scared to death. With only room in his boat for three souls, Death is faced with choosing which of them will get to live. The gambler suggests a game of cards, but the cleaner–" Before he could delve any further into the plot, Devon was silenced by the opening of the chamber's doors. In strode Milian, followed by a beautiful, poised young woman with dark skin, hair and eyes whom Trosclair had never seen before.

"Your Grace, please pardon the interruption," Milian said. "But I have the pleasure of introducing Lady Serena Parmida of Misty Vale." Serena curtsied in Trosclair's direction, and he acknowledged her with a nod of his head.

"We are pleased to make your acquaintance," the prince said. "Please, have a seat."

"Thank you, Your Grace," she said, as Armand stood and pulled out a chair for her.

"Have you eaten?" Trosclair asked, signaling for his squire, Antonin, to pour a glass of wine for his newest guest.

"Not yet, Your Grace," Serena answered as her cup was filled.

Trosclair looked to Antonin, and the boy volunteered, "I'll have the kitchen prepare another plate." Trosclair nodded his thanks, and the boy left the room. Milian bowed to the prince and followed the squire out the door.

Introductions were made all around, and then Ennio asked,

"So Serena, what brings you all the way from Misty Vale?" The city was on the other side of the kingdom.

"My father," the young woman replied. "He says it's time I made my debut at court."

"And so you shall!" Trosclair declared. "Tomorrow night, we'll have a ball formally announcing your arrival."

"Oh, there's no reason to go to such trouble," Serena protested, but Trosclair had already decided.

"Nonsense!" the prince said. "It's no trouble at all. Besides, what's the point of living in a palace if you don't throw lavish parties all the time?"

Serena nodded politely. "Your Grace is too kind."

Aleksey and his band of teenage adventurers arrived back at the train station with full stomachs and fifteen minutes to spare until their departure. Kaleb took the opportunity to sneak off and smoke from his pipe, claiming it would alleviate his indigestion from overindulgence. As they were all about to spend ten hours in the same cramped train compartment with the boy, no one begrudged him his curative. Darra and A.J. took their tickets and boarded the train early, while Aleksey paced up and down the platform.

When Kaleb came back around the corner sooner than expected, he looked spooked. "Soldiers!" he whispered to Aleksey, pointing back the way he'd just come. The pair quickly made their way toward the train, and Aleksey handed the two remaining tickets to the usher. The man examined them and handed them back to the half-elf.

"Compartment twelve," the usher said. "That's car number three."

Aleksey nodded, and as he and Kaleb entered the third train car, he saw several soldiers round the corner. He found a window and continued watching warily as they spoke to the usher. One of the soldiers held his fist over his heart in salute and then made for the first train car. Aleksey grabbed Kaleb by the shoulders and steered him down the middle of the car to their compartment. When he opened the door, Aleksey found Darra and A.J. sitting a little too close to each other for his comfort. He held his tongue, however, and closed the door behind Kaleb.

"Soldiers," he said. "They're searching car to car for

something."

"You think it's us?" Darra asked.

"We did piss off the commanding officer of this kingdom's military," Aleksey said. "I should've never risked bringing you to this city!"

"Well, we're here now," Darra stated flatly. "Dad, what are we gonna do?" Aleksey only looked up at the sunroof in answer. Darra rolled her eyes. "Oh," she said. "That old trick. Farewell, then, good hair day."

A few minutes later, the soldier made his way to compartment twelve - and found A.J. faking sleep and Kaleb reading a book. The soldier apologized for disturbing them and moved on.

When the train pulled away from the station a little while later, Darra opened up the sunroof and lowered herself back down through it onto one of the seats. She was followed by her father, who closed the sunroof behind him as best he could, since they'd broken its hinges to make their escape. As Darra had predicted, her hair was a windblown mess. She grabbed her brush from her satchel and started raking it through the tangles as the locomotive picked up speed.

Lilith lit a stick of incense at an altar as the Reaper moon rose over the horizon. In the center of the altar was the sketch of Aleksey and Darra. "Rebos," she prayed, eyes closed and hands clasped. "By your light, let me see!" Her eyelids fluttered open, and she stared up at the reaper moon with pupils so dilated, it seemed she had no color to her eyes at all. The light from her patron moon seemed to thicken as it cascaded all around her, forming figures that only she could make out. In this light, she found Darra and Aleksey in the train car as the father braided his daughter's hair. Next, she saw a small inn called *The Laughing Stocks.* The image shifted again, and she took in the unmistakable skyline of the Free City. "Thank you, my god," she said. "May your divine wisdom always guide me."

Aleksey and Kaleb exited the train first, followed by A.J. and Darra. Father and daughter had decided it was best if they walked separately, in case anyone was looking for them. Aleksey and Kaleb left the train station and headed not toward the heart of the city, but toward its eastern outskirts, Darra and A.J. following several hundred feet behind them.

"This city's even more impressive than the last one," A.J. commented. "How many people live here?"

"I think I've heard it's around half a million, these days," Darra said, and A.J. balked. "Lots of farmer's daughters and blacksmith's sons run away to make their fortune in the Free City, so it's always growing. Plus it's on the way to everywhere, so it's the center of continental trade, literally."

"And it's the Free City, so that means we've left behind the kingdom of...?" A.J. prompted.

"DuVerres," she said.

"Is that where you're from?" he asked.

"I'm sort of from everywhere," Darra answered. "We keep on the move."

"Oh, okay," A.J. said. "So you're like... roving adventurers?"

"Something like that," Darra confirmed. "We're a lot of things, when we need to be: warriors, thieves, explorers. We've even been called heroes a few times." Darra hoped she sounded impressive, but suddenly feared she was being a braggart. "Dad has been, anyway... He says we're just full-time tourists."

"So you don't, uh, have a boyfriend waiting for you back home somewhere?" A.J. asked as casually as he could, avoiding eye contact.

Darra smiled as she answered, "Nope. No boyfriend." A.J. smiled back.

Up ahead of them, Aleksey and Kaleb passed a street vendor selling candied treats from a cart. Aleksey caught Kaleb's eyes lingering on a lollipop, so he reached into a pocket and pulled out a one-credit coin. "How much?" he asked the elderly lady attending the cart.

"Four for a credit," she said, and Aleksey handed her the money.

"It's fate," he said to Kaleb, as he picked out a red sucker for himself and a green one for his daughter, who was mad for anything sour apple flavored. "Grab one for yourself, and one for the outworlder."

"You still don't trust him?" Kaleb asked as they resumed

their walk.

"I trust he's not a spy or a mercenary," Aleksey said. "But I wouldn't leave him alone in a room with my daughter, all the same."

"You don't allow her to date yet, do you?" Kaleb asked.

Aleksey shook his head in the negative. "I suppose you think that's too strict of me?"

"Kind of," Kaleb answered truthfully. "She's mature enough. In the tribe, she'd have already had her womanhood declared with a whole day's worth of ceremonies. She'd be free to marry, even."

"Your tribe thrusts adulthood on youths at too tender an age," Aleksey said.

"I don't know," Kaleb said. "Gram is as strict and old-fashioned as you are - no offense - and even she lets me have a girlfriend. Anybody who isn't dating at our age is sort of considered a... freak. You know, in the tribes."

"Right," Aleksey said, but the teen's words did give him a new viewpoint to consider. His own adolescence had been a long and tumultuous lesson in freakishness and ostracism, and the last thing he wanted was for Darra to suffer the same fate. "So you have a girlfriend, then?"

"Not right now," he said. "But I'm allowed to, in theory."

"Ah, I see," Aleksey said.

They continued until they rounded a final corner, and the city abruptly came to a halt about seventy-five yards in front of them. A steep cliff guarded this side of the city from any attack, and along this edge was the city's poorest district, appropriately named *Lastrow*. Smack in the middle of this small neighborhood stood *The Laughing Stocks*. It was large for a tavern, seating over a hundred and fifty when the house was full; but it was small for an inn, with only a half dozen rooms to rent. Aleksey and Kaleb waited outside the establishment for Darra and A.J. to catch up. Aleksey handed the green lollipop to his daughter, who gleefully unwrapped it and stuck it in her mouth.

"Green apple?" Aleksey asked, but Darra shook her head.

"Lime," she said, as the four of them entered together. Kaleb handed A.J. his own candy as they waited in the foyer.

"You're not afraid of being seen together here?" the pilot asked.

"Trust me, if anyone follows us as far as *The Laughing*

Stocks, we're already screwed," Aleksey said. "Soldiers rarely come out this far from the city center. And besides that, they know us here."

A young woman came out to greet them and then squealed with excitement on making eye contact with Darra. She rushed over to the teen and gave her a big hug. "Darra!" she said. "It's so good to see you! And Aleksey! Looking dapper as always."

"Thank you, Ani," Aleksey said.

"Who're your friends?" Ani asked, looking Kaleb and A.J. up and down.

"This young man is Kaleb," Aleksey answered. "And this is A.J. Boys, this is Ani; she runs this establishment."

"Well, with my brother," Ani said.

"Is Borri in, or...?" Aleksey asked.

"Oh, no. You know him. If the weather's fair, he's out hunting. So did you want a table or a room?" Ani asked.

"Sadly, we haven't the cash to pay for either," Aleksey confessed. "I was hoping Darra and Kaleb could stay here while we attend to some business in town. They'll work for their keep."

"We will?" Kaleb asked. Aleksey shot Kaleb a look, and the young mage mumbled, "I mean, we *will*."

Darra crossed her arms. "Why do we have to stay here? We've already proven we can be of use to you."

"And the crazy outworlder has proven to be a formidable threat," Aleksey said. "I won't put the two of you in any more danger."

Darra opened her mouth to argue some more, but Aleksey held up a hand to silence her. "I've already decided, Darra. Please make peace with it."

"Fine," Darra capitulated. "We'll stay here and work. That is, if you need us, Ani."

"Well, I can always use an extra waitress," she said, and Darra nodded her enthusiasm for the job. Ani turned to Kaleb and continued, "And I suppose I could put you to work in the back."

"Like the kitchen? That's fine. I'm actually a pretty good cook," Kaleb said.

"The kitchen? No, no, no. That's woman's work. I need you out back," Ani said.

"Doing what?" Kaleb asked.

"Oh, chopping wood for the stove, maybe mucking the stalls," Ani said. "You know, men's work. Excuse me," she said, as a middle-aged couple entered the foyer. Ani showed them into the barroom.

"Isn't Ani great?" Darra asked A.J. "She's like a sister to me."

"Yeah," he agreed. "She seems amazing. I mean, to run this place, with her... condition. It's really something."

"Her condition?" Darra asked.

"I don't know what you call it here, but in my world, we would say she has Down syndrome."

"She's touched by the Fae, if that's what you mean," Darra said. "But that doesn't slow her down any."

"I can tell," the pilot said.

"Darra, honey, say your goodbyes now," Aleksey instructed. "It's time the outworlder and I were off." Aleksey and A.J. left *The Laughing Stocks* and headed toward the science academy in the center of the city. Neither of them noticed the woman trailing them from a distance, her dark hair tucked away inside her cowl.

A knock came at Trosclair's private chamber door, interrupting the prince and his bodyguard as they lay in bed together. Ennio hurriedly slipped his clothes and boots back on, while Trosclair merely draped himself with a robe. He crossed to the door and looked back as Ennio tucked in his shirt and raised a thumb to signal his readiness. Trosclair gestured to his hair, and Ennio sought out the mirror and finger-combed his short chestnut hair back into place.

"Yes?" Trosclair called through the door.

"Your Grace, it's Milian," came the reply. "I was hoping I could have a word with you."

Trosclair opened the door just a crack and peered out at the Lord Advisor. "Now is... not a good time. I was sleeping."

Milian took in Trosclair's robe and spied Ennio over the prince's shoulder. "Yes, of course," he said. "But if Your Grace could find a moment later in the day, I would greatly appreciate it. I'll be in my study, when Your Grace is done... sleeping." A strange and subtle look crossed Milian's face, and Trosclair could not tell if it was a slight smirk or the beginnings of a scowl. The Lord Advisor bowed, turned, and strode away.

"Ugh," Trosclair said as he closed the door. "I suppose that means I'll have to get dressed and go be a prince now."

"You bear your burden so bravely," Ennio said, and Trosclair narrowed his eyes and shook a fist at the soldier playfully. Ennio crossed to Trosclair's closet and opened its double doors; it was like a small room unto itself, filled with clothes, shoes, and hats. There was even a whole section dedicated to capes and cloaks in every style. Ennio pulled a shirt from off the rack and held it up for Trosclair's approval.

"That's the wrong side, my love," Trosclair said, joining Ennio in the closet. He put the shirt back on the rack and gestured to an entire wall. "These are clothes I've already worn. And these," he said, indicating the other side, "Are the ones I have yet to wear." He drew a shirt out and held it up to his torso, then put it back.

"Ah, I forgot," Ennio said. "My prince would never be seen in public in an outfit he'd already worn."

"Heavens forefend!" Trosclair said. "I can only imagine the vicious gossip that would follow. 'The prince is a pauper!' they'd cry in the city streets."

Ennio placed an affectionate arm around Trosclair's waist and pulled him close. "I think you underestimate the love your people have for you," he said. "They'd follow you through feast or famine."

"It's a strange thing, to be idolized by people you've never even met," Trosclair said. "The expectations of perfection are easy to meet right now, while I have no real responsibilities. But after my coronation, I wonder how I'll manage. I've already angered one of my most important nobles."

"Lord Fallon?" Ennio asked, and Trosclair nodded. "That old fart can blow away with the wind!"

"My uncle used to say, 'As goes the noble, so goes his liegemen.' I worry Lord Fallon may poison the minds of his vassals against me before I even take the throne."

"You're the kindest, fairest person I know. You've been given the finest of educations, and you've quite a bit more wisdom than any other fifteen-year-old I've ever met. Whatever he poisons, your virtue will be the antidote."

"You really believe that, don't you?" Trosclair asked.

"I know it," Ennio said, as he pulled Trosclair in for a kiss.

Later, when he was fully clothed, Trosclair sought out Milian in the Lord Advisor's study. Ennio was back on duty; he held the door open for the prince and closed it behind him.

"Thank you for joining me, Your Grace," Milian said. "But I was hoping we could speak privately."

Trosclair looked to Ennio and then back to Milian. "Ennio has my trust," the prince said. "He will not repeat what is said in confidence."

"Of course, Your Grace," Milian conceded. "I asked you here today so that we could discuss Miss Parmida."

"Serena?" Trosclair asked, and Milian nodded. "What about her?"

"The girl is in a rather complex predicament," Milian said. "She is the oldest of her father's daughters, and the man has no male heir. Her father has his mind set on turning over his city to her when he dies. To that end, he's already gifted her half his holdings. But, as you are well aware, under current law, a woman cannot inherit a noble title directly."

"And Serena's father would have me change this law, so that Serena could inherit?" Trosclair asked.

"Precisely, Your Grace," Milian said. "And Lord Parmida is only one of a growing number of nobles who would support such a change. The late Duke was opposed to this idea, but Serena's father asked that I bring the matter up with you directly."

"Why did my uncle oppose it?" the prince asked.

"May I speak frankly?" Milian asked.

"Please do," Trosclair said.

"Your Grace's uncle was a very... conservative man," Milian said, choosing his words carefully. "He did not regard women as equally capable of ruling on their own."

"But you do?" Trosclair asked.

"My experiences have taught me not to underestimate the fairer sex," Milian said. "At any rate, you will not have to decide this matter now. I thought it merely prudent to bring it up beforehand, so that you could fully consider it before your coronation. And so you could take full measure of Serena herself, of course. What did you think of her, by the way?"

"She seems amiable enough," Trosclair said. "I've only just

met her, of course."

"And her looks?" Milian asked. "Did you find them pleasing?"

"I—I found her—She was beautiful," Trosclair stammered, caught off-guard by the question. "Why do you ask?"

"Lord Parmida requested, should you decide against allowing Serena to inherit, that you consider her for another role - that of your bride," the Lord Advisor said, and both the Prince and his bodyguard were visibly stunned.

Kaleb picked up a chunk of wood and placed it on the tree stump. The muscles of his chest and arms glistened with a fine sheen of sweat as he brought the axe down, but the blade only made its way through half the wood. Kaleb tried to pull the axe back, but it stuck. He placed a foot up on the wood and pulled again, and the blade came free. He hefted the tool far above his head, then swung down again - and missed the wood completely. The blade slammed into the tree trunk.

Watching the young man from a window above, Ani laughed. Darra, having just set a plate down for a hungry customer seated in the tavern's balcony, came to the window to see what the fuss was about.

"Ani!" Darra said when she spied Kaleb's futile efforts with the firewood. "Did you send him out there just so you could take in an eyeful?"

"Would that be wrong of me?" Ani asked.

"Yes, definitely," Darra said.

Ani just shrugged and resumed her ogling of the tribal lad. "Hey, if the gods didn't want us looking, they wouldn't have made young men's bodies so... sinewy."

"You fancy him, then?" Darra asked.

"He's a little skinny for my tastes," Ani said. "But he does bulge in all the right places."

"You're terrible!" Darra said.

"I am as the gods made me," Ani replied. "And don't play innocent with me! I saw the way you were with that other one."

"A.J.? He's just a friend," Darra said.

"So you wouldn't mind if I—"

"You keep your hands - and your eyes - off him!" Darra

commanded, and Ani held her hands up in surrender.

"So you do like him," Ani said.

"He's handsome, that's for sure," Darra said. "The other day, we almost kissed. I think. It's all really confusing."

"Love always is," Ani remarked, as she led Darra back down the stairs.

"Plus, there's my Dad," Darra continued. "He's dead-set against me dating."

"Then why are you travelling with two boys?" Ani asked. "I'd think he'd want to, you know - remove the temptation."

"Oh, believe me, if he could get away with it, I'd be locked up in a tower somewhere and never even see a boy!" Darra said. "As it is, he's just hoping to wrap up our business with A.J. as quickly as possible."

"Well, then, you'll have to make your move before that can happen," Ani suggested.

"I guess so," Darra said. "It's just - aren't guys supposed to make the first move? I mean, if he likes me—"

"Real love isn't like in the fairy stories, Darra," Ani said. "You have to grab it when it comes near, or you'll turn around, and it'll be gone." Darra contemplated Ani's advice as she wiped a table down with a damp cloth.

Aleksey led A.J. through the city streets, until they came upon the Middlestead Academy of the Sciences. The campus was itself the size of a small town, so Aleksey consulted a large directory near the entrance. He then walked confidently into the midst of the students on their way to and from class, A.J. trailing behind him, and they reached a building whose placard proclaimed it *Sturtevant Hall.*

"The buyer is in room four-thirteen," Aleksey said. "Or at least, that's where he had the pieces of your ship sent." The pair entered the building and made their way up the stairs. "Allow me to do the talking. Whoever this man is, he's rich, and I'd wager, powerful. Which, in this world, equates to dangerous, especially for you. He can't know you're an outworlder."

"Then maybe you should stop calling me that in public," A.J. suggested, as two students passed them, going down. Aleksey frowned and gave a slight shrug of one shoulder. "You don't like me very much, do you?" the pilot asked.

"Let's just say I've been made uneasy ever since your arrival, and leave it at that," Aleksey said as they reached the fourth and final floor. Room four-thirteen was at the end of the hall, and on its door was etched the name *Dr. C. H. Tillison.* Aleksey knocked twice, but there was no response. He tried the handle, and the door was unlocked. He poked his head inside and called out, "Dr. Tillison?" He saw and heard no one, so he entered the room, and A.J. followed. The pieces of his ship had been laid out on four long tables. A fifth table held weights and a large scale, as well as other measuring devices and a set of magnifying lenses. There were also several strange specimens on display, floating in large jars of pinkish liquid.

"Well, this is the right place," Aleksey said, examining a creature in a jar. The label read '*Fetal Orc,*' and once he had a name for it, Aleksey began to discern the unborn pig-man's hybrid features. "It appears our buyer has a taste for the exotic. And the macabre."

"Not really," Dr. Tillison said from the doorway as she entered. "I simply have an insatiable desire to explore the unknown." She crossed to Aleksey and held out her hand. "Dr. Cecelia Tillison."

Aleksey shook her hand and said, "Aleksey Fabian. And this is my associate, A.J."

Dr. Tillison shook A.J.'s hand next and gestured to a set of chairs. "Gentlemen, I hadn't expected you until tomorrow. Thank you for responding to my summons so quickly."

"Summons?" A.J. asked.

"You are the gentlemen from Morning's Peak who sold me my latest scientific curiosities, are you not?" she asked, indicating the fragments of the ship on the table.

"Of course," Aleksey said, sensing an opportunity.

"I just had to find out everything you know about it directly," Dr. Tillison said.

"What about the man that was sent here ahead of us?" A.J. asked. "What did he tell you about it?"

"The madman? He told me nothing but science stories about other worlds and flying ships."

"Is he still here?" Aleksey asked as casually as he could.

"Oh, heavens, no!" Dr. Tillison said. "He worked himself into such a state, I had to call the City Guard to have him removed from my office." A.J. shot Aleksey a worried glance, but the half-elf remained calm.

"Do you know if they detained him?" Aleksey asked, before tacking on, "He stole something from me, and I'd like to get it back."

"The last I saw, he'd eluded them, I'm afraid," Dr. Tillison answered. "He was headed west of campus." Dr. Tillison soon turned the conversation back to focus on the pieces spread out on her tables. Aleksey described the crash that had brought A.J. into this world in vague terms, as if he had merely seen the incident from afar. After questioning them for a few more minutes, Dr. Tillison figured she had all the information she was going to get from them. She thanked them and excused herself, and they showed themselves out of the building.

As they exited the campus, Lilith walked past them. Her face was still mostly hidden by her cowl, but something about the woman registered as familiar to Aleksey. He turned back to get a second look at her, and A.J. stopped to see what had caught the half-elf's attention. Lilith spun on one heel, threw back her cloak, and fired her longbow at Aleksey's heart. Aleksey caught the arrow by the shaft mere inches from his chest in a blurry move that clearly stunned the assassin. He threw the arrow down and crossed to her, drawing his sword.

"What's happening?" A.J. asked.

Aleksey ignored the pilot and swung at Lilith, who backed away, reached to her sides, and pulled a short scimitar out in each hand. The twin blades caught Aleksey's next attack high in the air, and Lilith used the momentary stalemate to kick Aleksey in the stomach. Aleksey was knocked back, but he stayed on his feet, which surprised Lilith again.

"You're tougher than you look," she said, as she took a few steps toward her target. "That makes it more fun for me!" She thrust both scimitars out toward his torso, but Aleksey swept them aside with his own blade.

"It won't be so fun for you when I inevitably win," he said. Aleksey head-butted the assassin, a move she clearly hadn't anticipated, and she staggered backward as her vision blurred.

Lilith looked around at the small crowd that had gathered on the street to watch the fight and said, "Now's not my moment." She pushed her way through the crowd and rounded a corner.

"Come on!" Aleksey said over his shoulder to A.J., and they chased after her. Aleksey turned the corner and scanned the street and the sidewalks. There were several carriages going to and fro and scattered pedestrians along both sides, but there was no sign of Lilith.

"Unholy Hells!" Aleksey cursed. "She's gone!"

"Do you know her?" A.J. asked.

"She seemed... familiar. But I can't recall–" Just then Aleksey did remember the encounter with the woman dressed as a nun several days before. "We have to get to back to Darra," he said.

"Why? Is that woman after her, too?" A.J. asked as he fell in line behind Aleksey, who was walking very briskly.

"She may well be," Aleksey said. "She's definitely seen us together."

"Then let's go!" A.J. urged, as he broke out into a run.

"Stop!" Aleksey commanded, and A.J. obeyed. "We've already caused one scene today. Running through the streets like your madman friend will only get us in more trouble, if the City Guard catches us."

"But Darra–"

"Has been schooled in self-defense since she could walk," Aleksey said. "I'm worried about her, too. But if we attract the wrong kind of attention, we'll never get to her." A.J. nodded his understanding, and the pair resumed their very brisk walk.

Further up the street, Lilith made herself comfortable in a carriage-for-hire, as the driver headed to the eastern outskirts of the city.

Kaleb had finished chopping the wood and was about halfway through mucking the stalls when Darra came out the back door.

"Ani wants to know if you're ready to eat," she said, holding out a glass of lemonade.

"Always!" Kaleb replied, as he put down his pitchfork and walked over to her. "But first, I should probably wash my... everything. Why do men have to do all the hard work, anyway? In the tribes, we all pitch in and get things done together. Your society's gendered division of labor stinks!"

"That's not the only thing," Darra said, breathing through her mouth to avoid Kaleb's reek. "Besides, women have it way worse. Men get to finish all their chores and call it a day; but a woman is on call to cook and clean and tend to children all day and all night."

Kaleb finished his drink and handed the glass back to Darra. "If it's bad for everybody, then why do they do it that way?" Kaleb asked, and Darra shook her head and shrugged.

"You go wash up, and I'll have the kitchen make you a plate," Darra said.

"Okay," Kaleb agreed, pulling his pipe out of his pocket. "Just let me work up an appetite real quick," he said, lighting the pipe with his finger-flame and inhaling deeply.

Darra returned to the kitchen with Kaleb's order and then spied a customer waiting in the foyer. She made her way out of the barroom and was pleasantly surprised to find she recognized the woman.

"Hey, I know you," Darra said. "I'm Darra; we met last week, remember?"

"Of course," Lilith said, holding out a hand. "Lilith. My, you're a long way from Shadowhaven."

"You too," Darra said. "Uh, can I get you a table, or a room?"

"I'd quite like a table," Lilith said, and Darra led her into the barroom.

"Are you here for the show?" Darra asked, and Lilith tilted her head quizzically. "The night's first performer is just about to start." Darra pointed to a small stage that was tucked up against the exposed brick wall of the building, where a man in a jester's collar and hat was rummaging through a pile of note cards.

Finding the one he wanted, the jester addressed the people in the barroom in a booming stage voice, "Welcome! Welcome, ladies and gentlemen, to *The Laughing Stocks*, Middlestead's premiere venue for off-the-wall comedy. My name is Killian, and I'll be your host for the evening. How many people in the audience tonight are married?" A quick round of claps, hoots and hollers answered the jester's question. "I love married people, I do. But what is it about being married that makes people let themselves go? You all know what I'm talking about. A guy gets married, he could be an athlete, a warrior even—but he slips that ring on, and the next thing you know, he's got a beer belly out to here." Scattered chuckles sounded throughout the barroom as the jester mimed having a large gut.

"He's not very original," Darra complained, as the jester started in on a riff about women and shopping. "So what brings you to Middlestead?" the teen asked Lilith.

"Work," Lilith said. "There's a Valeskan temple here that put out a call for volunteers, and I've come to answer it."

"You work for free, then?" Darra asked.

"My god is generous in compensation for my service, in ways I... can't quite express," Lilith said.

"Darra, hon," Ani called from a few tables over. "When you finish with her order, Kaleb's plate is ready."

"Okay," Darra said. "Did you want a whole plate, or just drinks? Wait, are you allowed to drink? Alcohol, I mean?"

"My vows make no prohibition against it," Lilith said. "And I'll take a plate, as well, please."

"You got it," Darra said. She turned and strode to the kitchen, where she put in Lilith's order and picked up Kaleb's food. As the teen made her way back outside, she didn't notice that Lilith had surreptitiously slipped out of her seat.

Night fell over DuVerres' capital city, and in the prince's private chambers, Trosclair and Ennio readied themselves for the ball. Trosclair had donned a dark blue tuxedo, and Ennio wore his ceremonial uniform. The soldier's shoulders were covered by large gold pads with fringe hanging down, connecting to a gold collar. He pinned two large eight-pointed stars to the charcoal gray material covering his chest, then turned to his prince and preened.

"You. Are. So. Hot!" Trosclair said, emphasizing each word. "Maybe I should order you to wear your dress grays all the time?"

"You'd best not!" Ennio said. "This material is positively stifling."

"I think it's worth it," Trosclair said. "Although there is something to be said for the ease of access provided by a nice, loose tunic." The prince placed a gentle hand over the front of Ennio's pants, and the soldier's eyes rolled into the back of his head with lust. The older boy cut the moment short, however, by removing Trosclair's hand.

A confused look crossed Trosclair's face. "We can be a little late," he said.

"It's not that," Ennio said. "I'm just—not sure I should even be going tonight."

"You're my best friend and my bodyguard," Trosclair said. "Your place is by my side."

"This ball is Serena's big night," Ennio said. "If I'm by your side all night, you won't get to know her at all."

"You don't seriously think I'd consider marrying the girl, do you?" Trosclair asked, pulling away slightly.

"If Milian is suggesting it, it's probably a smart move," Ennio said. "Sooner or later, someone is going to put the pieces together about you and me, assuming they haven't already. Having a wife would go a long way to covering that up."

"But I'd be living a lie!" Trosclair said. "I have no interest in Serena, or any other woman. I love you!"

"I love you, too," Ennio said. "But I'm nobody important, and you're a prince. Princes become kings, and kings must produce an heir, or the nobles will get nervous."

"Kings do as they please!" Trosclair said. "And I won't trick some poor girl into marrying me just to appease the nobility!"

"She'd be a queen. There are very few women in the kingdom who would turn that down."

"But can you imagine what her life would be like? Sentenced to a loveless marriage, kept around solely for breeding... Mark my words, Ennio: I'll not see any woman suffer that fate on my account."

"Oh, Trosc... You're too good for your own good," the older boy said, and he kissed the prince tenderly on his cheek.

Trosclair and Ennio finished adjusting themselves to their clothing and left for the ballroom. The prince was announced as he entered, and as usual, all eyes turned to him as he and his bodyguard walked down the wide staircase. They joined Armand and Devon at the edge of the dance floor and watched as couple after couple swung by in a swirl of skirts and jacket tails before dancing off again. Frederick and Alicia arrived a few minutes later, their entrance unannounced but their presence welcomed by Armand, who had grown tired of waiting on the sidelines watching others dance.

"Would you do me the honor?" he asked Alicia, and he grabbed her hands and pulled her onto the dance floor without waiting for a response.

"Lords and Ladies of the court, I present to you Lady Serena Parmida of Misty Vale," the announcer called out from the top of the steps. Serena stood beside him, looking stunning in a floor-length gown of emerald green. Because the ball was in her honor, there was a smattering of applause as she made her way down the stairs. She approached the prince and curtseyed, and Trosclair gave her a friendly smile in return. He suddenly wondered if she knew about her father's secondary proposition.

"She really is beautiful," Ennio whispered in Trosclair's ear. The prince's brows furrowed.

"Would you care to dance?" Devon asked Serena, and she looked ready to accept the invitation - before Ennio cut in.

"I'm afraid you must wait your turn, Devon," the soldier said. "The honor of the first dance is bespoken by the host." He took Serena's elegant wrist in his hand and presented the girl to Trosclair.

"Uh... Our apologies, Lady Serena, for our friend's exuberance," Trosclair said, retreating into the formal plural. "We are anxious to make your acquaintance, and a dance would honor us." Trosclair turned to Devon and handed Serena's wrist back to the playwright. "But please, do enjoy the first dance with our good friend Devon, while we refresh ourselves."

Serena smiled and said, "Thank you, Your Grace."

"Ennio," Trosclair said, spearing the soldier with a sharp look. "With me!" The command came out harsher than Trosclair had intended, but he made no apology for it as he crossed to a table loaded with refreshments. Ennio followed a few paces behind. Trosclair turned to face him, and the soldier was surprised to see tears welled up in the prince's eyes.

"What are you doing?" Trosclair asked in a whisper, shaking his head from side to side.

"It's important you get to know her," Ennio said.

"Are you really trying to... set me up with that girl?"

"I just thought she deserved a fair shot," Ennio said. "Not at you!" he added quickly, when Trosclair looked ready to object. "But a fair shot at, you know, proving to you she's capable of ruling."

"I've wondered what she really wants," Trosclair said, as he spied the subject of their conversation swinging on Devon's arm. "To be queen here, or to rule Misty Vale in her own right."

"So ask her," Ennio suggested, and Trosclair shook his head in agreement.

Kaleb had washed most of the stink off his body by the time Darra brought out his dinner. He had no way to wash his pants, however, so the smell of horse dung and sweat lingered on him, mixed with the distinct smell of the herb he'd smoked, as he ate. The meal was the same as lunch had been: a chunk of bread, two slices of white cheese, and a helping of brisket stewed with carrots and onions. Kaleb didn't mind the repetition, as it was the first meat he'd eaten since joining up with Darra and her father. The tribal lad devoured the food with little concern for table manners, since he was standing up. He ate the cheese first, in three quick bites, and shoveled down the brisket and vegetables with his spoon. He used his bread to sop up the juice left behind and unceremoniously handed the plate back to Darra. All in all, it had taken him about three minutes to finish his meal. Darra had watched him eat with a fascinated expression, which he only now noticed.

"What?" he asked.

"How do you eat so fast without choking?"

"In the tribes, you have to eat fast, or somebody else will finish your meal for you," Kaleb explained. "Why, is it... gross?"

"A little bit," Darra said, scrunching her face up sympathetically.

"Excuse me," Lilith said from behind them, and the teens turned to face her. "I wonder if you might help me with something?" she asked Darra, who nodded acquiescence.

"I can help you," Kaleb offered.

"Oh, that's very kind of you, but this job requires a woman's delicate hand," Lilith said, gesturing for Darra to follow her.

"I'm happy to help, but if you're looking for a seamstress or the like, I'm afraid you've got the wrong girl," Darra said. Lilith reached into her cloak and gripped her scimitar.

"Oh, I think I've got the right girl," she said as she started to draw the blade. The back door to the establishment slammed open, and Ani poked her head outside. Lilith let go of her weapon.

"Darra, the dinner rush has started," she said. "I could use you back inside."

"Of course," the teen answered, shrugging an apology at Lilith. "Sorry, my time is not my own right now. Can I help you later, after the rush?"

"Certainly," Lilith said, smiling. "I can wait."

Aleksey and A.J. made it almost all the way back to *Lastrow* before the sun went down. The pilot no longer gawked at the buildings they passed. In fact, he hardly noticed the city around them at all, so concerned was he for the safety of the girl he'd only met a few days ago. As they passed a blacksmith's shop, A.J.'s eyes caught on a sword, and it suddenly dawned on him that when they got to where they were going, he would have no clue what to do next.

"I need a weapon," he said, pointing to the shop displaying blades and tools of all kinds.

"You're in no danger," Aleksey said. "The assassin didn't even notice you were there."

"But I could help you fight her," A.J. replied. "It seemed like you and she were pretty evenly matched."

"What seems to be and what is are often at odds," Aleksey said. "Besides, I'm not spending the last money we have on a sword for someone who's never even held one before. You'd be as likely to hurt yourself as anyone else."

A.J. picked a spear off a shelf and gauged its weight and balance. "Do you have sports in this world?" he asked. When Aleksey shook his head in the affirmative, the pilot said, "I was on my school's track and field team for five years. And this bad boy works just like a javelin."

Darra finished bussing a table and returned the dirty dishes to the washing basin in the kitchen. She came back out and scanned the section of tables she'd been assigned. Her patrons had all been served, so she crossed to where Lilith sat.

"I'm free now, I think," Darra said. "At least for the next few minutes. What did you need help with?"

"A case," Lilith replied. "My fingers are too big to work the clasp."

"Sounds easy enough," Darra said.

"It's just out front," Lilith lied, as she led the teen out of the barroom, through the foyer, and into the night.

Trosclair sought out Serena for a dance – after first checking with the band to make sure no love ballads were on the playlist. The last thing he wanted was a slow, romantic dance with a girl who might have her sights set on marrying him. The two joined the other dancers in a *gorret,* a simple, mid-tempo dance that called for couples to slowly rotate in a circular motion around the dance floor. It was the perfect dance for making conversation, and Trosclair saw no reason to hold his tongue with the girl.

"So Serena," he began, "My Lord Advisor tells me you've your sights set on ruling one day."

"It's more my father who has his sights on it, Your Grace," the young woman said. "He built Misty Vale into the city it is today. He doesn't want to see his legacy passed on to a stranger."

"You have no personal ambition toward the post, then?"

"If Your Grace sees fit to let me inherit, I will do my best to rule Misty Vale as my father has – to the prosperity of all."

"And if I side with tradition?" Trosclair asked. "What would you do then?"

"I – I hadn't thought that far ahead, Your Grace," Serena said. "I suppose then my fate would be as any other Noble woman's, tied to the man I marry." Trosclair watched her features carefully, but he saw no sign of duplicity, trickery or veiled ambition in her expression. The prince proceeded to ask Serena about her family, her education, and her hobbies. When the dance was over, he thanked her and returned to Ennio confident about one thing – the girl was not here to seduce him.

Aleksey turned the corner onto *Lastrow* and saw that a small crowd had formed in front of *The Laughing Stocks.* He and A.J. raced over and made their way to the front of the crowd, where they found Ani and Kaleb watching helplessly as Lilith held Darra precariously close to the edge of the cliff, a scimitar at the young woman's throat.

"Let her go!" Aleksey called out. "It's me you're after."

"Actually, it's the both of you," Lilith said. "But one of you was much easier to corner. Drop your weapons!"

Aleksey obeyed, throwing down his sword, but A.J. hesitated.

"Don't even think about it!" Aleksey growled at the pilot, and the young man lowered his spear to the ground.

"Now walk to the cliff's edge," Lilith instructed Aleksey. When he was close enough to see the river rushing at the bottom of the canyon, he stopped. "Take a dive," Lilith said, "Or the girl goes first."

"What's to stop you from killing her once I've jumped?" Aleksey asked.

"Oh, I'm going to kill her," Lilith clarified. "My god demands that. But if you go quietly, I'll make it quick and painless for her."

"Your god?" Aleksey repeated. "You're a True Believer, then?"

"So you've heard of us?" Lilith asked. "That's impressive, in someone as young as yourself."

"I thought you'd all been killed during the wars," Aleksey said. He spied Kaleb out of the corner of his eye as the young mage made several slow, subtle gestures, then heard him whisper a few syllables in the old speak. A strobe of bright light flashed out from Kaleb's hands, temporarily blinding the assassin, and Aleksey made his move. The half-elf hurled himself at Lilith, but the woman held Darra out in front of her like a shield. He ended up slamming into both of them, and the two women fell backwards together over the edge. Aleksey reached out and caught his daughter's hand, and it took all his half-elven strength to keep her from tumbling down into the canyon. Lilith caught onto a thick root to stop her own descent. A.J. rushed over, grabbed Darra's free hand, and helped Aleksey haul his daughter back up onto the cliffside.

"Are you alright?" Aleksey asked.

"I'm fine," Darra replied.

"Help me!" Lilith cried, as the root she was holding onto started to give way. She made a futile attempt at scrambling back up, but the dirt and rocks clattered away as soon as her feet found purchase.

"Help yourself!" Aleksey spat at the assassin. "Or better yet, pray to your god for salvation."

"Please!" Lilith begged, as the root pulled out of the dirt a little more.

"Dad," Darra said, as she looked over the edge at Lilith in pity. "We're a lot of things, but... We're not killers, are we?"

"Darra, you have no idea how dangerous this woman truly is," Aleksey said.

"I'll be no threat to you any longer," Lilith pleaded. "In Rebos' name, I swear it!"

Aleksey exhaled deeply and rolled his eyes, then said, "Fine." He reached down and grabbed Lilith by the wrist, then yanked her up so that she could reach the top of the cliff. He let her crawl her way back up from there, and by the time she did, the half-elf was waiting with his sword in one hand and a section of rope in the other. A.J. held his spear out at her threateningly while Darra tied the woman's hands together.

"Alright, alright! That's everything to be seen out here," Ani said to the crowd of onlookers, who seemed to have no intention of dispersing.

"Should we call the city guard?" someone asked.

"No!" Aleksey said. "We'll handle this."

"Was that boy using magic?" another asked.

"Uh... Flash powder!" Aleksey lied. "My young friend is an amateur photographer." The half-elf shot Ani a desperate look.

"Half-priced drinks for the next ten minutes!" Ani bellowed, and the patrons began shuffling back inside.

"Thanks, Ani," Aleksey said.

"Yeah, we really owe you one," A.J. added.

"You owe me more than one," Ani replied. "I take gold, silver and credits."

A.J. pulled out his all-but-empty pockets and held up his lollipop. "I have this," he offered meekly.

Ani snatched the candy away. "It's a start. I'll put the rest on your tab," she said to Aleksey, before turning back to A.J. "Is it strawberry?" she asked hopefully.

"Smells like cinnamon," he replied, and Ani made a face.

"Keep it," she said, tossing the treat back to him as she went inside.

Trosclair and Ennio made their exit from the ball early. The soldier was looking forward to removing his formal attire, which had not relented in its stuffiness, and the prince was eager to remove it for him. They met Milian in the halls.

"How was the ball, Your Grace?" the Lord Advisor asked.

"Tiring," the Prince said. "We were just on our way to bed."

"Your Grace seems to be... resting quite a lot these days," Milian said with the slightest of smirks, as he took in both the prince and his bodyguard with his gaze.

"Yes, well...they say teenagers require more sleep than adults," Trosclair said.

"Of course," Milian said. "Your Grace, now that you've had a chance to take Lady Parmida's measure, may I ask which way you are leaning about Lord Parmida's proposal?"

"We are... still considering. However, we have determined that we will decide this matter based on our assessment of Lady Parmida's abilities and her aptness for rule, not her gender."

"So Your Grace is open to changing the laws of inheritance?" Milian asked.

"I suspect I'll change many laws over the course of my rule," Trosclair said, dropping the formal plural. "And I'll break with many traditions," he said, looking at Ennio.

"Any great ruler must, if progress is to be made," Milian said, and Trosclair beamed at the implied compliment. "Now, please don't allow me to continue holding up Your Grace's... sleep." As Milian bowed and left, he made prolonged eye contact with Ennio, and a strange smile crept over his face.

"Are you sure you can trust him?" Ennio asked, once they'd made it back to the prince's chambers.

"Who?" Trosclair asked. "Milian?" Ennio nodded. "He's always been loyal, as far as I know. Why do you ask?"

"It's just - he has a lot of power right now; he's practically ruling the kingdom until your coronation. Are you sure he'll be happy to just turn around and give that position up?"

"I hadn't really thought about it," Trosclair said. "But he's not power-mad. He let me decide that dispute between the Lords, and now he's consulting with me about future laws. That's more than my uncle ever did to include me in the affairs of state."

"Still, there's something he's hiding," Ennio said. "I'm sure of it."

"You think he's dangerous?" Trosclair asked.

"I think he... bears watching," Ennio answered.

"Okay, so I'll watch," Trosclair said. "Although I really think you're seeing devils where there are none."

"I hope so," Ennio said.

Aleksey had a room put on his tab, and the adventurers led Lilith upstairs. Once there, the half-elf sat the woman in the room's only chair and drew his sword.

"Now, I'm positively bursting with questions," he said. "And the only reason I let you live is because you're going to answer them."

"Fine," Lilith said. "Ask away."

"Who hired you?"

"A man named Milian Jaunet."

"I've never heard of him," Aleksey said. "Why would this man want us dead?"

"The full force of the Kingdom of DuVerres is after the two of you," Lilith said, indicating Darra. "Milian wanted you removed from the playing field, so to speak, so that Commandant Burke would waste more time looking for you."

"Commandant Burke?" Aleksey said. "He must still be after the DragonSword."

"No," Lilith said. "He's looking for you because they suspect you were involved in Duke DuVerres' assassination."

"The Duke is dead?" Darra asked.

"I can't say I'll miss him," Aleksey said. "He made the peasants poorer and the nobles richer. But why would they think we were behind his death?"

"It is a matter of crossed stars, I suppose," Lilith said, shrugging. "Our fates seem intertwined."

"*Our* fates?" Darra repeated. "You're saying you killed the Duke?"

"I did," Lilith confessed.

"You just go around killing people?" Kaleb asked. "For money?"

"Everything I do, I do in the name of Rebos, the Reaper," the assassin said. "I did receive compensation. But ultimately, I killed the Duke because my god told me it was his time to die."

"And your god said the same thing about us?" Aleksey asked.

"The two of you saved my life," Lilith said. "The Reaper's law commands that I repay the life debt I owe you in full."

"What do you mean? Repay how?" Darra asked.

"By saving your lives, of course," Lilith said.

Aleksey laughed. "True Believers," he said when he'd finished. "Their gods would have them killing us and saving us at the same time!"

"My god gives me power," Lilith said.

"Oh, I'm well aware of what you can do," Aleksey said. "That's why you're tied up."

"About that," Darra said, pulling her father aside. "What are we gonna do with her? We can't turn her over to the City Guard, and I don't feel comfortable sleeping next to her."

"I have an idea about that," Kaleb volunteered.

A few minutes later, the men stood outside one of the stable stalls, watching as Darra retied Lilith's bonds. This time she secured the assassin's hands and feet, then tied the other end of the rope to the hitching post.

"I trust you won't mind the lack of amenities," Aleksey said.

"I've suffered worse," Lilith said, as she situated herself on a pile of clean straw.

The adventurers left her there and returned to the barroom. Aleksey ordered a plate - with a salad in place of the brisket - and took it back up to their room to eat it. Kaleb followed, saying he wanted to get some studying done before bedtime. Darra brought out two more plates from the kitchen and sat down next to A.J. to eat.

"I guess now you can add 'waitress' to your résumé," the pilot said. "Is there anything you can't do?"

"I'm a terrible cook," Darra replied. "And I can't even pick up a needle and thread without drawing blood." A.J. picked up his fork and cut into the brisket, but Darra put her hand on his. "Wait," she said, and A.J. could tell she was suddenly nervous for some reason. "Before you get your mouth all... meaty, there's something

I've been wanting to do." With that, she leaned over and kissed the pilot on the lips. It was her first time, and she wasn't sure she was doing it right. And then it was over, and A.J. was staring at her with a smile on his face.

"Was that... okay?" Darra asked.

"Yeah!" A.J. said hurriedly. "Yes, that was... something I've wanted to do, too." The two stared at each other for a long moment, which started to turn awkwardly silent.

"I'm going to get us some drinks," Darra declared, lurching up off the bench on which she sat. As she made her way to the kitchen, she traced a finger over her lips and whispered, "Mmm, cinnamon."

That night, Darra and Kaleb won the coin toss and the right to sleep in the big bed. As she lay there with A.J. on the floor beside her, her thoughts invariably turned back to their kiss. When sleep finally took her, Darra dreamt of a large castle built right into the side of a mountain. She wandered through its halls, searching each room for A.J. She opened a heavy door and came upon the library. She walked in and began searching the stacks, but there was no sign of the boy she liked. She left the library behind and found a balcony, from which she could see a large valley spread out in front of her. "I know this place," she said to no one, as her lucidity increased. "It's near..."

"Morning's Peak," someone finished for her. She spun around, expecting to find A.J. - and instead found a handsome, swarthy stranger staring at her intensely. His dark eyes seemed to want to penetrate her, to see into her very soul. The stranger took her in his arms and brought her in close, and her heart started to race - though from fear or desire or both, she could not tell.

Darra woke just before the stranger's lips could touch her own. The dream had been so vivid, it took a moment for the teen to remember where she was. She stayed perfectly still, waiting for her heartbeat to settle, and wondered from what corner of her mind the stranger had been pulled. "*It's just a dream*," she finally told herself, as she closed her eyes once more.

CHAPTER FOUR
"BY ANY OTHER NAME"

A.J. awoke first and crept out of the room as silently as he could, given the creakiness of the floorboards. Ani was already up, and the pilot found her downstairs in the foyer, folding towels.

"Good morning, Ani," he said.

"You're up early," she observed.

"It's my service training," he said. "Ordinarily I'd be half-way into a ten-K by now." Ani stared at him uncomprehendingly. "That's a long run."

"Okay..." Ani said. "So what military did you serve with?"

"You've... never heard of it, I'm sure," he said, waving the topic away.

"Fine, fine, keep your secrets," Ani said. "You're certainly with the right group for it. Would you believe Aleksey told me he was an antiques dealer when we first met?"

"What makes you think he's not?"

"Listen, cutie, I'm a lot of things, but gullible isn't one of them," Ani said. "For starters, there's the assassin tied up in my stables. You don't hear about a lot of antiques dealers having contracts taken out on them. I mean, what'd he do, overprice a credenza?"

"I guess you have a point," A.J. admitted.

"I always do," she said, handing him a towel. "Breakfast isn't for another half-hour. If you wanna wash up first, we put in a shower out back."

"I'd love to! Thanks," A.J. said, and he made his way

through the barroom and out to the back of the establishment. He found the shower tucked up next to the building. It consisted of a simple stall with a round showerhead overhead, a large cistern above that, and a series of pipes leading down to a hand pump sticking up about four feet out of the ground. One fed the water through the pipes into the cistern and then pulled a cord to release the water in a steady spray. A.J. pumped the handle for several minutes, then quickly stripped off his clothes and set them outside the stall in a neat pile. He braced himself and pulled the cord; the water began flowing down on him, cold as expected, and he started washing as quickly as he could. A.J. was about halfway done when the stall door opened unexpectedly. Kaleb walked in, wearing nothing but a towel around his waist.

"Good morning," the tribal lad said sleepily, as he removed the towel and slung it over the top of the door. A.J. tried to hide his shock as he turned away from the mage, who took the opportunity to scoot under the showerhead with him. Kaleb shivered with the cold and shook his head, then wiped water from his face with a hand and began washing. "It's cold," he said.

"Yeah... yeah, it is," A.J. said. "So is this something you do in your tribe? Bathe together?"

"Of course," Kaleb replied. "It saves on water... Wait, you're not bothered by it, are you?"

"No! No, of course not," A.J. said.

"I mean, it's just us guys here, right?" Kaleb asked, and A.J. shook his head in agreement. They continued washing in silence for several moments, and then Kaleb asked, "Hey, A.J.?"

"Yeah?" the pilot responded.

"Get my back for me?" the younger boy asked. It took A.J. several horrified seconds to realize Kaleb was teasing him, and he punched the mage playfully on the shoulder.

At breakfast a little later, A.J. sat next to Kaleb and across from Darra, who was seated next to her father. Aleksey and Darra had eggs, biscuits and battered-and-fried apple slices, while Kaleb and A.J. enjoyed the same but also added bacon to the meal. Ani served the handful of other guests first and then brought out a plate for herself, settling in next to Darra.

"So, sexy Leksey," Ani said, looking over at the half-elf. "Do you mind telling me when you plan on removing the woman you're currently detaining in my stable?"

"I thought I'd take her some breakfast after we ate and send her on her way," Aleksey said.

"What?" A.J. asked in shock. "You can't be serious! She tried to kill you and your daughter, and you're just gonna let her go?"

"One night's detention isn't much punishment for attempted murder," Kaleb said.

"She's a True Believer. I don't expect an outworlder to know what that means," Aleksey said to A.J. "But suffice it to say, she worships the old gods - or the god of death, at least - and she invites danger with her mere presence. Best to be rid of her now."

"Couldn't you have her arrested?" A.J. asked. "There were plenty of witnesses."

"Not without giving an official statement to the city guard," Aleksey said. "And I don't fancy that, since the entire continent is now searching for my daughter and me for the Duke's murder." Ani looked shocked, so Aleksey quickly added, "We had nothing to do with it, by the way."

"I gotta say, Leks, it's a good thing I'm so fond of your daughter," Ani said. "Otherwise, I'd be throwing you out right about now."

"I know, I know. We bring a lot of potential trouble along with us wherever we go, it seems. Thank you, Ani, for your hospitality," Aleksey said.

"Just make your departure quick, so I don't have to explain any of this to my brother when he gets back," Ani said.

"He wouldn't want us here?" Kaleb asked.

"He can be a tad... severe, when he thinks I'm in any kind of danger," Ani replied. "It's an embarrassment."

"I know how you feel," Darra said, with a pointed look at her father. "Did you want to trade before we go?" she asked Ani.

"Of course!" Ani said.

"Trade?" A.J. repeated.

"Oh, I keep a lot of clothes here with Ani," Darra said, as she and Ani rose to leave. "That way I have something clean to trade out when I come through."

"And I get to borrow whatever I want in between visits," Ani said. "Everybody wins."

"Just hurry and get packed up," Aleksey said. "And we'll go see to the lady's comfort out back." The half-elf, the pilot and the mage made their way to the kitchen, where Aleksey asked the cook to serve up another plate. With the food in hand, the trio made their way to the back of the barroom and exited the building.

It was only a few steps to the stables, and they found Lilith where they'd left her, sitting on a pile of straw with her back against the stable wall. The rope that had tied her hands and feet was in a neat coil in front of the woman, who appeared to be resting with her eyes closed.

"So, you freed yourself," Aleksey said, scooting the ropes aside with a booted foot. Lilith opened her eyes and stared up at him blankly. "Why are you still here?" Aleksey asked, as he sat the plate of food in front of the woman. She snatched up a biscuit, tore a chunk of it off, and shoved it in her mouth.

"You knew those ropes couldn't hold me," she said, as she finished chewing. "Besides, I already told you: I owe you and your daughter a life-debt for sparing me. My god demands that I stay by your side until I've fulfilled it."

"Yeah, see, that's not really gonna work for me," Aleksey said. "My daughter and I have business we need to see to, privately. And our travelling party is already larger than I'd like. No offense intended," he said to A.J.

"I'm not asking for your permission," Lilith said. "Even if you leave me here, tied up, I'll find you again."

"And how exactly did you manage that, the first time?" Aleksey asked. "We've been on the move constantly."

"When he sees fit, my god grants me the longsight," Lilith answered.

"Ah, of course," Aleksey said. An idea suddenly occurred to him, lighting up his expression. "And this longsight of yours," he prompted. "Can you use it to find anybody?"

Trosclair and Ennio were in the study, the large middle chamber in the prince's suite. The walls were lined with bookshelves filled to capacity with fiction, such as the *Brothers in Blood* series, and nonfiction, like biographies, histories and books of art. There was also a whole section devoted to science stories, which were all the rage both at court and abroad. One corner of the room had also been converted into a large cage that was the home of a parrot with a red body and yellow and blue wings. The bird had been a gift from the King of Vilmos for Trosclair's tenth birthday, and on most days, it was a chatty, chittery little thing – which is why Trosclair had the cage built in his study and not his bedroom or his parlor, where it could potentially disturb his sleep or his guests, respectively. Today, however, it wouldn't make a sound, in spite of Ennio's coaching.

"Say it," the bodyguard instructed the bird. "Come on, Ignatius, you've said it before."

"Yeah, like a million times," Trosclair said, looking up from his book. "Maybe he's as sick of saying it as I am of hearing it."

"Aw, you love it, and you know it!" Ennio teased, glancing over his shoulder at the prince, who rolled his eyes, shook his head and resumed reading. Ennio turned back to the bird and held up an orange slice. "If you say it, I'll give you a treat."

"That's never gonna work," Trosclair said without looking up.

"Hey! Ignatius and I don't need that kind of negativity," Ennio said. "Besides, if you can teach a dog or a monkey to do tricks for food, surely you can teach a parrot the same way."

"I don't think so," Trosclair said, placing his finger on the page to mark his spot. "There's a reason they call stupid people 'birdbrained.'"

Ennio's jaw dropped exaggeratedly. "Cover your ears, Ignatius! Do birds have ears?"

"I think just about everything has ears."

"Then cover your ears, Ignatius! Your owner's just called you dumb."

"You're the dummy," Trosclair said.

"Oh, yeah?" Ennio asked, as he put the orange slice in the bird's feeding bowl. He stalked toward the prince with fingers wiggling, poised to tickle.

"Yes," Trosclair said, putting his book aside and picking up a pillow to shield himself with. "Birds have ears. But they can't cover them because their wings don't bend that way," he said, lifting his brows in a smug, know-it-all look.

Ennio reached Trosclair and grabbed at the pillow, but the younger boy pulled it close to his chest. "No! Ennio, no!" Trosclair squealed, as Ennio reached around the pillow and tickled him. "I give up! I give up!" the prince said, laughing. The young soldier ended his assault and leaned in to peck Trosclair quickly on the lips.

A knock at the door interrupted their play. Trosclair stood up and straightened his vest, then crossed to the door. He swiped a hand in front of his smiling face and said, "Prince face." He opened the door wearing the blandest of expressions. "Yes?"

"Morning, Your Grace," said Mrs. Applebaum, a matronly older woman with long silver hair down her back. She shuffled into the study without waiting for an invitation and wrapped the prince in a tight hug. "Are you ready for your haircut, my boy?"

"Has it been three weeks already?" he asked.

"Almost four," she said. "And we can't have a shaggy little prince running around the palace, now, can we?" She scooted Trosclair toward his desk, where he pulled out his chair and sat down obediently. Mrs. Applebaum ran a hand through the prince's red and gold hair, the fiery trait for which the DuVerres royal family was known.

"So, what kind of trouble have you been getting into?" she asked, as she pulled a pair of scissors from her smock and began measuring Trosclair's hair with her fingers.

"No trouble," Trosclair said, holding up his hands. "I have been taking on more responsibilities, though."

"Well, that's wonderful!" Mrs. Applebaum said. "I suppose you'll be running the whole kingdom proper, by summer."

"That's the plan," the prince replied.

"Oh, Ennio!" Ignatius said from the corner, and one could hear the swoon in the parrot's imitation of a human voice. "My hero!"

"Yes!" Ennio said, pumping his fist in triumph.

"Pay him no mind," Trosclair instructed Mrs. Applebaum, rolling his eyes again. "He's touched in the head."

Aleksey and his band of teenage adventurers followed Lilith out of the Free City. They crossed the bridge over the Sylvan, the large river that bordered Middlestead to the west, and began trekking through the woods. This technically meant that they had crossed back into the kingdom of DuVerres. It was a tactical decision Aleksey dreaded, but Lilith had sworn her god's vision showed her a young man with a dusky complexion and a wild look in his eyes – Tarun – speaking to another man in the forest here. When Aleksey questioned her about the second man, she said only that he was there and gone in an instant, as if by magic.

"You'd best not be trying any tricks," Aleksey warned the assassin.

"I don't need tricks," she replied. "My god grants me actual power."

"How does that work?" Darra asked.

"I offer obeisance three times a day," Lilith said. "I observe all of Rebos' holy days, and I live by the vows I took when I became a True Believer. In return, Rebos answers my prayers."

"What, you mean you just – ask for something, and it happens? Like magic?" Darra asked.

"Not exactly," Lilith said. "A mage draws upon his or her own life energy to cast a spell. But a True Believer's powers come from the gods themselves. It never wavers or falters, as can happen with magic."

"Tell me about it," Kaleb said.

"You're strong," Lilith said to Darra. "Any god would be lucky to have you as a follower. If you're interested, I can explain my vows to you."

"Whoa!" Aleksey said, stepping between his daughter and the assassin. "Keep your proselytizing to yourself, if you don't mind. I'm lucky to be blessed with a daughter with a good head on her shoulders, and I won't have religion creeping in to confuse everything."

"You don't have to protect me from this, Dad," Darra said. "I can make my own mind up about things, you know. I'm not some dumb kid anymore."

"And she has an independent streak," Lilith commented. "I'm starting to see why my god chose to spare you."

"Fine, fine," Aleksey said, stepping back out of his daughter's way as she passed him. "Make nice with the lady who almost killed you yesterday. Just don't go calling for dear old dad when the cult comes to claim you."

"So you were saying," Darra prompted, ignoring her father.

"Right. My vows," Lilith began. "First comes the vow of obedience. I have vowed to make myself a vessel for enacting Rebos' will..." The assassin continued listing her vows, and Darra listened intently, if only to annoy her father. They made it into the thick of the forest before the sun set.

"How close are we?" Aleksey asked Lilith.

"I'm not a bloodhound," Lilith replied. "I can lead us to the place where I saw your friend in my vision, but he may have moved on. I'll consult with my god again tonight. It's a process." Lilith continued leading them in the dark, until they reached the clearing she had seen in her vision. Aleksey sniffed the air and caught a whiff of Tarun's scent, but it was weak and scattered, indicating that he had moved on hours before.

"Alright," Aleksey said. "We'll make camp here tonight."

"Oh, thank god!" Kaleb said. "I didn't want to slow us down, but I am starving! And I saw a blackberry bush not too far back."

"Okay then, we'll forage our dinner and meet back here," Aleksey said.

"I can't live on a handful of berries. I'm going hunting," Lilith declared.

"Hunting, huh?" A.J. asked. "Mind if I tag along? I'm pretty anxious to take this bad boy out for a spin," he said, hefting his spear.

"I'd like to help, too," Kaleb offered. "In return for some meat."

"Just try and keep up," Lilith said, as she turned and walked back into the trees. A.J. and Kaleb followed after her. After about twenty minutes of silently stalking through the trees, Lilith heard a rustling movement from the bushes in front of her. She signaled to the young men behind her to stop and readied an arrow in her longbow. The rustling came again, and a rabbit the size of a large dog hopped out of the bushes. "Now's your chance, hunter," she whispered to A.J. The pilot raised his spear and took aim, then let the weapon fly. It struck a tree several yards behind the rabbit and clattered to the forest floor. Lilith laughed as the rabbit leapt away. "Perhaps you'd be better at gathering firewood," the assassin suggested as she moved on.

A.J. took the hint and retreated back the way they'd come. Determined to be of some use, he picked up scattered sticks and twigs along the way and had an armful by the time he made it back to the clearing. He put down his weapon and the wood and then went back into the trees to find more. His attention was caught by a sweet smell hanging heavy in the air. He rounded a tree and found a large flower about four feet high. The sweet smell grew stronger the closer he got to the plant, which was a single thorny stem topped by a red and purple blossom made up of seven large, droopy petals. It was, in A.J.'s opinion, the prettiest flower he'd ever seen. He knew immediately that he wanted to present it to Darra. He crossed to the flower and grabbed the stem; careful though he was, he nevertheless pricked himself on a thorn as he bent and broke the flower off. He pulled his index finger back and examined it as blood swelled at the site of the tiny injury. A.J. wiped his finger on his pants as he made his way back into the clearing.

Lilith and Kaleb made it back next. Kaleb carried a large pouch full of blackberries, and the assassin had a large dead squirrel with an arrow sticking out of its eye slung over her shoulder.

"Geez, is everything here so... huge?" A.J. asked as Lilith laid the creature out on the ground. Its head and body were just over three and a half feet long, and its fluffy tail was almost as long as that again. Lilith gripped the arrow in the animal's skull, and there was a slow sucking sound that made A.J. flinch as she pulled the arrowhead clear.

"This one's not that big," Lilith said.

"Yeah, I've seen a lot bigger," Kaleb agreed. "Oh, you should have seen it though, A.J.! She said a prayer, closed her eyes and shot - I hadn't even seen the squirrel in the bushes - and it fell over, dead in an instant."

"Well, of course it was instantaneous!" Lilith said. "I worship the god of death, not the god of making animals suffer. Rarely does Rebos allow my hands to deliver anything other than a clean killing blow."

"That's good to know," Aleksey said, as he and Darra came up behind Lilith into the clearing, each carrying a linen bag of something. "It smells like death, so I take it your hunt was successful?"

Lilith pointed to her kill. "Once it's stripped, cut, salted, seasoned and wrapped, I'll have meat for days. You, boy," she said, looking to Kaleb. "You're of the Tribes, are you not?" When he nodded, she said simply, "Skin and cut this, if you want to earn your share."

"No problem," he said, as he drew a knife from the inside of his robes. "What did you guys find?"

"Well, as it so happens, we found a peach tree and a faerie garden," Aleksey said, obviously quite proud of himself. "There were onions, carrots, potatoes – even a tomato plant! So my daughter and I will be eating like royalty for the next few days."

"You're not gonna share?" Kaleb asked.

"We'll be happy to trade for some blackberries," Aleksey said. "Don't look so hurt, Kaleb. I'm just trying to teach you about the barter economy."

"Oh, I forgot," A.J. said, as he reached into his pack and pulled out the flower, careful not to poke himself again. He presented the flower to Darra – and her face froze in terror. She jerked her hands back.

"Drop that right now!" she commanded.

"Why?" A.J. asked.

"It's poison!" Darra answered, her voice frantic. A.J. stood dumbfounded for a moment, then looked at the flower. He let go of it, and it fell to the ground.

"Poison?" he repeated.

"Darra, honey, what's going on?" Aleksey asked, and then the sweet smell hit him. "Good gods, you picked a Cursed Knight?"

"I don't know what that is," A.J. said.

"It's a flower," Darra said. "That flower, specifically. And every school child knows it's poison!"

"Haven't you ever heard the song? Purple and red, petals of seven, soon you'll be dead and gone up to heaven," Kaleb sang.

"I'm not from here, remember?" A.J. said defensively. "Besides, it was just a tiny prick. I don't feel sick or anything."

"The plant drew blood?" Aleksey asked. A.J. nodded, and Aleksey said, "You've got six, maybe seven hours before the symptoms set in. I'm sorry."

"No," Darra said, tears welling in her eyes. "No!"

"Are you saying I'm... gonna die?" A.J. asked, disbelieving, but the grave looks that greeted him forced him to reconsider.

"Every time the Cursed Knight draws blood, the poison sets in," Aleksey said.

"Well, surely there's a cure? An antidote, something?" he said.

"I've never heard of one," Aleksey said. "The problem is

that the poison is mystical in nature."

"Well then, can't magic cure it?" Darra asked, turning to Kaleb hopefully.

"I do know a healing spell – it's the first thing Gram teaches anyone who shows an aptitude for magic," the tribal lad said. "But it's more for cuts, bruises, burns – external injuries."

"Please, Kay – you have to try!" Darra begged, and Kaleb shook his head in agreement. The young mage went to his pack and pulled out his spellbook. He found the correct page and started practicing the hand gestures and intonations that would complete the ritual.

"Give me your waterskin," he said, and Darra rushed to retrieve it. Kaleb performed the spell, his eyes flashed amber, and a strange sort of energy the same color coursed through the water. "Okay," he said, handing the waterskin to A.J.

"What am I supposed to do with it?" the pilot asked.

"Well, ordinarily, I'd pour the water over a wound," Kaleb said.

"But the poison is in his bloodstream now," Aleksey said. "Best to have him drink it."

"That was my thinking, as well," Kaleb said. A.J. lifted the waterskin to his lips and took a long, deep swallow. He took another drink, and then another.

"There," he said, handing the empty skin back to Darra. "Am I, you know, cured now?"

"I guess we'll just have to wait and see," Aleksey said.

"If you wait much longer, he'll be dead for sure," Lilith said.

"What do you mean?" Darra asked.

"My god grants me many gifts," Lilith said. "One of these is the knowledge of impending death. Rebos is still coming for you; I can see your fate in your eyes."

"Then it's hopeless?" Darra asked.

"Not necessarily," Lilith said. "I have seen the look of certain death before. Your fate, however, seems to be wavering."

"You're saying there's a way to save him?" Aleksey asked.

"Half-elf, there is almost always a way," the assassin replied.

"So point us in the right direction," Aleksey said. "Ask your god how to save the boy."

"It doesn't work like that," she said.

"I think we were on the right track before. Use magic to fight magic, and all that," Kaleb said.

"But she said it didn't work," Darra said.

"Kaleb's spell was taught to beginners," Aleksey said. "There are more powerful healing spells in the world."

"I wish Gram were here," Kaleb said. "She could probably cure you in her sleep."

"So all we need is a more powerful spell, then?" Darra asked. "Where can we find that?"

"I... may know of a place," Aleksey said.

"Really, Dad?" Darra asked.

"It's possible. There's a shop back in the city that might have what we need," Aleksey said.

"Well, then, let's hurry!" Darra urged. The party began packing up their food and belongings, and Lilith looked down at her squirrel.

"I guess I'll take this to-go, then," she said, and she slung the carcass over her shoulder.

Trosclair, Ennio and Armand were seated at the table in his parlor playing *Queen's Tower*, a game that called for the players to assemble a "tower" of ascending numerical cards while also "battling" each other with their face cards.

"Seven-eight-nine," Armand said, as he built his tower to near-completion.

"Ennio, check his pockets and his sleeves," Trosclair said. "He's hiding cards; I'm sure of it."

"Now, now - there's no reason to get bitter, just because I'm going to win again," Armand said. The prince laid out a king and a jack to battle, but the merchant's son topped him with two queens. Trosclair held up his cards, their backs to Armand, and Armand picked one from the middle of his hand. Trosclair handed the card over with a sigh.

"How do you always know the card I least want you to pick?" the prince asked.

"Aha!" Armand said, as he flipped the card over to reveal a ten. Armand laid out two more cards, a jack and another queen.

"Come on, Ennio," Trosclair said. "Tell me you have that last queen."

"Sorry," Ennio said as he laid out two kings. Trosclair glared at him, and the soldier held up his hands in a gesture of helplessness.

"Haha!" Armand exclaimed, as he laid the ten down to complete his tower. "Victory!"

"Nobody likes a gloater," Trosclair said.

"I guess I'll just be taking this," Armand said, as he scooped up the three gold coins in the pot with a smug look.

"Another hand?" Ennio asked as he gathered up the cards.

"I'm out of gold coins," Trosclair said. "Should I call my squire and have him bring some more?"

"As much fun as it would be to continue taking your money, I'm afraid I have to get going," Armand said. "Alicia and I have tickets to the opera."

"*The Mystery of Santo Mori*?" Trosclair asked, and Armand nodded as he stood and pushed in his chair. "Oh, you're in for a treat. Delphine Loew is among the most gifted sopranos I've ever heard."

"At a hundred credits per seat, I should hope so!" Armand said, as he crossed to the door. He spotted something on the floor and bent to retrieve it. When he came back up, he was holding a small white envelope. "Somebody must have slipped this under the door while we were playing," he said, offering it to Ennio. The envelope was sealed, with Trosclair's first name written on the front in an elegant hand.

"Thank you," Ennio said, as Armand waved a goodbye and left the parlor. The soldier handed the envelope to his prince, who wasted no time opening it. He pulled out a thick white card written in the same elegant hand and began reading.

"It's an invitation," he said, as a confused look crossed his face. "To a salon."

"Oh?" Ennio asked. "What's the topic?"

"Forbidden love," Trosclair said. "And there's no signature."

"Forbidden love? You don't think whoever sent this is implying something about us, do you?" Ennio asked.

"More than implying," Trosclair answered. "There's an addendum at the bottom: 'Perhaps Your Grace and his favorite bodyguard should attend?' it asks."

"It doesn't say that!" Ennio said, snatching the note to read for himself. When he'd finished, his shock competed with worry for control of his features. "Who - who could have sent this? And why?"

"Isn't it obvious?" Trosclair asked. "Someone's found out about us, and they're mocking me. They're probably planning to blackmail me."

"I'll ask around the royal guard," Ennio said. "Someone must have seen the person who left this behind."

"Oh, Ennio, you can't!" Trosclair said. "The more people who know about this, the likelier it is that we'll be found out. And you know how gossipy court life is."

"Then what do you propose we do?"

"We'll have to consider our options carefully," Trosclair said. "But I'm sure of one thing, Ennio: Whoever sent this note is going to regret it."

Aleksey and the other adventurers kept moving long into the night, but in the dark, travel was slower than in the day. After about five and a half hours, Darra noticed A.J. was using his spear as a walking stick. He was sweating profusely, and his breathing was labored.

"Hold up," she said, and the party came to a halt.

"What is it?" Aleksey asked.

"A.J.'s feeling the poison. Aren't you?" she asked. The pilot nodded.

"I'm so hot," he said. "It's like my blood is... burning."

"That would be the first symptom of the Cursed Knight's poison: an unnatural fever," Aleksey said. "We're not far from the city. If you can make it to the Sylvan, you'll be better off. Immersing yourself in water will slow the fever down."

"Okay, then," A.J. replied, and the group walked on. "You said the fever was just the first symptom, right?"

"Unfortunately, yes," Aleksey said over his shoulder.

"So what can I expect next?" A.J. asked. "Nausea? Headaches?"

"Nothing like that," Darra said.

"Aren't you going to tell him the story?" Lilith asked.

"Oh, I - I wouldn't want to worry him," Darra said dismissively.

"What story?" A.J. asked.

"The story of the Cursed Knight, of course," Lilith said. "I mean, if I was dying from the slow poison of a curse, I'd want to know where that magic came from. Aren't you curious?"

"Well, I am now," A.J. said. "So what's the story?" he asked Darra, who still seemed hesitant. "Come on, I can handle it," he assured her.

"Okay then," Darra said. "In the olden days, there lived a knight whose valor was renowned throughout the kingdoms, though his name is now lost to history. The knight was called to a crusade, and he was separated from his true love for years on end. When he finally returned, he found his betrothed had been abducted by a cruel and powerful sorcerer. The knight knew no fear of magic, for his sword had been blessed to cut through spells and the like."

"Another gift from the gods," Lilith put in.

"The knight confronted the sorcerer," Darra continued. "The battle they fought was among the greatest the world had ever seen. They were too evenly matched for one to gain advantage over the other, and too strong-willed to call the battle off before they were exhausted. In the end, they each delivered a killing blow at the exact same moment, ensuring that both would perish. But the sorcerer had enough strength left in him to curse the knight, and with his dying breaths, he uttered the incantations that created the flower we now call the Cursed Knight. The flower's poison brings fever, as you already know. Next, you'll begin to see and hear things that aren't there. And finally, the Cursed Knight himself will appear before you."

"And...?" A.J. prompted. "What happens after that?"

"I—I'm not going to let it get that far," Darra said.

"But what happens?" the pilot asked again.

"The knight is bound by the curse to kill everyone who sees him," Kaleb said. "Death usually comes while the victim is unconscious."

"I see," A.J. said.

"What I don't get is how you found a Cursed Knight to begin with," Kaleb continued. "It takes a powerful sorcerer to create one."

"That's a question for another time," Aleksey said, as they cleared the last of the trees. The banks of the Sylvan spread out before them, and in the distance, the bridge back into the city was visible. "Let's set up camp here until morning comes."

"Shouldn't we move on into the city?" Darra asked.

"I don't think the outworlder will make it that far," Aleksey said.

"Outworlder?" Lilith said. "My, my – this party is certainly more interesting than a first glance would suggest." The assassin plopped down on the ground, pulled a knife from her bag, and started skinning her squirrel.

"Besides, the shop I'm headed to won't be open until mid-morning," Aleksey said.

"You mean the shop we're headed to, don't you?" his daughter asked, readying herself for an argument.

"Honey, we're talking about a dealer of magics – which, in the cities, is exclusively black market stuff," Aleksey said. "I don't wanna mix you up in it."

"I'm already a wanted fugitive," Darra said. "Please, Dad, just let me help you with this. I have to do something."

"Fine," Aleksey capitulated. "If you lie down and get some rest, I'll wake you, and you can go to the shop with me."

"But who'll look after A.J.?" Darra asked.

"We'll take turns," Kaleb said.

"You two will," Lilith said. "I'm going to eat and go to bed."

"Are you really so callous?" Aleksey asked. "My daughter may lose a friend, and you're not even going to try to help us?"

"Without my help, you would not have come this far," Lilith responded. "I make death with my hands nearly every day. How did you expect me to react to its proximity? With tears and pathetic sentiments?"

"How about just a little humanity?" Aleksey replied.

Lilith stared Aleksey down for a tense, silent moment. "What do you know about humanity, half-elf?" she finally said under her breath.

"More than I'd like," Aleksey said. "Darra, honey, go ahead. Sleep. I'm gonna help A.J. into the river to cool off."

"That sounds amazing," the pilot said.

Darra pulled out her bedroll and spread it on the sand. As worried as she was for A.J., she was also very tired, and it didn't take long for her to fall asleep.

For the second night in a row, she dreamt lucidly about the castle carved into the mountain near Morning's Peak. She was again searching the castle room by room, but this time, she was searching for the stranger, the swarthy young man who tried to kiss her in her previous dream. She found him in the same spot, staring out of a portico at the night sky with his arms clasped behind his back. He turned his head a fraction of an inch toward her, and her stomach leapt.

"Whenever I look out at the heavens, I always feel like I'm supposed to be thinking great thoughts," the stranger said. "But they seldom come." The stranger turned to face Darra and then gestured to a bench near him. "Please, sit."

"I prefer to stand," Darra heard herself say.

"That's fine, too," the stranger said. "You're here. In the end, that's all that matters."

"But why am I here?" Darra asked. "I mean, I know I'm not really here, here." The stranger crossed over to Darra. "This is just a dream."

"Yes, and no," he said, as he held out a hand for her own. "You are dreaming, that much is true. But while your body is... elsewhere, your mind is here with me - a fact I'm grateful for, since I spend the majority of my days here alone."

"You brought me here?"

"I can assure you, the meshing of our psyches was brought about by no one other than yourself."

"Who are you?" Darra asked. "You seem... familiar."

"My name is Volos," the stranger said. A shooting star raced across the night sky. "And too quickly, it seems, our time has once again come to an end."

"What are you—"

"We'll see each other again soon," Volos said, and then he took Darra by the arms and gently shook her.

"Darra," Aleksey said, shaking her, and his daughter's eyes snapped open. The sun was already rising. "Darra, it's time we got going." Darra sat up quickly as the urgency of the morning settled in on her.

"I'm coming too," Kaleb said from A.J.'s side. "If you're headed to a magic shop, you've got to take your mage. I even talked to Lilith about it last night; she's willing to watch over A.J. until we get back."

"Well, that's more generous than I thought her capable of being," Aleksey said.

"For fifty credits," Kaleb added, and Aleksey snorted.

"Of course she wants money," the half-elf said. "There's no such thing as charity any more, is there, sweetie?"

"Hmm? Oh, no I - I guess not," Darra said. "How is he?" she asked Kaleb, as she looked down at A.J. If it weren't for his sallow complexion and ragged breathing, it would've seemed like he was merely sleeping.

"I'm not gonna lie," Kaleb said. "It got... pretty bad. The delusions have set in. He was seeing snakes and spiders everywhere he looked. I brewed up a sedative tea, and that's what finally got him to sleep."

"Thank you, Kay, for taking such good care of him," Darra said, placing a hand on the tribal lad's arm. "We're lucky to have you with us."

"I'm sure he'd do the same for me," Kaleb said. Aleksey woke up Lilith and then led Darra and Kaleb over the bridge and back into the city.

The assassin had an easy morning. She skewered several chunks of squirrel with two long, sharp metal pins and roasted the meat over a fire. She bathed in the Sylvan, and she prayed, on her knees with her hands clasped and her eyes closed.

By midmorning, A.J. was starting to come around. Lilith tried to get him to eat, but the pilot pushed the food away.

"Stomach hurts," he mumbled. "Everything hurts."

"I'm... sorry," Lilith said. "Are you still seeing things?"

"No," A.J. said, but from the wild look in his eyes, Lilith knew he was lying.

A.J. drifted in and out of consciousness. He awoke a couple hours later just in time to see a shadow fall over Lilith. He tried to make out the figure that was blocking the sun, but his vision was too blurred. He rubbed at his eyes and looked again, and this time, he saw the figure clearly. It was a man in a full suit of armor and helmet, his sword drawn, looking down at him. A.J. tried to warn Lilith about the man behind her, but his throat seized up, and he could feel the blackness at the edges of his perception that meant he was about to pass out again. With enormous effort, he waved a frantic hand at the assassin, pointing behind her as the darkness took him.

Lilith turned around and saw nothing out of the ordinary.

If she'd scanned the trees a little longer, she might have seen Tarun as he skulked about, waiting for his moment.

Trosclair and Ennio were seated in the back of a hired carriage as it rolled through the capital city's streets. Whenever the prince left the palace, he usually rode in one of his personal carriages. Today's outing, however, called for discretion, thus the hired coach.

"Are you sure you want to go through with this?" Ennio asked. "No one's seen us. It's not too late to turn around and go back."

"We can't go back," Trosclair said. "If we are being blackmailed, we've got to face it, not run from it."

"I'm not suggesting we ignore the threat altogether," Ennio said. "But to show up at the time and place designated by the invitation – it's madness. What if we're walking into some sort of trap? They could be planning to hold you for ransom, or worse."

"I don't think whoever's behind this is expecting me to actually show up," Trosclair said. "And besides, my curiosity has been piqued. It won't be satisfied until I see for myself what's waiting at this address."

"We could've at least brought some of the royal guard to back us up."

"Too risky," Trosclair said. "We're conspicuous enough without an army behind us. And anyway, Commandant Burke says you're the best sword he's seen in generations. You have all my faith."

"He said that?" Ennio asked, a smile lifting one side of his mouth.

"His words exactly," Trosclair said. The carriage slowed to a stop, and Ennio peered out of the window.

"This is the address," Ennio said. "It's a house." Trosclair leaned over Ennio to see for himself.

"A nice one," Trosclair said, as he took in the structure. "Look at that yard, and the fountain! Whoever lives here has money to spare."

"So..." Ennio prompted. "We've seen the place. We can easily find out who owns it and have them arrested."

"But what if whoever lives here isn't behind all of this?" Trosclair asked, reaching for the carriage door. "The only way to know for sure is to take their measure ourselves." The prince opened the door and climbed out of the carriage, followed by Ennio. The soldier told the driver to wait at the end of the block and handed the man a gold coin.

Trosclair approached the house and walked up the marble steps to the front door, followed by his bodyguard. The prince struck the knocker three times against the door, and almost immediately, it opened. A butler, a plump little man with a genial expression, held the door wide open and gestured to admit the two young men.

"Welcome," he said, as Trosclair and Ennio entered and removed their hats. As soon as Trosclair's hair came into view, the man's face lit with recognition - and fear.

"Your Grace, I–I–" the man stammered, before giving up on the sentence. "What are you doing here?"

"We were invited," Trosclair said, handing the man the invitation. "Are we not welcome?"

"Oh, no!" the man said, his smile slowly returning. "No, of course not, Your Grace." The man handed both Trosclair and Ennio a black facemask. "The salon has already begun. May I show you to the parlor?"

Trosclair looked to Ennio, who was just as surprised as he was to find out the salon was a real event. "What are these for?" the prince asked, indicating the masks.

"They're provided for privacy," the man said, as he led Trosclair and Ennio down a short hallway. "This is, strictly speaking, an anonymous affair." The young men donned their masks, and the butler swung wide the double doors. Inside the large room, there were perhaps fifty people, all seated and listening to a man at a podium as he lectured. Several guests turned to see who had opened the doors, and as Trosclair and Ennio took seats near the back, the guests started whispering. Trosclair was used to his presence creating a stir; wherever he went, whispers seemed to follow. But today, in front of this faceless crowd, he felt especially exposed.

"—and so they have criminalized our love," the lecturer was saying. "This is nothing new. People often reject what they don't understand. One has only to examine the plight of the elves to witness this firsthand. Gentle and peaceful by nature, the elves were nonetheless excommunicated from our society because we simply refused to understand them." The speaker paused as he looked directly at Trosclair, and a hard swallow was the only sign of his recognition of the prince. "If I might, I'd like to pause here for a quick intermission. We'll resume in five minutes."

Most of the guests stood, taking the opportunity to stretch or make casual conversation. One guest, however, made a beeline toward the prince and his bodyguard.

"What are you doing here?" the guest asked, as he pulled off his mask.

"Frederick?" Trosclair said, as he hugged his friend and cousin. "I could ask you the same question."

"Oh, I—I just thought the topic was interesting," Frederick said, his cheeks reddening.

"It's okay," Trosclair said. "Ennio and I... find it interesting, as well."

Frederick's grin widened. "I knew it!" he said. "Well, I didn't know, know. But I suspected."

"Are you the one who invited us here, then?" Ennio asked.

"Oh, no," Frederick answered. "No. I haven't even told my sister that I'm—you know..."

"Queer?" Ennio whispered, removing his mask, and Frederick nodded.

"So everybody here is... like us?" Trosclair asked.

"Not everybody," Frederick said. "Some folk just come to support our cause, or to commune with like-minded individuals."

"Your cause?" Trosclair asked.

"To have the right to love as we see fit, of course," Frederick said. "And I suppose with the king on our side, that'll soon be a reality."

At the front of the room, a guest shook the hand of the lecturer and removed his mask - and Trosclair was shocked to see it was Milian.

Aleksey, Kaleb and Darra reached the middle of the city,

and the half-elf led them into a small restaurant.

"This is where we're gonna find a healing spell?" Darra asked, as the three sat down at a booth.

"No, this is where we're going to eat a proper breakfast," Aleksey said.

"Dad, we don't have time for—"

"The apothecary shop," Aleksey said, pointing out the window and across the street. "That's where we're headed, and it's not open yet. From here, we'll be able to see the moment the owner arrives. So please, honey, eat something."

"Shouldn't we be saving our money?" Darra said. "To buy the spell?"

"I don't think the seventeen credits I have left to my name is going to go very far, at black market prices," Aleksey said.

"So what, then?" Kaleb asked. "Is this a heist? Because I'm ready to get my hands dirty."

"Calm down, Kay," Aleksey said, as a waitress passed out paper menus. "I know the owner. Or I used to know her, a long time ago. I'm hoping she'll extend me a line of credit."

"How long ago did you know this woman?" Darra asked.

"I haven't seen Marika in, oh, I'd say a good fifteen, twenty years," Aleksey said.

"Dad, that's a lifetime ago!" Darra said. "Will she even remember you?"

"I'm counting on my being unforgettable," Aleksey said. The waitress came back and took their order, then retreated to the kitchen. A few minutes later she returned from the kitchen carrying all three plates at once. They ate slowly, paid the bill, and loitered around out front for another fifteen minutes before they saw a woman unlocking the door to the apothecary shop.

"Finally!" Darra said, and started toward the shop. Aleksey grabbed her hand to stop her.

"Hold on, honey," he said. "If we go rushing over there asking for a healing spell, she'll know we're desperate, and likely raise the price. We'll give it a minute, and then let me do the talking." The teens both nodded their understanding. After another few minutes of waiting, they crossed to the apothecary shop and entered. Kaleb was astonished by the range of the shop's goods, which consisted of everything from medicinal plants and herbs, which lined an entire wall, to scented candles, creams and perfumes, which were on display on a table in the middle of the shop.

The owner, a tall, heavy-set woman with dirty blonde curls framing her round face, came out of a room in the back of the shop. "Good morning!" she greeted the customers cheerfully. "What can I help you with today?"

"Marika?" Aleksey said, holding his hands out wide for a hug that was not forthcoming. He lowered his arms awkwardly as the woman looked him up and down.

"Aleksey?" she finally asked in a thin voice.

"Yep," he said proudly. "It's me!"

Marika promptly slapped the half-elf, who brought up a hand to rest against his cheek.

"I don't think we're getting that line of credit," Darra whispered to Kaleb.

"You're supposed to be dead!" Marika said.

"Well... aren't you happy that I'm not?" Aleksey asked. Marika's jaw jutted out as she shook her head from side to side.

"Unbelievable," she said. "You are utterly unbelievable... Who's this?" she asked, as she peered around Aleksey at Darra and Kaleb.

"This is my daughter, Darra," Aleksey said proudly.

"Very nice to meet you," Darra said, as she stepped forward to shake Marika's hand.

"And you," Marika replied.

"And this is our friend, Kaleb," Aleksey said, pulling the young man forward. "He's a budding mage, and he needs a new spellbook to learn from. I was hoping you were still in the trade."

"Oh, yeah, sure," Marika said, gesturing for them to follow her. She drew the curtain to her back room, a cubby with a small table and chairs in front of a single shelf, covered by a heavy cloth. She pulled the cloth away, revealing a small collection of books and scrolls, as well as an assortment of magical items. "Grimoires are up top," she said. "Help yourself."

Aleksey turned to Kaleb and said, "Have a look through these and see if any will do, while I get reacquainted with Marika." Kaleb crossed to the shelf and picked out the first book.

"They're arranged by price, so if you're on a budget, stick to the front," Marika said.

"About that," Aleksey said. "I don't suppose there's any way you could see to extending me a line of credit?"

Marika blinked exaggeratedly and shook her head. "Same old Leksey," she said, as she snatched the book from Kaleb's hands. "Sorry, but I have bills to pay, like everybody else."

"Come on, Marika, you know I'm good for it," Aleksey pleaded.

"I don't know a thing about you anymore, except that you didn't care to show up and tell me you were alive until you needed something!" Marika said.

"I was busy raising my daughter," Aleksey said. "And I wanted to put my old life behind me. I'm... sorry if I hurt you."

"No, it's fine, it's just - the shop is struggling," Marika said. "I have creditors breathing down my neck. If you have something to trade, I'm willing to barter, but I can't just give away my inventory."

"I'm afraid we don't have anything of value," Aleksey said.

"That may not be true, strictly speaking," Darra said.

"What are you talking about, honey?" Aleksey asked. Darra hesitated, then reached into her pocket and pulled out the gem she'd been hiding for days.

"You trade in magics, right?" Darra asked. "What will you give us for this?"

Marika whistled in appreciation as she examined the gem carefully.

"Is that from the dragon's hoard?" Aleksey asked. Darra nodded guiltily. "That gem could be essential to returning the outworlder to his world. Why would you hide it?"

"I don't know," Darra said, avoiding eye contact with her father. "I guess I just wanted... more time."

"Well, if your intention was to prove you're too immature to date, you've succeeded admirably," Aleksey said, and Darra turned away from the criticism. "You can't force fate, honey. I know you like this boy, but it's just not meant to be."

"I think I've found what I was looking for," Kaleb said, holding out another spellbook.

"This is a mighty pretty looking gem. It positively reeks of power," Marika said, as she handed the bauble back to Darra. "But I can't take it."

"Why not?" Darra asked.

"I don't trade in cursed objects," Marika said. "Well, I do, but only if I've cursed them myself."

Darra looked at the gem and frowned. "Cursed? Are you sure? I mean, it's so... pretty."

"So you're not gonna give us the book?" Kaleb asked.

"I didn't say that. I'll be happy to make the trade for... something else," Marika said, looking to Aleksey.

"Unholy hells," Aleksey said, as he began rolling up a shirt sleeve. "How much?"

"That book is... not cheap," Marika said. "A couple pints will do me."

"Fine," Aleksey said. "Just don't drain me to the point of death, like last time." Marika left the little room.

"What's happening?" Darra asked.

"She wants my blood," Aleksey said.

"Why?"

"A half-elf's blood is thick with magical properties," Kaleb said. "But it's mostly used in dread magic rituals."

"I never said Marika was a saint," Aleksey said, as the woman returned with a jar and a tube attached to a needle.

As the Cursed Knight's mystic poison slowly spread through A.J.'s veins, he dreamed. He was on a battlefield, or at least, he thought he was, from all the bodies scattered around. As he looked closer, however, he saw that each corpse had been laid out with their arms crossed, and each held a single thorny, purple and red flower in their dead hands. A.J. wanted to run, but there was nowhere to go – there weren't even trees to hide behind. He heard the slow clop of a horse's hooves coming to a halt, and he turned to face the rider. The Cursed Knight sat atop his horse and looked down at A.J. with a grim expression. He climbed down from his steed and faced the pilot; although A.J. was over six feet tall, the Cursed Knight towered over him. A.J. backed up a couple of steps.

"You–you're him," A.J. said. "The Cursed Knight." The knight nodded and began to draw his sword. "Wait!" A.J. exclaimed. "You don't have to do this."

The man reached out and placed his gauntleted hand on A.J.'s shoulder. "Unfortunately, child," the knight replied, "This is all I do."

Confident that her charge was in the last stage of the poison, which always induced unconsciousness, Lilith left A.J. alone and stepped into the trees. Tarun took the opportunity to run to A.J.'s side. He knelt in the sand next to his co-pilot and best friend. "I'm sorry," Tarun said, tears welling in his eyes, as he put his hands around A.J.'s throat and squeezed. The pilot's face turned dark red as his circulation was cut off.

The knight began choking A.J. The pilot clawed at the hands that strangled him, but the knight felt nothing through his gloves, and his grip was too strong for A.J. to pull his arms away. The pilot felt blackness on the edges of his perception again, but he somehow knew that if he gave in to it this time, he would not wake up. He struggled to keep his eyes open.

Lilith returned from the woods and saw Tarun choking A.J. "Can't even take a piss," she said under her breath as she raced over to them and pulled Tarun off the pilot, throwing him down into the sand. She drew a scimitar from its sheath at her side. "You're him," she said, as she recognized Tarun from her vision. "You're the one they're looking for." Tarun roared as he threw a handful of sand into Lilith's eyes and grunted as he launched himself at her. They tumbled to the sand together, but Lilith was quick to roll the pilot off of her. As Tarun tried to stand, Lilith swung a leg and brought him back down again. She stood and held her sword inches from Tarun's neck.

"Please," the pilot begged. "Don't kill me!"

The Cursed Knight threw A.J. down and backed up a pace. A.J. took several urgent breaths, and then he asked, "Does this mean you're not going to kill me?"

"It means you have been given more time," the Cursed Knight said. "But it is my curse to kill all who have seen me."

Trosclair's instinct was to hide from Milian, but it was too late; they'd already made eye contact. When the lecture was over, the audience stood, and many people began removing their masks again, including Milian. The Lord Advisor kept Trosclair in his line of sight as he spoke, leading the lecturer toward the prince and his friends. When he reached them, Milian bowed and said, "Your Grace." His mood was as calm as if he had run into Trosclair in the halls of the palace and not at a clandestine meeting. "May I introduce you to today's host, Mr. Justin Martine?"

"Of course," Trosclair said, holding out his hand. The man seemed hesitant at first, but then he shook the prince's hand vigorously.

"Your Grace honors me with your presence," Mr. Martine said.

"Nonsense," Trosclair replied. "It is you who honors us with your hospitality. Do you host events like these on a regular basis?"

"We have an alternating schedule of hosts and topics," Mr. Martine answered. "But we always aim to set an example for social progress."

"Your Grace?" came a familiar voice from behind, and Trosclair turned to find Mrs. Applebaum. The old woman hugged the prince, then stood back. "I see you two got my invitation."

"Your invitation?" Trosclair repeated, dumbstruck.

"I'm sorry if it caused any confusion, but the rules of our little society have us adhering to strict anonymity." Trosclair looked to Ennio and raised his eyebrows slightly.

"We appreciate the gesture," Trosclair said. "And by 'we,' I mean Ennio and me."

"It was nothing," Mrs. Applebaum said, as she took in both Ennio and the prince with her gaze. "I just want to see my boy happy."

Trosclair smiled. "So how long have you been a member of this... society?" he asked.

"We call ourselves the Alliance for Progress," Mr. Martine said.

"Oh, I've been coming to these salons for years," Mrs. Applebaum said. She leaned in conspiratorially and whispered, "My brother was queer. He and his lover introduced me to the Alliance."

"That's amazing," Trosclair said. "I had no idea people actually lived like this."

"How do you mean, Your Grace?" Mr. Martine asked.

"You seem to live your life so... openly," the prince said. "I envy you that freedom."

"It's funny that you should use the word "freedom," Your Grace," Mr. Martine said. "For that is exactly what we queer folk, as individuals and a community, lack. Just the other day, I was accosted as I left a saloon known to welcome queer folk. If my bodyguard had not been present, I might have been killed. What can you promise to do to make such establishments safer to frequent and operate?"

"I—I don't know what to say," Trosclair stammered. "I had no idea such places even existed."

"Now, Justin, you're rushing things," Milian said. "At least let the prince have his coronation before you ask him to solve all the kingdom's ills in one fell swoop."

"Forgive me if I come on a bit strong," Mr. Martine said. "But we've invested all our hopes in your fairness and wisdom, Your Grace. Other rulers have not been as agreeable to us or our cause."

"Well, you can trust that by midsummer, you'll have an ally on the throne," Trosclair said. "Beyond that, I cannot promise much. I can change laws, but changing people's minds is another matter."

"My work brings me into contact with a wide assortment of citizens," Mr. Martine said. "And I say with certainty, Your Grace is beloved by both rich and poor alike. Where you lead, your people will follow."

"Let us hope so," Milian said, as the butler brought around a tray sporting several glasses of sparkling wine. After the drinks were distributed, the Lord Advisor raised his glass. "To tomorrow's gifts," he said, and the reference to his nickname made Trosclair blush.

Aleksey, Darra and Kaleb took a carriage to the city's edge, after the half-elf talked Marika into paying for it - and throwing in the healing spell's required ingredients for free. "My blood is worth it," he'd said, and she'd agreed. During the ride, Aleksey ate two peaches from Darra's bag, but he was still lagging behind when they exited the carriage. They made it halfway across the bridge over the Sylvan before Aleksey's knees buckled and he nearly fell. He steadied himself against the bridge's side rails.

"Go on," he said. "I need to rest, but I'll just be a few minutes behind you."

Darra nodded, and she and Kaleb raced across the bridge

and out of Aleksey's sight. They didn't stop running until they reached their campsite, where Lilith was still standing guard over A.J.

"Is he okay?" Darra asked as she struggled to catch her breath.

"His death is near. I can feel it," Lilith answered.

"How fast can you work this spell, Kay?" Darra asked.

"It's a complicated spell," Kaleb said. "And I'm just a beginner. If I rush it, I could mess it up and put us all in danger."

"I understand," Darra said. "Can I help?"

"Sure," Kaleb said, handing her a jar of sacred sand. "Pour this around his body." Darra took the jar and poured it slowly, walking in a rough oval around the pilot. Kaleb practiced the gestures he would use first, and then he read aloud the words in the old speak that would complete the spell. It was by far the longest casting sequence he had ever attempted, and he struggled to memorize it as quickly as he could.

"Your time has come, child," the Cursed Knight said as he crossed over to A.J. The knight swung a gloved fist at the pilot, who ducked and let the blow swing harmlessly over his head. The knight was impossibly fast even in his heavy armor, and as A.J. tried to back away, the cursed man swung again, this time landing a blow to the young man's stomach. The pilot doubled over in pain. "Fighting back may prolong your life," the knight said. "But it will also increase your agony. Go gently, child; there is no dishonor in it." The knight drew his sword.

Aleksey shuffled over to the campsite, and the first thing he noticed were the boot prints in the sand. Believing them to be A.J.'s, he asked, "He was up and about?" Lilith shook her head in the negative and broke eye contact suspiciously. "There's only one other person with boots like his," Aleksey said. "I know, because I've been tracking him for days. It looks like there was a fight?"

"There was," Lilith said.

"So where is he?" Aleksey asked. "There's no way he defeated you."

"You are correct," Lilith replied. "I let him go."

"You let him–?" Aleksey began, but then he abandoned the

question. "You know what? I'm not even going to act surprised. May I ask why?"

"The search for him will bring danger," Lilith said. "Danger I can save you from, to release me from my debt."

"You vile, self-serving–"

"I serve Rebos, and only Rebos," Lilith cut in. "And without me, this outworlder friend of yours would already be dead. Which reminds me: Do you have my fifty credits for babysitting?"

"You'll get your money," Aleksey said.

"Dad," Darra called, and Aleksey turned to face her. "Kaleb's ready." Aleksey came over to watch as the young mage took a place beside A.J. and put the book down on the sand, facing him. Kaleb gestured slowly and deliberately and pronounced each syllable carefully, so as not to make any mistakes. When he was done, Kaleb's eyes glowed amber; he clasped his hands together, and they also started to glow, as if a bright light were being shone through them. He placed his hands flat on A.J.'s chest, and the glow passed from his hands into the pilot's body. It spread up and down rapidly, covering him from head to toe, and then faded.

"Did – did it work?" Darra asked, after a few moments of silence. She looked to Lilith, who studied A.J. for several seconds.

"It might have worked," Lilith said. "He has a fighting chance now."

The Cursed Knight threw A.J. to the ground and raised his sword above his head, ready to stab it down through A.J.'s chest. Seemingly out of nowhere, a spear materialized in A.J.'s hand. The knight seemed shocked by the aberration and froze mid-strike. A.J. instinctively swung his weapon, aiming for the space between the knight's helmet and chest plate. The spear sliced through the knight's neck, and the giant man fell to his knees.

"I'm sorry," A.J. said, as he got to his feet.

The Cursed Knight grabbed A.J.'s arm, then looked straight into the pilot's eyes and mouthed the words, "Thank you." One by one, the corpses spread out around him began to disappear, and the Cursed Knight himself began to dissipate, until all that was left was A.J. and a field strewn with thorny, purple and red flowers.

A.J. opened his eyes and saw Kaleb, Darra and Aleksey

staring down at him.

"It worked!" Darra squealed, as she hugged Kaleb.

"Welcome back to the land of the living," Aleksey said, holding out his hand. A.J. took it and pulled himself upright.

"You—you did it," A.J. said, looking to Darra. "You cured me."

"Actually, it was all Kaleb," Darra replied, and the young mage blushed. "And Dad."

"I also saved the outworlder's life," Lilith put in.

"What do you want, a cookie?" Aleksey asked.

"Not unless it's a fifty-credit cookie," Lilith mumbled.

"Thank you," A.J. said, as Darra helped him to his feet. "All of you." The pilot hugged Kaleb and then turned to Lilith.

"I don't hug," she said, holding up a hand to ward him off.

"That's okay," he said, as he took her hand and shook it vigorously.

"So you're not feeling any lingering symptoms from the curse?" Darra asked.

"No. No, I feel great," A.J. responded.

"Good," Aleksey said. "Now we can catch up to your friend and, with any luck, send you both on your way home - after I get back our gold, of course."

"Send me home?" A.J. asked, looking from Darra to Aleksey. "Have you figured out a way to do that?" Darra held her breath, afraid of another embarrassing reprimand from her father.

"The gem that opened the first portal. We've... come upon another one," Aleksey said, raising his eyebrows at his daughter. "Go ahead, Darra, show him." Darra reached into her pocket and pulled out the gem for A.J.'s inspection.

"Wow," A.J. said. "How does it work?"

"We're not exactly sure," Aleksey said, as he snatched the gem from Darra and put it in his pocket. "But we should be focusing on finding your friend, since we know he's close," he said, before turning to Lilith. "Can you find him with your longsight?"

"Rebos does not rise for another six hours," Lilith said, looking to the horizon. "Without his light to guide me, the visions will not come. Besides, half-elf, you look like you can hardly stand."

"She's right, Dad," Darra said. "You should take the day to recover." Aleksey considered it for a moment and then nodded.

"I suppose one day's head start won't get him very far," he said. Aleksey spent most of the rest of the day sleeping, although he did wake to eat some of the stew Darra tossed together from the vegetables they'd found the day before. Kaleb spent the afternoon reading from his new spellbook, but when the sun began to set, he joined Darra and A.J. for a walk alongside the Sylvan.

"I'm glad to see your nose out of that book, Kay," Darra said. "I thought we'd lost you to it."

"You just might," he warned. "It's fascinating. The mage who compiled it wrote all kinds of notes in the margins about the origins of each spell and the theories associated with their creation."

"That sounds less than fascinating," Darra said.

"Oh, no, it is!" Kaleb insisted. "That's where real the power of magic lies: in shaping raw mystical energy into spells of your own design. If I can learn to do that, I'm sure I can find a way to send you home."

"That would be amazing," A.J. said.

"How close are you to figuring that out?" Darra asked.

"Ordinarily it takes years, maybe even decades, to build up that kind of skill," Kaleb said, and Darra was silently relieved. "But I'm a real fast learner. There may even be something in my new spellbook that points the way."

"Well, that's good," Darra said, trying to sound enthusiastic. A.J. took Darra's hand and laced his fingers in her own.

"You don't want me to go, do you?" he asked.

"I just met you," Darra said. "Of course I don't want you to go."

"What, uh... What's going on here?" Kaleb asked, a knowing smile on his face as he pointed to their clasped hands. "Are you two together now?"

"Yes?" A.J. replied, looking to Darra for confirmation.

"Yeah, I guess we are," Darra said, smiling, before turning deadly serious. "Don't tell my dad."

"I wouldn't dream of it," Kaleb said. "Ah! I forgot my pipe. I'm just gonna... go get that." Kaleb walked away, still sporting his knowing smile.

"Look," A.J. said. "I may not have very long here." Darra looked to her feet. "Or, I could be stuck here forever."

"Would that be so bad?" Darra asked, meeting his gaze

again.

"I've been here less than a week, and I was almost killed by a flower," he said. "I may not be cut out for this world. But there are definite upsides to being here, too."

"Oh, yeah?" Darra asked.

"Definitely," A.J. said, as the two leaned in to kiss.

Upstream, at the campsite, Aleksey was enjoying another helping of stew when some paternal instinct told him to check in on his daughter. He stood and scanned the banks until he found her - in the arms of the young pilot.

CHAPTER FIVE
"SPELLBOUND"

It was nearing midnight, and Kaleb was reading from his new spellbook by the light of the campfire and the many moons. He'd taken first watch so that he could keep studying after dinner, and although his shift had ended an hour ago, he hadn't yet woken Aleksey to take his place. He'd found a spell toward the back of the book that intrigued him, but the translation of the text was going slower than he'd like. The spell was titled simply "Release," and below that was a strange symbol that the mage couldn't translate; it looked like a circle with serpents coming out of it. Kaleb hoped the spell would be the right one for releasing the mystical energy stored in the gem that might be A.J.'s only chance of getting home. A cloud passed over the Giant's Moon, and Kaleb lost his place as his eyes adjusted to the darker skies. "Verres," he said, which meant 'fire' in the old speak, and he made a single gesture toward the campfire. The flames leapt higher in response, and he resumed reading.

Fire needs fuel, however, and Kaleb failed to notice that the flames had already consumed the wood he'd placed in the pit. The flames flickered and danced hungrily, desperate to obey their magical compulsion to grow, and soon rivulets of fire were snaking their way out of the pit and burning the grass around the center of the campsite. Kaleb kept reading, oblivious, until he noticed that his right leg was significantly warmer than his left. He glanced up and saw the flames had spread, coming close enough to singe his leg hairs. Kaleb dropped his book, jumped up and started stomping out the stray bits of fire before they could reach his sleeping companions' bedrolls.

The commotion Kaleb made containing the fire woke Aleksey, and the half-elf sat up and rubbed the sleep from his eyes. He watched as Kaleb kicked dirt over the last of the runaway flames, and then he stood and stretched his arms high above his head. "I'm up now, Kay," he said. "You better get some sleep."

"I just want to finish this passage," the mage replied.

"Is that the same passage you were translating at dinner?" Aleksey asked, and when Kaleb nodded, he took the book from the young man's hands. "Get some sleep," Aleksey repeated. "You can put fresh eyes to it in the morning." Kaleb nodded again and lay down on his bedroll.

When he awoke the next morning, it was to the sounds of arguing.

"I never said your god was a failure," Aleksey said.

"You questioned the veracity of my visions," Lilith replied. "It's the same thing."

"Look, we've been following your visions for a week now, and still we haven't caught up to the other outworlder," Aleksey said, holding up a hand to stop Lilith's forthcoming rebuttal. "I know, I know – 'It's a process.' But surely you can see how this is frustrating for me?"

"For you?" Lilith asked. "What about for me? I've given up my services to you for free, half-elf, only because, for the moment, it suits my needs."

"And a fat load of good it's done us!"

"Your quarry has kept on the move. It seems he almost never stops to eat or sleep," Lilith said. "That's not my doing."

"Just tell me where he is now," Aleksey said as A.J. and Darra began to stir.

Lilith gritted her teeth at the command, but nonetheless turned her face up to the Reaper's Moon as her pupils dilated. When she'd finished communing with her god, her eyes returned to normal. "He's still headed due west," she said.

"That makes the third day in a row he's followed the road west," Aleksey said, as he began drawing a crude map in the dirt with a stick. A.J. came over to listen. "He'll come upon the Greenbanks by midday," the half-elf said, drawing a curvy line to indicate the river. "If he turns south, he'll hit Roderik Canyon. He'll have to head north eventually, which will put him straight on the path to Morrigen's Plot."

"Is that another city?" A.J. asked.

"It's a settlement," Darra said, joining the group. "It moves along the Greenbanks."

"This time of year, they'd be about here," Aleksey said, as he notched a spot on the line indicating the river and then began drawing a diagonal line through the dirt map. "If we cut through the forest, we can finally get ahead of your friend and block his escape route."

"Sounds like a plan," A.J. said.

"We'll gather a quick breakfast, then, and be on our way," Aleksey said.

"Can I have my book back?" Kaleb asked. "I'd like to get some more studying in before we leave."

"About that," Aleksey began, "I took a look at the book last night. It was clearly compiled by a dread wizard of some power. I'm sorry, Kay, but your grandmother entrusted you to my care, and I can't have you working from a tainted spellbook."

"But not every spell in the book is dread magic," Kaleb protested. "I mean, the healing spell worked, didn't it?"

"It did, by some miracle," Aleksey said, and Kaleb frowned.

"But I'm close to figuring out how to use the gem," Kaleb said.

"Not to downplay your magical prowess, but you're still a beginner," Aleksey said. "And Marika said the gem is cursed. It must be very dangerous if even she's not willing to work with it."

"But–"

"I'm sorry, Kaleb, but my decision is final," Aleksey said, before his attention was stolen by Darra and A.J., who were trying to sneak off into the woods together. "Darra, with me, please," he said, before he headed into the trees himself. Darra mouthed an apology to the pilot and then followed behind her father. As the two scanned the trees, bushes and ground for edibles, Aleksey turned to face his daughter. "I've been meaning to talk to you," he said.

"Uh-oh. That's never good," Darra replied.

"I saw you and our outworlder friend, back on the banks of the Sylvan," Aleksey said, and Darra's face froze up. "Clearly, you've begun a romance with this boy, even though I expressly forbade it."

"So that's why you've been keeping us apart," Darra said. "I thought you were just in an especially bad mood these last few days."

"Well, watching the constant flirtations between you two certainly hasn't helped any," Aleksey said.

"So... am I in trouble?" Darra asked, after a few seconds of awkward silence.

"I'm not going to punish you, if that's what you're asking," Aleksey said. "I still think you're making a mistake. What you're feeling is infatuation, not love. But I suppose you're old enough to face your first heartbreak."

"Really?" Darra asked excitedly.

"But neither will I allow you two to sneak off together," Aleksey said.

"The world's not going to end just because I have a boyfriend, Dad," Darra said. "I see how happy Eliza makes you, and I just want the same thing."

"Actually, Eliza and I decided - mutually - that we should take a break from each other," Aleksey said, turning half-way away.

"Oh... I'm sorry," Darra said, putting a hand on her father's back. They came upon a brushberry patch and started plucking the juicy morsels from the thorny plants.

"Darra, I realize that we've never had 'the talk,'" Aleksey said, and Darra cringed.

"Oh gods," she said. "We're not about to have it now, are we?"

"If you're going to be dating, you need to know how everything works," he replied.

"I know how everything works, Dad," Darra said, rolling her eyes.

"You do?"

"Of course! I do have friends, and they gossip. Especially Ani. But seriously, A.J. and I just met. Nothing's gonna happen between us, if that's what you're worried about."

"That's good to hear you say, sweetie," Aleksey said. "But at your age, feelings can intensify quickly. It can be... overwhelming, and you can't always maintain control of yourself. As your father, it's my job to make sure you don't do anything you'll later regret."

"And here I thought your job was to love and support me, no matter what I choose to do," Darra said.

"That's a given," Aleksey said, pulling his daughter into a hug. "But I'm a talented man. I can do both at the same time."

Trosclair sat at his desk in his study, listening to Mr. Summers, a thick, balding, bespectacled man in his fifties, as he lectured from the front of the room. Alicia, Frederick, Armand, Devon and Serena had filled out the informal class, while Ennio stood watch at the door. Today's topic was the government, both its functions and the theories behind its structure.

"—and so, the Lord Advisor's Council plays an important role in checking the absolute authority of the monarch," Mr. Summers said, glancing up to make sure the prince was still listening. Alicia raised her hand with a question, and Mr. Summers nodded at her.

"But if the king has the favor of the gods, shouldn't his will reign supreme?" she asked.

"Ah! You've brought up an interesting philosophical dilemma," Mr. Summers said. "The great thinker Alfred Dabney would agree with you."

"But wasn't he a noble?" Armand asked, and Mr. Summers nodded again. "His claim to power rests on the authority of the king. By saying 'the king has a divine right to rule,' Dabney's really reinforcing the idea that nobles like himself are also favored by the gods."

"Excellent observation!" Mr. Summers enthused. "And Dabney's self-serving philosophies were later refuted by the Industrialists, who taught that a strong work ethic and meritocracy were the keys to building a sustainable society."

"But meritocracies are problematic in and of themselves," Trosclair said. "Someone decides the worthiness of the individual, whether that be a king or a committee, and so there is always room for bias. Also, the Industrialists were notoriously apathetic to the plight of less-gifted individuals, who they saw as a drag on society."

"True, Your Grace," Mr. Summers said. "But without their push for the promotion of commoners to the Lord Advisor's Council, the kingdom might well have fallen apart under any number of unfit rulers - no disrespect meant to Your Grace's ancestors, of course."

Trosclair waved away the imagined insult, and Mr. Summers resumed his lecture, describing the function of each of the nine Lord Advisors in detail. When he'd finished, he thanked the prince for his attentiveness, gathered up his books, and left the roomful of teenagers to their own amusements.

"Now my brain hurts from big thinking," Alicia said, and Frederick flashed his sister a sarcastically sympathetic smile.

"If your head hurts, it's because you two were up all night drinking," Frederick said, indicating Armand. The banker's son merely shrugged in response.

"You're lucky to have such an engaging tutor," Serena said. "Mine back home could talk a rabid dog to sleep."

"I'm just glad he didn't quiz me like he usually does," Trosclair said. "I hate to get even one question wrong."

"That's your perfectionist nature," Ennio said from across the room.

"I'm not a perfectionist," Trosclair replied. "I don't want to be known as 'The Dunce King,' is all."

"The Dunce King," Devon repeated, pulling out a notepad and writing down the phrase. "You may have just inspired a new comedy, Trosc."

"Oh, great!" Trosclair said. "Just don't model your monarch after me."

"You're not afraid of a little political satire, are you?" Devon asked.

"In your hands, Devon, satire is as deadly as a sword," the prince replied, and the playwright smiled.

The adventurers found Morrigen's Plot just where Aleksey said it would be. The encampment was made up of hundreds of tents spread out in a large field along the east side of the Greenbanks.

"Stay with me," Aleksey said, as they walked into the tents. The villagers here wore clearly homemade clothing underneath thick animal skins. The earthy people all stopped in the middle of their daily routines to stare at the party of strangers as they walked past, headed more or less toward the center of the village. Eventually, a bullish man stepped in front of them to block their path, an ax held casually in front of him.

"Evening," he said. "How can I help you folk?"

"My name is Aleksey Fabian," the half-elf said. "And we're just passing through. I don't suppose Haben's still running things around here?"

"Haben died, three winters past," the man said.

"That's the trouble with getting older," Aleksey mumbled. "Everyone around you starts to die off."

"His daughter's here, though," the man added. "Follow me." Aleksey and the others fell in line behind the man, who led them to a large red tent. "Yuma!" he yelled at the tent, and a few seconds later, the flap parted to reveal a middle-aged woman with long, thick plaits in her black hair.

"What?" she asked the man.

"Visitors," he said, pointing to Aleksey over his shoulder. "Says he knew your pa." Yuma looked Aleksey up and down, then walked forward and held out her hand, which Aleksey shook.

"I'm Yuma."

"Aleksey."

"So you knew my father?"

"He and I were old war buddies."

"You don't look old enough to have fought in the wars," Yuma said, squinting at the half-elf suspiciously.

"Looks aren't everything," Aleksey said, pushing his hair back to reveal the pointed tip of an ear. Yuma's face lit up with recognition.

"Ah!" she said, smiling. "Come in, come in," she urged, waving the group into her tent. When they were inside, she drew the flap down and said, "I've heard many stories about the half-elf who saved my father's life. It's an honor to meet you."

"The pleasure is all mine," Aleksey said.

"So what brings you to Morrigen's Plot?" Yuma asked.

"We're searching for someone," Aleksey said. "My associate and I are headed back out into the forest—"

"So I'm your 'associate,' now?" Lilith asked. "Is that a euphemism?"

Aleksey ignored her and continued, "I was hoping my daughter and her friends could stay here overnight."

"No problem," Yuma said. "We have plenty of food right

now, and we always keep an extra tent or two open for guests. Not that we get too many. Most people don't even know we exist all the way out here."

"I thought that was the idea," Aleksey said. Yuma led the group to another tent and left them to settle in. Darra and A.J. entered first, followed by Lilith, but Aleksey grabbed Kaleb by the arm and held him back.

"I need to ask you for a favor," the half-elf said to the mage.

"Sure," Kaleb said. "What is it?"

"Lilith and I will likely be out late tonight," Aleksey said. "I need you to keep an eye on Darra and the outworlder."

"Oh, I'm not sure I–"

"I'm counting on you, Kaleb, to be my eyes and ears while I'm gone," Aleksey said. "I know you think of Darra like a sister, and she considers you family, too. I'm not asking you to do anything a brother wouldn't do."

"Um... okay, I guess," Kaleb said, and Aleksey slapped him on the back.

"That's my boy," the half-elf said, as he ducked into the tent, followed by the young mage. There was a thick bearskin rug covering most of the ground inside the tent that A.J. stared down at.

"Is this all from just one bear?" he asked, and Darra nodded. "How do you even kill a bear that size?"

"One shot, straight through the eye, into the brain," Lilith answered matter-of-factly, as she and Aleksey stowed their belongings along the far wall of the tent. Aleksey said goodbye to the teenagers, and then set out with the assassin along the Greenbanks, headed south. As soon as her father was out of sight, Darra turned to Kaleb with a wild look in her eyes.

"So how close are to you to figuring out that spell?" she asked.

"I–I think I'm close," Kaleb said. "But your dad told me not to work from that book anymore."

"My dad will come around when he sees what a powerful sorcerer you are," Darra said, as she stooped to rummage through Aleksey's pack. "Ow!" she cried, pulling her hand out of the bag. "Stupid sword!" she said, as she wiped blood from her index finger onto her pants. "I don't know why Dad is still carrying this thing around." She pulled out the largest piece of the DragonSword, which was now just a fragment of blade attached to a hilt, and set it aside. Next she pulled out the grimoire, and after searching the pack's front pockets, she found the gem. She handed the book and the jewel to Kaleb.

"We don't have a lot of time, Kay," she said. "You better get to studying."

"I thought you didn't want me to go," A.J. said. "Now you're pushing for it to happen tonight? What gives?"

"I was just thinking, with my Dad gone, maybe—if we got the portal opened tonight—that maybe I could go with you."

"Really?" A.J. asked, smiling.

"I've always wondered what other worlds were like," Darra said.

"You'd really run away forever?" Kaleb asked.

"Of course not!" Darra said, before turning back to A.J. "But you said your people have machines that fly through the stars to find other worlds, right?"

"Yeah. They're called 'spaceships.'"

"So I could go with you through the portal, and you could bring me back," Darra said, taking A.J.'s hand. "It would be like the ultimate quest."

"It might be more complicated than that," A.J. said. "I don't even know what galaxy we're in."

"What's a galaxy?" Darra asked.

"It's a really big group of stars," A.J. said, waving the topic away. "The point is it could take years to find this planet again, if it's possible at all. I couldn't ask you to leave your whole world behind."

"Oh, my father would find a way to bring me back, count on it. I just... don't want to lose you so soon," Darra said, blushing and looking away. A.J. cupped her chin, turned her face back towards his own and kissed her. Kaleb, squatting on the rug with the book open, ignored them for several seconds and then cleared his throat. The couple broke off their kiss.

"Sorry, Kay," Darra said, wiping her lips. "We'll just go ask Yuma about dinner." Darra led A.J. out of the tent by the hand, and Kaleb resumed his reading.

Kaleb worked furiously for the next three hours to memorize the gestures and syllables he hoped would activate the gem's latent magical properties, stopping only to scarf down the dinner Darra brought him. When he finally decided he was ready, he called Darra and A.J. back into the tent. Kaleb placed the gem on the rug in front of him as he sat cross-legged, his book open at his side. Darra and A.J. took up positions facing him on the other side of the jewel. The mage began his incantation and flashed a series of strange signs with his hands. His eyes began to glow amber. Darra and A.J. held their breath, waiting for the gem to show any sign of magical activity – but Kaleb finished his spell without eliciting so much as a sparkle from the gem. Kaleb's eyes returned to normal; he looked to Darra and the pilot and shrugged.

"Did you do it wrong?" Darra asked, and Kaleb shook his head.

"No way," he said. "I was very careful. I guess I wasn't close to figuring it out after all. Sorry."

"That's okay," Darra said. "Running away was probably a stupid idea, anyway. Especially now that my dad has given me permission to date."

"Are you serious?" A.J. asked. "He actually said that?"

"More or less," Darra answered.

"I guess I'm growing on the guy," A.J. said, smiling.

If Kaleb had glanced down at his book, he would have noticed that the strange symbol he couldn't translate had begun to move, the snakes around the circle writhing and striking at the blank page surrounding it. Instead, he closed the book without another look, and the teenagers began spreading out their bedrolls and preparing for sleep.

Without their belongings and the teenagers to slow them down, Aleksey and Lilith had covered a lot of ground. When they were several miles from Morrigen's Plot, Lilith turned to face the half-elf. "We should stop here," she said.

"Why?" Aleksey asked. "Don't tell me you're tired already."

"My god grants me endurance even you could never match, half-elf," Lilith said.

"Now, see, when you call me that, it hurts my feelings," Aleksey said. "I have a name. How would you like it if I called you 'True Believer' all the time?"

"I am what I am, as are you," Lilith said. "There is no point in hiding our true natures from each other. And I suggested we stop so we could set a trap."

"A trap?"

"Your quarry will come through here eventually," Lilith said. "We should be hidden and ready to pounce when he does."

"I suppose you are the expert on hunting humans," Aleksey replied. "Don't you ever get tired of it?"

"It?"

"All the killing," Aleksey clarified. "You're not exactly personable, but you don't seem like an especially cruel woman, either. And yet you worship death."

"I worship the god of death," Lilith corrected. "Who is also the god of rebirth. With each soul I send him, my own life is renewed."

"How do you mean?"

"How old are you, half-elf?" Lilith asked in reply.

"I'll be seventy-nine by autumn," Aleksey answered.

"And yet, you look barely more than a teenager," Lilith said. "It is the same with me. I was in my thirties when I found my calling. I've dedicated my life to Rebos for over twenty years, and I haven't aged since the day I took my vows."

"You'll live forever, then?" Aleksey asked.

"Everyone dies eventually, half-elf," Lilith said, as she crouched behind a tree.

As Kaleb slept, he dreamt he was sitting in a dimly lit grotto, warm water spilling down from a waterfall like a curtain over the cave's mouth. A human figure approached on the other side of the waterfall, blocking the sunlight, and entered through the cascading water. Kaleb caught his breath as the most beautiful young woman he had ever seen appeared. She had long dark hair and blue eyes that stood out among her otherwise dark features, and she was clad in a thin wrap dress that clung to her wet body obscenely. Kaleb found himself staring at her full breasts as they heaved hypnotically with her breathing.

"Hello, stranger," the young woman said, a finger playing idly at her cleavage as if to keep his attention there.

"Uh... hi," Kaleb managed, meeting her gaze for the first time. He noticed a strange intensity in her eyes. "Do I know you, or...?"

"Not yet," the young woman replied as she waded over to Kaleb. "But I know you. You're the mage who released me." She grabbed her belt and loosened it, then pulled the flaps of the dress apart to reveal her nakedness. Kaleb's eyes went wide as he took in the sight of the woman's body. "I was hoping I could do the same for you."

"Uh, I–I... yeah," Kaleb stammered. "Release is... good." The woman grabbed Kaleb's hand and drew it to her breast, which filled his cupped hand. Her body was hot to the touch, and Kaleb felt a familiar stirring in his groin as he gently massaged her. She tossed her head back and shrugged off her dress, and only then did Kaleb realize that, beneath the water, he was naked and exposed as well. "I–I've never–" he began, but the woman leaned down and silenced him with a kiss.

"I know," she said. "That's okay. I'll take over from here." She placed her hands on the young man's shoulders and lowered herself down onto his lap, wrapping her legs behind his back. She reached beneath the water and took him in her hand before sliding forward, and Kaleb gasped at the ecstatic sensations of entry. She waited a few seconds for the young man to adjust to this new pleasure and then began writhing her hips. The added friction was too much for Kaleb, and he knew he was nearing an embarrassingly early climax. Suddenly, the sun grew brighter outside the cave, until the entire grotto was bathed in light.

Kaleb opened his eyes and saw a female figure standing just outside the tent, holding the flap open to the early morning sunlight. He thought the woman he'd dreamed was really there, and he froze. As the figure came into the tent, his vision cleared, and he saw that it was actually Yuma, delivering breakfast.

She looked down at Kaleb and smiled wickedly. "Sweet dreams?" she asked, as she placed the platter she was carrying on the rug. He didn't know what she meant until he noticed the tent in his bedroll just below his stomach. He rolled onto his side as fast as he could, but it spared him no humiliation, and his complexion darkened as the blood rushed to his face. Yuma slipped out as quickly as she'd come in. Kaleb looked over at Darra and A.J., but both were still asleep. He took the opportunity to check his undershorts and was grateful there was no mess to clean up. After his lingering physical excitement subsided, he pulled his bedroll down and sat up to eat breakfast.

Frederick knocked on Trosclair's study door around noon, and Ennio smiled broadly when he opened the door and admitted the young man inside. Frederick carried with him a thick book, clutching it to his chest as if it were precious.

"I thought you might be interested in this," he said, as he held the book out to the prince. Trosclair glanced at the cover and read the title: *A Thousand Pardons.*

"I've already read it. It's up there somewhere," Trosclair said, pointing to the bookshelves all around the room.

"Just open it," Frederick said, and Trosclair took the book and obeyed. He found the pages had been hollowed out, and inside was another, smaller book. Its cover showed a photograph of a nude, muscular man with an erection, and Trosclair's jaw dropped.

"What is this?" he asked, as he withdrew the book and began thumbing through its pages. Ennio came over to get his own look, and an equally shocked expression covered his face.

"Erotic poetry," Frederick answered.

"The Warrior and the Farmer's Son," Trosclair read aloud. "The warrior fierce was known as savage/The farmer's son he soon would ravage/No tender kiss did twixt them pass/As warrior plundered tight young– I can't finish this," Trosclair said, shaking his head as he broke off his reading and looked back to Frederick. He set the book down on his desk, and Ennio quickly scooped it up.

"Well, it has my interest piqued," the soldier said as he started reading silently.

"Where did you find such a thing?" Trosclair asked his distant cousin.

"I happen to know of a bookshop in town with a healthy subversive section," Frederick said. "If it interests you, you can borrow it."

"Oh, I can't - I have the Poet's Curse," Trosclair said.

"What's the Poet's Curse?" Frederick asked.

"You've heard of the poet Claudette Beckett?" the prince asked, and Frederick nodded.

"Wasn't she one of the Romanticists?" he asked.

"One of the best," Trosclair said. "But what many people don't know is that she had a love affair with my great-great-grandfather, Kind Aldric. Family legend has it that when he broke it off with her, she sought out a sorceress and had him cursed. They say that's what drove him mad in his final years. And the curse passed down the family, so now I have it. I can't read more than a few lines of poetry without becoming consumed with it. It preoccupies my mind for days afterwards."

"That doesn't sound like much of a curse," Frederick said. "That just sounds like you really like poetry."

"No, it's a real affliction," Trosclair said. "Sometimes I even start to accidentally rhyme – in iambic pentameter."

"And that just sounds like you want to be a poet," Frederick said.

"Maybe I'm explaining it wrong," Trosclair said. "Ennio, tell him how sensitive I am to verse."

"Hm?" Ennio mumbled, as he looked up from the book to the prince. "What?" Trosclair shot him a grumpy look. "Sorry, I got caught up. I just want to make sure I'm doing everything right."

"I've got no complaints so far," Trosclair said. Ennio smiled and leaned in to peck him quickly on the cheek.

"Aw," Frederick mewed appreciatively. "I wish I could find somebody like you two have."

"Is there no one you've got your eye on?" Trosclair asked.

"Well... there is someone I fancy, but he's never even noticed me," Frederick said. "I don't even know if he's queer."

"Who is it?" Trosclair asked. Frederick hesitated. "Come on, Freddie," Trosclair urged. "You can trust us."

"It's not that, it's just—I'm embarrassed," Frederick said. "He's older than us."

"In that case, you've got to tell me!" Trosclair demanded.

"Okay, fine," Frederick capitulated. "It's Lord Advisor Milian." Trosclair tried to hide his surprise. He'd never thought of the slight, nerdy Advisor in sexual terms – not even when he'd seen him at the secret meeting of the Alliance for Progress.

"Well, that's great," Trosclair said.

"I know he's not the most handsome man, but there's something about him that drives me wild," Frederick said. "Which, knowing my luck, probably means he's not queer at all."

"You never know," Ennio said. "At the very least, he's open-minded."

"I thought the same thing," Frederick said. "But then I worried I was just deluding myself. You know, setting myself up for heartbreak."

"I've never seen him with a woman," Trosclair said. "Not romantically, anyway. And men his age are usually married or at least dating. You might have a real shot."

"You think?" Frederick asked hopefully, and both Trosclair and Ennio nodded.

Aleksey and Lilith had waited the night away behind the tree. They took turns sleeping only a few hours at a time, as they were both eager to establish which of them had the greater stamina. When morning also came and went without any sign of Tarun, Aleksey grew frustrated.

"Damn it!" he said, seemingly out of nowhere. "He should've come through here hours ago. He must've changed course. We're wasting our time."

"I could consult with my god again," Lilith offered.

"Good idea," Aleksey said. "Let's keep depending on the nonexistent deity who's consistently led us to nothing for the past week."

"Do you really believe, after all you've seen me do, that Rebos and the other old gods do not exist? Surely even you are not that foolish."

"Magic comes in many forms," Aleksey said. "Your god is not made any more real to me just because you say his name in your spells."

"They're prayers, not spells," Lilith said. "And for a man who's lived so long, you are shockingly ignorant of the world around you. Can you truly look on the Artist's Moon, with its vast swirls of purple and pink, and not see Kesari's talented hands at work? Don't you taste the love of Arol in every plant whose fruit you eat, or feel the strength of the Undying Mother in the very ground beneath your feet?"

"I don't know what love tastes like," Aleksey said. "Strawberries, maybe? Or cherries in chocolate."

"You mock me," Lilith said. "But deep inside, you know the

gods are real. You fear it, because their existence makes you feel small and insignificant."

"Hey, I'm large and very significant, lady!" Aleksey said. "And say it's true: there are divine beings up in the heavens looking down on us, controlling our fates. Should I thank them for killing my father in the Elven Wars, before I ever really knew him? Or capsizing the boat my mother was on when I was just a boy? Do I owe your god for those debts, or another?"

"You fought in the wars alongside your father, correct?" Lilith asked, and Aleksey nodded. "You must have still been young, the equivalent of a human adolescent. I'd say you owe Fela, goddess of luck and fortune, that you were not killed in battle with him, and that you did not accompany your mother on her fateful voyage."

"You think I'm lucky?" Aleksey asked.

"As a half-elf, you've a natural strength greater than most other mortal beings," Lilith said. "Even your birth defied the odds, as most hybrid children die within the womb."

"My elven family looks at me like I'm a freak of nature, and if human society found out about my dual heritage, I'd be killed on the spot," Aleksey said. "But please, continue to educate me on how fortunate I am."

"Now you're just sulking," Lilith said, turning away. "You're worse than a teenager."

"I do not sulk!" Aleksey said. "And I won't kowtow to the big sky bullies, either."

"You have more bluster in you than bite," Lilith said. "Are you always in such a bad mood, or did you wake up angry because of Eliza?"

"What do you know about Eliza?"

"Only that you said her name twice in your sleep," Lilith said. "What should I know about her?"

"Not a damn thing," Aleksey answered. "I keep my personal business personal, thank you very much."

"Fine, half-elf," Lilith said. "I was only making conversation. There's no need to get defensive."

"Let's just head back to the village," Aleksey said, as he turned and strode away.

A.J. had woken not long after Kaleb, and the pilot was quick to try to shake Darra awake, but the young woman had resisted. "Mmm," she'd grunted angrily with her eyes still closed.

"Darra," the pilot had whispered into the young woman's ear. "It's time to wake up, babe." She'd smiled and squinted her eyes open to look up at him.

"Babe?" she'd repeated.

"Just something I'm trying out," he'd said. "If you don't like it, I could call you something else. Cutie-patootie. Hottie with a body. I've got options." A.J. had leaned down to kiss her, and thus had begun an epic three hour make-out session that Kaleb was forced to bear witness to, lest it should become something more. The couple had stopped only to eat breakfast and occasionally exchange a few whispered sentiments. Kaleb chalked it all up to teenage lust until he stepped outside of the tent to get some fresh air around mid-day.

Everywhere he looked, villagers had coupled up, and they all wore the lovesick expressions he'd seen on Darra and A.J.'s faces. Some were merely holding hands, while others pawed at each other lustily, mouths locked together and eyes shut tight. A few had even laid themselves out in the grass to make love in broad daylight. A group of teenagers giggled as they gawked at one such couple from around the corner of a tent.

"Release," Kaleb said under his breath, a suspicion dawning on him. "Oh, crap," he said, as he raced back inside the tent. He opened up the grimoire and hurriedly found the page with the spell he'd tried on the gem. The strange serpentine symbol was still writhing and striking on the page, and Kaleb realized that the spell had been successful - it had released something into the world. He wasn't sure what that something was, but he could tell from the symbol that it was not a benevolent entity.

"What're you up to, Kay?" Darra asked, breaking away from A.J. momentarily.

"I, uh—I think I did... something bad," the mage said, as he sat down. "But I'm gonna handle it." He began translating the footnotes and the handwritten scribbles around the edges of the page, hoping there was some clue to reversing the spell in the bits he hadn't had time to study before. "Does that say 'reversal'?" he asked himself hopefully. Out of the corner of his eye, he saw A.J.'s hand move from the middle of Darra's back to her buttocks. Kaleb stood up and said, "Whoa, A.J.! Getting a little hands-y there, don't you think? Can I just have you two scoot apart for like, ten minutes?"

"Are we grossing you out?" Darra asked.

"More like stressing," Kaleb said. "But it's not your fault. I think you're under some sort of spell."

"A spell?" A.J. asked. "I don't feel like I'm under a spell. Unless it's yours." He put his forehead against Darra's own and stared into her eyes. "Are you a witch?"

"More like an enchantress," Darra said, before kissing the pilot again.

"See, that's what I'm talking about," Kaleb said. "You two can't go three seconds without locking lips. It's like you're under some sort of love spell."

"You don't think our love is real?" Darra asked, the hurt evident in her voice.

"I—I didn't say that—"

"You're just like my dad!" Darra said, as she stood and pulled A.J. up with her. "Come on, A.J." She stormed out of the tent, leading the pilot by the hand.

"I really don't understand women," Kaleb muttered, as he resumed reading.

"Well, that much was obvious from my first glimpse of you," came a familiar female voice from behind Kaleb, startling him. He turned to see the woman from his dream, standing there in her wrap dress, her head tilted and an inviting smile on her lips. "But you don't need to understand a woman to please her."

"You!" Kaleb practically screamed, as he stood up. "Are you really here? Did I fall asleep?"

"You're not dreaming, loverboy," the woman said. "And I'm sort of here and not here at the same time."

"What do you mean?" Kaleb asked.

"I used to exist only in dreams," she said. "But your spell changed that. I'm in the hearts and minds of this whole village now, and with every passing moment, my power grows. By nightfall, I'll have driven this whole kingdom mad from love or lust. When it's done, I'll be worshipped as a goddess. And you can rule at my side. There's just one more thing I need from you first."

"What?"

"It's a simple gift, really," she said. "You almost gave it to me last night. You see, I can appear before you because you summoned me." She lifted her hand to stroke Kaleb's cheek, but her hand had no mass to it, as if she were composed entirely out of light. "But I can't take full physical form yet. Not until I've brought you release, as your spell commands."

"—and it's not that she didn't love me, I could say that with some certainty," Aleksey said. "Eliza never hid her affections or her wrath from me. If she felt a rage, she wouldn't deny it. But she could also be—"

"Long-winded and lovelorn?" Lilith interrupted, hoping to get a rise out of the half-elf, but Aleksey just shook his head.

"No, I was going to say, 'compulsively driven.' There was very little she cared for in this world more than her music and her businesses," Aleksey continued. "Not that she was greedy. Her main concern was providing a comfortable living for her employees. An admirable ambition, to be sure, but it did distract somewhat from—"

"Half-elf, are you feeling okay?" Lilith asked. "You seem... not yourself."

"Honestly? I just really miss Eliza."

"So you've said... a lot," Lilith observed. "You must be the type of man who loses himself in love."

"And I suppose you're the type of woman who scorns romance?" he asked.

"There's nothing wrong with having a good tussle in the sheets," Lilith said. "I just don't lose my head for the sake of my loins."

"I ought to have known you'd equate sex with violence," Aleksey said.

"I'm sexually liberated, that's all," Lilith said. "You're so old-fashioned, it borders on repression, and that's no reflection on me."

"Oh, spare me your condescension!" Aleksey said. "I've had my fair share of dalliances. I just grew out of that phase."

"Are you calling me immature?" Lilith asked. "Because there's nothing so immature as a lovesick pup like yourself."

"Lovesick?" Aleksey repeated. "Are you kidding me? I've moved on."

"Yeah, right!" Lilith replied. "Dreaming of her—"

"One can't help what one dreams."

"—and pining over her virtues. You may as well be writing poetry for her."

"Are you jealous?" Aleksey asked. Lilith slapped him in response. The half-elf composed himself and then said, "Yep. You're jealous." Lilith's jaw jutted out and she gave a frustrated grunt before she sped up and put Aleksey behind her.

Kaleb squirmed under the young woman's intense scrutiny. "I—I don't think I'm supposed to, you know... release with you," he said, backing away a step. His fear competed with his lust for control of his actions. "I mean, how would that even work, if you can't take physical form?"

"I can always put on a show for you," she said, as she drew her dress open and let it fall to the floor. "I'm even strong enough now to lend you a hand." With that, she put her hand down the front of his pants and began stroking him.

"No," he said, but his breathy voice lacked conviction. "We should stop."

"Is this form not pleasing to you?" she asked. "Because I can always take another." The young woman shimmered like a heat vision, and Kaleb watched as her body changed from the soft curves of the young woman into the taut, lean muscles of a handsome young man. The man continued the work the woman had begun in Kaleb's pants, but with a firmer grip, and the mage swooned in spite of himself.

"Okay," Kaleb mumbled. "This just got a whole lot more confusing."

Trosclair decided he'd take a walk in the gardens at sunset, and as always, Ennio was at his side. They made their way down the palace steps and walked in a half-circle around the large fountain before ducking into the hedge maze. They hurried to the center of the maze, which sported a gazebo, but they were disappointed to find another couple had already claimed it. Though the man and woman were still fully clothed, the man lay on top of the woman, her legs spread open to him, as they kissed with their eyes closed. Trosclair signaled to Ennio, and the teens moved back into the maze.

"I guess we'll just have to do this standing up," Trosclair

said, as he threw his arms around the young soldier's shoulders.

"Is that even possible?" Ennio asked.

"I don't know," Trosclair answered honestly, a stumped expression on his face. "Anyway, I thought you were the expert now, after reading all those poems."

"I wouldn't say I'm an expert," Ennio said. "Although I do have a few new things I wanna try out."

"Like what?" Trosclair asked.

"Have you ever heard of a Sailor's Delight?"

"I can't say I have."

"It's when two men—" Ennio began, but he stopped mid-sentence as a flash of motion behind the prince caught his attention. The soldier gently nudged Trosclair aside and drew his sword.

"What is it?" Trosclair asked.

"Someone was watching us," Ennio said. "Follow me." With that, the soldier sprinted away in the same direction as the figure. Trosclair ran as fast as he could, but he soon lost sight of Ennio as the soldier rounded a corner. The prince kept moving along the familiar path back to the fountain, and before long, he heard the sound of metal scraping on metal that could only come from a sword fight. Trosclair rounded a few more corners, and the scuffle came into view. Ennio was locked in a duel with another uniformed soldier, a middle-aged man with a short white beard and a terrified look on his face. He caught sight of the prince, and the momentary distraction was all Ennio needed to knock the sword from the man's hand. The man held up his hands in surrender and lowered himself to his knees in front of the bodyguard. Ennio pointed the tip of his blade at the man's throat.

"Who are you?" the young soldier demanded.

"M—my name is Flavius, milord," the man said.

"I'm no Lord. Why were you spying on us, Flavius?" Ennio asked. "Was this another assassination attempt?"

"Assassination? No! No, of course not," Flavius said. "I was just on my way to my Lady's house - it saves me time if I cut through the gardens - and I happened upon you two by accident. I swear it."

"But you were watching us?" Trosclair asked, as he stepped forward.

"Y—your Grace," Flavius said, bending at the waist to bow as best he could. "I– I meant no harm."

"Then why did you fight me?" Ennio asked.

"Your pardon, young master," Flavius said. "But you drew on me first. I was defending myself the only way I knew how. There's no harm done, now, is there?"

"Unfortunately, we can't agree with you," Trosclair said, using the formal plural. "Irreparable harm has been done to our privacy. The question now becomes, what shall we do with you to make sure no further breach of our trust occurs?" Flavius swallowed hard as the prince's question hung in the air.

The young man got down on his knees and looked up at Kaleb seductively. "Let me show you what else this body's good for," the man said, as he lowered his face toward Kaleb's midsection.

"No," Kaleb said, firmer this time. "This doesn't feel right." The mage removed the man's hand from his pants, and the man's image shimmered and shifted until the young woman was again looking up at Kaleb.

"So you do like girls, then?" she asked.

"Of course I like girls," Kaleb said. "But that's not what I meant. And you're not really a girl, are you? You're not even human."

"Oh, so now that you've summoned me, you've decided I'm not good enough for you because I'm not human, is that it?"

"No! No, I–"

"All I've ever tried to do was please you - and take over the world by enslaving humanity - and now you're dumping me? Well, if you think I'm going quietly, you summoned the wrong succubus," the woman said. "You like to play with magics, don't you, loverboy? Wanna see what real power looks like, when love breeds hate?" The woman snapped her fingers and disappeared.

"Uh-oh," Kaleb said under his breath.

Aleksey and Lilith reached the village just after dark. The assassin was still ahead of the half-elf, so she was the first to notice the omnipresent couplings taking place in the village. A group of children raced by in front of her, laughing and screaming, as they played without adult supervision. Lilith rounded a tent and stopped in her tracks, her mouth dropping open as the burly man who'd led them to Yuma the day before appeared before her, his axe in one hand and his stiff member in the other.

"Fancy a go?" he asked, his voice breathy with lust. Lilith consciously closed her mouth, her jaw set sternly, and then kicked the man between his legs. The man yelped in pain, dropping his ax and doubling over, and Lilith grabbed him by the shoulders and slammed him facedown at the same time she brought her knee up. The blow to the head laid the man out on his stomach, and Lilith drew her scimitar. She raised it back, but a hand grabbed her wrist from behind before she could swing it down to deliver the killing blow.

"Don't," was all Aleksey said.

"He accosted me - sexually," Lilith replied. "That kind of abuse deserves punishment."

"I don't think it's his fault," Aleksey said. "Look around you. Everyone here is consumed with lust."

"I had noticed that, thank you," Lilith said. "It's as if Veleska herself has come to this village."

"Somehow I don't feel this is the work of the goddess of love," Aleksey said, before he spotted a familiar blonde head lying in the grass - cuddled up close to and kissing A.J., who had his arms around her. "Darra!" he yelled as he crossed over to her, and the young woman broke off her kiss and turned to him in fear.

"Dad!" she said. "Did you, um - did you find Tarun?"

"Get up this instant, young lady!" he commanded, ignoring her attempt at deflection, and Darra obeyed. A.J. stood up awkwardly behind her, wishing he could disappear. "I leave you alone for one day, and this is how you repay that trust?"

"Can't you see we're in love?" Darra cried.

"And you!" Aleksey said, spearing A.J. with an ice-cold gaze. "I hope you've come to like this world. Because as of this moment, we are done helping you, protecting you, feeding you—" Aleksey stopped in the middle of his threat as a half-naked man ran into view.

"Help!" the man cried, as an angry-looking woman ran up behind him. She threw a cooking pot at the man, but it sailed harmlessly past him. "You're crazy!" the man yelled before resuming his flight, and the woman chased after him.

"You can't make me abandon him, Dad," Darra said defiantly.

"I can, and I most certainly will!" Aleksey replied.

"Then I'll run away!" Darra said. These words came almost like a physical blow to Aleksey, instantly extinguishing the fire in his eyes.

"Darra, you—you can't be serious," he said.

"I am," she said, taking pleasure in the pain she was causing her father. "I almost ran away last night, but Kaleb's stupid spell didn't work."

"Spell?" Aleksey repeated. "What spell?"

Kaleb had translated all the text, and he thought he'd found what he'd hoped to find - a passage on the reversal of the summoning spell. It called for the same hand gestures as the first spell, delivered in reverse order, with an entirely new incantation. He quickly practiced both the motions and the words, committing them to memory. The flap to the tent flew open, and Aleksey stormed inside, followed by Lilith, Darra and A.J.

"Alright, Kaleb, what did you do?" Aleksey asked.

"I, uh—I accidentally summoned a succubus," the mage said, standing.

"Of course," Lilith said, looking to Aleksey. "It all makes sense now. Your lovesickness and the amorousness in the air - a succubus fans the flames of those feelings, to feed on the chaos it creates."

"Why didn't you succumb to it, then?" Aleksey asked. "Wait, let me guess - you don't have a heart to manipulate?"

"How droll," Lilith said dryly. "But you're not far off. My heart, mind and soul belong to Rebos, and no other entity may lay claim to them, not even a succubus."

"So you've fought one of these things before?" Aleksey asked.

"Technically, it was an incubus," Lilith said. "But they're essentially the same creature. And I didn't fight him so much as date him."

"You dated a demon?" Aleksey asked. "Why am I not surprised?"

"It was just the one date," Lilith said. "And I didn't know he was a demon until I saw his true form."

"So how do we kill it?" Aleksey asked.

"I'm not sure," Lilith admitted. "But I'd assume it's like most other demons, vulnerable to fire, or beheading, maybe a sacred object."

"You won't have to kill her - I mean, it," Kaleb said. "There's a reversal spell." They heard a scream from outside the tent, and Aleksey turned back to the mage.

"I don't know, Kaleb," Aleksey said. "Your magic is... unpredictable, at best. And we don't have a lot of time."

"Well, I have to try, don't I?" the tribal lad asked. Aleksey considered it for a moment and then nodded. Kaleb began the series of hand gestures, but before he could start the incantation, the succubus shimmered into existence, causing everyone inside the tent to start.

"Trying another spell, are we?" the succubus asked. "Are you sure that's the wisest move, loverboy?"

"Just ignore it, Kaleb," Aleksey said.

"You can see her?" Kaleb asked.

"Everyone can see me now, in all my glory," the succubus said, as she casually crossed over to Aleksey and looked him up and down. "My, my - I've never smelled a man with blood like yours before. Maybe when I'm done with the mage, I'll add you to my stable."

"Kaleb, the spell," Aleksey instructed, not taking his eyes off the demon. Kaleb began his spell again, gesturing slowly and deliberately, as the intonations of his incantation rose to a crescendo. The mage's eyes glowed a bright amber color as the mystical energies passed through him.

"Oh, fine," the creature said. "We'll do this the old-fashioned way." She shimmered and disappeared, leaving the room in empty silence.

"Did - did it work?" Kaleb asked, before his attention was stolen by the book he was holding. The strange serpentine symbol began to glow and lifted off the page, floating into the air. The glow intensified as the symbol grew in size, until the entire apparition shimmered and shifted. Where the symbol had been, there was now a roughly spherical mass of loose-hanging, quivering flesh floating in the air, with dozens of snakes writhing and striking out in all directions.

"Unholy hells," Aleksey said, drawing his sword. "I don't think it worked, Kay." The succubus floated toward the half-elf, who hacked at the striking snakeheads. He chopped off several with one blow, but almost immediately, the snakes grew new heads, and Aleksey had to duck and weave to keep from being bitten.

"Allow me," Lilith said, as she gathered her longbow and arrows from her belongings. She nocked, took aim at the creature, and let the arrow fly. It thudded deep into the monster's sagging flesh, but the creature merely wrapped one of its snakes around it like a tentacle and broke the wooden shaft in two. The creature suddenly swooped toward A.J., but Darra tackled the pilot, pushing him out of harm's way. Her heroism was rewarded with a strike on the shoulder from one of the creature's serpents, and she screamed in pain.

"Verres!" Kaleb yelled, gesturing, and flames enveloped the creature. The succubus squealed in pain, and Kaleb had time to wonder where its voice came from, since it had no discernable mouth. The creature veered away from Darra and slammed into the side of the tent. It flopped and twisted against the material until the flames were smothered. Its singed snake-appendages all recoiled, drawing tightly back against the ball of flesh, as the creature floated menacingly toward the mage.

Crouched down beside Darra, Aleksey saw the hilt of the DragonSword sticking out of his pack and was struck with inspiration. "Sacred object," he said, as he grabbed the broken weapon. The succubus had Kaleb cornered. Aleksey hurled the half-sword at the creature, and the fragmented blade sliced it wide open. The succubus squealed again, and instead of healing like it had before, it began to disintegrate; within a few seconds, there was nothing left of it.

"—four hundred, four hundred and fifty, five hundred," Milian counted out in credits, which he then scooted with his arm all the way across Trosclair's desk toward Flavius. A religious man, the soldier was silently thanking Fela for this fortunate turn of events. "I assume that's enough to keep you from mentioning this night to anyone?" the Lord Advisor asked, and Flavius nodded enthusiastically as he scooped up the coins and filled his pockets with them.

"I'll just show our new friend out," Ennio said, and Flavius jumped up, bowed, and fell in line behind the young soldier.

"One more thing," Milian said, and Flavius turned back around to face him. "I don't think I have to say what might happen if anyone else finds out about this. But let's just say it wouldn't be a good day for you."

"You don't have to worry about that, milord," Flavius said. "I know which side of the mountain the giant sleeps on, as the saying goes."

"That's good," Milian said, and Flavius bowed again and departed.

"Was it really necessary to threaten the man, after we'd just paid him off?" Trosclair asked.

"I find the best sportsmen are the ones who play both offense and defense, Your Grace," Milian said.

"Ugh, sports metaphors are utterly lost on me. But thank you, Milian, for doing this for me," Trosclair said to the Lord Advisor, as Ennio moved back to his side.

"For us," the young soldier corrected, taking Trosclair's hand.

"I'm just glad you came to me with this," Milian said. "But whatever possessed you to display your affections in public?"

"I–I'm not sure," Trosclair said. "It was like something just came over me. An intensity I can't quite put into words, now that it's passed."

"It was the same for me," Ennio said.

"Hmm," Milian said, frowning a little as he considered. "Well, please do try to see that it doesn't happen again, alright?"

"That's all you're going to say?" Trosclair asked. "You're not going to lecture me?"

"I've come to know you quite well, Your Grace, and you are anything but stupid," Milian said. "You know what such displays could do to set the palace, the city - even the whole kingdom -- aflame with rumor and innuendo. But I must admit I felt the same strange... compulsions you spoke of tonight; had I still been a youth myself, I might have given in to them as well. You'll find no judgment in me for Your Grace acting upon natural urges."

"That's kind of you to say," Trosclair said.

"Now, if you'll excuse me, I was just about to take my dinner," the Lord Advisor said. He bowed and headed toward the door.

"Oh, Milian?" Trosclair said, working up his nerve.

"Yes?"

"I've been meaning to ask you, ever since I saw you at the Alliance for Progress," Trosclair began. "That is to say, if it's not too personal a topic– Are you... you know..."

"Ah," Milian said, recognition in his voice. "It's a fair question, Your Grace. And I did attend an all-boys secondary school, if you catch my meaning. But no, I do not consider myself queer. I merely support the advancement of the rights of queer people."

"That's truly honorable of you, Milian," Trosclair said.

"Thank you, Your Grace," Milian said. The Lord Advisor smiled that unreadable smile of his, bowed again and left the room. Ennio turned to Trosclair and brought the prince's hand up to his lips for a quick kiss.

"That was close," the soldier said.

"Too close, Ennio," Trosclair replied. "We could have lost everything tonight."

"Not everything," Ennio said. "The world might crumble around us, but we'd still have each other." The prince kissed the soldier, who responded by picking him up and carrying him into the bedroom. He dumped the young man onto the bed playfully and said, "Now let's make some poetry!"

Aleksey dabbed blood from Darra's wounded shoulder and examined the skin around the snakebite, but he could discern no discoloration.

"Does it hurt?" he asked, as he pressed the skin around the wound.

"Not really," Darra said.

"That's good. It means the bite probably wasn't venomous," Aleksey said. He wrapped a strip of cloth around her shoulder so that if fell over the wound and tied it off tightly. "We'll keep an eye on it tonight." The half-elf turned to Kaleb. "What were you thinking, Kay? I specifically forbade you from working from that book just so something like this wouldn't occur."

"I–I don't know," Kaleb said, looking at his feet. "I just thought, since the healing spell worked, that I was ready. I'm really sorry."

"And what am I supposed to do with you now?" Aleksey asked. "How would your grandmother punish you?"

"Punish?" Darra asked. "No, Dad, you've got it all wrong. Kaleb didn't even want to do the spell."

"Then why–"

"I made him do it," Darra confessed. "If anyone should be punished, it's me." Aleksey looked from the mage to his daughter, considering his options.

"Fine," the half-elf said. "You're both grounded."

"Okay," Darra said, a confused look on her face. "But we're travelling adventurers. How exactly are you going to ground us?"

"Easy. Kaleb, please hand over your spellbook. I don't want you doing any magic for the next two weeks," Aleksey said, and the young mage moved to comply. "And Darra, I suggest you say 'goodbye' to the outworlder. You won't be getting any time alone with him again."

"You're grounding me from my boyfriend? But that's not fair!" Darra protested. "You just said I was old enough to start dating."

"And I was proven wrong," Aleksey said.

"Lilith, tell him he's being unreasonable," Darra said, looking to the woman for aid.

"I'm sorry, little one," the assassin replied. "Although I do agree with you that your father's worldview is... outmoded, he is still your father. It's not my place to question his judgment."

"Thank you, Lilith," Aleksey said. "That may be the first time you've said something I agree with wholeheartedly."

"Okay, fine," Darra said, grabbing A.J. by the hand. "We'll just be outside, saying our goodbyes." She led the pilot out of the tent and far enough away so that even her father's hearing would not detect them, then turned to the pilot with that wild look in her eyes again. "We'll go," she said. "Tonight. Just the two of us."

"You mean, run away?" A.J. asked, and Darra nodded. "I–I don't think that's a good idea."

"Why not?" Darra asked.

"Well, for one, your dad would just come after us," he

answered. "And I don't really want the man with the sword on my bad side, you know?"

"You don't have to be afraid of him," Darra said. "He'd never hurt someone I cared about."

"It's not just that."

"Then what?"

"I just think... maybe he's right," A.J. said, and Darra drew away slightly.

"Right about what?" she asked.

"About us," A.J. said. "Maybe we are rushing things. I mean, we just met, and now we're talking about running away together? That's a huge decision. It'd mean giving up on Tarun, and I'd be stuck on this planet, maybe forever."

"But you'd be stuck with me," Darra said. "Doesn't that make it any better?"

"Of course it does," A.J. said. "But that's a problem, too."

"What do you mean?" Darra asked.

"Back home, I always stayed on top of things, you know? School, sports, my training – I had it all under control," he said. "And then I wound up here, where I can't control anything. Not even my own thoughts and feelings. Today, when that thing was controlling us, it was like I lost myself in you. I didn't care about Tarun, or getting home, or anything – except you. I still sort of feel like that."

"I feel the same way," Darra said.

"But I don't think we're supposed to... lose ourselves," A.J. said. "Maybe taking a step back from 'us' is the right thing to do. Just until we've gotten to know each other better." Darra struggled not to show her disappointment.

"Yeah," she said, turning halfway away. "Yeah, you're probably right... Um, I should go... check on dinner now." She tried not to walk away too quickly, lest A.J. suspect her true impulse to run away at top speed.

"Darra," A.J. called, and she turned back to him. "I still care about you. I want you to remember that."

"I... care about you, too," she said, without meeting his gaze. She wandered up to the village center, where a large bonfire was burning in a square, stone-lined pit. Some of the villagers roasted meats and vegetables on long skewers over the flames, but she spied

Kaleb simply lighting a stick on fire. She walked up to where he sat on a long, thick log and sunk down beside him. "Hey," she said, as the mage used the flame at the end of his stick to light his pipe.

"Hey," he said, holding in his breath. After several seconds, he exhaled, and a huge cloud of smoke blew out of his mouth like fire from a dragon. "Thank you for coming to my defense in there. And I'm sorry you got bit - and grounded."

"Thanks," Darra said. "But it was my own fault. I never should have pushed you to do that spell, Kay."

"No kidding," Kaleb replied. "I think I may have lost my virginity to that thing. When she looked like a girl, of course. Because I only ever saw her as a girl."

"And you really... did it with her?"

"Kind of. Does it count if it was just a dream?"

"No way," Darra said, remembering her own vivid dreams of the man who called himself Volos. "Dreams do not count."

"That's a relief," Kaleb said. "In the tribe, we don't get overly worked up about sex. It's just something people do, like eating or going to the bathroom. But I still didn't want my first time to be with a demon."

"So what was it like?" Darra asked, blushing just a little.

"It was... intense," Kaleb answered. "And kind of confusing."

"Oh," Darra said. "That sounds a lot like the day I've had, actually." Yuma came by and offered them each a skewer laden with food, which the teens gratefully accepted. They began roasting the skewers over the fire.

"Things got pretty wild here today," Yuma said.

"Uh, yeah," Darra said. "Yeah, we noticed."

"It isn't always like that here, just so you know," Yuma said. "I hope we haven't made a terrible impression on you."

"No need to worry about that," Darra said. "I'm sure all we'll remember of our time here is your hospitality." Yuma smiled and left the teens alone again.

"And the soulless succubus that almost killed us all," Kaleb said. "I'll probably remember that part, too." Darra nodded her agreement.

"Trade you my meat for your tomatoes," she offered.

"Deal," the tribal lad replied.

CHAPTER SIX
"DANCE WITH A DRAGON"

Aleksey and Lilith slashed their way through a thicket, and the teenage trio traipsed along behind them. They'd been on the move ever since they left Morrigen's Plot. Aleksey made sure they'd taken full advantage of the daylight, or the little of it that managed to shine through the thick foliage above their heads, foraging and eating breakfast and lunch as best they could while still moving steadily to the west. They'd only stopped late at night to eat dinner and sleep, and the increased pace had worn the teenagers out.

"Are you sure we shouldn't keep looking for Tarun?" A.J. had asked on the first day, after Aleksey had announced the change in their plans.

"Your friend has proven quite skilled at evading us," Aleksey had answered. "But Kaleb's gram is an expert in magic. She'll be able to track down your friend and tell us more about the gem. She might even be able to send you home herself." This plan had satisfied the pilot, and they'd made excellent time since then. They'd covered six days' worth of ground in four and a half when they came upon a break in the trees, and A.J. headed toward the sunlight of a large clearing.

"Wait," Aleksey said, placing a hand on the pilot's shoulder to stop him before he emerged from the woods. The half-elf stared up at the sky warily.

"What is it, Dad?" Darra asked.

"There," Aleksey said, pointing up at what appeared to be a

far-off bird.

"I don't see anything," Lilith said, but as the creature flew closer, she could tell by the mechanics of its large wings that it was no bird. "Is that–"

"A dragon," Aleksey said. "It's a dragon."

"But they only live in the mountains," Darra said. "What's it doing all the way down here?" The dragon flew almost directly over them, and Aleksey got a good look at its underside.

"Isn't it obvious?" Aleksey asked. "It's looking for us."

"You think it's the same one I crashed into?" A.J. asked, and Aleksey nodded.

"You crashed into a dragon? And you're still alive?" Lilith asked. "Fela favors this group, for certain. It's no wonder I'm having such a hard time fulfilling my oath."

"There's no question, it's the same dragon," Aleksey said. "I saw the scars. It's probably come looking for payback."

"I don't understand," Kaleb said. "Dragons possess powerful innate magics. If it's looking for us, why doesn't it just snap its fingers and make us appear?"

"Do dragons have fingers?" A.J. asked.

"They have talons," Aleksey said.

"But can they snap them?" A.J. asked. Aleksey rolled his eyes and turned away from the pilot.

"I don't know why it hasn't found us yet. Maybe it's still recovering from its injuries," Aleksey theorized.

"So what do you propose we do?" Lilith asked. Aleksey looked out over the clearing and pointed to the trees on the far side.

"The Tribe should be just a few miles that way," the half-elf said. "But we can't cross without making a meal of ourselves. And if we move any farther north, we'll enter the capital city's hunting grounds."

"And since the kingdom's soldiers are out in force hunting for you, you obviously aren't going to do that," Lilith said.

"We'll stick to the trees and head south, then cut back to the west when we have some cover," Aleksey said.

"But... south of here is orc territory," Kaleb said.

"What's an orc?" A.J. asked.

"Pig-people," Darra said, without quite making eye contact with the pilot. "They live in clans, they're very warlike, and they hate humans. Some people even say if they catch you, they'll eat you."

"Hmph!" Aleksey grunted. "Who told you all that?"

"Ani," Darra said. "She said her brother ran into some while he was hunting and barely got away. And you know how strong Borri is."

"Well, I've actually known a few orcs in my day, and they were nothing like you've described," Aleksey said. "They were a peaceful, kind family who took me in and treated my wounds during the war. Gods, I haven't thought of them in years."

"Well, pleasant reminiscences aside, you must agree that most orcs are adverse to humans crossing their lands," Lilith said.

"We'll stick to the outskirts," Aleksey said. "Besides, if it's between meeting an orc or a dragon, I'll take the pig-man any day."

Admiral Brandt began her work as she had every day since the portal opened up and swallowed her nephew and his co-pilot, with a visit to the command deck. She stared up at the anomaly, her hands clasped behind her back, as she listened to Gracie deliver a summary of the statistical analysis of the anomaly's overnight activity, which was almost exactly the same as the ones she'd heard every morning since the event. The anomaly had entered a period of deep stasis, and she knew it.

After her daily briefing, the Admiral would take coffee in her office and hear any concerns from her crew. She'd heard everything from complaints about the food served in the cafeteria to projections of how much fuel they would use in their prolonged stay here. After this, Admiral Brandt would usually attend yoga classes. Lately, however, she'd found the incessant instructions to relax only tensed her up more.

She'd started replacing the classes with long runs. There was a track that ran around the outer edges of the recreational deck for just such a purpose. It had sporadic sections of large windows so joggers could look out at the stars. One window had a clear view of the anomaly, and with each lap, Admiral Brandt found herself staring up at it again as she passed, as if she might notice some small change that would be the clue to finding her missing pilots. She took a quick shower, careful to keep her shoulder-length brown hair out of the water, and took lunch back in her office, where she scanned brief daily activity logs from each of the station's departments.

Around two, there was a knock at her door. "Come in," she said, and Myra's bespectacled face appeared.

"Do you have a free moment?" the older woman asked.

"I have nothing but free moments of late," the Admiral replied. "Please, have a seat." Myra complied, sliding down into one of the two chairs facing the Admiral's desk. "What can I do for you?"

"I finished my treatise on the anomaly. I was hoping I could go over it with you before I sent it in," Myra said.

"Of course," Admiral Brandt replied.

"As I've mentioned before, the major premise is that the anomaly seems to be the work of an unknown, sentient alien entity or civilization," Myra said, and the Admiral shook her head in agreement. "There are no less than seven observations that suggest this. The first is the anomaly's location. It is beyond coincidence that the anomaly was found within a solar system that boasts several potentially terraformable planets, including one which is already known to support a vast variety of non-terrestrial flora and fauna and is hospitable to human inhabitation. The second observation to suggest the intelligent design of the anomaly is its size. It's extremely small on a cosmic scale, and yet, when it activated, it was the perfect size for swallowing a spacefaring vessel."

"I hadn't considered that before, but you're right," the Admiral said. "If it is a mechanism for travelling through space-time, it must expend a massive amount of energy. Keeping the anomaly small likely reduces the amount of energy it uses in both its active and dormant state."

"So you would agree that the anomaly has gone dormant?" Myra asked, and the Admiral shrugged.

"Unless you have a better word for the way it just sits there, pulsing," the Admiral said. "It almost seems like it's waiting for... something. A cue, or a catalyst, maybe."

"You've brought up an important point," Myra said. "I think it's now time to admit that we are at the mercy of the anomaly's creators or operators. There seems to be little we can do from this side to utilize the anomaly's portal functionality."

"Which puts any hope of another rescue attempt down to a waiting game," Admiral Brandt said. "And, given that we know nothing about this alien entity or civilization, that wait could be days, months or even years."

"I'm glad you've thought all of this through so thoroughly, Alyson," Myra said, reaching across the desk to briefly place her hand on top of the younger woman's. "I always hate to be the bearer of bad news, especially where family is concerned."

Aleksey scouted ahead of the rest of his group by about a tenth of a mile. Kaleb and A.J. came next, as Lilith had taken it upon herself to guard the rear and Darra had hung back to keep pace with her.

"I notice you're not at the outworlder's side, like usual," Lilith said. "Is that because of your father's grounding?"

"No, actually," Darra said, her back straightening so she stood just a little taller. "A.J. and I just decided we're better off as friends."

"Ah," Lilith said knowingly. "Well, at least it was your decision, and not your father's."

"Yep," Darra said, faking cheerfulness. "One hundred percent my decision. I am in control of my life. Honestly, I'm trying not to even think about it. I'm just here for the mission: get A.J. and his friend back to their world."

"And what will you do after?" Lilith asked. "Have you given any thought to my suggestion that you take the vows before a god? It wouldn't have to be Rebos; with your fighting skills, you'd make a fine follower of the god of war."

"Ew, Obelix?" Darra asked. "No way! He's such a woman-hating jerk. He kidnapped his own sisters, for the sake of the heavens! Besides, as the god of war, he's also the god of rape. I could never worship him."

"Good point. Forgive me if I sound surprised, but you're well-educated for a non-believer."

"Thanks," Darra said. "That's all Dad's doing. He home-schooled me. Not that we ever had a home to speak of."

"Sorry if I seem pushy about taking the vows. I just hate to see so much potential go to waste," Lilith said. "To reach your full potential as a great warrior, you need to follow a path to power, in my opinion."

"Oh, I've already chosen a path," Darra said. "Dad said when I turn sixteen, he'll pay for my tuition to the Pentonese

Warrior Women's Academy – if I prove to him I'm mature enough. Have you heard of them?"

"Of course," Lilith said. "Their chi-fighting technique is legendary."

"I saw an exhibition match between two graduates one time, and they were doing all kinds of crazy things, like smashing thick boards and concrete blocks with their bare hands. I've wanted to train to be one ever since."

"I've always wanted to face one in combat, just to see if they live up to their reputation."

"Well, give me a few years," Darra said, and Lilith smiled.

Up ahead, Kaleb led and A.J. followed close behind. While Kaleb tried to keep Aleksey in his sights, A.J. made a habit of glancing back at Darra. "She hates me now," the pilot said to the tribal lad in a low voice. "She's barely looked at me the last few days."

"Darra doesn't hate people, especially you," Kaleb said. "She just doesn't know how to act around you now. The same thing happened when my girlfriend and I broke up, even though we swore we'd stay friends."

"I can't imagine not being her friend," A.J. said. "Maybe I should talk to her."

"Sure," Kaleb said. "Like, what would you say?"

"That I'm sorry," the pilot answered. "That I never meant to hurt her."

"I think she knows that," Kaleb said. "She just needs time to adjust."

"That's the problem," A.J. said. "If your grandmother really can find Tarun and send us home, I don't have a lot of time here left. And I don't want to leave things on these terms."

"So don't," Kaleb said. "When we get to the Tribe, pull her aside and let her know how important her friendship is to you."

"The direct approach," A.J. said. "Has that ever worked?" Kaleb just shrugged.

Prince Trosclair and his friends had taken a carriage to Westbury Street, the main business strip of the capital city's arts district. It was Kesari's Week, as the Artist's Moon was in its full phase for the last time this year, and there was a corresponding arts festival to celebrate it. Everywhere along the street there were stalls set up. Most had paintings on display, but there were also more than a few framed photographs, as well as booths devoted to pottery, jewelry, weavings, fabrics and fashions, face painting, and of course, cuisines. The all-men's a cappella choir *The Knightingales* were even performing from the marble steps of the museum.

Ennio was feeling especially nervous to have Trosclair out in the crowd so soon after the Duke's assassination, and no less than eight guards circled the prince and his friends as they made their way down the crowded street. Whenever commoners noticed the prince next to them, some bowed and others called out to him, while still others were starstruck into wide-eyed silence. Trosclair made sure to make eye contact with the people around him, merchants and peasants alike, and he spared them a smile more often than not. It was the least he felt he could do for these folk, who would likely one day tell their children and their grandchildren the story of their run-in with the prince.

Alicia pulled the group into a stall with several artists at stools and easels, working on caricatures. "It'll be fun," she said. "Plus, it'll commemorate our time together." She then began arranging the group for the picture. She pulled Armand, Frederick and Devon to the back, as they were the tallest, and put Trosclair in the front middle between herself and Serena. "Ennio," she called, and the bodyguard stopped scanning the crowd. "Get in here."

"Oh, no," he protested. "I'm on duty."

"But we need you for balance," Alicia insisted. "It won't look right without you." Ennio capitulated and took his place beside Devon in the back.

The artist took in the group and, bowing, said, "Your Grace honors me with your patronage. I've always wanted to do a royal portrait." He then reoriented his sketch pad sideways to better fit the group on the page and began scraping the paper with his colored pencils.

"Just don't accentuate this blemish," Trosclair said, pointing to a red spot on his chin, and the artist smiled and nodded. "I swear, every time I'm to have my picture done, my face revolts, and I break out. I had a photograph done on my birthday last year, and I had a big red pimple on the very end of my nose."

"I don't recall that," Ennio said.

"Well, it's not like I showed it to anyone!" Trosclair said.

"Speaking of photographs, did you see the one with the owl passing in front of the Giant's Moon?" Serena asked, and Trosclair shook his head. "It was carrying a snake. I don't know how the artist managed to capture it in the moment of action like that."

"Why didn't you buy it?" Trosclair asked.

"I'm pretending to be ambivalent so I can talk the price down," Serena said. "It's a negotiating tactic my dad taught me."

"Ah," Trosclair said. "How shrewd."

"I don't suppose you've ever had to haggle yourself, have you, Trosc?" Armand asked.

"The crown always pays a full and fair price for its goods and services," the prince said. "Like today: We're the major sponsor of this festival, yet I still brought a hefty bag of gold to shop with."

"You brought?" Ennio asked. "I'm the one who has to carry all this money around with me. And it is hefty." He lifted his shirt to reveal the two large coin purses tied to his belt.

"You've got the muscles for it," Trosclair said. "My delicate frame is unsuited to such menial labor."

"If you're too delicate to shop, how will you ever survive?" Devon asked.

"Simple," Trosclair said. "I'll pay someone to shop for me."

"Ooh, ooh!" Alicia said. "I want that job."

"Get in line, sister," Frederick said. "I was born to spend other men's money." A trumpet and a snare drum sounded at the end of the street. The trumpet's melody was instantly recognizable as the military marching song, and it clashed with *The Knightingales'* gentle number about a singing blackbird. The choir eventually stopped performing altogether as the musicians marched into view, leading a long, thick line of soldiers.

"It sounds like Commandant Burke is back with his brigade," Ennio said.

"That's a good thing, right?" Armand asked. "Now he can hunt down whoever killed your uncle."

"Yeah, you're right. But it also means I have to cut the day short. Sir," Trosclair said, catching the artist's attention. "How close are you to finishing? We have to be going soon." The artist turned his picture around to face the prince, and Trosclair was impressed. In the few short moments he'd been given, he'd depicted the prince with a burning crown of fire that blended perfectly into his red and gold hair. Most of the other figures were still in the early stages of being sketched.

"Just need a few more minutes, Your Grace," the artist said, as he turned the sketch pad back around and resumed his work.

"I suppose that'll give Burke time to settle in, anyway," Trosclair said, and Ennio nodded.

Aleksey made his way back to Kaleb and A.J. as the sun began to set. "The way forward is clear," he said. "Where is my daughter?"

"Dad!" Darra called as if in answer from the trees just behind them, and Aleksey noted the tension in her voice. He sprinted past both mage and pilot and found his daughter with her crossbow aimed at an orc. It was a young thing, not quite a child but not fully grown either, and it was kneeling on the ground in front of Lilith, its hands raised in surrender. The assassin had her scimitar drawn on it.

"Look what we found lurking on our trail," Lilith said.

"But I wasn't lurking, I was hunting," the orc said. "And I didn't know I was on your trail until you came at me with your weapons drawn!"

"If you're hunting, where's your weapon?" Aleksey asked.

"That's not my job," the orc said. "I'm just supposed to flush out the game for the others."

"Others?" Lilith asked. "How many?"

"Lots," Aleksey said, as the orcs came out of the woods from all directions around them. They were poorly armed with only wooden clubs and spears, but there were more than a dozen of them.

"Gentlemen," Aleksey began in his most charming voice. "There seems to be a misunderstanding here."

"There's no misunderstanding, human," one of the orcs said. "You're on our lands, threatening harm to one of our own. Did they hurt you, Chiron?" The young pig-man shook his head in the negative.

"See? No harm done," Aleksey said, helping the young orc to his feet. "We were just crossing through. You can let us go, and we'll be off your lands in five minutes. This doesn't have to get nasty."

"Might get nasty for you," another orc said. "Won't get nasty for us." Lilith suddenly grabbed the young orc and raised her scimitar to his throat.

"Are you sure about that, pig-man?" she asked.

"What are you doing?" Aleksey hissed.

"Giving us some leverage," the assassin answered through bared teeth. "Drop your weapons and let us pass, or I'll gut the youngling." The other orcs stood their ground, readying themselves for battle.

"I'm sorry, Chiron," said the first orc. Slowly, the pig-men tightened their circle around the adventurers. When the first ones were within striking distance, Lilith threw the young orc forward into her attackers.

"So much for that idea," she said, as she blocked a swinging club with her sword.

"If you knew anything about orcs, you would've known threats wouldn't work," Aleksey said, ducking underneath the jab of a spear. The half-elf caught the shaft of the weapon in one hand and butted it back into the forehead of the orc holding it. The pig-man let go of the weapon and stumbled backwards. "Haven't you ever heard the word 'pigheaded' before?" Two more orcs charged Aleksey, and he used the spear to sweep the legs out from under one and block the attack of the other.

"Can you do something, Kaleb?" A.J. asked, as five orcs stalked toward the teens. "Like a spell?"

"I haven't studied my spellbook in a week," Kaleb said as he held up his hand in a familiar gesture. "But I still know how to do this: Verres!" Flames leapt up between the orcs and the teens, and the pig-men fell back, grunting in fear.

"A mage!" one of the orcs squealed. "There's a mage among them!"

"And a powerful one, at that!" Kaleb said.

"I thought you were just a beginner?" A.J. whispered, and Kaleb shot him a silencing look.

"And since you orcs fear magic, maybe you'd better just turn around and leave right now," Kaleb said.

"Yeah," Darra said. "Or he'll turn you into real pigs." One of the orcs leapt through the fire, his club raised high above his head.

"I do not fear fire!" he bellowed. "Or mages!" The orc struck Kaleb over the head, and the tribal lad fell to the ground, as his fire faded with his consciousness.

"Kaleb!" A.J. cried.

"What about steel?" Darra asked, her crossbow pressed against the back of the orc's neck. "Do you fear that?"

"You kill him, and I'll crush you," said another orc, his club raised behind the young woman's head.

"And then I'll stab you, right through the neck," A.J. threatened, his spear held up toward the second orc.

"I don't want to kill anybody," Darra said.

"Yes, well," Lilith said, side-stepping a jab from a spear. "Sometimes the gods take that decision from you." She stabbed the spear-wielder in the stomach, then yanked her blade back out to block another incoming blow with it.

"No!" Aleksey cried out, but it was too late. The injured orc fell to the ground next to Kaleb's slumped form.

"Aurick!" yelled one of the orcs, as he rushed to his fallen companion's side.

"What have you done?" Aleksey asked, throwing down the spear and raising his empty hands. "Stop!" the half-elf commanded. "Everyone lay down your arms! It was never our intention to harm you."

"Tell that to Aurick!" said the orc by his injured friend's side. "He's bleeding out. You've killed him!"

"You attacked us," Lilith said.

"Shut up!" Aleksey snapped at the assassin. "You've done enough harm already, thank you very much!"

Admiral Brandt was reading the captains' logs from the various ships dispersed throughout the solar system when another knock sounded at her door. This time she got up and crossed to open the door herself, and when she did, she found Andre standing there, arms folded across his chest and looking uncomfortable. "May I come in?" he asked.

"Of course," she said, holding the door wide for him.

"You asked me to take an informal survey of morale," Andre said. "I had the department heads discuss it with their crews, and the news is... mixed."

"Well, give me the bad news first, then," the Admiral said.

"The majority of the crew thinks we may be wasting our time on this extended rescue operation," Andre said. "They feel like the shuttle may be gone forever."

"They're scientists," Admiral Brandt said. "They think in cold, rational terms about statistics and variables. As their leader, I have to approach this another way."

"And how is that, Admiral?"

"I have to hold on to hope and trust my gut. And my gut says that anomaly will open back up - eventually - and we will find our pilots alive."

"I truly hope so, Alyson."

"So what was the good news?" the Admiral asked, deflecting the offered sympathy with a half-waved hand.

"In spite of their fears about the shuttle, the crew is still excited about this mission and its evolving objective," Andre said. "Specifically, they're excited that the anomaly may lead to our first contact with a sentient, intelligent non-terrestrial species. It's no overstatement to say we could all be on the verge of going down in history together."

"Trust this crew to find the bright side," the Admiral said. "Well, whatever gets them out of their pods in the morning. I'm just glad I don't have the makings of a mutiny on my hands. I expected backlash from the crew because A.J. was - is - my nephew."

"On the contrary," Andre said. "This crew is behind you all the way, Admiral."

"Really?" the Admiral asked, and Andre nodded. "That means the world to me, it really does. And if my new plan is going to work, I'm going to need more than a few brave souls willing to follow me out into the great unknown."

"So you do have a plan," Andre said.

"Don't sound so surprised," the Admiral said. "We've been sitting here for two weeks. I've had nothing but time to consider all our options."

"And?" Andre prompted. "What have you decided?"

"I was just about to make an announcement, but I suppose I can tell you now," the Admiral said. "The gist of it is, I've asked for and received permission to modify our mission parameters."

"Sure," Andre said. "I expected as much. How much longer will we be staying here?"

"Actually, the station will move on as scheduled late tonight," Admiral Brandt said. "I've already had the transport team begin preparing for the leap."

"God, I hate the leaping," Andre said. "It always leaves my stomach in flutters. But what will you do about A.J. and Tarun? Surely you'll leave some presence behind, in case they reappear."

"Of course. More than a presence, actually – a force," the Admiral said. "I'm staying here, Andre – with the *Morningstar*. Congratulations; you'll be taking over command of the rest of the fleet for the remainder of the tour."

Prince Trosclair caught up to Commandant Burke as the older man was sitting down for what was either a late lunch or an early dinner in the banquet hall. Half a dozen soldiers dined with him. The men were laughing and talking in booming voices, but Burke kept himself aloof, merely watching the soldiers. When Ennio announced the prince's entrance, all of the men stood except the Commandant, who kept spooning stew past his thick beard and mustache into his mouth. Trosclair decided to ignore the slight and walked up to face Burke as the rest of the men took their seats. "Commandant," he said. "I was hoping we could have a word. In private."

"These are my top men," Commandant Burke said. "We can speak freely in front of them."

"Very well," Trosclair said. "I witnessed your arrival back in town. You've quite a force at your command. I take it there were no problems raising the troops for your brigade?"

"Actually, I did run into some reluctance on the part of Lord Parmida of Misty Vale to call up his men."

"Really?" Trosclair said. "That surprises me. He's always seemed loyal to the crown."

"Yes, well, I made up the difference with an extra battalion from Lord Fallon's men. It'll leave his own city's forces stretched thin, but he was eager to demonstrate his staunch support for this cause."

"I'll have a messenger send my thanks," Trosclair said. "And I'll send another one to see what Lord Parmida has to say for himself."

"If you wouldn't mind, allow me to send my own men to Misty Vale," Commandant Burke said. "It was me Lord Parmida defied, after all, and I feel inclined to demonstrate my authority in this matter."

"Fine," Trosclair said. "But don't allow the situation to escalate. I'm sure he felt he had a good reason for denying you the troops. I'm just eager to hear what that reason is."

"Yes," Burke said. "As am I."

"And how is the hunt for the fugitives going?" Trosclair asked. "It's been two weeks, and I haven't heard a word about them."

"I was informed they may have been sighted in Morning's Peak," Burke said.

"And...?" Trosclair prompted. "Did you follow up on that lead?"

"Of course," Burke said, before slurping down another spoonful of stew. "But they've not been seen since. It's likely they know we're after them, and they're steering clear of the cities."

"Then how will you find them?" the prince asked.

"Rest assured, I do have a plan in place," Burke said. "Although I prefer not to show my cards before the game has been called."

"With all due respect, Commandant, this is not a game," Trosclair said. 'The reputation of the kingdom itself is on the line. DuVerres will not be known as a place where high crimes go unpunished."

"Well said, Your Grace," Burke replied. "I agree with you completely."

"Kill them!" ordered one of the orcs, and the others moved in to comply.

"Wait!" Aleksey yelled. "Our mage - he can heal your man."

"Is that the mage, on the ground?" one of the orcs asked, and Aleksey nodded. "Looks like he needs a healer himself." Aleksey help his hands up slowly to show he meant no harm and then took his shirt off over his head.

"We need to pack and tie off the wound, to slow down your

friend's bleeding," the half-elf said. "It'll buy us more time for our mage to recover." Aleksey dropped to his knees and began treating the wounded orc. Darra reluctantly lowered her crossbow, and the orcs around her and A.J. lowered their weapons as well. Kaleb groaned and began to stir, and Darra knelt down beside him.

"Kay," she said, and the mage seemed to hear her. He lifted his eyebrows and his mouth fell open as if he might speak, but no words came out. "Kaleb, you have to wake up." The mage opened his eyes into twin slits.

"Head hurts," Kaleb said, before closing his eyes again.

"Yeah, I know it does," Darra said. "But we need you to stay awake." The tribal lad's eyes snapped open wider.

"I'm awake," he said. He tried to sit up, but his wince revealed the pain this tiny movement caused him.

"Just clear your head before you try to sit up, Kay," Darra said.

"So the mage will live?" one of the orcs asked. "You must be getting old, Keeran. I remember the days when a blow from you would crush a man's skull."

"He's just a boy, Sabiq," Keeran said. "I felt sorry for him."

"Your mage friend is lucky, then, youngling," Sabiq said to Darra.

"I'd say you're the lucky ones," Darra replied. "If you'd seriously hurt my friend, I'd have—"

"Darra," Aleksey said. "I need your help more than they need your threats. Please, put your hands right here and apply pressure evenly." Darra scooted over and did as she was instructed. Aleksey went to his pack and pulled out Kaleb's spellbook. He handed it to the mage, who sat up more easily this time.

"So am I un-grounded, then?" the tribal lad asked.

"You've been given a temporary reprieve," Aleksey said. "We need a healing spell, obviously. How long will it take you to prepare for it?"

"Maybe fifteen minutes," Kaleb said.

"He may not have fifteen minutes," Aleksey said.

"I don't understand," A.J. said. "You said you know dozens of spells."

"I said I know *a* dozen. And anyway, knowledge of magic is... fleeting," Kaleb said. "Every time I do a spell, it's like it's wiped clean from my mind. And I have to study from my spellbook every day to keep the mystical energies flowing through my body."

"So stop explaining it and get to it," Aleksey instructed.

"Right," Kaleb said, and he lowered his head into his book. He didn't look back up again until the orc on the ground beside him started coughing up blood several minutes later.

"Kaleb," Aleksey said in an urgently rising tone. "It may be now or never for your spell."

"I–I'll try," Kaleb said. He pulled off his waterskin and placed it on the ground before him, then balanced his book on his lap. He started the sequence once but faltered on a hand gesture. He took a deep breath and began the sequence again, adding the incantation the spell called for when the time came. The mystical energy flashed in his eyes and coursed through the water. "Here," he said handing the waterskin to Aleksey. "Pour it over the wound."

Aleksey removed his blood-soaked shirt from the wound, and more blood gushed forth. The half-elf quickly poured the water over the gash, and as the blood rinsed away, the wound began to close up. Soon Aleksey was pouring water over a four-inch scar and nothing more. "Drink the rest of this," he told the orc, handing him the waterskin. "It'll take care of any remaining internal injuries." The orc obeyed, and soon Aleksey was helping the pig-man back to his feet. "See, now? Calmer heads have prevailed, and we're all better off for it."

"There is still the matter of you trespassing on our lands," Sabiq said.

"Oh," Aleksey said. "That."

"And now that you've laid down your weapons and healed Aurick, what's to stop us from executing you right here, right now?" Sabiq asked.

"I was hoping common decency," Aleksey said.

"Well, your hoping was in vain," Sabiq said, as he stepped in closer. The wind picked up, and with it came a strange scent that Aleksey found oddly familiar. The orcs smelled it too, and they immediately started grunting in the guttural quasi-language they lapsed into when they felt deeply threatened.

"What's going on?" Darra asked, as the orcs began backing up. A figure appeared from around a tree, and the orcs' grunting reached a fever pitch as they sprinted away and out of sight.

"Volos?" Darra asked the figure incredulously. "What are you doing here?"

"Looking for you," Volos replied.

"Darra, who is this man?" Aleksey asked.

"Forgive me," Volos said, extending his hand toward Aleksey. The half-elf looked Volos up and down before he finally shook the offered hand. "My name is Volos."

"Aleksey," the half-elf said. "And if you'll forgive my directness, how is it exactly that you know my daughter?"

"Well, technically, I don't. This is our first time meeting," Volos said. "It's... complicated. But I can assure you, I mean you no harm."

"And those orcs," Aleksey said. "What was it about you that made them scatter like that?"

"They say orcs can smell powerful magic," Volos said. "And that they fear it."

"So you're a sorcerer, then?" Aleksey asked.

"Of a sort," Volos replied.

"And what is it you want with Darra?" Aleksey asked.

"Just a few minutes of conversation," Volos said. "We have important private matters to discuss."

"It's okay, Dad," Darra said. "He just wants to talk."

"Fine," Aleksey said. He reached down, picked up Darra's crossbow and handed it to her. "But at least take this. In case the orcs come back. And stay within shouting distance."

"Of course," Darra said. Volos offered her his arm, and Darra placed her hand inside his elbow as if she were a fine lady and not a forest brat who'd gone days without a proper wash. When they'd walked out of earshot, A.J. approached Aleksey.

"I don't trust him," the pilot said.

"Don't trust him, or don't like him?" Lilith asked.

"Neither," the pilot said. "I mean, both. Just look at the way he showed up out of nowhere and scared off those pig-men."

"So you're angry that he saved us, then?" the assassin asked. "And it has nothing to do with jealousy?"

"Jealousy?" A.J. said. "Yeah, right. I'm just worried he's gonna hurt Darra."

The massive gymnasium on the space station's recreational

level was where all mandatory crew meetings were held, as it seated five thousand. There was still overflow, as there were just over seven thousand crew members, and those who couldn't fit in the gymnasium - as well as the skeleton crew that remained in place to operate the station's vital functions - would be watching over the various monitors and screens of their pods and workstations. Admiral Brandt entered onto the basketball court, headed for the podium that had been placed there for this occasion. The crew rose to their feet, and all conversation stopped as they stood at attention. The sharp *click-clack* of the Admiral's short heels on the polished wooden floor was picked up by the microphone attached to her lapel, but nothing could be done except to continue walking and ignore it. When she reached the podium, she said, "At ease. Please, be seated." The crew collectively relaxed and sat back down. "I called you here today to announce a deviation from our scheduled tour of duty. As you should all be aware by now, in less than seven hours, this space station will move on to the next star system on our route. But our flagship, the *Morningstar*, will remain behind." A light murmur moved through the crowd as people reacted to this news. "I'll take command of the vessel myself, and we'll embark on a mission of indefinite length to wait out the re-opening of the portal and resume our search and rescue operations for our missing pilots. This mission has also been designated by headquarters as a possible candidate for first contact, as we've been given direct orders to enter the anomaly if and when its portal functionality activates again." The murmurs grew louder with the crew's excitement. "Now, obviously, I can't ask the regular crew of the *Morningstar* to uproot their lives for the sake of this mission. I know many of you are anxious to end the tour and get back to your families and loved ones. So the crew for this mission will be comprised of an all-volunteer force." There was controlled pandemonium as the crew began to discuss their inclination to join the new mission or carry on with the old one. "There are a couple more things to consider," the Admiral said, and the crowd quieted down enough to hear her. "The first is the time frame of this mission. The *Morningstar* is a self-sustaining ship, and headquarters is willing to invest a substantial amount of time in watching the anomaly. Realistically, it could be years before the anomaly opens again, if it opens up again at all. Before you volunteer, make sure you're ready to devote what could be a good portion of your life to this cause. And second, there is the prospect of first contact itself. As I'm sure you're all aware, it brings with it certain inherent dangers, as we know nothing about the entities or civilization we may come into contact with. This could easily turn into a life or death mission for us, as it already may have for our lost pilots. I'd be a failure of a leader if I didn't warn you about that reality. Now, to orient you to the altered scope of the station's continuing mission, please welcome your new commanding officer, Vice Admiral Johnson." The crew gave a polite round of applause as Andre entered onto the court, and the Admiral scurried to the side, glad the sound of the clapping covered that of her shoes. She removed the microphone from her lapel and switched it off, glad to be out of the spotlight, and approached Gracie, who was standing alone by the doors.

"Very well done," Gracie said. "I think you've piqued the interest of everybody on this station with that bit about first contact."

"Every word of it was true," the Admiral said.

"But we both know you're not telling them everything," the younger woman said.

"A good leader rarely does," Admiral Brandt replied. "Are we on for chess tonight?"

"Wouldn't miss it," Gracie said.

Darra and Volos walked arm in arm through the trees in silence. Just before it turned awkward, he said, "I imagine you're wondering why I'm here."

"Sure," Darra said. "Let's start there."

"I've been searching for you ever since we last dreamed of each other," Volos said.

"Why did we dream together?" Darra said. "That's never happened to me before."

"For the same reason I've had such a hard time tracking you down," Volos said. "You carry my gem with you."

"Your gem?" Darra repeated. "No, no. I took that from a... dragon." Volos merely lifted his eyebrows. Darra pulled her arm away from his and turned to face him, raising her crossbow to his chest. "Who are you?"

"I've already given you my name," Volos said. "And from your reaction, it seems you've guessed that this is... not my natural form."

"You're really him?" Darra asked. "You're the dragon?"

"A dragon, certainly," he said. "But there's really no need for this." He pushed her crossbow so that it pointed away from him. "I hope my behavior up until now has earned me a modicum of trust."

"You attacked us," Darra said. "You spat fire at my dad."

"You woke me up with your thieving, and I saw that your father carried the DragonSword," Volos said. "I was acting in self-defense, or at least I thought I was."

"So why have you come now?" Darra asked. "And why do you look human?"

"Many mystical creatures prefer to walk as humans from time to time," Volos said. "It is, after all, a largely human world. And I thought it would put you at ease. As to why I've come, I can only say I felt... compelled to see you in person. After sharing such an intimate experience as dreaming, I wanted to meet you in real life. I hope that doesn't upset you."

"No," Darra said. "No, it's only natural to be... curious, I guess."

Not too far away, Aleksey was deep in concentration, his ear cocked in the direction his daughter had left in. "Half-elf, are you spying on your own daughter?" Lilith asked.

"Not spying," Aleksey said. "Monitoring. Chaperoning. But not spying. Now be quiet. I can barely hear them as it is, and I think they said something about the dragon."

"Someone should explain to him the privacy concerns of young adult women," Lilith said to A.J. and Kaleb. Both teens just shrugged.

"Right," Lilith said. "I forgot. I'm surrounded by men."

"Enlightened men, I like to think," Kaleb said. "My tribe is a matriarchy, after all."

"Hey, half-elf," Lilith said. "You'll tell me if he attacks, so I can save her, right?"

"If he attacks her, he'll be the one who needs saving," Aleksey said.

Prince Trosclair left Commandant Burke to his meal and returned to his own rooms. He hadn't been completely satisfied by the Commandant's evasive answer about his plans for finding the fugitives, but he didn't think it was worth challenging him, either. Trosclair knew from Commandant Burke's days serving under his uncle that the man did not like to be lorded over; he liked to be the one doing the lording. For now, that was fine with Trosclair - although after his coronation, he planned to have a conversation with Milian about the possibility of replacing the Commandant.

Ennio had been called away for a mandatory military exercise, and his absence had Trosclair feeling especially lonely. He sent Antonin to fetch Frederick, but the squire came back to the prince's parlor with word that the older boy wasn't in his room.

"What about Alicia? Did you see her?" the prince asked.

"No, Your Grace," Antonin said. "I was told she went out with her brother."

'Well, I'm at a loss, then," Trosclair said. "I don't suppose you'd like to play a game of cards?"

"I'm not supposed to gamble, Your Grace," Antonin said.

"We won't use any real money," the prince replied, as he fished a deck of cards out of a drawer.

"Okay, but... I only know how to play Kingsies and Downfall," the boy said.

"That's alright," Trosclair replied, as he sat down at the table and started shuffling. "We'll play Kingsies." Although the game was overly simplistic and could get monotonous, Trosclair decided it was infinitely better than Downfall, which was basically a lesson in counting meant for young children like Antonin. The prince began dealing out the cards, seven for each of them.

"So how are your lessons coming along?" Trosclair asked.

"Fine," the boy said. "Mr. Summers is nicer than my tutor back home, but he also assigns more homework."

"Well, you are the squire to the prince," Trosclair said. "You deserve to be taught by the finest minds, and being challenged intellectually is part of that."

"Yes, Your Grace," Antonin said, and Trosclair could tell from the boy's tone and his downturned face that he'd been looking for sympathy.

"I'm sure the workload will lessen once Mr. Summers sees all the hard work you're putting in," Trosclair said.

"I hope so," Antonin said.

"Oh!" Trosclair said, as a thought came to him. "Before we start playing, I have one more errand I need you to run."

"Sure. I mean, of course, Your Grace," Antonin said. "What is it?"

"Find Commandant Burke and ask him when Ennio will be returning to my guard duty," Trosclair instructed.

"I can deliver the message to one of the Commandant's men," Antonin offered. "But on my way back from Frederick's room, I saw Ennio and Commandant Burke leaving with a bunch of other soldiers."

"Just my luck today," Trosclair said. "Oh, well. You go first."

"Do you have any eights?" Antonin asked.

"Nope," Trosclair replied. "Fight, or flee?"

"Flee," the boy said, drawing a card from the pile.

"I need to ask you for a favor," Volos said.

"What's that?" Darra asked.

"I can sense that one of your companions still has my gem," Volos said. "I would like it back, if you don't mind."

"Oh," Darra said. "About that... You wouldn't happen to be able to open a portal like back at Morning's Peak, would you? My friend is lost, and I was hoping–"

"I know all about the outworlder who travels with you," Volos cut in. "And as much as I appreciate the predicament he is in, the gem is precious to me. I invested a significant amount of my mystical energies in its creation, and I cannot afford to waste it returning one lost sheep to his flock."

"Well, can you make another one?" Darra asked. "We could find a way to pay you back."

"Sadly, the art of gem magic is a lost one," Volos said. "The elves were always the masters of the craft, but their society has given up on magic. I only dabbled in the creation of the gem and its sisters, and their magic has always been unstable, at best. If I tried to send the boy home with it, he could end up tormented, like his poor friend, or stranded in interspace for infinity."

"If it's unstable, why do you want it back so bad?" Darra asked.

"Call it a last resort," Volos said. "There's a great war coming to Ona, Darra. Not just a war of men, but a war of ideas.

The magical creatures of this planet were targeted before with crusades and genocide, and I fear that may be the case again. The gem is my way out of this world, if the time ever comes that there's nothing left for me here."

"Where would you go?"

"To a new world. There's no magic in it, so I would be stranded there. And there are no other people - or dragons. But there are plenty of fish and chickens to eat, and I could live out the rest of my life in peace, if I had to."

"That sounds like an awful fate," Darra said.

"I said it was a last resort," Volos replied. Another almost-awkward silent moment passed, until Volos said, "I also wanted to apologize for the first time we dreamt together. I should never have tried to kiss you like that."

"Why did you?" Darra asked.

"I could say I was overwhelmed by the dreamscape, but that wouldn't be the whole truth," Volos said. "Oh gods... I can't believe I'm telling you this, but I've always tried to be forthright."

"What exactly are you trying to say?" Darra asked.

"Do you believe in love at first sight?" Volos asked in return, and Darra's eyes went wide.

"Well, half-elf?" Lilith prompted. "What are they up to? They've been gone long enough to make you a grandfather."

"Mind your tongue!" Aleksey said.

"Yeah, don't - don't say that," A.J. said.

"They're out of my earshot now," Aleksey said. "But I heard enough to know he isn't planning to hurt her."

"That's a relief," A.J. said.

"How did a half-elf come to adopt a human baby, anyway?" Lilith asked, lifting an elegantly arched eyebrow.

"It's a long story," Aleksey said.

"We've got some time on our hands," Lilith said.

"Darra's birth parents were casualties of the last Elven War," Aleksey answered.

"Like mine," Kaleb added.

"Exactly," Aleksey said. "Darra's mother entrusted her to my care before she died. She's been my daughter ever since."

"That wasn't a long story at all," Lilith said. "There must be more to it that you're not telling."

"How very perceptive of you," Aleksey said. "I am, in fact, holding back on the more gruesome details of my daughter's parents' deaths. But I suppose you wouldn't find it gruesome at all. You'd probably revel in it."

"I do not 'revel' in death," Lilith said. "I respect it. That's an important difference you've still not picked up on. I'm beginning to question your powers of observation."

"And I'm questioning why I've allowed you to come with us this far," Aleksey said.

"Allowed me? Please," Lilith said. "No man decides my fate, least of all you."

"I seem to recall a moment when you were dangling from a cliff, and I quite literally decided your fate," Aleksey countered.

"That decision was your daughter's," Lilith said. "Your problem, half-elf, is that you think you can control everything around you, including people. Take your daughter, for instance..."

"What about Darra?" Aleksey said. "She's a perfectly normal, healthy teenage girl – and I'm proud to see how she's grown up."

"She is an empowered young woman whose main goal in life appears to be liberating herself from the control of an overbearing patriarch," Lilith said.

"You say that like I'm Darra's enemy," Aleksey said. "But she knows deep down that everything I do is for her. Besides, every young person chafes at parental control. Just look at Kaleb."

"Me?" Kaleb asked. "What did I do?"

"You ran away from your gram and your tribe, I heard," Aleksey said.

"Yeah, but there were... extenuating circumstances," Kaleb said.

"There always are," Aleksey said. "With young people, everything seems bigger and more urgent, more dangerous or exciting or alluring. Self-discipline isn't always a big consideration for youths. Believe me; I speak from experience."

"Wait, are you saying 'Mr. Repression' himself had a wild side growing up?" Lilith asked.

"I'm not repressed," Aleksey said. "Old-fashioned, maybe."

"And yet so immature," Lilith said. "I guess it's

understandable, considering the lifespan of half-elves. You're barely more than a youth yourself."

"Uh, guys," A.J. said, pointing to a stirring among the foliage several feet in front of them. "It looks like we have company."

"Have the orcs come back?" Kaleb whispered, as he drew his throwing knives out of his robe. A.J. raised his spear, Aleksey drew his sword, and Lilith nocked her longbow, and all the weapons were trained on the figure moving through the trees toward them.

"Tarun?" A.J. asked, when the figure's face came clear. "We've been looking all over for you!" A.J. lowered his spear and stepped closer to Tarun, who froze in place with a look of fear on his face.

"Stay back, outworlder," Lilith said to A.J. "This man is dangerous."

"He's my best friend," A.J. said.

"He tried to kill you while you were sick from the Cursed Knight," Lilith said.

"What?" A.J. asked. "No, that can't be true." The pilots locked eyes for a brief moment, and A.J. read the guilt in Tarun's expression. "Tarun? Did you try to kill me?"

"I—I'm sorry," Tarun said. "Ever since the portal, I don't always know... what's happening around me."

"He seemed in full control of his faculties when he had his hands around your throat," Lilith said.

"I was delusional, alright?" Tarun said testily. "But I'm better now. I found a way to live in this world in safety and security. Luxury, even."

"Live on this world?" A.J. repeated. "Tarun, you may not have to. We've been trying to find a way to get home. Or, you know, back to the station. Kaleb's grandma might be able to open another portal and—"

"No!" Tarun said. "I won't go through any portal, ever again! Have you even thought about what it was like for me the first time? My consciousness trapped in my body by day, and spread out across infinite worlds by night. I travelled to dozens, maybe hundreds of worlds just like this one – I couldn't touch anything, but I could appear before people, and I tried to help them all, at first. Like a guardian angel. And then the tyrants always came. Giants or wizards or despotic kings and queens, and they inevitably killed the people I had been guiding. It made the dreaming seem pointless, and eventually, I stopped trying to help the people and realized what I had become: a prophet of death."

"You dreamt of impending death?" Lilith asked. "That's a rare gift, and a heavy burden. It's no surprise you went mad from it."

"But I really am better now," Tarun insisted. "I figured out that in worlds like these, the only thing that matters is power. And now I've aligned myself with the most powerful person I could find."

"Who?" A.J. asked.

"Volos," Tarun said. "The dragon."

"Are you saying you're in love with me?" Darra asked, both flattered and flabbergasted - and, somewhere in the back of her mind, a little frightened. She pushed all those emotions away and tried to stay in the moment.

"Truthfully?" Volos asked, and Darra nodded. "I don't know. I've never felt the way I feel about you. I barely know you. And yet I knew from my first glimpse of you on the mountainside that you were strong, and brave - and, of course, beautiful."

"Beautiful?" she said, smiling even as a rosy blush came to her cheeks.

"Beyond words," Volos said, staring straight into her eyes. "I knew from that moment that I would never love another woman as much as I could love you, if you'd let me. Even after the outworlders' craft crippled me, all I could think of was finding you. It took a while for me to heal, but as soon as I could fly I came for you. And now I'm here, pouring my heart out to you, hoping you feel something for me, too."

"Uh, I—I just met you," Darra said, shaking her head. Volos looked crestfallen. "I mean, sure, in the dreams, there was a... pull, I guess, that led me to you." Volos seemed hopeful again. "But I'm barely allowed to date, and honestly, my dad would freak out if I was dating a dragon."

"If you asked it of me, I would take on a human form forever, and live a human life with you," Volos said. "Our children would be fully human."

"Children?" Darra asked. "Wow. That's intense. I mean,

I'm still a child myself, technically."

"Oh, no!" Volos said. "I didn't mean right away. We would wait, of course, until you were older. I'd never rush you."

"But that's sort of what you're doing now," Darra said. "You're trying to turn a... a spark into a wildfire."

"Isn't that how all wildfires start?"

"You know what I mean," Darra said. Volos sighed and looked away.

"I recently made a friend, and he warned me not to take the direct approach with you," Volos said. "I never should have used the word 'love' so soon."

"No, I'm glad you did," Darra said. "It's nice that you were so honest with me."

"So is there no chance for us, then?" Volos asked.

"I don't know what to say," Darra said. "I have plans for my life, you know? I want to be a great warrior. I'm... not even thinking about settling down. But I'd like it if we could be friends."

Volos smiled. "I'd like that, too. And on that note, I have a gift for you."

"A gift?" Darra asked. "That really isn't necessary." Volos pulled a heart-shaped locket from his pocket and held it up for Darra's inspection. "That's beautiful, really. But I can't take it. I mean, I've already stolen enough jewelry from you."

"I insist," Volos said, as he lowered the silver chain and charm into her palm. "I made it especially for you, so we could keep in touch. You just have to put it on, and no matter where you are, it will summon me."

"Thank you," Darra said, as she slipped the necklace into her own pocket. "I'm sorry I don't have anything to give you in return."

"Nonsense," Volos said. "The gift of your friendship means everything to me."

Admiral Brandt finished moving her belongings into the captain's quarters of the *Morningstar* around seven, and she had just about everything stowed away by the time the ship pulled out of the space station for the last time. She'd said her goodbyes to Andre and Clayton, and the actuary had issued an apology for not volunteering to stay behind. "It's my grandkids," he'd said. "They're growing up without me, and I won't have that. I hope it doesn't leave you short-handed."

"Don't worry about it," she'd replied. "We're fully crewed up. I actually had to turn away three-quarters of the volunteers. We'll be fine."

The *Morningstar* flew a few hundred kilometers away, so as to be clear of the wake from the faster-than-light leap the station was preparing to make, and then it idled, roughly equidistant from both the anomaly and the station. The Admiral made her way to the command deck, and once there, she found Myra and Gracie discussing the inhabitable planet nearby.

"—and so many roots, fruits and insects, it would make a monkey's paradise," Myra said. "But there was nary a primate to be found. Nor were there very many apex predators, but birds, fish and small mammals abound."

"I wonder if there's a correlation between the lack of dominant predation and the prospect of an alien presence," Gracie said. "If the planet had been terraformed by an alien species, it would make sense to exterminate the apex predators and larger life-forms that might pose physical threats to the population. And the predominance of edible species of flora and fauna would be a huge benefit to any burgeoning population there."

"You two just can't stop brainstorming, can you?" Admiral Brandt asked. "Take a moment to ponder the significance of the station leaving. For me, it means no more rec deck, which means if I want to jog, I'll have to use the treadmills in the gym."

"Mmm," Gracie grunted sympathetically. "No more taco buffets in the caf."

"On the bright side, you're the only student aboard this vessel," Myra said to Gracie. "Which frees me of virtually all my academic responsibilities."

"And opens up your time for entertaining all the wild, brilliant thoughts that pop into your head," the Admiral said. "Honestly, I was surprised you volunteered for this mission, Myra. Don't get me wrong, I'm thrilled to have you on-board. It just seems like a long-term commitment for someone as close to retiring as you are."

"About that," Myra said. "I've reconsidered my life plans. I don't think an old age of leisurely retirement is going to suit me.

Certainly not when the prospect of first contact is dangled in front of me like a diamond."

"Ah," the Admiral said. "So you're here to make history, are you?"

"You know it," Myra said. A bright light flooded the command deck.

"The station's powering up for its leap," the Admiral said. "No more chances to back out now."

"I think we're both content to be right where we are," Gracie said, and Myra nodded her agreement. All three women watched as the light intensified around the station one last time, and then suddenly, it was gone.

"Do you play chess, Myra?" Admiral Brandt asked.

"No, but I've always wanted to learn," Myra answered.

"Please, come with us, then," the Admiral said. "Gracie can teach you something for a change."

"That sounds like fun," Myra said, and the three women headed for the elevator.

A knock sounded at Trosclair's parlor door, and the prince's squire jumped up to answer it, inadvertently leaving his cards face-up on the table.

"Lady Serena," Antonin said, as he held the door wide for the young lady. She entered with a distracted smile on her face.

"Your Grace," she said, curtsying in Trosclair's direction.

"Oh, there's no need to be so formal," Trosclair said. "I'd like to think we've become friends."

"Of course we're friends," Serena said. "That's why I came to you first."

"First?" Trosclair asked. "What do you mean?"

"I have to leave the palace, tonight," Serena said. "By my father's orders. I just got word."

"That's unfortunate," Trosclair said. "You've made quite an impression in your short stay here at court, especially among the young, eligible bachelors."

"That's... interesting, but I don't have time to talk about boys right now," Serena said. "There was another part to my father's message. You should read it for yourself." Serena handed Trosclair a slip of paper, which he dutifully read out loud.

"The Commandant means to make a move against the prince," he said. "Is this true?"

"My father seems to think so," Serena said. "His messenger said that's why my father refused to call up his troops. He didn't want them used against you."

"And I'd wager Lord Fallon sent twice as many troops just so he could have a larger hand in my undoing, the ungrateful old bastard," Trosclair said. "It's all starting to make sense now. Gods, I don't even know the guard posted outside my doors right now. Do you think that's why he took Ennio away? To leave me vulnerable?"

"Probably. That's why you should come with me back to Misty Vale," Serena said. "My father is offering you sanctuary. He says his men could hold off a siege indefinitely, no matter how strong the Commandant's forces."

"I can't leave without Ennio," Trosclair said. "And besides, plenty of the palace guard are loyal to me, I'm sure of it."

"Have you left your chambers today?" Serena asked.

"Barely," Trosclair said. "Why?"

"The Commandant's called all the regular guards away for those stupid military drills," Serena said. "He's put his men in their place, I'm sure of it."

"Antonin," Trosclair said, and the boy snapped to attention. "I need you to find Milian, immediately. Tell him I need to speak to him urgently."

"Yes, Your Grace," Antonin said.

"And Antonin," Trosclair called after the boy, and he turned around to face the prince. "I don't think I need to tell you not to mention anything you just heard to anyone else. This is a solemn secret between a prince and his liege man."

"Of course, Your Grace," the squire said, beaming at having been called a man. The boy turned and left the room.

"I don't mean to sound pessimistic, but what do you expect the Lord Advisor to do against an army?" Serena asked.

"I've learned he has a certain skillset that's likely to be useful in this situation," Trosclair said. "If anyone knows how to handle the Commandant, it's Milian. And he is fiercely loyal."

"That's it," Aleksey said. "I'm through waiting."

"What're you gonna do when you find them?" A.J. asked.

"I'm going to make sure the creature stalking my daughter doesn't hypnotize her and fly off with her," Aleksey said.

"You're gonna take on a dragon?" Lilith asked. "Well, it looks like I'll be fulfilling that life debt sooner rather than later. Or, more likely, dying in the attempt."

"It is pretty insane to face a dragon without a powerful mage present to counter the dragon's magic," Kaleb said. "That's how they used to hunt them in the old days."

"And are you up to the challenge?" Aleksey asked.

"Not even close," Kaleb said. "Even if I had time to study all my spells, I'd just get us all killed."

"That's okay, Kaleb," Aleksey said. "It's good to know your own limits."

"And do you know yours, half-elf?" Lilith asked. "Taking on a dragon is a tall order, even for your kind, and the DragonSword is in pieces. The best you could hope for is a quick death."

"If you don't want to help—"

"Dad!" Darra called from several yards away. "It's okay. We're back."

"Are you okay?" Aleksey asked.

"Of course," Darra replied. "Volos was a complete gentleman."

"He's not a man at all, honey," Aleksey said, stepping between his daughter and Volos. "He's the dragon."

"I know," Darra said. "He told me everything."

"And what exactly is it that you wanted with my daughter?" Aleksey asked the dragon-man.

"I merely wanted to ask a favor," Volos said.

"Oh, right," Darra said. She walked over to her father's pack, reached into the front pocket, and pulled out the gem. She handed it over to Volos, saying, "Here you go. Sorry for stealing it in the first place."

"But that's my best chance at getting home," A.J. said.

"No, it isn't, A.J.," Tarun said. "It's your best chance at getting lost. Forever. Trust me, I know."

"So what, you're just gonna... live with a dragon, now?" A.J. asked his co-pilot. "In a cave?"

"I have a castle, actually," Volos said. "Carved right into the mountain. And I'm quite pleasant company to keep, in spite of what you may have heard about dragons. I make life very comfortable for my friends. You should come by sometime. For a visit."

"Maybe we will," Darra said.

"I'd like that," Volos said, gazing into Darra's eyes again. "We should be going now, I think, so you can get on with your journey. But don't hesitate to reach out if you should run into any more trouble along the way. I'll be there to help in an instant."

"Thanks again," Darra said. "I'll keep that in mind."

"Tarun, my friend," Volos said, holding out his hand to the pilot.

"Oh, I hate this part," Tarun said.

"It'll be over in an instant, I promise," Volos said, and Tarun took the dragon-man's hand. The two of them began to fade, as if their very molecules were disappearing one by one. "Goodbye, Darra. Until we meet again, stay safe." The two men vanished completely, as if they'd never been standing there at all.

"I can't believe Tarun actually went with him," A.J. said. "Also, did they just teleport?"

"They likely travelled far in an instant," Kalbe said. "Is that what telebort means?"

"Teleport," A.J. said. "With a 'p' as in pony."

"Aww," Darra said wistfully, as the group picked up their belongings and started moving again. "I had a pony once."

"Buttercup," Kaleb said. "I remember. Whatever happened to her?" Darra's eyes began to mist up.

"I don't really like to talk about it," the young woman said. "But the short version is, she died. And it was all my fault."

"Honey, we've been over this a million times," Aleksey said. "It was not your fault. I'm the one who let her out to pasture that night. If anyone is to blame, it's me."

"We'll just have to agree to disagree on this one, Dad," Darra said, wiping at her eyes. "Let's talk about something else."

"Okay, uh...," Aleksey said. "We haven't had a study session in a good long while. How about a pop quiz? I'll stick to the arts, history and culture. You always liked those lessons best."

"Okay, shoot," Darra said. "But ten questions, max."

"Deal," Aleksey said. "Number one: Who was the king of Vilmos who was deposed by The Faith in the eleventh century for his lecherous behavior with underage girls?"

"Ugh. Old King Hurley," Darra said.

"Good," Aleksey said. "That lesson was over a year ago. I'm glad you remembered."

"You were very descriptive about his lechery," Darra said. "It made me want to hurl. Get it? King Hurley?"

"Yes, I get it," Aleksey said. "That's a clever way of remembering it."

"It's called a mnemonic device," A.J. said. "We used them in school to memorize everything from capital cities to mathematic formulas."

"Number two," Aleksey said. "Name the three great 'B's of romanticist poetry."

"That's easy," Darra said. "Baldwin, Beckett and Burgheart. You know I have the mind of a poet, Dad. You could've asked me to recite verses from each one, and I'd have still gotten it right."

"Maybe I'll try a harder one, then," Aleksey said.

"We're here," Kaleb said. "This is the border of the Tribe's land. Our main camp is just a few more miles."

"You lead the way, Kaleb," Aleksey said, and the tribal lad moved to the front of the group. "Okay, number three: In what year did the—" Aleksey broke off his question as the wind sent dozens of competing scents his way. "Everyone arm yourselves," he said slowly, as figures began to move out of the trees all around them.

"Is it the orcs again?" A.J. asked. "Did they follow us?"

"No," Aleksey said, as the soldiers - including Ennio and Commandant Burke - came into clear view. "These are just men. Lots and lots of heavily armed men."

CHAPTER SEVEN
"AFFAIRS OF STATE"

"Do you like games of chance, half-elf?" Commandant Burke asked as a silver, lidded platter was placed on the table in front of him. The muscular soldier who carried in the platter had a large bandage on his shoulder that stuck out of the collar of his tunic. Aleksey, chained to a chair opposite the Commandant, raised his eyebrows as the man exited the room.

"I've played my fair share of them, yes," Aleksey said. "Are we to play cards to earn our supper? Because I won't eat anything with parsley in it. Too bitter, I say." The muscular soldier came back in, put down another identical platter and left again.

"Hmph," the Commandant grunted. "There's that smart mouth of yours. I understand now that you use it to try to rile up your opponent. I won't allow myself to succumb to my anger, like the first time we met. In fact, I've come to enjoy your... spunky defiance."

"Unholy hells," Aleksey said. "I was aiming for angst-ridden insubordination. I'll have to recalibrate my tone." The soldier came back in with a third platter and placed it on the table.

"Thank you, Bidzil," the Commandant said, and the muscular soldier nodded and took up a place against the wall behind Burke. "You might remember Bidzil from our last encounter."

"Of course I remember him," Aleksey said. "I never forget a lumpy face." Bidzil lowered his hands into fists and took a few steps toward the half-elf.

"Yes, well, he remembers you, too," the Commandant said, holding up a hand that stopped the big man in his tracks. "You managed to get him stabbed, and he's volunteered to demonstrate how far along his recovery has come by... convincing you to confess."

"With a buffet service for one?" Aleksey asked.

"Actually, yes," Commandant Burke said. "Although the only thing on the menu is pain, served up in every flavor. One of these platters contains an object that is hot. Another, one that is sharp. And finally, the third has an object that is blunt."

"It's a smorgasbord of torture," Aleksey said. "Yummy."

"If you cooperate, we won't have to use any of them," the Commandant continued. "Bring in the woman." Bidzil left the room again and came back a few moments later with Lilith in tow. She was shackled at her hands and feet, and she had to take tiny shuffling steps to accommodate the chains. Bidzil pushed her down into an empty chair next to Aleksey.

"This woman was found carrying a longbow with arrows of the same length and material as the one that killed the Duke," Commandant Burke said. "The fletching on her arrows was even the same: two black feathers and one red on each shaft."

"So?" Lilith said. "I bought those arrows from a craftsman here in the city. If you let me out of these chains, I'll take you to him, and he can tell you who else he's sold them to. That's where you'll find your assassin."

"Yes, yes," Burke said. "I've heard your denials. But I don't believe in coincidences so great." Burke turned back to Aleksey. "If you testify against her, I'll see to it that your life is spared. You'll be banished from this kingdom, of course, but you'll live to see another day."

"You're a terrible liar," Aleksey said. "Your face scrunches up, and those worry lines on your brow appear. It's a dead giveaway. Besides, I barely know this woman, and even I can tell she isn't capable of murder. She worships Valeska, for the sake of the heavens!"

"Alright, then," Commandant Burke said, turning back to the table with the trays on it. "Shall I pick the first platter? Or shall I let Bidzil have the honor? He's really the one with the greater grievance. Your killing of the duke actually worked out very well for me, personally. Bidzil?" The big soldier took his time looking from tray to tray before pointing to the one in the middle. Commandant Burke held his hand on the knob of the platter's lid until both Aleksey and Lilith were looking at him, and then he lifted the lid with a dramatic flourish. "Ah. Blunt it is."

"What do you think they're gonna do with us?" Kaleb asked, his face pressed up against the bars of the large cell. Darra and A.J. sat across the dimly lit room on a long bench, with three loud, laughing women and a man slumped up against the wall, snoring.

"There's only one punishment for assassinating a noble, Kay," Darra said. "They're gonna kill us."

"Oh, I know that," Kaleb said. "I just meant, how do you think they'll do it? Beheading? Public hanging?"

"I don't know," Darra said. "I'm trying not to think about it, so I can focus on finding a way out of here."

"You never give up, do you?" A.J. asked. "You keep fighting until the very end."

"If the alternative is waiting to be hacked apart or hung, I'd rather go out fighting, that's all," Darra said.

"Hey, little girl," the woman in the middle of the trio hollered. "What're you in here for? My sister says she heard the guards say you killed the Duke DuVerres."

"I didn't kill anybody," Darra said. "We're being framed."

"Oh, I see," the woman said. "My sister and my friend here, we're innocent, too."

"What did you do?" Kaleb asked.

"Nothing!" said the woman on the right.

"Just what the gods intended for men and women to do, and nothing more than that," the woman in the middle said.

"We're charged with solicitation," the woman on the left said.

"That doesn't sound like a very serious offense," Darra said. "I've known plenty of women in the profession. In some kingdoms, it's not even illegal."

"It's all because our man didn't pay the constable off this month. Drank it away, we think," the woman in the middle said.

"And yet, he's out walking free, while we're stuck in here."

"More like stumbling about free, or falling over free, knowing him," said the one on the right, and all three of the women laughed.

"I hope he lands in the sewers, headfirst," said the woman in the middle.

"It would only serve him right," the woman on the left said.

"And what's this guy in for?" A.J. asked, as the sleeping man slumped over onto the pilot's shoulder. A.J. tried to gingerly push him back upright, and the man stirred.

"G'way!" he growled, with his eyes still shut tight.

"Can't you smell it?" the woman in the middle asked. "He's drunker than the poet who just got paid, as the old song goes."

"He was fighting all the guards on his way in here," the woman on the right said. "Then once he sat down, he was out within a minute."

"He's the type of man I like for a customer," the woman on the left said. "If only they'd all fall asleep so fast, right, girls?"

"What about you, cutie?" the woman in the middle asked A.J. "Are you looking for an experience you'll never forget?"

"Mmm, yeah," said the woman on the right. "I could polish his sword all night long."

"I–I... have a girlfriend," A.J. said, blushing.

"Is that you, then, love?" the woman in the middle asked Darra, who glanced at A.J. for her cue. His eyes widened ever-so-slightly, and she decided to come to his rescue.

"Yes," Darra said, taking A.J.'s hand. "That's me. I'm his girlfriend."

"I figured as much," said the woman in the middle. "I saw the way he was looking at you. Oh, well. The good ones are always either queer or taken."

"He was looking at me, was he?" Darra asked, smiling over at A.J.

"Like Valeska herself had stolen his heart and given it to you," the woman in the middle said.

"I was not looking... like that," A.J. said.

"It's okay, love," the woman continued. "There's no shame in a man being a romantic."

"All our best customers are," the one on the left said. A

guard came in the door at the end of the corridor, pushing a cart with a large pot and several small bowls and spoons. When he reached the cell, he ladled up a bowlful of gloppy food, threw a spoon into it, and shoved it through the bars at Kaleb.

"Here," the guard said, shaking the bowl for emphasis. "I won't hold it out to you all day. You can eat off the floor for all I care." Kaleb took the bowl and backed away from the bars as the three women got up and formed a line. Even the drunk man in the corner woke and hopped up behind the women. Darra and A.J. were the last to get in line and, a few moments later, the last to be served.

"Is this supposed to be oatmeal?" Darra asked, as she let a spoonful droop and plop back down into her bowl.

"I think so," Kaleb said, sniffing his own bowl.

"They always feed us the food that's about to spoil," the woman in the middle said as she sat back down to eat. "It's not great, but it won't kill you, either."

"No," Kaleb said under his breath. "The Commandant's men will do that."

"Don't be so pessimistic, Kay," Darra said. "My dad will find a way to get us all out of here. He always finds a way."

"I hope so," Kaleb said. "But what if he doesn't?"

"Well, I've been thinking, and I have a plan," Darra said. "Half a plan, anyway."

"Okay," A.J. said. "Spill it."

"The gist is this: if we can get to our stuff, I can summon Volos," Darra said.

"Volos?" A.J. asked. "Are you sure that's a good idea?"

"He said he'd find me in an instant, no matter where I was, if I was ever in trouble," Darra said. "And there's no way a bunch of soldiers could take on a dragon."

"But your Dad said dragons are dread creatures," Kaleb argued. "That they don't have souls, like demons."

"I don't know anything about theology, or any of that," Darra said. "I just know he's been nothing but nice to me."

"Aside from the time he tried to kill us," Kaleb said.

"Yeah," Darra said. "Aside from that. So what do you say, Kaleb? Do you have a spell that will open up these locks, or something?"

"I was grounded from studying my spellbook, remember?" Kaleb said. "I've got about enough magic in me to light a pipe, and that's it. Oh, gods, why did I say pipe? Now I'm fiending. I don't want to die sober."

"Even if we got out of this cell, we don't know where they put our stuff," A.J. said. "I think we may be on our own here."

"This is all very troubling," Milian said, after Trosclair had related the entirety of Serena's message. The Lord Advisor crossed to the parlor doors and checked to make sure they were locked. "You should have taken Serena's father up on his offer of sanctuary and fled with her to Misty Vale while Commandant Burke was out of the palace."

"But, Ennio–"

"I would have sent him along, when it was safe," Milian said. "I know what he means to you."

"So what do we do now?" Trosclair asked.

"Commandant Burke has an army behind him, literally surrounding us," Milian said. "Given your popularity, many of those soldiers would stay loyal to the crown. But Burke has surely filled the palace with his most loyal men."

"My bodyguard certainly has a shifty look about him," Trosclair said.

"He's likely been placed here to watch you," Milian said. "We can't do anything to arouse his suspicion."

"What if he's been put here to do more than watch?" Trosclair asked, as he began pacing back and forth through the middle of the room. "What if he tries to assassinate me? Gods, a thought just occurred to me: Do you think Commandant Burke was behind my uncle's murder?"

"I... don't know, Your Grace," Milian lied. "But it's best to stay focused on the immediate danger in front of us."

"Of course," Trosclair agreed.

"First, I'll have my own men keep an eye on both you and your shifty bodyguard," Milian said.

"But the Commandant ordered all our regular guards out for field exercises," the prince said.

"I employ a number of men as part of a private security ensemble," the Lord Advisor said. "They'll fight for you, if it comes to it."

"Are there enough of them to get us out of the palace?" Trosclair asked.

"Not if the Commandant's men are in full force against us," Milian said. "We'll have to time everything about this just right. Possibly leave in the middle of the night."

"Tonight?" Trosclair asked.

"No," Milian answered. "The Commandant's men are all still up, celebrating their capture of the fugitives. We'll have to wait until tomorrow night."

"What am I supposed to do in the meantime?" the prince asked. "I can't just hide in here all day. The Commandant will know I'm onto him if I don't question him about the fugitives."

"That's what you'll have to do, then," Milian said. "I know you're a patron of the arts, Your Grace. How good are your acting skills?"

"I guess we'll see tomorrow," Trosclair said. "Will you be there with me? I think I'd do better with an ally in the room." Someone knocked on the parlor door, and Trosclair jumped, his head spinning toward the sound. Milian crossed to the door again and opened it to find Ennio.

"Ennio!" Trosclair cried, rushing over to him as the soldier came through the door. "Thank the gods, you're back!"

"I take it you missed me?" Ennio asked, as the prince hugged him tightly.

"Ennio, so much has happened - or it's about to, anyway," Trosclair said. "The Commandant means to make a move against me."

"Burke?" Ennio asked. "That can't be true."

"That's why he wanted to gather the troops for his brigade himself," Trosclair said. "To ensure they were loyal to him and the army first."

"Has he done or said something to make you think this?" Ennio said.

"Serena's father sent a message to warn me about him," Trosclair said. "We're leaving tomorrow night to take sanctuary in Misty Vale."

"Okay," Ennio said. "Then what?"

"Then I'll have Serena's father raise forces of our own, and we'll take down the Commandant's brigade in battle," Milian said. "If we visit every city, I guarantee we can come up with more men than the Commandant has – and that's before those loyal to the crown desert him."

"I hate to see blood spilled on my account," Trosclair said.

"I'm afraid the Commandant has forced our hands, Your Grace," Milian said. "We all want peace, but we'll never have it if that traitor manages to depose you."

"He's right, Trosc," Ennio said. "A battle may be inevitable. And I want you as far away from it as possible."

"A good king leads his soldiers onto the battlefield," Trosclair said.

"But a better one trusts to the strengths of others when the need arises," Milian said. "Ennio can lead your forces. No one will think lesser of you for it."

"You expect me to cower in safety while the man I love fights my battles for me?" Trosclair asked.

"I expect you to survive," Milian said. "By any means necessary. With you rests the entirety of my hopes for the future of the kingdom."

"I've had training with a sword," Trosclair said. "And knives."

"Yes," Ennio said. "But to be honest, you didn't show much potential. And I was going very easy on you."

"You said I had 'a certain grace' about me when we sparred," Trosclair said. "Now you're saying I'm weak?"

"No, it isn't that," Ennio said. "But you don't have a – a killer instinct inside you. You're too intellectual, and too driven by your compassion. You'd hesitate in a fight, and it would get you killed. I couldn't live with that." Trosclair sighed and looked away.

"Fine," the prince said. "But if I can't lead the troops in battle, I will lead them up to that point. I won't send Lord Parmida on my behalf; I'll travel the kingdom and raise my own forces."

"That sounds like a wise compromise, Your Grace," Milian said. "And it will likely inspire even more men to volunteer. And war, like the movements of the heavens themselves, always comes down to the numbers."

"That's enough for now, Bidzil," the Commandant said, and

the muscular man backed away from Aleksey and put his bloody cudgel back down on the middle platter. The half-elf was on his knees in the middle of the room, still chained at the hands, and his shirt had been ripped off. His right eye was swollen shut, and he had a large gash dripping blood from somewhere on his scalp onto his face, as well as large red welts and bruises on his arms and back. Commandant Burke picked up a pitcher of water and walked over to Aleksey. He overturned the pitcher just above Aleksey's head, so that one big splash soaked the half-elf, rinsing the blood from his face. "There. That's better. Now I can see your face again. I think that's important for proper communication, don't you?"

"Roast in hell," Aleksey said.

"Yes, well, I probably would someday, if such a place existed," the Commandant said. "I never claimed to be a righteous man. And if you won't testify against this woman, maybe I'll have Bidzil play the little game again on her until she confesses."

"You would torture a woman?" Aleksey asked.

"Oh, heavens, no!" Commandant Burke said, chuckling. "I haven't the stomach for it. Inevitably I picture my own daughters, and I can't go through with it. But Bidzil, he's a different sort of fellow altogether. You'd hurt a woman, wouldn't you, Bidzil?"

"I like hitting women," Bidzil said. "I like it when they scream at me. Like cats when you pull their tails."

"You'll be disappointed, then," Lilith said. "I'm not a screamer, and I don't have a tail."

"We'll see about that, in due time," the Commandant said. "For now, I'm content to let you sweat it out." Burke turned back to Aleksey. "I've heard the healing powers of half-elves are remarkable. I'll give you until tomorrow. If it's true, and you're recovered, we'll play the game again." The Commandant crossed to the door, turned back, and said, "Pleasant dreams." He exited the room, and Bidzil followed behind him. Aleksey flinched at the twisting of the lock from the other side of the door and then collapsed face-first onto the wet, bloody floor.

"Half-elf," Lilith said, as she got down onto her knees on the floor beside him. "Are you okay?"

"Just need a – a minute," Aleksey said, turning his head to look up at her.

"He could've killed you," Lilith said.

"No, he couldn't have," Aleksey said. "Not with a cudgel, anyway. My bones are hard as steel. It's one of the reasons half-elves are so strong."

"You still bleed like everybody else, though," Lilith said. The assassin pulled on her sleeve until it ripped and then peeled the scrap of cloth from her arm. She found the gash on Aleksey's head and gingerly pressed the cloth to it.

"Are you my nurse now?" Aleksey asked.

"Is that question really a complaint?" Lilith asked.

"It's just... not the role you usually play in our little group," Aleksey said. "Caretaker."

"Fully half of my work as a True Believer of Rebos is devoted to saving lives," she said. "I've worked in hospitals, I've fed the poor – I even worked as a bodyguard for a while. Part of respecting death is knowing how and when it can be prevented and working toward that."

"So you could give up murdering, then?" Aleksey asked. "And still honor your vows?"

"It doesn't quite work like that," Lilith said. "As a True Believer, I deliver death when and how I'm called to by my god. And my god is just. I've only ever been tasked to kill very evil people. Men, mostly."

"What about my daughter and me?" Aleksey asked.

"Rebos saw to it that I failed at that task," Lilith said.

"And the Duke DuVerres?" Aleksey asked. "Was he an evil man?"

"I was told he was an unrepentant serial murderer of young women," Lilith said.

"Oh," Aleksey said. "That – that is evil. But still, you didn't have to take it on yourself to be the one to kill him. Have you ever heard of the Pentonese concept of karma?" Lilith nodded. "I believe something bad would have happened to the Duke to stop his murders anyway, and then you wouldn't carry the karmic burden of killing another sentient being, like you almost did with that orc."

"That was the heat of battle," Lilith said. "I didn't want the pig-man to die, but more than that, I was going to live. And besides, I happen to believe I've been acting as an agent of karma, of sorts, delivering much-needed justice when social systems fail."

"An 'agent of karma,' huh? That's a very strange way of

saying you murder bad people," Aleksey said. "I think you're deflecting."

"Half-elf, you are absolutely exhausting," Lilith said. "But you also protected my life, again, at the cost of your own well-being. Thank you." She leaned down and kissed Aleksey on his left cheek, careful of the bruising on his right.

"If you wanted to show your gratitude, you could stop calling me 'half-elf' and start using my name," he said.

"I'll consider it," the assassin said.

"Where do you think they took your dad and Lilith?" A.J. asked Darra in a whisper. The three women and Kaleb had stretched out on the hard floor to sleep, and the pilot didn't want to disturb them.

"They've got to be questioning them somewhere nearby," Darra whispered back. A.J. leaned out toward the cell bars and spied the guard asleep in his chair at the end of the wide corridor.

"Looks like the guard's out for the night," A.J. said. "We should test the door." The pilot got up and leaned into the bars on the cell door, pushing slowly but firmly. The metal creaked, and he glanced back up at the guard, but the man didn't stir. "It does have some give to it, but I doubt I'd be able to break it down by myself. Maybe if Kaleb and you helped..."

"Hmm-mm," Darra grunted. "Better to wait until someone opens the door, then rush them all at once, before they can draw their weapon."

"But we don't know when they'll open the doors next," A.J. said.

"Those ladies said they were getting out in the morning," Darra said. "They'll have to open it up for them."

"Okay," A.J. said. "I guess that means we should get some rest, so we're ready in the morning."

"The thought of putting my body down on this cell floor is grossing me out," Darra said. "And I've gone weeks in the forest without a proper bath before."

"Well, here," A.J. said, as he slid off the bench and stretched out on the floor in front of it. "You can have the bench."

"Thanks," Darra said, lifting her feet onto the bench and reclining onto an elbow to look down at the pilot. "This is... slightly better."

"It's the least I could do, after you saved me from those women," A.J. said, smirking. "So thank you."

"It was nothing," Darra said. A few silent moments passed, and Darra repositioned herself onto her back to stare up at the dingy grey ceiling.

"They were right, you know," A.J. said.

"About what?" Darra asked.

"I was looking at you," the pilot said. "Like that."

"Oh," Darra said, turning her head to face him. "Well, it's only natural to have some... lingering feelings. Sometimes I look at you like that, too."

"But they're not lingering feelings," A.J. said. "They're current ones."

"What are you saying?" Darra asked.

"I think I messed up," A.J. said. "When that succubus messed with our emotions, I thought we should cool things off. But I never meant to break things off with you completely."

"You didn't?" Darra asked.

"And then, seeing you walk arm-in-arm into the sunset with Volos, I got... jealous, I guess. I know, it's stupid – he's a dragon, for Pete's sake."

"Who's Pete?" Darra asked.

"It's an expression," A.J. said. "But I was just being stupid, right? I mean, there's nothing between you and Volos... is there?"

"No," Darra said, a little too emphatically for A.J. to fully believe her. "I mean, he did... say he loved me."

"I knew it!" A.J. said in a louder voice. "I knew from the way he tried to get you alone that he had an ulterior motive."

"Shh!" Darra admonished him. "You'll wake the others. Besides, you have nothing to worry about. It takes two to make a romance, and I'm not interested in Volos in that way."

"Really?" A.J. asked.

"Really," Darra said. "Now stop talking to me so I can get some sleep."

"Okay," A.J. said. "Sorry." A few more silent moments passed, and then Darra rolled onto her side to face the pilot. She reached out her hand and placed it on his chest, over his heart.

"A.J.," she said. "I'm glad you said something. About... how you feel."

"Do you think we could try and start over, then?" A.J. asked.

"I'd like that," Darra said. "Goodnight."

"Goodnight," A.J. echoed back, as he lifted her hand to his lips and gave it a gentle kiss.

The teens - as well as the women on the floor and the drunk in the corner - awoke the next morning to the sound of the cell door unlocking and swinging wide open. "Alright, ladies," the first of three guards said from the corridor. "Time to go home." The women hurried to get up off the floor and then took turns straightening each other's hair and dresses. One of them had slipped off her shoes to sleep, and she rushed to sling them back on one foot at a time as she held herself up against the wall.

"You too," the guard said to the man in the corner. "Unless you still feel like taking a swing at me?" The man pushed himself off the bench and stood up.

"No, sir," he said in a meek voice. He wobbled just a little, and then he shuffled into line behind the first two women.

"Hurry up, Patricia," said one of the women.

"I'm coming, I'm coming," Patricia said, as she finished hooking her second foot into its shoe. She followed her companions out of the cell as she waved goodbye to the teens, who were still rousing themselves from their slumber. "Good luck, loves." The former prisoners followed the guards down the corridor, through the door, and out of sight.

Darra sat up on the bench, an irritated look on her face. "So much for rushing the door," she said, looking down at A.J. "Why didn't you wake me, Mr. I'm Up With The Sun Every Morning?"

"I would have," A.J. said. "But there's no sun down here."

"Sure there is," Kaleb said through a yawn, as he stood up. He pointed out of the bars and down the corridor, where a tiny window situated at the very top of the wall looked out on the palace lawn from just above ground-level. "Well, maybe not right now," Kaleb said, as he took in the blackness of the world outside the window. "I think it's still early."

"Well, what do you propose we do now that our window of opportunity has closed?" Darra asked.

"I'm not sure," A.J. said. "Maybe when they bring us

breakfast we can... figure something out."

The prince took his breakfast in his parlor with Ennio, who had spent the night, in spite of technically being off-duty. The soldier was supposed to resume his military exercises today, but he'd refused to leave Trosclair's side for even a moment. After breakfast, Trosclair had a very brief study session with Mr. Summers. It was brief both because no other young members of the court were in attendance, and because the teacher recognized that Trosclair's attentions were elsewhere this morning. "I'll stop boring you now, Your Grace," the older man said, after concluding a short lecture on daily life in the early days of the kingdom.

"It's not you, Mr. Summers," Trosclair said. "I'm not feeling well today, that's all."

"Oh?" the older man asked. "Would you like me to call the court physician?"

"No, thank you," Trosclair said. "It's just a headache. I'll have some strong tea, and it'll likely get better on its own."

"Okay, then," Mr. Summers said, rising with the notebook he lectured from clutched in one hand. He bowed to the prince, crossed to the door, and exited. Ennio crossed to Trosclair and sat down on the couch next to him.

"I know you're worried about everything that's happening," Ennio said. "But you can't look this distraught in front of the Commandant, or he'll know something's going on." Trosclair raised his hand above his frowning face and then swiped it down, his expression changing with the motion. Now he wore a slight, tight smile that he hoped was unreadable.

"Is this better?" the prince asked in a sunny tone.

"Much," Ennio said. "We can't put it off any longer. Are you ready to face him?"

"As ready as I'm going to be," Trosclair said. "You know, I was thinking, Ennio - maybe when we get to Misty Vale, we could resume our training? I know you think I'm hopeless with a weapon—"

"I didn't say hopeless," Ennio interjected.

"—but I should keep trying," Trosclair finished. "If nothing else, it will boost morale for the troops to see a sword in my hand."

"I'll keep teaching you, if that's what you really want," Ennio said. "But you were better with knives. And if you show your training half the dedication you give to your schooling, I'm sure you can improve. But that doesn't mean I'll change my mind about you fighting."

"I understand. Okay," Trosclair said, as Ennio put his hand on the parlor door. "Let's do this." Ennio opened the parlor door, and Trosclair turned his face up ever-so-slightly in the perfect imitation of a haughty prince.

"Your Grace," the soldier posted outside his chambers said with a bow. Trosclair nodded to acknowledge the man, and the soldier followed behind the prince and Ennio as they strode down the hallway. "May I ask where we're headed?"

"To see the Commandant," Trosclair replied.

"Then we're going the wrong way," the soldier said. "He's not in his chambers. Last I saw, he was headed out to the barracks."

"Thank you," Trosclair said, and the soldier led them in the opposite direction, toward the back of the palace. They exited through the main ballroom onto the back steps, then descended and passed in front of the fountain. The barracks were on the other side of the hedge maze, but before they could enter it, Commandant Burke and Milian exited in front of them. About a dozen men followed behind them, half in soldiers' uniforms and half in plain clothes.

"Ah, Your Grace," Milian said. "We were just discussing what to do with the fugitives."

"That's just what I've come to ask the Commandant about myself," Trosclair said. "I take it you've questioned them?"

"The man and the woman, yes," Burke said. "It hasn't gotten us a confession or a testimony, but I'm confident our efforts will be rewarded in time."

"How did you find them, anyway?" Trosclair asked.

"Simple," the Commandant said. "I knew they had an accomplice in that Tribal witch they freed. So I had my men watch the borders of the Tribe's lands, and the fugitives wandered right into the trap."

"Well done," Trosclair said. "Very well done."

"Thank you, Your Grace," the Commandant said.

"I was saying to the Commandant that a public hanging seemed most appropriate," Milian said. "To make an example out of them."

"But I'd prefer to use them as target practice for our new troops," the Commandant said. "Nothing like a moving target, and one that can fight back, to train an archery."

"You are nothing if not practical, Commandant," Trosclair said, and Burke's already thin lips stretched into an evil smile.

"Yes, I agree," the Commandant said. "And so, when the Lord Advisor told me of your plan to flee to Misty Vale in the dead of the night, I knew I needed to secure you right away."

"What?" Trosclair asked, as all the color drained from his face. "Milian?" Ennio drew his sword as the men in the background formed a half-circle around the prince and himself.

"I'm sorry, Your Grace," Milian said. "I truly am. But after hearing Commandant Burke's plans, I've had a change of heart."

"You traitor!" Ennio spat. "I'll kill you myself!"

"Come now, Ennio," Milian said, as he signaled for his men to move forward. "There's no need for this to get bloody."

"Ennio, put down your sword," Trosclair said. "They'll kill you if you don't." Ennio hesitated but ultimately obeyed, throwing his weapon down onto the ground, and two of Milian's men grabbed the soldier by the arms and led him toward the steps that led down to the dungeon. Another pushed Trosclair along from behind with the handle of his knife on his back.

"They say Rebos rewards those who betray their kings with especially horrible deaths," Trosclair said as he passed Milian.

"Yes, well," the Lord Advisor said, looking away. "You're not a king yet, now are you, Your Grace?"

"Guard!" A.J. called out, and the soldier at the end of the corridor rolled his eyes and sighed.

"Yeah?" he yelled back. "What is it?"

"It's my friend," the pilot said. "She's sick. She needs medical attention." The guard got up and walked down to the cell. He saw Darra stretched out on the bench, face down and softly moaning, while A.J. and Kaleb stood on opposite sides of the cell door. The man tilted his head and gave A.J. a disbelieving look.

"Gods," the guard said with sarcastic gravity lilting his voice. "Whatever shall I do with a sick prisoner? Maybe I should open up this cell door and see for myself that she's really sick. Is that the thick of it, lad?"

"I–"

"You're not the first prisoners who've tried to fake an illness to gain my sympathy," the guard said. "Now sit back down and keep quiet, or you won't get your lunch."

"But she really is sick," Kaleb said. "She could die."

"And that would be a shame, wouldn't it?" the guard asked. "To die before she can be executed." The guard shook his head and started back toward his chair, and the door at the end of the corridor flew open. Ennio and Trosclair entered first, followed by the Lord Advisor's hired men and a few soldiers.

"By Arol's bright and shiny beard!" the guard said. "Is that the prince?" One of the soldiers moved to the front of the group and held out his hand expectantly. Darra sat up and brushed the hair out of her face to see what was happening.

"The key to the cell," he said. "Give it to me, soldier."

"Y-yes, sir!" the guard said, fishing the key out of his pocket. He handed it to the other soldier and stepped back as the man unlocked the cell door. A.J. looked to Kaleb, but the mage subtly shook his head in the negative.

"Too many," the tribal lad whispered, as both teens backed up to make room for Trosclair and Ennio, who were pushed unceremoniously into the cell. The soldier then locked the cell door behind them and gave the key back to the guard.

"They're not to be let out for any reason," the soldier told the guard. "By direct order of the Commandant."

"But... what's the reason they're in there?" the guard asked. "What did they do?"

"The Commandant say these two helped plot the murder of the Duke DuVerres," the soldier said. "Apparently, the Duke found out they were queer, and they murdered him to keep their perverted secret."

"That's a lie!" Trosclair said. "Nothing the Commandant says can be trusted. He's a power-mad traitor and nothing more."

"Better than being a queer," the soldier said, before turning and walking away with his companions in tow. One of them made some sort of gesture that had the others laughing as they exited the corridor.

"Are you really a – a prince?" Kaleb asked, as he backed

away timidly.

"We are the prince, yes," Trosclair said, holding his head high. "Who are you?"

"Me?" Kaleb squeaked. "I'm nobody."

"That's not true, Kay," Darra said. The prince turned to face her, and recognition washed over his features as she spoke. "His name is Kaleb."

"Kaleb what?" Ennio asked. "What's your family name?"

"I–I don't have a last name," Kaleb said. "I'm of the Tribe."

"I know you," Trosclair said to Darra. "You're the girl who made a fool out of me pretending to be Eliza Dell. I realized almost immediately after you left that she's decades older than you."

"Yeah, about that," Darra said. "I never meant to - make a fool out of you. We just had to get out of the city."

"Because you killed my uncle?" Trosclair asked.

"No!" Darra said. "We had nothing to do with that."

"I heard the woman you were travelling with had arrows matching the one that killed him," Trosclair said. "Please don't insult my intelligence by telling me that's just a coincidence."

"I didn't kill your uncle," Darra said. "I didn't plan it or help in any way. I swear it!"

"Yes, well, the word of a murderer doesn't count for much, now does it?" the prince asked. Darra rolled her eyes.

"Fine," she said. "Don't believe me. I could care less what some snooty prince thinks."

"You'd better mind your tongue, girl," Ennio said. "People don't speak to royalty that way."

"Oh, yeah?" Darra asked. "What are you gonna do about it? Throw me in the dungeon?"

"There are other means to silencing someone," Ennio said.

"Was that a threat?" A.J. asked, drawing a step closer to the soldier.

"If it needs to be," Ennio said, puffing up his own chest to match the pilot's posture.

"Ennio, please, calm down," Trosclair said. "There's no need to threaten anyone over this girl's lack of manners."

"This girl has a name. I'm Darra."

"And are you also of the Tribe, Darra?" Trosclair asked.

"No," Darra answered.

"Where are you from, then?" the prince asked.

"My dad and I move around a lot," Darra said. "I'm not really from anywhere."

"And you?" Trosclair asked A.J., as he took a seat at the end of the bench. Ennio moved to stand next to him. "What's your name, and where do you hail from?"

"I'm A.J.," the pilot said. "And I'm... not from around here."

"Okay then," Trosclair said. "Kaleb, Darra, and A.J. I am Trosclair, and this is my – this is Ennio. And it appears we all have something in common."

"Something besides being stuck in this cell together?" Darra asked.

"Yes," Trosclair said. "We all also want to find a way out of here, am I right?" Darra shrugged and nodded. "Then I suggest we stop squabbling and work together."

Lilith watched out the tiny window at the top of the room as heavy rain splashed down onto the puddle-covered lawn. From her viewpoint, Lilith had a perfect angle on the way each raindrop sent the water in the puddles up into the air, only to plash back down in a pattern that made concentric circles on the surface. She stared at the ground, but she'd moved to the windows to get a view of the skies. And when the clouds cleared in the right patch of afternoon sky, she caught a glimpse of the Reaper Moon. She couldn't see her patron moon in full, but a large section of it was visible, and that was all her prayer required. "Rebos, hear my plea," she began, and Aleksey perked up in his chair.

"Okay, now, here we go," Aleksey said. "What exactly are you up to?" Lilith ignored him and kept her eyes on the heavens.

"Grant me strength which no man may possess," she said. Her eyes dilated, and she turned away from the window and looked down at the shackles on her wrists. She pulled her arms apart, and to both her own and Aleksey's delight, the links on the shackles began to bend. Lilith grunted long and deep, and one of the links gave way to the impossible strength with which her god had imbued her. Her arms flew open wide, and she smiled triumphantly at Aleksey. "What do you think of my god now, half– Aleksey?"

"How long will it last?" Aleksey asked, as Lilith crouched

down and began pulling on the shackles around her ankles.

"As long as Rebos shines down on me," Lilith said. "So if you want me to break you out of your chains, you're going to have to come over here into the light. And I'd hurry. Those clouds are moving fast."

Aleksey obeyed, and within a few moments, Lilith had broken the shackles around her ankles and started to work on the lock on Aleksey's chains. "I can't quite get a grip on it," she said, after several attempts to pull the lock open with the two fingers that would fit inside the hasp.

"What about the chain itself?" Aleksey asked. "Can you pull it apart?"

"It's three times as thick as the manacles I just broke out of," Lilith said. "Even god-given strength has its limits." The clouds finished shifting over the last bit of the Reaper Moon, and Lilith's pupils returned to their normal size. "I'm sorry. The Reaper is gone."

"Can you say your prayer again, when the clouds clear?"

"That prayer can only be answered once per lunar cycle."

"Damn it!" Aleksey said. "Well, at least you got yourself free."

"I'm hardly free yet," Lilith said. "Although now I will be able to put up a fight when they come back, at least."

"I can still help you," Aleksey said. "If I can get a sword in my hands, I'll just swing it two-handed." Lilith crossed to the table, where the platters were still spread out. She picked up the cudgel and tested its weight. Next, she lifted the lid on the platter on the right - and smiled.

"There's no sword," she said over her shoulder, before she spun to face Aleksey with a weapon in each hand. "But you can have your pick: Cudgel or dagger."

"Dagger," Aleksey said. "I try never to use a weapon that has my own blood on it."

"Sound policy," Lilith said. She crossed to the half-elf and handed him the knife. "So now, we wait." Lilith took a seat in the chair next to Aleksey's, facing the door, and she crossed her legs and rested the cudgel across her lap. "You spoke of karma before," Lilith said. "Are you Pentonese?"

"My father was," Aleksey said. "I was raised in the Elven

Isles. I didn't move to the continent until I was what you'd consider a teenager."

"I'd like to travel there, someday," Lilith said. "I hear the elves welcome human tourists with open arms."

"That they do," Aleksey said. "Although the price of accommodations is outrageous, especially in the capital city, which is where all the sights are. So what they're really welcoming is your gold."

"I've heard nothing but good things about elven society," Lilith said.

"Oh, their society has plenty of social ills, believe me," Aleksey said. "Crime and poverty, for example - elves are just too proud to talk about that sort of stuff."

"So you get your pride from your elven side, then," Lilith said.

"My pride?" Aleksey asked. "Hmph. I take pride in having almost none."

"And yet you wear the latest designs, so as not to seem your real age," Lilith said.

"Fashion is an underappreciated art," Aleksey said. "Besides, you dress younger than your real age, too. We'd stick out like a giant in the tub if we didn't."

"What do you think it says about us, that we put so much effort into looking like something we're not?" Lilith asked.

"I'd say it makes us like just about everyone else in the world," Aleksey said. "Everyone wears a mask of some kind, at some point in their lives. It's necessary. You and I are just - surviving in style."

"I guess we're more alike than one would first suspect," Lilith said. "We're both warriors, older than we look, and stronger, too. Your bruises are barely visible today. I had no idea half-elves healed so fast."

"My father always said it was because half-elves possessed more chi than other creatures," Aleksey said.

"And is it true, what they say about a half-elf's other... remarkable feature?" Lilith asked, a playful smile on her lips.

"Lilith!" Aleksey said, as if she had caused him some offense. "Are you referring to that vulgar rumor about the anatomy of my kind?"

"You're the first of your kind I've ever met," she said, and Aleksey couldn't tell if she was blushing from the topic or just flushed with heat from the stuffy room. If she was blushing, she certainly wasn't shying away from the half-elf. In fact, she was leaning in seductively. "It's natural for a woman to be curious."

"Well, I find that kind of filthy gutter talk utterly reprehensible," Aleksey said, as he let the dagger fall to the floor. He brought his face slowly toward hers, and they kissed. Lilith threw her hands around his shoulders. After several seconds of passionate awareness of only each other, they broke apart.

"Are we really gonna do this?" Aleksey asked in a breathy timbre. "Right now?"

"I'm up for it if you are," Lilith said, as she removed her shirt over her head. "Besides, you'll hear anyone coming before they get here, right?"

"In theory," Aleksey said, taking in the sight of her breasts in her black bra. "If I hear anything at all. I tend to become consumed with the task at hand." Lilith stood, straddled his legs, and then sat down on his lap. She leaned forward and kissed him again.

"That's a good thing," she said, pulling back slightly to give his hands access to her chest.

"Sorry about the chains," he said.

"That's okay," she replied, as she fumbled with his belt. "I like to be in control anyway."

"Sounds about right," he said.

Commandant Burke reassembled the pieces of the DragonSword on a long table in a conference room. His men sat around the table, and one of them began copying the scribbles in the old speech on the fragments of the blade. Milian stood near a window, his hands clasped behind his back, looking out at the afternoon sun as the Giant's Moon began to eclipse it, casting its dark shadow over the city. "This sword was supposed to be indestructible, according to legend," the Commandant said. "I wonder what possible force could have shattered it?"

"Will you still be able to find your way to the treasure?" Milian asked.

"I've got my best man working on it," the Commandant said, and the man copying from the sword beamed. "And all the pieces are there. The half-elf was kind enough to bring it all back to me. We should be able to follow the directions, if the translators get all the phrasings correct."

"I can lend one or two of my men to the task," Milian offered. "I have some scholars on the payroll. I just hope the treasure it leads to is enough to compensate for all the time and energy we've put into this project."

"Getting the gold was only one of the Duke's objectives for the sword," Burke said.

"What else did he plan for it?" Milian asked.

"He never revealed the entirety of the plan, but it involved a witch from Middlestead," the Commandant said. "And it would not have ended well for the prince."

"The boy really has been in a precarious position his entire life," Milian said.

"Yes," Burke said. "And he's far too weak - of will and body - to be a proper king. What kind of liegeman would bow down before a poncy little queer like that?" Milian shook his head and shrugged. "I think I'll have the metallurgists take a look at the sword, to determine if it can be re-forged. And if so, I might seek out that witch from the Free City."

"What for?" Milian asked.

"I've always wanted to go on a dragon hunt," the Commandant said. "And killing a dragon would demonstrate to my men - and to all the people of DuVerres - that I was meant to lead them." An urgent knock sounded through the door before it swung wide open. An anxious-looking soldier entered.

"Have you no manners?" Burke asked. "This is a private meeting."

"I'm sorry, Commandant," the man said. "But there's something going on in the city."

"Yes?" Burke prompted. "What is it?"

"It seems word has gotten around that you've locked up the prince," the soldier said. "It's the people, sir - they've taken to the streets. Some of them are rioting. We've had reports of vandalism, fires, thieving—"

"Call the city constabulary, then," the Commandant said. "That's what they're there for."

"It's just that—many of the rioters are constables, sir," the soldier said. "They're just as angry as the rest of the citizenry."

"Gods damn it!" the Commandant cursed. "Fine. I'll handle it myself."

"I knew there would be blowback from the people," Milian said. "I just didn't expect it to happen so fast."

The Commandant moved to the head of the table and addressed his men. "Gather your battalions," he ordered. "We'll divide the city into six sections, one for each of you. I want patrols along every major street."

"Yes, sir," said one of the men, and they all raised their fists to their hearts. They started for the door, but it swung open again, this time with no warning knock at all.

Another breathless soldier practically shouted, "Sir! The barracks – they're on fire!"

Out in the city streets, the people roamed about, looking for an outlet for their collective rage. They'd grown up or grown old with one person at the center of all their hopes and dreams, efforts and endeavors, and they were not about to sit idly by while he was deposed. Most of the people travelled in small groups of ten or fifteen, but at the busiest intersections, these numbers swelled into the hundreds. Some marched with burning white candles held high that represented their loyalty to the crown. Others carried swords and spears, and there were more than a few improvised weapons, from pitchforks to kitchen knives.

Several military posts were scattered around the city, practically overflowing with the extra soldiers Burke had brought in, and these were the focus of much of the rioters' attentions. At one such outpost, they crowded around the building and yelled profanities at the soldiers huddled inside, daring the men to come out and face them. One group of teens picked up a trash can from the sidewalk and hurled it through the building's bay windows, sending shards of glass and splinters of wood raining down, and still the men inside did not move to come out. "Cowards!" yelled one of the teens through the broken window. "My prince is no murderer!"

"He's innocent!" yelled another, practically on the verge of tears. Her friend rubbed her back supportively. "We'll kill you all if he's harmed!"

Inside the building, the men debated whether or not to go

outside and try to disperse the rioters. Some of the soldiers wanted to seek out their commanding officers at the palace for orders. Others wanted to go to the prince's aid, or to flee the city and abandon the army altogether out of disgust for what they viewed as an institutional act of treason.

"I'd rather die by my own sword than follow a queer!" one of the men said.

"There's no proof of that," said another.

"I'll take the Commandant's word for it," said the first man.

"My sister likes women," said one of the soldiers. "I don't give a pair of shits if he's queer or not. He's my prince, damn it! And yours too!"

"There hasn't been anyone but a DuVerres to lead this kingdom for over three hundred years," said an older soldier with a graying beard. "And after the Duke, I was ready for a change. I'd hoped the young prince would be better, but if it's not in Fela's plan for him..."

"Fela can kiss my hairy little ones goodnight!" one of the men near the back wall said, and several men laughed, while others took offense.

"Ought not to talk about the gods that way," the older soldier warned. "It brings their wrath."

"Shut up, old man!" said one of the younger soldiers. "Nobody cares about your stupid gods – or your queer prince!" A loud thump sounded at the front door as the crowd outside battered it with something heavy.

"They're getting in!" one of the men yelled, and the others scrambled to flee or find a weapon.

Outside the palace gates, the crowd was even thicker. The sea of candles was interspersed with those who had come looking for a fight, and they were packed twenty deep against the entire perimeter of the palace, with hundreds lined up along the street that led to the arching golden gates. The Commandant himself had only a few hundred men marching behind him as he rode his horse across the palace lawn toward the gates. The rest were all occupied with putting out the fire in the barracks. He knew if he could get to the other outposts and collect his men, his coalesced forces would be strong enough to fight back this little rebellion; but to do that, he had to first pass through the angry crowd in front of him. "Archers, to the front!" he called, and several dozen men jogged up to form a line in front of the Commandant. "Kill anyone who comes near me," he ordered, and the men all saluted their understanding.

Commandant Burke raised his hand to the gatekeeper, and the man nodded and pulled a lever, unlocking the gate. It opened from the force of the crowd pushing against it, but the rioters were wary to go inside the palace grounds, with so many arrows nocked and pointed right at them. The crowd shuffled back as the archers slowly made their way forward, clearing a path down the street that the Commandant and the troops behind him followed. The crowd on either side of the street booed and hissed as Burke passed. Some cursed at him, while others simply yelled the prince's name as a rallying cry. One teen picked up a rock and threw it at the Commandant. It sailed past him harmlessly, but he still flinched and almost lost his seat in the saddle. "Faster!" he yelled, and his men obeyed, the pace of their march increasing to double-time. Soon they were out of the thick of the rioters. Commandant Burke looked back at the gates, which had been closed and locked behind the last of his men, and signaled to one of his Colonels. The man marched over to the Commandant. "Leave a few dozen men to guard the gates."

"Yes, sir!" the man said, saluting. He ran to the back of the line of soldiers and rounded up about thirty men. He told them the job they'd been chosen for, and they drew their swords and formed a single line in front of the gates. The Commandant and his men continued down the road, and the crowd swarmed back together in their wake.

When the last of the soldiers marched out of sight, someone in the crowd yelled, "For the prince!" Many members of the crowd echoed back the call. Suddenly, throughout the crowd, people began pulling out and donning black masks. These masked men and women moved through the crowd toward the gates, until over two hundred of them were all lined up facing the soldiers. Although their identities were concealed, most of the people wore finely tailored clothing that revealed them to be people of means, perhaps even nobles. They were all armed.

"Gods," one of the soldiers said, as he backed away from the ominous rioters. "Who are they?"

"Stand your ground!" barked another soldier, and the first raised his sword again obediently.

"We don't want to hurt you!" yelled one of the masked women. "Lay down your blades!" Several soldiers moved to do just that as the crowd of masked rioters lurched forward at them. Those soldiers who surrendered were spared, but the others were outnumbered seven to one, so they never really stood a chance. The rioters surrounded the soldiers, who had no way of retreating because of the position they'd taken against the gates.

"Yield!" yelled one of the soldiers, throwing down his sword. "I yield!" One by one, his companions followed suit. A young woman began gathering all the soldiers' swords and redistributing them throughout the crowd, who lifted them high and cheered their victory. As soon as the soldiers were out of the way, a man moved forward from the back of the masked group. He withdrew a roll of fabric which, when unrolled, revealed an array of locksmith's tools, and he immediately went to work on the gate.

Aleksey and Lilith were on the cement floor, lying on their sides facing one another. "Well, that was... fun," Lilith said.

"Thank you," Aleksey said.

"And educational," Lilith said, smiling. Aleksey cocked his head and lifted a curious eyebrow. "Now I know the rumors are true."

"Well, you won't know for sure until you bed another half-elf," Aleksey said. "It could be I'm just favored by Fela, as you suggested."

"Oh, that's for certain," Lilith said. Something caught Aleksey's attention, and he perked up an ear.

"What is it?" Lilith asked, as she sat up and reached for her clothes with one hand and the cudgel with her other. "Is Burke coming back?"

"No," Aleksey said, standing and crossing to the window. "It's out there. Something's happening. I heard men and women shouting."

"If Burke's men are distracted, this could be our moment," Lilith said, as she pulled on her pants. "What do you think our chances of breaking down this door are?" She picked up her shirt and slipped her arms into it, then began buttoning it up.

"If we both throw our weight against it, it should give eventually," Aleksey said, crossing to the door and examining its metal frame. "The noise will probably bring someone to investigate, though."

"And they'll have to open the door, expecting me to be bound and you to still be recovering. It's a plan. But Aleksey?"

"Yes?"

"You should probably have some clothes on for this," Lilith said. "Unless your plan is to distract them. Or seduce them." Aleksey nodded and moved to pick up his undershorts with his chained hands.

"Sir!" Trosclair called to the guard, and the man stood and slowly approached the cell door.

"Yes, Your Grace?" the man asked.

"Sir, I saw the way those other soldiers forced you into locking us in here," Trosclair said.

"I–"

"And I can tell from your politeness that you have some lingering loyalty to the crown," the prince continued. "If you were to let us all out of here, I'd see to it that you were honored throughout the kingdom. You'd be a hero."

"But the Commandant would kill me," the guard said, genuine torment showing on his face. "I'm sorry, Your Grace."

"And of course, there'd be payment," Darra chimed in, jumping up off the bench. "Right, Trosclair?"

"Oh. Right!" Trosclair said. "Of course, there'd be payment. Name your price."

"Dead men can't spend any credits, Your Grace," the man said.

"Are you married, or do you have children?" Trosclair asked.

"No," the guard said.

"Then you could come with us," Trosclair said. "To somewhere the Commandant can't reach you at. I give you my solemn vow that you'd be protected as if you were royalty yourself." The man thought about it for several seconds, and then said, "I'll get my keys." He turned and started toward his chair. The teens inside the cell brightened in unison, and Trosclair smiled over at Darra.

"Thank you, for reminding me of the power of gold to move men's hearts," Trosclair said.

"No problem," Darra replied. "Thank you for including us in your escape." The guard came back with the key, but before he could unlock the cell, the door at the end of the corridor opened. In strode about a dozen people in fine clothes and black masks.

"We've found them!" one of the masked men yelled. "You!" he yelled at the guard, shaking his pitchfork threateningly. "Open it up."

"Now, just stay calm, now," the guard said, as his shaky hand moved the key toward the door. "I was just about to, I swear. There's no need to harm me."

"He's telling the truth," Trosclair said. The guard opened the cell door, and the teens filed out.

"Who are these people?" A.J. asked.

"It's the Alliance," Trosclair said. "Aren't you?" The man with the pitchfork lowered his mask, and Mr. Martine's face came into view.

"Quite right, Your Grace," Mr. Martine said. "When we heard about your... predicament, we assembled immediately and came up with a plan." Next to him, a woman with a cooking skillet removed her mask, and Trosclair cried, "Mrs. Applebaum?" The old woman hugged the young prince.

"You didn't think I was going to let them hurt my boy, now, did you?" she asked.

"I should've known better," Trosclair said.

"We should probably hurry, Your Grace," Mr. Martine said. "There's no telling how long the Commandant's forces will be gone."

"But they're holding my dad and our friend somewhere else," Darra said.

"By Valeska's own breath," Mrs. Applebaum said as she looked Darra up and down. "Who are you?"

"This is Darra," Trosclair said. "She's a – a friend."

"I wouldn't worry about your dad," Mr. Martine said. "We split into groups so we could search the entire palace at once. Wherever he is, they'll find him." The group of masked women and men led the teens out of the corridor.

Aleksey and Lilith stood side by side in front of the door. "Ready?" Aleksey asked, and the assassin nodded. "On three. One... two... three!" They both slammed against the door with their shoulders, and it creaked in response. "Again!" They rammed into it a second time, and it seemed to give a little more. Lilith prepared to slam into it a third time, but Aleksey held up his hand to stop her. "Wait," he said, putting his ear to the door. "Someone's coming." Lilith snatched their weapons from the table and handed Aleksey his dagger. They took up positions on opposite sides of the door as they heard the key turning in the lock. The door opened, and they both leapt back in front of the door, weapons drawn, only to find a half dozen men and women in masks.

"Aleksey?" asked one of the women in a thick accent that he immediately recognized. Eliza took off her mask and rushed in to hug the half-elf. She drew back and placed a kiss directly on his lips, and Aleksey couldn't help but kiss her back. When it was over, he glanced at Lilith, who looked away.

"How did you know I was in here?" Aleksey asked.

"I didn't," Eliza replied. "We were looking for the prince."

"The prince?" Aleksey asked. "What do you want with him?"

"I'll explain everything on the way," Eliza said, replacing her mask. "Come on," she said, and Aleksey and Lilith followed her out of the room. As they exited the building they were in – a sort of guest compound that also sometimes housed overflowed troops – Eliza explained the Commandant's move against the prince. "The last information we had put Trosclair in the dungeons," Eliza said.

"That's where they had my daughter, as well," Aleksey said as they crossed the courtyard. A group of men and women in masks came into view around a corner ahead of them, and Aleksey spotted his daughter's pale blond hair. "Darra!" he cried, as he rushed over to her. They hugged, and then Aleksey reached a hand up to ruffle Kaleb's hair.

"You!" Mrs. Applebaum yelled, pointing a bony finger accusingly at Aleksey.

"Me?" he asked.

"Yes, you!" Mrs. Applebaum said. "I know you!"

"I just have one of those faces," Aleksey said, stifling a look of panic.

"Oh-ho, you certainly do!" the old woman said. "And I remember it like it was—"

"So!" came a booming male voice from across the lawn. It was Bidzil, with ten other soldiers behind him. "The little kitties got out to play."

"Turn around and leave us," Mr. Martine said. "We have more men than you." Aleksey did a quick count and came up with just under twenty masked rioters.

"You have a bunch of soft, lazy men and old women with cooking utensils against my trained men with swords," Bidzil said. "I'll take those odds!" The muscular soldier lunged forward with his sword, stabbing Mr. Martine through the chest. Mr. Martine cried out in pain, fell to the ground, and almost immediately began spitting up blood.

"Mr. Martine!" Trosclair cried as he started for the man's side, but Ennio held him back. Mr. Martine's body jerked convulsively several times, and when his head slammed against the ground, it was clear he was dead. Next Bidzil approached Mrs. Applebaum threateningly, but Aleksey stepped in front of her protectively. Bidzil slashed at him, but Aleksey caught the thrust with the blade of his dagger. Bidzil had the advantage of leverage, since Aleksey was still chained at the wrists, while Aleksey had the greater strength, and in the end they were deadlocked. The other soldiers approached the group, but before they could engage, Milian and eight of his hired men showed up on the lawn behind the soldiers brandishing swords.

"Ha!" Bidzil said, seeing the reinforcements. He stepped back out of Aleksey's reach. "Now we'll see who—" Bidzil was cut off midsentence by the surprise move Milian's men made - against the soldiers. They slashed into the men from behind, stabbing most of them in the back, and in no time, Bidzil was the only one in a guard uniform left standing. His eyes went wide with fear as Lilith approached him with the cudgel.

"Milian?" Trosclair asked in a shocked voice, as Lilith dispensed justice to Bidzil in the background. "I thought you'd switched sides!"

"I'm sorry, Your Grace," Milian said. "But the situation forced my hand. When I spoke to the Commandant this morning, it was clear he was going to make a move on you sooner rather than later. I thought the safest place for you was right under his nose, until I could summon your allies from the city, and I had to give him something to make him think I was on his side."

"We'll head to Misty Vale now, then?" Ennio asked.

"I'm afraid that plan won't work anymore," Milian said. "The Commandant has already sent a third of his troops to place Misty Vale under siege. We'd never make it there in time." Milian waved to a group of women waiting on the palace steps, and they came down onto the lawn, laden with several bags, packs and satchels.

"We'll start raising troops in another city, then," Trosclair said.

"The Commandant has his men stationed at every train depot and coach stop in the kingdom," Milian said. "That's why his forces here in the capital are so small. You'd be caught. You're much better off sticking to the woods and the back roads, maybe the smaller villages if you must enter society at all."

"I can't raise an army hiding in the woods," Trosclair said.

"I've been looking over the treaties, and none of the cities are legally bound to help you until you come of age," Milian said. "The raising of your army may have to wait until this summer. By then, you'll be a full king in your own right, and not only will the cities have to lend you their support, but several other kingdoms will be bound to come to your aid as well. We'll crush the Commandant's forces without losing too many of our own."

"You expect me to wait a half a year to take back the throne with other kingdoms' forces?" Trosclair asked.

"If the alternative is a civil war you might lose, then yes, Your Grace," Milian said. "I expect you to always act in the best interest of your kingdom, and so far, you've never disappointed me." He placed a hand affectionately on the prince's shoulder. The women passed out the baggage, and Aleksey was pleased to see the DragonSword's fragments had been placed back in his pack. Kaleb was even more thrilled when he found his pipe. He lit it with his finger-flame and took a long, deep drag.

"That's illegal here," Trosclair said, wafting away the smoke from Kaleb's exhalation.

"The herb or the fire spell?" Aleksey asked, as the locksmith started to work removing the chains from his wrists.

"Both," Ennio said.

"Don't care," Kaleb said, as he tamped down the contents of his bowl and took another hit. "It's medicinal."

"Thank you for returning our belongings," Aleksey said to Milian.

"Actually, it comes with a condition," Milian said.

"And what's that?" Aleksey asked. The locksmith popped open the padlock, and the chains fell from the half-elf's wrists. "Thank you," Aleksey said, and the locksmith nodded and moved to start on the broken shackles still encircling Lilith's wrists and ankles.

"Help see the prince to safety," Milian said. "And I'll see to it that you are paid handsomely."

"How handsome?" Aleksey asked. "Are we talking just good looking, or a real stunner?"

"I'll pay you one hundred thousand credits upon the safe return of our prince this summer." The Lord Advisor turned to Lilith. "If you help, I'll pay you the same."

"Please, Leks," Eliza said, taking the half-elf's hand. "Do this for me. You're the only one I trust to keep the prince safe. You know the dangers he's facing."

"Fine," Aleksey said. "He can travel with us until he comes of age."

"Then I'm coming, too," Ennio said.

"Who are you?" Aleksey asked.

"I'm Ennio," the soldier answered. "I'm the prince's... bodyguard."

"And boyfriend," Trosclair added after a moment, his nose tilted up just a little defiantly.

"Oh, that's - good for you," Aleksey said. "Well, if we're going, we'd better leave now, before the Commandant returns."

"Agreed," Milian said, as he took the last bag from the women and handed it to Ennio. "I packed everything you'll need." Trosclair glanced down into the bag.

"There're no clothes in here," the prince said.

"It's mostly gold and credits, Your Grace," Milian said. "You can buy a more inconspicuous wardrobe when you get to – wherever you end up going." The group started walking en masse through the south palace lawn, where another smaller gate would let them out into the city.

At the city's wall, the guards proved loyal, and they opened the gates immediately for the prince and his party. Aleksey hugged Eliza goodbye as Trosclair and Ennio bid farewell to Mrs. Applebaum and Milian.

"Darra," Eliza said, as she hugged the teen next. "Now you keep your father out of trouble, okay, darling?"

"I always try," Darra said. Aleksey and Lilith led the teens away from the city wall and into the forest.

"So who was she?" Lilith asked without looking at Aleksey.

"Eliza Dell?" Aleksey asked. "Surely you've heard of her music."

"Ah," Lilith said. "And are you and she... together?"

"We broke up," Aleksey said. "It's just hard, sometimes, to make a clean break."

"I understand," Lilith said. Several moments passed by, until Lilith finally said, "I'm leaving."

"Why?" Aleksey asked. "Because of Eliza?"

"Of course not," Lilith said. "I've just been feeling... off. At least twice now, I've needed my own life saved by others."

"There's no shame in that," Aleksey said. "Friends help each other. That's how good conquers over evil."

"But it's not how my powers are supposed to work," Lilith said. "I need to make a pilgrimage."

"To where?" he asked.

"A temple, in the Free City," Lilith said. "I should find the answers I'm seeking there."

"What about your life debt? And your promise to the Lord Advisor to watch over the prince?" Aleksey asked. "You're supposed to stay with us and save our lives and all that."

"If you're in danger of dying, Rebos will warn me in time to help you," Lilith said. "But I must make this trip. I can't stand feeling powerless, like I was back there."

"Is that why you - why we—"

"No, of course not," Lilith said. "I meant what I said: I had fun. I hope you can say the same, and that it won't make things awkward between us."

"I'll be the very picture of normalcy," Aleksey said.

"Don't make promises you can't help but break," Lilith said.

CHAPTER EIGHT
"DROPS TO DRINK"

Aleksey led the five teens due south, through the capital city's hunting grounds, and after several hours, into tribal territory. They foraged what they could along the way, as Aleksey hadn't eaten all day, and they came up with a passable meal consisting of pecans, slightly overripe red apples, and brushberries, which were always plentiful, even late into the fall. Darra noticed that Trosclair and Ennio weren't eating, and she held out a small bunch of the berries toward them. "You've got to be hungry," she said. "You should eat something."

"I—I can't eat that," Trosclair said.

"Brushberries?" Darra asked. "Are you allergic or something?"

"No, it's just - they're dirty," the prince said, scrunching his face. "I'll wait until we can wash them."

"Hmm," Aleksey said, frowning. "That may be a while. We've passed two dried-up streams in as many miles."

"At least have some pecans," Darra said. "They're clean, I promise. They come wrapped in their own little shells and everything."

"Thank you," Ennio said, as he took a handful from the offered bag.

"I've never eaten a raw brushberry before," Trosclair said.

"They're good," A.J. said. "Kinda of like a cross between a cherry and a blueberry."

"My chef prepared a lovely marmalade from them one summer," Trosclair said.

"Dad's brother is a chef," Darra said. "For the elven royal family. His food is out of this world."

"So you've been to the Elven Isles?" Trosclair asked.

"Sure," Darra said. "We haven't been in a few years, though. Dad says it's too expensive. And he'd never admit it, but he gets seasick crossing all that water."

"I do not!" Aleksey called back over his shoulder. "I was just regular-sick."

"See?" Darra said, raising her eyebrows and shaking her head. Ennio held a tree branch out of the way for Trosclair, and Darra smiled. "So how long have you two been together?"

"Gods, I don't even know," Trosclair said. "It kind of feels like we've always been together."

"We grew up as friends," Ennio said. "And even when I was away at the military academy, Trosclair would send me letters and care packages almost every week. Then when I graduated and moved back to the palace to be his bodyguard, it just became something more."

"You lived in the palace as a child, then?" Darra asked. Ennio nodded. "Are you a noble?"

"Oh, gods, no!" Ennio said. "My mother worked in the kitchens, and my father in the stables, before they retired. I wouldn't even have been able to afford the academy if Trosc hadn't pitched in."

"What about you two?" Trosclair asked, indicating Darra and A.J.

"We're... just starting out," Darra said.

"I only met her a few weeks ago, actually," A.J. said. "But I knew right away I'd never met anyone like her." Darra blushed.

"That's great," Trosclair said.

"We're here," Kaleb said, pointing to a set of wooden stairs that led up into the branches of a *himari* tree. The species dominated this section of the forest. They grew upwards of one hundred and fifty feet tall, with trunks as thick as eight or nine feet in diameter, but the aspect that made the tree really distinct was its remarkable branches. They were broad and flat, about a foot thick and anywhere from six to twenty feet wide. They wrapped around the trunk and fanned out about fifteen feet in all directions. They were also green, as the branches themselves caught the sunlight to provide the tree with energy, and during the day, they cast a deep shadow onto the forest floor only punctuated here and there with the occasional strand of sunlight. On these platform-like branches, the tribe had built their homes - and a civilization. Stairways and bridges connected branch to branch, tree to tree, and level to level. Each branch also had a bamboo hut with a thatched roof and heavy beaded curtains hanging down over the doorways and windows. One tree might be home to a dozen or more families, each with their own hut. The Tribe stuck to building on the lower and middle levels of the trunk, so that the trees still got plenty of sunlight on their upper branches. Kaleb led them to a tree with two ribbons, one brown and one white, tied around its massive trunk at about eye level. "Gram!" he called up into the tree. "Gram, it's me! I'm back!"

After a few seconds, Ramla poked her head out of the doorway of one of the lower huts. "Kaleb?" she yelled down at him. "What are you doing back here so soon?"

"Waking us up!" yelled someone from a nearby hut, and there was the faintest sound of scattered laughter from above.

"We need some advice," Aleksey said. "And you're the only one who can give it to us."

"I see," Ramla said. "Come on up."

"So," Ramla said, as Aleksey and the teens sat cross-legged in a semicircle facing the witchy woman inside her hut the next morning. "I have been considering what you told me last night about the outworlder, and I think I understand now... You have ships that sail through the heavens." Ramla looked pleased with herself, like she'd figured out something terribly important.

"Like in the science stories," Trosclair said.

"Well, they don't sail, so much as make faster-than-light leaps through space-time," A.J. said.

"Did what he just said make sense to everyone but me?" Ennio asked.

"Nope," Kaleb said.

"Okay, good," Ennio said.

"Look, it's not important how our ships work," A.J. said. "I just need to know if you can get me home."

"Hmm," Ramla said, as she considered. "Without the gem you described, I would not even know where to begin. My strength lies in spells of the earth and the air, not the heavens."

"So it's hopeless?" A.J. asked.

"Not necessarily," Ramla said. "I will meditate on it more throughout the days ahead, and perhaps Ona will enlighten me." She twisted to face Aleksey. "It is fortunate for us that you've come through here at this moment. I need your help with something."

"What is it?" Aleksey asked.

"One of our women has been kidnapped," Ramla said.

"That's awful!" Darra said.

"It gets worse," Ramla said. "The woman is our Tribe's most powerful water-witch. And it has become apparent that the men who took her are torturing her."

"How do you know that?" Aleksey asked.

"The rains," Ramla said. "They aren't falling on our lands. The dark clouds form in the sky, but the water doesn't fall."

"And that means this woman is hurt?" Aleksey asked.

"It means she is dying," Ramla said. "Of thirst. And she is so intimately connected to the water cycle of this environment, her thirst is reflected in the dryness of the land."

"Why are these men doing this?" Aleksey asked.

"This is our rainy season," Ramla said. "We normally get three-fifths of our yearly rainfall over the course of the next few weeks. My assumption is that they are trying to wage war on our water supply, with the goal of starving us out when the forest stops giving fruit."

"You said this woman was powerful," Aleksey said. "Do you know how they took her in the first place?"

"The only witness was her nephew, and he said one of the men simply waved his hand in front of her face, and she fell over," Ramla said.

"So they've got a mage working for them," Aleksey said. "Good to know."

"You'll help?" Ramla asked.

"Of course!" Aleksey said.

"I want to help, too," Darra said.

"And you'll need a mage to counter theirs," Kaleb said.

"I'm in," A.J. added.

"I appreciate the enthusiasm," Aleksey said. "But none of you are going with me."

"But these men sound dangerous, Dad," Darra said. "And even you can't take on more than a few at a time. You'll need our help."

"I do need help, but not yours, sweetie. Not this time," Aleksey said. "We're surrounded by a tribe full of warriors and hunters. I'll have all the help I need."

"He's right," Ramla said. "You should stay here, where I can keep you safe." A middle-aged woman appeared in the doorway. She was tall and thick, with both muscle and a little extra weight, and her curly brown hair was cropped short. Instead of a dress, which many women of the tribe wore, she wore pants, a brightly colored shirt, and a red robe that belted at the waist and fell to just above her knees. It was the look Kaleb and most of the men of the tribe sported, but it seemed to fit this woman well. "Landa!" Ramla greeted the woman cheerfully. "Please, come in." The woman obeyed, and Ramla stood, so Aleksey and the teens followed suit.

"Aleksey," Landa greeted the half-elf with a friendly nod. "I thought I heard your voice last night. And Darra, it's nice to see you. Haven't been around in a while."

"We've been very busy," Darra said. "Landa, this is my boyfriend, A.J."

"Oh, well, look at you," Landa said in a rising tone, as she shook A.J.'s hand. She pulled the pilot in close and mock-whispered, "You better treat her right. If you hurt her, I'll carve you up myself."

"You'd have to get in line," Aleksey muttered under his breath.

"That won't be a problem," A.J. said, although he winced a little from all the attention.

"And this is Ennio," Darra continued.

"Are you a soldier?" Landa asked, as they shook hands. "Or did you just steal the uniform?"

"I–I don't know how to really answer that question," Ennio said. "I was a soldier, until yesterday. Now I'm just here to protect Trosclair."

"Trosclair?" Landa repeated, looking to the redheaded teen with wide eyes. "As in, Prince Trosclair?"

"That's me," the prince said.

"Ramla, what - what is the prince doing here?" Landa asked.

"Taking refuge," Ramla said.

"There was a coup," Trosclair explained. "It's not safe for me at the palace anymore."

"Do I - am I supposed to bow or curtsy or something?" Landa asked. "I've never met royalty before!"

"Landa, compose yourself," Ramla said. "You are, after all, a sort of royalty yourself." Ramla looked to Trosclair. "It was decided last year that, when I retire, Landa will take over as Chief of the Tribe."

"That's wonderful, Landa!" Darra said.

"Congratulations," Aleksey said.

"Thanks," Landa said. "I just hope I can be as strong a leader as Ramla the Ominous, here. I already know I won't be as famous."

"You mean infamous," Aleksey corrected, and Landa and Ramla both smiled.

"Kaleb!" came an angry, feminine voice from outside the hut on the ground below.

"Uh-oh," the mage said.

"Who's that?" Darra asked.

"Kaleb, if you're in there, you better come out right now!" the voice cried.

"That's Bessa," Kaleb said. "My ex-girlfriend."

"Well, are you gonna answer her?" A.J. asked.

"I was thinking I might just hide in here until we leave, actually," Kaleb said, as he crossed to the window and peeked down below. He glimpsed Bessa's dark hair blowing in the wind and immediately lurched back.

"Kaleb!" Bessa called again. "I saw you! I know you're up there!"

"Gods damn it!" Kaleb whispered. He composed himself, put on a happy smile, and leaned back in front of the window. "Bessa?" he called down in a soft, surprised voice. "Oh my goodness! It's been forever. How are you?"

"Oh, nice try, buddy!" Bessa said. "You better get down here. Or do you want the whole Tribe to hear our business?

Because I'll keep yelling."

"No," Kaleb said. "You're right. I'll be down in a second."

"She sounds upset," Ramla commented, as her eyebrows lifted. "What did you do to anger her so?"

"Want a list?" Kaleb asked, as he headed out the door.

"Landa, I'm going to take Aleksey and gather the warriors for Talia's rescue," Ramla said. "Would you please show the prince and his companion around? I'd like them to get a feel for how we live here."

"I'd be honored," Landa said, looking to Trosclair and gesturing toward the door.

"The honor is all ours," Trosclair said, as he and Ennio exited the hut, followed by Aleksey and Ramla.

"I think I'm gonna tag along with the prince," A.J. said to Darra. "I wanna see what Tribal life is like."

"Are you sure?" Darra asked, her lips pouted playfully. "We were just about to get some alone time."

"Alone time?" A.J. asked. "I like the sound of that even better." He put his arms around her waist and pulled her in close for a kiss.

A few minutes later, Ramla had gathered a dozen of her Tribe's most experienced warriors. They assembled in a large, empty bamboo hut that was on the forest floor, although it still backed up to a tree. The tribe used huts like these for things that couldn't – or shouldn't – be done higher up, such as butchering and curing meats, as well as for storing bulky farming equipment. There was a lingering gamy smell in the air just strong enough to offend Aleksey's delicate olfactory sense, but he ignored it as best he could.

"You all know why you're here," Ramla said. "Talia's life is in danger. She is being tortured, but she is still alive."

"How do you know that?" asked one of the warriors.

"If she were dead, her connection to Ona's water cycle would be severed, and it would rain," Ramla said. "She is alive. Which means, likely, that she is being raped. And the Tribal punishment for rape is death."

"I thought we were forming a rescue party," Aleksey said. "Now it's an execution?"

"More than one," Ramla said. "Talia's nephew said there

were three men, in addition to the one who ensorcelled her."

"Look, Ramla - I'll help free your friend," Aleksey said. "But I won't take part in murdering people, no matter how evil they are."

"What would you have us do, alternatively?" Ramla asked. "We don't have jails or dungeons here. When someone commits a very serious crime, there are only two punishments: exile and execution. And these men are not of the Tribe, so they can't be exiled."

"Whatever happened to just, you know - beating a man within an inch of his life to teach him a lesson?" Aleksey asked.

"You are not a woman," Ramla said. "You cannot understand the true horror of rape."

"That's not fair, Ramla," Aleksey said. "I may be a man, but I also have a daughter. I'm not trying to downplay what these men are guilty of."

"Good," Ramla said. "Because rape is about inflicting pain. These men would probably cut your ears off and sell them, if they could."

"How will we find them?" Aleksey asked.

"That is the easy part," Ramla said. "Tora?"

"Yes?" the warrior woman answered.

"Find Talia's nephew and ask him for something of hers," Ramla said. "An item of clothing or a piece of jewelry will suffice."

"I'll be right back," Tora said, as she exited the hut.

"*Kiris col fera,*" Ramla said in the old speak, as she flashed a series of gestures with her hands. Her eyes glowed crimson, and she stomped her foot down onto the earth. A circle of dirt about four feet wide suddenly sprang up into the air several inches, and when it fell back down, it had the appearance and texture of a relief map of the surrounding areas. Aleksey could make out the location of the tribe, the orc's territory, and all the other land south of the capital city. He was astonished by the detail of the map; it showed trees where the forest grew tall, fell flat to represent the clearings, and mimicked the curves of every hill and stream precisely.

"Very impressive, Ramla," he said.

"When Tora returns, I'll do a spell to locate Talia," Ramla said. "And then these men will see what tribal justice looks like!"

Tora and her husband, Amall, led the way to the spot Ramla's spell had indicated. Aleksey was wary, as they were headed back north, toward the capital city. They wouldn't be going all the way to the walls, however, as Ramla's spell had put the missing water-witch smack in the middle of the cluster of farms that surrounded the city. Still, Aleksey kept himself ready for anything. He'd donned his skullcap, and even though it was hot, he kept it on to better hide his pointy ears. The sight of a group of Tribals moving through the farmlands was not entirely uncommon, as the Tribe sometimes traded with these farmers when their fertile lands yielded more than even the capital city could devour. But these were obviously warriors, and they were armed, so they drew plenty of long, nervous looks from the scattered farm folk they passed along the way.

"So how long have you known Ramla?" Tora asked.

"Oh, we go back decades," Aleksey said. "We met during the Second Elven War."

"Gods," Amall said. "That's before we were even born."

"Are you trying to make me feel old?" Aleksey asked, and the warrior couple smiled.

"It's just hard to imagine Ramla as a young woman," Amall said.

"And not Chief yet," Tora added. "What was she like?"

"She was... different," Aleksey said. "Less disciplined. Quicker to temper."

"Quicker to temper?" Amall asked. "Yikes."

"But she was also funny," Aleksey said.

"Really?" Tora asked, and Aleksey nodded.

"Nobody could make me laugh harder," the half-elf said.

"She's always had a quick wit," Tora said. "Though she tends toward seriousness."

"Yes, but she had a different sort of humor back then. Less cynical, more shocking," Aleksey said. "Then when her husband and children died, she just... stopped making jokes."

"That's so sad," Tora said.

"If I lost you, I'd be the same way," Amall said, and Tora smiled.

"You'll never lose me, dear," she said. "We're almost there. Ramla's spell put Talia just over that ridge." She pointed to the small hill that blocked any view of the road ahead of them. "Stay here," Tora said to the other warriors, as she and Amall ascended the slope, hunching down so as not to be visible from the other side. Aleksey moved to follow them.

"We're just scouting," Tora whispered. "We got this part covered."

"I have elven sight and hearing, remember?" Aleksey whispered back. "I might catch something you don't."

"Fair enough," Tora said. When they neared the top of the hill, the other side came into view, and Aleksey held back a curse. There were about ten large covered wagons led by a team of four horses each lined up down the road. The wagons had come to a stop in front of a tiny creek about six feet wide. The water trickled along gently, just a few inches deep in most places, but there was no bridge; the road simply led straight through the creek. About half a dozen men were gathered around the first wagon, talking, but many more lingered around the other wagons.

"Damn it!" Aleksey whispered.

"You're in big trouble, Kaleb," Bessa said, but her tone was less angry than before. Kaleb still shrunk into the collar of his robes. They'd relocated to one of the empty huts on the forest floor for a more private conversation.

"I know," Kaleb said. "I'm sorry."

"What exactly are you apologizing for?" Bessa asked. "Running away without telling me first? Or kissing Ophelia?" Kaleb's eyes went wide.

"She told you?" he asked.

"No," Bessa said, crossing her arms across her chest. "Her sister told me. She saw you."

"She kissed me, I swear," Kaleb said. "I would never do that to you."

"You talk like we're married," Bessa said. "I don't care that you kissed her."

"She kissed me."

"Whatever. My point is, we never said we'd be exclusive," Bessa said, as she brushed a strand of hair out of her face.

"So you aren't mad?" Kaleb asked.

"I'm not mad that you kissed," Bessa said. "I'm mad that

you turned it into something so huge, you had to run away rather than face it."

"That's not why I ran away," Kaleb said.

"Then why?"

"I just... needed to get away," Kaleb said.

"From the Tribe?" Bessa asked. "Or from me?"

"Both, sort of," Kaleb said.

"Did I do something?" Bessa asked.

"No!" Kaleb said. "It wasn't you... it was your father."

"Oh, gods," Bessa said, shaking her head. "What did he do now?"

"You say we're not married," Kaleb said. "But after your womanhood ceremony last spring, he kept hinting that we should."

"Get married?" Bessa asked, her eyebrows arching high.

"Yep," Kaleb said. "He even threatened to tell my gram about the time he caught us behind the chicken coop if I didn't propose."

"He didn't!" Bessa said as she buried her face in her palm.

"I'm not making it up," he said.

"I'll kill him!"

"But honestly, that wasn't the only reason I left."

"Okay," Bessa said. "What else?"

"It's just, all this," Kaleb said, gesturing all around him. "Tribal life is so... limited. I want to be a great mage, and to see the world. I can't do either of those things here."

"I get it, Kay," Bessa said. "I really do. It just hurt that you didn't even say goodbye."

"I know. I'm sorry," Kaleb said. "But I'm back now."

"For how long?" she asked.

"Not too long," he said. "A couple days, maybe."

"Then I guess we better not waste any more time fighting," Bessa said, as she leaned forward and kissed him.

"That was nice," he said, when it was over. "Does this mean we're back together, or...?"

"Not if you're leaving in a few days," she said. "Let's just say we're friends."

"Friends that kiss," Kaleb said.

"Exactly," Bessa said, as she leaned in again.

Trosclair and Ennio followed Landa through the trees. The prince marveled at the tribal women's dresses. "Where do you get your fabrics?" he asked. "I've never seen dyes in all these colors before."

"We trade for some of it," Landa said. "But we spin and weave most of it ourselves, from hemp, cotton and bamboo fibers. The dyes come from a range of forest plants."

"How industrious of you," Trosclair said.

"Yeah, well, we don't have a lot else to do around here," Landa said.

"What do you do, you know, day to day?" Ennio asked. "How do you stay busy?"

"We hunt, we forage, we fish," Landa answered. "We patrol our borders. Other than that, it's a pretty laid back way of life."

"I can tell," Ennio said, as a pair of children ran by, squealing.

"Do you hate the cities?" Trosclair asked. "For kicking your ancestors out all those years ago?"

"No, of course not," Landa said. "The way I see it, they did us a favor. I hear in the cities, you have to work all day long just to pay for the things we get for free. And we get to spend much more time with our families and loved ones."

"Not a bad trade off," Ennio said.

"And speaking of loved ones," Landa said, as another middle-aged woman approached them. She had dark hair in braids that ran along her scalp and dark skin that contrasted beautifully with the bright purple and yellow dress she wore. "This is my wife, Heradia. Heradia, this is Ennio and Prince Trosclair."

"Oh my goodness!" Heradia said. "What is a prince doing in our little Tribe?"

"Wait a second," Trosclair said. "Did you say she's your wife?"

"Yes," Landa said, draping an arm casually around her wife's waist. "This spring we'll have been married five years."

"And your Tribe supports you in this?" Trosclair asked.

"Of course," Heradia said. "I know everyone outside the Tribe thinks it's wrong, or shocking or whatever. But our people have always recognized the fluidity of gender and sexual attraction."

"That's amazing," Trosclair said. "I wish my own people

were equally as enlightened."

"That's good to hear you say," Landa said. "Since, technically, you'll be king of us one day, too." They continued their tour, and Landa pointed out the various communal areas. There were fire pits and stone ovens scattered all around, as well as several small to medium-sized ponds. They came upon one such body of water that was almost a perfect circle. Several children laughed and shrieked as they splashed around in the shallows. Trosclair was surprised by how clear and clean-looking the water was. "These ponds are where we get our water, and they are one-hundred percent manmade. Or actually, woman-made."

"How do you make a pond?" Trosclair asked. "I mean, I had a pool back at the palace, but that took almost a year to build."

"Ramla shapes the earth into a crater, and Talia raises the groundwater to fill them," Heradia said. "Together, they can get it done in a day or two."

"Wow," Ennio said. "I guess I've been underestimating the power of magic my whole life."

"We also do some fish farming in them, and, as you can see, we reserve a few for bathing and for the little ones to play in," Heradia said. "Frankly, I don't know what we're going to do if Talia doesn't make it home. The Tribe can't survive without her."

"Don't think like that, hon," Landa said, clutching her wife's hand. "She'll be home soon. I know it."

"I hope you're right," Heradia said.

Aleksey concentrated, and soon he could make out the men's conversation. He listened carefully for many moments before he brought his attention back to the warriors next to him.

"Well?" Tora asked. "Can you tell what they're saying?"

"They're afraid their wagons will get stuck crossing the creek," Aleksey said.

"Are we sure these are the men that have Talia?" Amall asked. "Her nephew said there were only four of them."

"They definitely have her," Aleksey said. "I heard one of the men mention a witch."

"What did he say?" Tora asked.

"He was afraid crossing the water would give her some sort of strength," Aleksey said.

"We should attack now, while they can't flee," Amall said.

"Are you insane?" Aleksey asked. "I counted over twenty of them, against our thirteen. And we don't know how powerful their sorcerer is."

"Every moment she's with them, Talia's in agony," Amall said. "We didn't come here just to leave her behind."

"No, but we didn't come here to die, either," Aleksey said. "Or at least I didn't. The Tribe's not too far back. You go and get reinforcements. The others and I will stay here and keep an eye on these men."

"I think he's right," Tora said. "We'd lose too many of our own if we tried to take them on now, and possibly Talia with them."

"I guess so," Amall said. "I'll go tell the others." Amall slid back down the hill toward the warriors.

"I don't like leaving Talia to suffer at their hands, even for a moment longer," Tora said.

"I'll sneak up through the woods as close as I can get," Aleksey said. "If there's an opportunity to slip in and get your friend out, I'll take it."

"Thank you," Tora said, before she went back down to join the other warriors. As Aleksey headed for the tree line, he saw Tora and Amall break off in a sprint back down the road. He crept through the trees toward the men, careful to use the whisper-foot technique his elven mother had taught him to move across the leaves and twigs almost completely silently. It meant moving slower, but he had plenty of time. He was glad he had been cautious when he spotted a log snake stretched out perfectly still on the path in front of him. Instead of smooth scales, the serpent had rough, craggy bumps all along its back that mimicked the texture and color of a log. Even its head was shaped and colored like a leaf in fall. It was the perfect camouflage for the forest floor, and the snake's paralyzing venom was not a trouble Aleksey wanted to contend with. The half-elf picked up a rock and threw it at the snake, which reared its head back and up at the empty air around it, hissing. Unable to sense where the danger came from, the snake slithered quickly away.

When Aleksey got within view of the men again, he saw that they'd begun shoveling dirt into the creek in two thick lines clearly meant for their wagon wheels to roll over. Other men had begun gathering large rocks, which Aleksey assumed would be placed on top of the loose soil to give the wagon wheels a firmer surface to pass over. Water flooded out of both sides of the little creek as they dammed it with the dirt, but of course the men didn't care about the minnows and tadpoles this would dislocate and kill. "Get her out," Aleksey heard one of the men tell another. "Holleran wants her."

The half-elf heard something small moving through the brush in front of him, and he prepared himself to see a rabbit or squirrel emerge. Instead, a small black and brown dog with shaggy fur that was matted in several places and ribs that showed through its thin skin bounded out of the foliage. Aleksey's heart sank for the awful condition the animal was in. The dog growled quietly at him, and he immediately dropped to his knees to try to avoid threatening the animal.

"Shh!" he whispered at the dog, who danced back and forth excitedly. "Stay quiet, boy... That's a good boy..." Aleksey reached out a tentative hand and petted the animal down its back. "I'm sorry I don't have any treats to give you." Suddenly the dog began to bark in its loudest voice. "Unholy hells!" Aleksey stood up and turned around in time to see a shovel swinging at him. It clocked him across the side of his head and opened up a small gash just behind his temple, and the half-elf fell to the ground, unconscious.

"Holleran!" the man with the shovel yelled over his shoulder. "We got a problem!"

A cone of floral-scented incense burned in a tray on a bamboo shelf, one of only three pieces of furniture in Ramla's hut, the other two being a small, square table and a chair pushed up against the eastern window. One corner of the room had a thicker pile of furs than the rest of the room, as well as a blanket and a pillow, but Darra didn't want to make out with her boyfriend on Ramla's own bed. So they lay on their sides facing one another on the floor, A.J. with his hand on the curve of Darra's waist. As they kissed, he moved his hand down to rest on her hip. Darra pulled away slightly. "Maybe we should stop," she said. "We're supposed to be taking things slower this time."

"Okay," A.J. said, as he leaned back and pulled his hand off her body.

"I just don't want to be too forward, like that slutty snake monster that seduced Kaleb," Darra said. "And I don't want to be what she turned me into, either – a mindless, lovesick drone. Does that make sense?"

"It does," A.J. said, sitting up. "Maybe if we hurry, we can catch the tail end of that tour."

"Actually," Ramla said from the doorway. "I need to ask you some questions first."

"Sure," A.J. said. "What about?"

"Your home world," Ramla said, as she crossed to the chair and sat down. "What is it called?"

"I'm originally from New Titan," A.J. said. "But we were literally light-years away from there when we got sucked through the portal." Ramla stared at him, unblinking and uncomprehending. "That's a really long way. In a different star system."

"And is this New Titan like Ona?" Ramla asked.

"Not even remotely," A.J. said.

"But you speak our language," Ramla said. "More or less. And you seem to recognize the names of our animals, and our foods. So allow me to rephrase my question: Does your world have mountains and plains, forests and seas, snow and rain, like ours? Does it have only humans, or are there a multitude of creatures and races? And most importantly, does your world have magic?"

"Oh, wow. Let's see," A.J. said, as he thought about her questions in order. "Yes, we have mountains and seas and all types of different weather. But there are only humans there. And no, we definitely do not have any magic."

"Hmm," Ramla said, as she looked out the window. "And yet you sail – or leap, as you say – from star to star, through the heavens. That's a feat I did not think science capable of achieving, and it does not bode well for the future of Ona."

"Why?" Darra asked.

"Our planet is on the brink of another great war," Ramla said. "A war between those who understand magic, and those who fear it."

"I have a – a friend who said virtually the same thing," Darra said.

"And scientists, by and large, fear magic," Ramla continued. "Because they cannot understand it."

"I'm a scientist," A.J. said. "And I don't fear magic. In fact,

I'm fascinated by it."

"As are many scientists," Ramla said. "But I have witnessed firsthand that this fascination is derived from a desire to dominate the magic, and with it, the world. And since scientists cannot dissect a spell or observe the inner working of the mage's mind when she casts it, they will ultimately reject magic." Tora suddenly appeared in the doorway, and Ramla turned to her. "Well? How did it go?"

"There were too many of them," Tora said. "We've come back to get more warriors."

"How many do you need?" Ramla asked, as she rose from her chair. Darra and A.J. stood up, too.

"There were over twenty of them," Tora said. "We'll need at least twice that to make sure no one is hurt."

"Where's my dad?" Darra asked.

"He stayed behind with the other warriors to keep watch," Tora said.

"If you're taking that many people, this time I'm definitely coming with you," Darra said.

"Your father told you to stay here," Ramla said.

"I'm gonna have plenty of warriors around me to protect me," Darra said. "And Dad almost always needs my help, whether he likes to admit it or not."

"Hmph," Ramla said. "You are every bit as obstinate as he is, I see. It actually reminds me a bit of your mother, too."

"I—I didn't know you knew my mom," Darra said.

"We met very briefly, just before you were born," Ramla said. "But, much like you, she left a lasting impression. Very well. You can go with the warriors to rescue Talia."

"Thank you, Ramla!" Darra said, beaming.

"But you are to stay behind when the warriors confront the men," Ramla said. "And if your father gets angry, I'm telling him that you snuck out without permission."

"Deal!" Darra said.

The farmers had been made nervous by the first group of warriors crossing their lands, but the sight of an entire war party sixty people strong had them in an all-out panic. Several scared farm hands dropped their tools and vegetables and hurried away as they passed, while others stood perfectly still, like the tattered scarecrows scattered throughout their fields. Darra and A.J. brought up the rear of the party, along with Kaleb and Bessa.

"Thanks for joining us, Bessa," Darra said. "It's nice to have another young warrior woman around."

"Oh, I'm not really a warrior," Bessa said. "But I am a pretty good huntress, so I'm a fair shot with a bow."

"I never got the hang of a regular bow," Darra said.

"If you want, I could teach you," Bessa said, offering her bow to Darra. The young woman waved the weapon politely away.

"No thanks," Darra said. "I always end up hurting my arm when I try to use one. Besides, I'm pretty attached to Madeline here." She lifted her crossbow to show it off.

"You named your crossbow?" A.J. asked.

"Yeah," Darra said. "So what? Guys name their swords all the time."

"Yeah, but they name them, like, 'Stormbreaker' and 'the Annihilator,'" Kaleb said. "Why'd you give it a girl's name?"

"I got it when I was eight," Darra said. "I'd asked for a doll for my birthday, but Dad's always been the type to give very practical gifts. I thought giving it a girl's name would remind him what I really wanted. And it worked. He bought me a doll not two weeks later."

"Aw, that's sweet," A.J. said.

"It was, wasn't it?" Darra asked. "Of course, a few months after that, I got mad and used the doll for target practice. Dad wasn't too sweet when he found out about that."

The warriors came to a stop, and the teens turned their attentions ahead. A group of about ten farmers had stretched across the road in front of them. The farmers weren't armed with weapons, but they had their tools with them, and their forbidding postures indicated they wouldn't let the Tribals pass. Darra and the other teens kept moving toward the front of the group, so they could hear the exchange.

"Fine day," one of the farmers greeted the warriors. "What business do you have over here, with so many of you?"

"A woman of our Tribe was kidnapped," Amall answered. "We're just going to get her back from the men who took her." The farmer consulted with the man next to him in a quiet voice, then turned back to Amall.

"We won't try and stop you, then," the farmer said, as they

cleared a path for the Tribals. "Can I ask who you think took her?"

"There's a caravan," Tora said. "They looked like merchants of some kind."

"You mean those boys with the covered wagons full of pipes and hoses?" the farmer asked.

"We didn't see what they were transporting," Amall said.

"They're selling irrigation supplies," the farmer said. "They have a scientist with them, and he's predicting a drought."

"More like creating one," Darra said, and Bessa nodded.

"It's not surprising," Bessa said. "Rape is all about having power over someone else, and not caring about the harm you do to them. These men don't care about the suffering they cause from harming the environment, either."

"It's almost like they don't have souls, like that succubus," Darra said.

"Succubus?" Bessa repeated. "You guys met a succubus?"

"More than met it," A.J. said.

"We fought it," Darra said. "Dad killed it."

"But I thought a succubus could only appear in men's dreams?" Bessa said.

"It's a long story," Kaleb said.

"We've got time," Bessa said, raising an eyebrow. "Don't get all secretive on me now, buddy." Kaleb began to tell Bessa the story as they continued down the road. When he got to the part about his erotic dream, he summarized it without mentioning the act in which he'd engaged with the demon. Darra and A.J. shared a knowing glance and a smile.

They reached the ridge and the warriors they'd left behind, and Tora and Amall crept up the slope again. This time, when their line of sight crested the hill, they saw nothing but an empty stretch of road and the muddy, gravel-strewn path the wagons had taken over the creek, water and tiny fishes still spilling out of both sides.

Ramla had two more chairs brought up to her hut, as well as a kettle of hot tea, when Landa brought Trosclair and Ennio back from their tour. The two teens took seats at the little table by the window, while Ramla sat a few feet away.

"So," Ramla said. "How was your tour?"

"It was very enlightening," Trosclair answered. "You've

carved out a wonderful little world here."

"Thank you," Ramla said. "I must admit, I had ulterior motives in sending you out with Landa as your guide."

"Oh, really?" the prince asked.

"Yes," Ramla said. "I wanted you to get to know Landa personally. Someday, you and she will run this kingdom and this Tribe, respectively. Historically, as you are well aware, there has always been animosity directed toward the Tribe by city dwellers. I thought maybe if you two got to know each other, it would create a dialogue between our two communities."

"I see," Trosclair said. "Well, I found Landa to be very personable. And I think you were right to introduce us. It will make living so close to one another easier for all of our people, knowing we have allies at our borders instead of enemies."

"Good," Ramla said. "I also wanted you to get a feel for how we live here so that you could understand how, with a strong foundation of trust, we might better help one another's people."

"What did you have in mind?" the prince asked.

"The first issue is trade," Ramla said.

"I don't mean any offense," Ennio said.

"That phrase is often followed by something offensive," Ramla said.

"But you don't have merchants here, do you?" Ennio asked. Ramla shook her head. "Then what do you have to trade?"

"Plenty," Ramla said. "I hear your noble women like to wear furs, and that they pay outrageous prices for them. We have more furs than we can use. I have huts and huts full of them, stacked higher than you stand. And we would not charge you much. Your people could all be dressed warmly - and fashionably - in winter, instead of just the rich women."

"That sounds like a fantastic idea!" Trosclair said, before he blew on the top of his tea cup to cool it.

"Next, there is our food supply," Ramla said. "In spring and summer, the forest provides more nuts and fruit than we could ever eat. And these are foods that are not easily grown in the farmlands. I hear pomegranate seeds and swellfruits are considered delicacies by your people. We could provide hundreds of pounds of these a week, without depleting the forest in the slightest."

"What would you want in return?" Trosclair asked.

"Corn, wheat -- the foods we can't grow here, for lack of sunlight and open space," Ramla said. "And of course, we'd need carts and horses to move all these goods back and forth."

"That sounds easily accomplishable," Trosclair said.

"I'd also like to begin an exchange of people," Ramla said.

"People? What do you mean?" the prince asked.

"Our Tribe has a custom of sending young folk away to live in other villages within the Tribe," Ramla said. "This provides each village with vital new blood, both literally and figuratively. But it also strengthens the bonds between the villages. I feel our societies could benefit from a similar exchange."

"Like the fostering of noble youths as squires and ladies-in-waiting brings together kingdoms and cities," Trosclair said.

"Beyond the good will this will create, there is also the prospect of exchanging our disparate knowledge and expertise," Ramla said. "I want a fountain outside my window, and walls to protect small herds of cattle, sheep and horses from the forest predators. But we do not practice masonry here. If some of your skilled workers could live with the Tribe long enough to build these things for us, I would repay the effort by sending some of my mages to the cities."

"Oh I–I don't think that's a good idea," Trosclair said. "Magic is outlawed in the cities because people are afraid of it."

"That is because all they have known of magic is its misuse, during the Elven Wars," Ramla said. "But perhaps if they saw the way sorcery can heal, and create, they would not be so afraid it."

"I'll... consider it," Trosclair said, and Ramla smiled.

"That's all I ask," she said.

As Aleksey began to regain consciousness, the first thing he noticed was something warm and wet swiping against his cheek. He squinted his eyes open and a blurry, furry little figure came into view right in front of his face. The dog lifted its muzzle and barked once, and Aleksey flinched from the pain the sound brought pounding into his skull. He tried to move his arm and realized both his hands and feet were bound by ropes tied to hooks screwed into the wagon bed he was stretched out on. The dog licked his cheek again, and Aleksey was powerless to stop it. "You little traitor," he said to the animal.

"You're awake?" came a hoarse female voice from behind him, and Aleksey shifted to try to get a glimpse of her. All he could see was the back of her head, but he was sure it was the missing Tribal woman. She sat propped upright against the front of the wagon, her torso completely swaddled with blankets and tied tight with ropes. The dog moved away from Aleksey, to the corner of the wagon, and began chewing on a broken bone.

"Talia?" he asked.

"How did you know my name?" she asked weakly. "Who are you?"

"My name is Aleksey," he said. "Ramla sent me to free you." Talia chuckled joylessly.

"Guess she should've sent someone with you," she said.

"She did," Aleksey said. "But we needed reinforcements. They should be here any moment. Are you hurt?"

"I need water," Talia said. "If I had just a cupful, I'd show these men who they're really dealing with. But they won't let me have more than a few drops at a time. If I weren't a water-witch, I'd already be dead."

"Their mage," Aleksey said. "What did he look like?"

"He was tall, with dark features," she said. "Other than that, I couldn't really tell you, it all happened so fast. I was confronting the men about trespassing on Tribal land, and then he just appeared out of nowhere in front of me. The next thing I knew, I was wrapped in these disgusting blankets, literally dying of thirst, and then the men... started doing things that made it even worse."

"I'm sorry," Aleksey said.

"I don't want your pity," Talia said. "I want out of here. Are you a mage?"

"No," he said.

"Then why did Ramla send you?" she asked.

"I'm half-elven," Aleksey said. "And I do have one idea for getting us out of here."

"I'm listening," Talia prompted.

"I haven't tried this in a long time, so I may be a bit rusty," Aleksey said. "But there's an elven technique for communing with domesticated animals. I used it on my horses during the Elven Wars, to make us move as one entity in battle."

"I don't think the dog is going to be much help scaring off

these men, if that's what you're getting at," Talia said. "The poor thing is far from threatening. And I've seen the way the men treat it. They'd kill it in a heartbeat, no question."

"I don't want the dog to frighten them," Aleksey said. "I want it to bring me that sharp bone it's playing with, so I can cut myself out of these ropes."

"Anything's worth a shot," Talia said.

Aleksey closed his eyes and concentrated, then opened them again and said in a lilting tone, "Come here, boy!" The dog looked up at him from across the wagon bed.

"It's actually a girl," Talia said. "I saw its nipples."

"Come on, then, girl!" the half-elf said, before he made several kissing noises at the dog. "Come on!" The dog began to wander cautiously back over to him. "That's it, girl," Aleksey said, and when the dog was within reach of his bound hands, he threw them around it too quick for the animal to get away. The terrified dog started barking again, but Aleksey ignored it as he brought the animal's face up to his. He stared into its dark brown eyes, and as he held it, he pictured his own mother, and the hugs she used to give him as he sat on her lap. He remembered the strange warmth that would cascade through his body from these embraces. It was the closest thing he could imagine to a physical embodiment of love, pure and strong, and he imagined passing that same warmth and sense of safety and security through his own hands into the animal. The dog stopped barking and started making a low, throaty noise that sounded like he was suddenly very curious. As he held the animal's gaze, Aleksey visualized the dog bringing him the bone. He repeated the visualization several times. Next, he pictured himself giving the dog treats of beef, sausage and chicken, and the animal's legs began to shake excitedly. "Okay," Aleksey said over his shoulder. "I think we're getting somewhere."

The sun was low in the sky, and the warriors and the teens trailing along at their rear had made it almost all the way back to the Tribal village before Bessa stopped questioning Kaleb about the encounter with the succubus. Somehow he had made it through her grilling without lying or revealing the full truth of his encounter with the demon, a feat of editing and obfuscation at which Darra and A.J. marveled. "Well, I'm just glad you weren't hurt," Bessa said, when she was satisfied she had gotten the whole story. "I just hope we can say the same for Talia."

"I hate that we had to come all the way back here just so Gram can do her spell again," Kaleb said. "If I were a real mage, I'd know a locating spell, and Talia would be on her way home."

"Hey, you are a real mage," Bessa said.

"I hardly know any spells by heart," Kaleb said. "And the more complex a casting is, the less control I have over it."

"But your gram says you have plenty of power," Bessa said.

"Gram sad that?" the mage asked.

"She said if you study and practice hard, you could even surpass her abilities someday," Bessa replied.

"Wow," Darra said. "That would be something to see."

"She was probably just exaggerating," Kaleb said. "You know how she likes to brag about my accomplishments."

"She does still talk about how quick you were to potty train," Bessa said, and Kaleb cringed.

"Don't sell yourself short, Kaleb," A.J. said. "I wouldn't be standing here if you didn't have some pretty awesome abilities."

"And you saved that orc, too," Darra said.

"Oh, that sounds like a fun story," Bessa said. Suddenly an arrow whizzed past the teens. It almost hit one of the warriors ahead of them, but she happened to veer slightly to the left as she walked, and it saved her getting an arrow in the shoulder. The warriors and teens turned in unison to see a wall of hundreds of soldiers in the distance. Many were arming their bows, but some were charging at the warriors head-on, swords drawn.

"*Min dikai lyng*," Kaleb said in the old speak, as he gestured with his right hand. The soldiers groaned and cursed as a bright white light flashed out of Kaleb's palm.

"Run!" Tora said, and the Tribals and teens sprinted away as the soldiers rubbed at their eyes. They managed to stay just out of range of the soldiers' arrows, and when they got back to the tree village, they rushed up the stairs and into the lower-level huts.

Trosclair nearly spilled his tea when he heard Tora calling out in her loudest voice, "Attack! We're under attack!" Kaleb and the other teens soon raced into Ramla's hut, and Darra and Kaleb immediately took up positions by the western window.

"What's going on?" Ennio asked.

"Soldiers!" Darra said. "Hundreds of them!"

"The Commandant must be looking for us," Trosclair said.

"Or us," Darra said, as she loaded her crossbow. "He found us on Tribal lands before; I guess he figured we'd come back here." She looked out the western window, found a soldier approaching through the trees with his bow nocked, and took aim. When the man pointed his bow upward to shoot at one of the last Tribals fleeing into a hut, Darra squeezed Madeline's trigger, and a split second later, the soldier was on the ground screaming, a bolt imbedded in his thigh.

"Wait here!" Ramla said, as she rushed out of the tent at a speed Darra hadn't thought her capable of at her age. The old woman raced down the stairs to the ground floor of the forest. Several soldiers aimed their bows at her.

"Surrender!" shouted one of the soldiers. "We don't want to kill an old lady, but we will!"

"*Arrit marg cho*," Ramla said, gesturing with one hand, and the wind suddenly picked up and shifted directions. The soldiers fired at her, but the air itself came to Ramla's defense, deflecting the arrows. "*Ri tor mosa*!" Ramla yelled, and as she lifted her hands, several large rocks flew up from the ground and at the men.

"Fall back!" one of the soldiers yelled. "She's a witch!" More soldiers approached Ramla, but she held them off using the earth and air as her weapons and shield. She could only take on so many, however, and most of the soldiers got past her. They didn't try to storm up the stairs to raid the tree huts. Instead, they formed a rough line, took a knee, and started nocking their bows. More soldiers came up from behind, placed large shields in front of the archers, and then crouched down with them. Finally, a pair of soldiers holding torches started moving from archer to archer, lighting the tips of their arrows ablaze.

"Damn it!" Darra said, as she spied the flames from the window. "They're gonna try to burn us out!"

"Almost done," Aleksey said, as he worked the sharp end of the bone through the last few strands of the ropes around his feet. He quickly got to his knees and crawled over to Talia. He started sawing the bone into the ropes around her torso. "You'll be free in a minute." The wagon slowed and came to a halt, and Aleksey heard one of the men dismount from the drivers' seat.

"What'd we stop for?" yelled one of the men outside.

"Holleran's gonna take another turn on her before we do 'em," another man yelled back. Aleksey heard someone approaching the back of the wagon, but he was only halfway through the rope binding the water-witch. He yanked on it, and it tore apart. The half-elf then quickly moved to the back end of the wagon, and when the flap of the cover shifted open, Aleksey grabbed the man on the other side by the shirt and head-butted him as hard as he could.

"Ahh!" the half-elf immediately cried. "I shouldn't have done that with a head injury!" Aleksey pulled the man into the back of the wagon, which bounced up and down with the added weight. The dog mimicked Aleksey's attitude and began barking at the man. "So you're Holleran, I take it?"

"Y-yes," the man answered. "Please don't hurt me!"

"He's not the one you have to worry about," Talia said, as she finished removing the constrictive, suffocating blankets. She lurched forward, grabbed the bone from Aleksey's bound hands and pressed the sharp end to Holleran's throat. Next she went for the canteen hanging from a hook at his belt. She unscrewed the lid and turned it over in her mouth. Large dribbles fell down the sides of her face as she guzzled its contents.

"Slow down!" Aleksey said. "You'll make yourself sick." Talia ignored him and kept drinking until she began to spit up a little.

"Please don't let her kill me!" Holleran begged, and Aleksey shrugged.

"You run this little operation?" Aleksey asked, and Holleran nodded.

"But it wasn't my idea to kidnap the witch!" Holleran said. "I swear! The mage told us to do it."

"You expect me to believe you were ensorcelled?" Aleksey asked.

"Not ensorcelled, just... enticed," Holleran said. "We were just trying to sell our supplies, and he came up out of nowhere and told us of a way we could make ten times as much profit. I couldn't say no to that."

"But you could say yes to raping me?" Talia asked. "I see

the kind of man you are!" Talia pushed the bone into the man's neck flesh and drew blood, and the man screamed. Aleksey punched Holleran, which silenced him by way of knocking him out.

"Why did you do that?" Talia asked angrily. "I was going to get justice!"

"You were going to murder him," Aleksey said, as he held out his hands. Talia started untying the ropes around them. "I won't stand by and watch you do that to yourself."

"Then close your eyes or turn your head, half-elf!" Talia said. "Because I will have my revenge for what they've done to me!"

"See? Even you admit you're after revenge, not justice," Aleksey said.

"Sometimes the two align perfectly," Talia replied. The half-elf and the water-witch stared at each other for a long moment, and finally he relented.

"Okay," Aleksey said. "Are you going to need any help? There are a lot them. I won't kill them, but I could take some out for you."

"No, thank you," Talia said, as she crawled to the back of the wagon and peeked out of the flaps. "*Ri ta perla*," she said, making a fluid motion with her hands. The water in the canteen, as well as that which she had spilled on the wagon bed, floated up and swirled in front of her. She closed her fists, and the water separated and froze - into a half dozen floating ice daggers. "This is all the help I'll need." She started to move out of the wagon, then stopped and looked back to the half-elf. "Just... stay ready, in case the mage comes back."

"I will," Aleksey said. Talia crawled out of the wagon, and soon the night was filled with shouts and cries for help. Aleksey sat in the back of the wagon petting the dog, trying not to remember the last time he had heard the sounds of a slaughter. A man screamed out in pain, and the dog whimpered sympathetically. "I know, girl. But at least this time it's rapists, not innocents," he whispered to the animal on his lap. After a few minutes, it grew eerily quiet outside the wagon, and Aleksey knew it was over. He got out, put the dog on the ground, and moved to the front of the wagon to start unhitching the horses without looking directly at the bodies strewn out all around him, while Talia came back to take care of Holleran.

The Tribals had put windows into their huts for more than just allowing air and light inside; they were also the perfect size for shooting a bow out of, and that's just what they did as the soldiers took aim. Most of the Tribal arrows struck the shields the men were crouched behind, but occasionally a soldier would fall.

"Draw!" one of the soldiers yelled, and the archers drew their flaming arrows and took aim at the huts. Bessa aimed her bow at the commanding soldier, but she was a split-second late on the release, and the man managed to give his command to fire before her arrow hit him in the shoulder. The archers sent their arrows high into the trees, and the flaming shafts struck the roofs and bamboo walls of the huts. One arrow pierced the roof of Ramla's hut, and the dry thatching ignited almost immediately.

"The roof!" A.J. said. "It's on fire!"

"Uh, Kaleb?" Darra asked. "Can you do something about that?"

"I'll try," Kaleb said.

"Try?" Bessa repeated, covering her mouth with her sleeve to filter the smoke that was already filling the hut. "You're a fire mage. It should be easy."

"I can create fire, no problem," Kaleb said. "Quelling it has always been harder for me." He gestured at the flames overhead and said, "*Ercha!*" The fire did not respond. Kaleb repeated the attempt, but again nothing happened. Bessa put her hand on his arm, and he looked over at her.

"You can do this," she said.

Kaleb looked back to the flames, gestured a third time and repeated the word for "extinguish" in the old speak. This time his eyes glowed amber, and the fire obeyed.

"Thank the gods!" Bessa said. She gave Kaleb a quick hug, but the mage pulled away when something outside the eastern window caught his attention. He moved to it and saw flames had taken hold of several huts. Most of the families inside ran across the bridges and up or down the stairs to other huts, but one family's door frame had caught fire, trapping them inside. The mage worked his spell on the doorway, and as soon as the fire was out, the family ran to the relative safety of another hut. Kaleb turned his attention to the other flaming huts and began working to save them one at a time.

"I wish I had a bow," Ennio said. "I feel useless, trapped up here with just a sword."

"You may get to use it soon," Darra said, looking out the window. "They're moving forward." The soldiers stood, still hiding behind their shields, and took a few tentative steps forward at a time, firing their arrows at each interval. The Tribals returned their fire sporadically, and they had better luck landing their shafts now because the shields could not cover the men entirely when they stood. But for every soldier who fell, there were twenty more behind him, ready to take his place.

Aleksey and Talia brought their horses to a stop at the edge of the woods near the northern end of the Tribal village. "Is that fire?" Talia asked, as she caught glimpses of orange glowing through the trees.

"Yes," Aleksey said, smelling the faint smoke in the air. "And I hear shouting. The Tribe is under attack!" He slid off his horse, pulled the dog out of the saddlebag she'd been riding in, and let her down onto the ground. He held out an arm to Talia, which she took to steady herself as she got off the horse. "Come on!" Aleksey said.

"You go ahead," Talia said. "I'm too weak to run. But there is one way I can help." She looked skyward, flashed a gesture at the dark clouds, and said "rain" in the old speak. It took a few seconds, but soon Aleksey felt a drop on his cheek, and another on his head.

"Are you sure you'll be alright?" he asked.

"I'll be fine," Talia answered. "Go! Help them!" Aleksey looked down at the dog, which was faithfully following his every move.

"Stay, girl," Aleksey commanded. "Guard." The dog barked once, short and crisp, as if to signify her understanding, and Aleksey took off through the trees. As he ran, he noticed the rain getting heavier and heavier, until it was pouring so hard that he could barely see fifteen feet in front of him, and that was with his keen elven eyesight. The fires had all gone out by the time he reached the village, and he dashed toward the western edge, where Ramla's hut was located.

Most humans would find it almost impossible to function in this weather, and the soldiers were no exception. Their torches had been doused by the rain, which left them practically blind in the dark. They stopped firing and started yelling to one another, looking for orders, and because no one could clearly hear beyond their immediate vicinity, it quickly devolved into chaos. This presented an opportunity that Ramla couldn't pass up. She waved her hands and said a few syllables in the old speak, and the very ground beneath the line of archers and shieldsmen buckled, throwing them off their feet and into the muddy earth. They fell out of line, and Ramla smiled as she heard one of the men yell, "Retreat!" Soon others were repeating the call, until the soldiers started scrambling back in the direction from which they'd come.

Ramla's smile disappeared when a soldier lunged out of the rain in front of her, swinging his sword. The tip of the weapon grazed her upper arm as she jumped backwards. "Gonna die now, witch!" the man growled, as he stalked toward her. A fist holding a sword slammed into the man's head from behind, and when the soldier fell, Aleksey was standing there, drenched and smug.

"Miss me?" he asked.

"I had him right where I wanted him," Ramla said, clutching her bleeding arm. They made their way back to the stairs that led up to her hut, and Ramla bellowed into the trees, "My people! Grab your weapons, and fight!" The warriors and hunters of the Tribe obeyed, emerging from their huts with their weapons in hand. They made their way to the forest floor and amassed behind Ramla. "Disarm them and subdue them if you can," Ramla said. "But kill them if you must." The Tribals split into small groups and moved cautiously through the trees, looking for those soldiers who had not yet retreated. After an hour of searching and skirmishing, Ramla was satisfied that all the soldiers had either fled or been killed, and she called her people back to their homes.

She made her way up the stairs to her hut, and when she entered, she craned her neck upward to survey the damage from the fire. A steady flow of rainwater drizzled down through the hole in the thatching, soaking the fur carpet. Ramla crossed to the shelf, picked up a large bowl, and placed it under the leak.

"Gram," Kaleb said. "You're bleeding!"

"Oh," she said. "Right." She performed a spell on the bowl of rainwater in front of her, and then poured it over her shoulder. The wound closed up, leaving a very thin scar, and she replaced the bowl under the falling water.

"So we won, I guess?" Kaleb asked.

"We beat them back," Ramla said. "For now."

Aleksey appeared in Ramla's doorway, holding the dog, which was shivering from the cold rain that had soaked it. Aleksey let it down onto the floor, and it shook off some of the water clinging to its fur.

"Aww," Darra said, kneeling down to pet it. "Whose dog is this?"

"Ours," Aleksey said.

"Really?" Darra asked, a huge smile stretching her lips wide. "I thought you didn't like dogs?"

"I never said I didn't like dogs," Aleksey said. "I just prefer cats. But this little girl and I have... bonded. She saved me and helped me free Talia."

"And Talia saved us all," Ramla said.

"Ramla, do you have anything to eat?" Aleksey asked. "She's starving, and I made her a promise earlier."

Ramla went to her shelf and took the lid off a ceramic jar. She reached into it and pulled out a handful of some sort of jerky. The scent of dried meat hit Aleksey and the dog at the same time. The animal barked and wagged its tongue, then began jumping up on its hind legs at Ramla's feet. The half-elf crossed to take the treats from the tribal woman. "Thank you," he said, as he dropped to his knees to feed the dog by hand.

"What's her name?" Trosclair asked, as Darra scooted over to pet the animal some more.

"I don't know," Aleksey answered. "Her previous owners never mentioned it."

"Previous owners?" Darra asked, giving her father a suspicious look. "Dad, is this a stolen dog?"

"No!" Aleksey said, waving her suspicion away. "Although as bad a shape as she's in, I'd have had every right to liberate her. But this little girl is an orphan."

"Like us," Kaleb said, and Aleksey nodded.

"Well then, I claim the right to name her," Darra said.

"Okay," Aleksey said. "But with that comes the responsibility of cleaning up after her."

"Oh, I would, but I think I heard A.J. say he wanted that

job," Darra said, pointing to the pilot.

"I did, huh?" A.J. asked, smiling. "Sure, I guess I can help out."

"While you're here," Aleksey said, and the pilot's mood suddenly plummeted.

"Yeah," A.J. said, looking to his girlfriend, who was still petting the dog but was no longer smiling. "While I'm here."

By early the next morning, the skies had cleared, at least for a little while, and A.J. and Darra took the dog for a walk. The pilot expected them to be the only ones up, as it was before sunrise, but the people of the Tribe were scattered across the forest floor, collecting the bodies of the soldiers too stubborn or stupid to flee when they had the chance. The men and women of the Tribe didn't want their children to wake up to the grim reality of war, so they piled the bodies onto wheelbarrows and carried them far into the forest.

"What will they do with them?" A.J. asked, as a Tribesman pushed a wheelbarrow past the teens.

"They'll give them a proper burning," Darra said. "I still can't believe the Commandant was willing to slaughter a whole village just to get at us."

"I can," A.J. said. "The guy seemed like a sociopath." Darra gave him a quizzical look. "That's a really bad type of person."

"Men like him are the reason I decided to become a warrior," Darra said. "Somebody has to stand up to tyrants, and I'm gonna be ready when I do. Have I told you about chi-fighting?"

"No," the pilot said.

"It's a style of self-defense that draws on the body's own natural mystic energy, sort of like a mage does when they cast a spell," Darra said. "It allows a warrior to accomplish awesome feats of strength, speed and agility. I once saw a woman do this flying kick higher than your head, and the board she broke with it was three fingers thick."

"That's amazing," A.J. said.

"Dad says when I turn sixteen this summer, I can study at the academy that teaches it," she said.

"So you're going away?" he asked. "That's a definite bummer."

"It's not for another half a year," Darra said. "Besides, you could be gone by then yourself."

"I don't know," A.J. said. "The way things are going, I might be here a while. And the more I get to know you, the less terrible that possibility sounds." Darra smiled and took A.J.'s hand, and as they walked, the sun began to rise.

Aleksey and Ramla met in her hut after breakfast. The tribal woman gestured to an empty chair, and Aleksey took a seat. "I guess we'll be heading out today," Aleksey said. "Hopefully the battle last night taught the Commandant not to mess with the Tribe. But... what if he comes back?"

"I have decided to start training my mages in spells of self-defense and attack," Ramla said. "Last night was just the first battle in what may be a very long war, and my people will be ready to survive it."

"I'm sure of that," Aleksey said.

"I've spent all morning meditating on your outworlder's predicament, and I think I have come up with the most obvious solution."

"All morning? It's barely past ninth," Aleksey said.

"If we cannot open another portal from this side to return him home, his rescue will have to come from the other side," Ramla said. "His flying ships will have to leap through the heavens to our world, if he is ever to see his own again."

"That's a fine plan," Aleksey said. "Except his people have no way of knowing where he was sent when he passed through the first portal. How do you expect them to launch a rescue operation with no knowledge of our world?"

"I don't," Ramla said. "The key will be getting a message back to his people."

"And you can do this?" he asked.

"No," she said. "But I may know of a way it can be done."

CHAPTER NINE
"A UNIQUE HORN"

Aleksey led his band of teen adventurers - and their newly adopted dog, which had been groomed and was filling out nicely - into a clearing with a wide stream running through it. The reflections of several moons rippled on top of the water, which ran gentle and clear, so that the dark black stone that composed the bed of the stream was visible even with a depth of eight or nine feet in some places. "Well," the half-elf said. "We're here."

"This doesn't look like the ruins of an ancient city," Darra said.

"Oh, we won't make it there until midday tomorrow, at the earliest," Aleksey said. "If Ramla's information is good. I just thought we could all use a bath."

"Is that a polite way of saying we stink?" A.J. asked.

"I wasn't going to say it," Aleksey said as he began undressing. "It's just proof that your little teenage bodies are working properly. It's been a hard week of travelling."

"I'll say!" Trosclair said. "My feet aren't used to walking so many miles every single day. They're covered in blisters."

"Why didn't you say something earlier?" Ennio asked.

"I didn't think there was any point," Trosclair said. "There's nothing that can be done about it."

"We could've slowed down," Ennio said. "Or I could've carried you."

"I'm nearly as heavy as you are!" Trosclair protested. "And

you're not my litter bearer – you're my boyfriend!"

"Still, you have to admire his enthusiasm," Darra said.

"I can bandage your feet, to cushion the blisters," Kaleb offered while he stripped down. "Once you wash them off."

"Thank you," Trosclair said. "But I don't think I can bathe in this water. It's freezing out here!"

"That's why I brought us to this particular part of the stream," Aleksey said as he waded into the water in his undershorts. "It's a hot spring."

"That sounds amazing!" Trosclair said. "It's just what my feet need."

Kaleb soon joined Aleksey in the water, followed by the pilot. Ennio and Trosclair peeled off their clothes, and the former gingerly removed the latter's boots, whistling when he saw the raw sores on the young man's feet. Then the soldier made good on his offer and carried the prince into the water. Darra was the last one in, as she had ducked behind a tree to change into her bathing tunic. The teens swam around for a while, before they started scrubbing their bodies underneath the surface. Aleksey left the water to retrieve a jar from his pack. When he returned, Darra swam over to him, and he smeared a glop of pale yellow goo onto her head, working it all the way through her hair from the scalp to the ends.

"What is that?" A.J. asked. "It smells amazing!"

"It's a mixture of chamomile, lemon juice, and *pistari* resin," Aleksey said.

"It's to lighten my hair," Darra said.

"So you're not a natural blonde?" Trosclair asked.

"Nope," Darra said. "My natural hair color is pretty close to yours, actually. But I was almost caught during one of Dad's jobs a few years ago. The constables got a good look at me and put up fliers and everything. So we decided to dye my hair to better hide my identity."

"Well, now there's a whole kingdom looking for you as a blonde," Ennio said. "Maybe you'd have better luck as a brunette." Aleksey chuckled, and Darra splashed the soldier playfully.

The next afternoon, Aleksey consulted the map Ramla had drawn and declared, "We should be coming up on the outskirts of this city any time now. Keep your eyes open."

"What exactly are we looking for?" Trosclair asked. "I read that the Great Cataclysm destroyed all of the ancient civilizations."

"Ruins. Crumbled structures, underneath all this vegetation," Aleksey said. "So you've studied the Great Cataclysm?" The prince nodded. "That's an advanced topic for a human."

"My tutor wanted me to know how the ancient societies failed," Trosclair said. "So I could learn from their folly."

"He sounds like a wise man," Aleksey said.

"He was - or, I mean, is," Trosclair said. "Gods, this is the first time I'm even thinking about what happened to the people loyal to me in the palace!"

"Commandant Burke would have no reason to harm them," Ennio said as he patted Trosclair on the back. "I'm sure they all fled to somewhere safe, just like Serena."

"So, how did the ancient societies fall?" Darra asked.

"It's a long story," Aleksey warned. "Though I suppose we do have time for a history lesson. It all started with a great war over a thousand years ago. The humans, elves and other races lived alongside one another back then, though of course they had natural enemies, like the ogres and the denizens of the Dread Continent, who still plague the elves to this day. But the war with the frost giants took a greater toll than any of their other struggles, and the people grew desperate for a way to beat them back. They looked to magic, and to the Magus Prime, for a solution."

"I don't know what that is," Ennio said.

"The Magus Prime is a title given to the greatest sorcerer in all of Ona," Kaleb explained. "It passes from mage to mage, and generation to generation, through a process including multiple trials and ritual combat."

"That's right," Aleksey said. "And there is only ever one at a time. But the Magus Prime at the time of the frost giant wars was an old man, weak with a sickness of the bones even his magic could not cure. So the tournament of mages was held, and one mage rose through the trials and magical battles to become the clear successor to the old man. Only men were allowed to compete for the title back then, but when this mage won, she dropped her illusion and revealed herself as a woman. The other mages were equally stunned and furious that a woman had entered the tournament and bested them. The old Magus Prime even refused to perform the ritual that would see her ascend to the title, and she left the tournament, vowing to create her own tradition of magic.

The old Magus Prime decided he would deal with the frost giants himself, and he created a spell that would move the planet itself closer to the sun. He knew this would raise the temperatures across the globe, and that wherever the frost giants had come from, they would suffer. But he also had an ulterior motive. He knew the change in Ona's climate would wreak havoc on the environment, and he and his school of dark wizards knew the people would become dependent on their magic just to survive. Their goal was to dominate the world, and to make themselves inconceivably rich in the process. So the Magus Prime cast his spell, and Ona's orbit was forever altered. But he died in the attempt, and his spell went awry. It killed the frost giants well enough, but it also threatened to destroy all other life on the planet - including the men who'd aligned themselves with him. Only the intervention of the woman the mages had rejected saved the planet and its people from total annihilation. She assumed the title of Magus Prime, but without direct knowledge of the old Magus' spell, she was powerless to reverse it. The best she could do was shift the positions of Ona's twelve moons, aligning them to eclipse the sun and provide the continent with patches of shady relief. She also melded her consciousness with the flora and fauna of the planet, directing it to spontaneously evolve to survive the sudden changes in climate and sunlight."

"Is that why the plants and animals here are so big?" A.J. asked.

"Precisely," Aleksey said.

"What happened to the woman who became the Magus Prime?" Darra asked.

"Some say she died correcting the old man's mistake," Aleksey said. "But others say she merely retired, her powers having been exhausted by the enormous effort of saving the world. In any case, the Great Cataclysm, as it's now known, is the reason the Tribes, the elves and all the other magical races were kicked out of the new kingdoms that arose - the humans blamed them for the magic that had ripped apart their world. Even the elves shunned magic, not out of fear but in penance."

"So there are no elven mages?" Kaleb asked.

"Oh, there are still a few elves out in the world who practice magic," Aleksey answered. "You just wouldn't want to meet them. But the Great Cataclysm also brought to light the sexism rampant in elven society, and my mother's people changed their attitudes toward women for the better. Now elven women enjoy all the same rights as their men, at least as far as the law is concerned."

"I've considered trying to move my own kingdom toward the same end," Trosclair said.

"Really?" Darra asked excitedly. "What would you change first?"

"I think the laws of inheritance need a reexamination," Trosclair said. "And I'd like to see women rise to the Scientific Advisory Council. If a man's intelligence can earn him a title of nobility, I see no reason why women shouldn't enjoy the same opportunity."

"I think I'm gonna like it when you become king," Darra said.

"Well, Mrs. Applebaum – that's my nanny, or she was, when I was little – she always says, 'A good king gives the peasants what they want and the nobles something to do.' And I feel like my people – the majority of them, anyway – expect a progressive agenda from me."

"That will be healthy for your kingdom, and the rest of the continent," Aleksey said. "Where DuVerres leads, the other kingdoms follow."

"I just hope the conservative noble faction doesn't—*aagh*!" Trosclair tripped and fell to the forest floor.

"Are you okay?" Ennio asked, crouching down to help him up. The dog bounced over toward the prince, who patted the animal on its head.

"Yeah," Trosclair said, rising. "I just tripped on this stupid branch and banged my knee. It's no big deal."

"It's not a branch," the half-elf said, examining the bump on the forest floor covered in moss and leaves. It ran in a straight line about twelve feet long, then turned at a right angle and continued for a few more feet. "You just found our first foundation wall."

"That's it?" Darra asked. "That's all that's left of a whole building?" Ennio approached Aleksey, a frown on his face.

"All this travelling is too much for the prince," the soldier said. "We need to stop moving around and find someplace to hide out for the next six months."

"We're on a quest to return the outworlder to his home world," Aleksey said. "We'll stop when the quest is complete."

"I don't mean to sound ungrateful, but you're being paid to protect the prince," Ennio said. "That should be your top priority."

"I'm great at multitasking," Aleksey said. "By sticking to the forests as much as we can, we avoid human contact, which helps protect the prince. And we are headed to a place where you two can take long-term sanctuary. We're just making a few strategic stops along the way."

"Where are you taking us?" Trosclair asked. Aleksey hesitated and then smiled.

"The Elven Isles," he said.

"What?" Ennio asked incredulously. "Are you insane? That's all the way across the continent!"

"Which means we're basically halfway there," Aleksey said. "We'll risk a train for most of the journey, after we get out of your kingdom, where there's less chance we'll all be recognized. And when we get to where we're going, you'll be welcomed with open arms, in a style befitting a future monarch. I promise you, the elves will find the prospect of entertaining you for the next half a year too exciting to resist."

"How do you know that?" Ennio asked.

"The elven king is very old – almost two thousand," Aleksey said. "He was already on the throne at the time of the Great Cataclysm, and he longs for the days when elven royalty socialized with their human counterparts."

"I suppose it makes sense," Trosclair said. "Milian did pack several letters of introduction with the royal seal on them, just in case we took refuge in another kingdom. I just never imagined it would be the Elven Isles!"

"If you agree to the plan, it could sow the seeds of harmony between humans and elves," Aleksey said. "Who knows? They might even lend you a hand in taking back your kingdom." Trosclair looked to Ennio, who shrugged.

"It's your decision," the young soldier said. "Although it would be nice to have the elves as allies rather than enemies." Trosclair chewed on his lower lip as he considered it.

"I'm in!" he finally said. "I'll never have another opportunity like this."

"Yes!" Kaleb said, pumping his fist. "I've always wanted to see the Elven Isles."

"I think that's a wise choice," Aleksey said to the prince. "Now, since you were kind enough to find our first structure, we're on the lookout for a doorway that will lead us underground."

"How do you know that?" Ennio asked.

"It's part of a very old song the tribal elders sometimes sing," Kaleb said. "It's supposed to point the way to an ancient oracle."

"Well, go on," Trosclair prompted. "Sing it for us."

"Oh, I – I don't really know how to sing," the tribal lad said.

"Just try," Trosclair said.

"Okay, fine," Kaleb said. He cleared his throat and then sang in a surprisingly high tenor, "The city fell when Ona spun toward her love, the burning sun. But Arol's fire could not burn through the double doors of maple hewn into the hillside under oak, bespelled with magic words mage-spoke to offer hope, a guiding light. The Oracle can clear the night away. Just with her words comes day."

"Wow," Trosclair said. "You have a really nice voice."

"Thanks," Kaleb said, blushing. "There's more to it, but you get the idea."

"So we're looking for doors in a hillside, under an oak tree," Darra said. "That shouldn't be too hard to find."

"Except the song was written a millennium ago," Aleksey said. "That oak tree is long dead."

"So how are we supposed to find the doors?" Kaleb asked.

"We'll just have to search all the hills in the area," Aleksey said.

"But that could take days," Ennio said.

"So we'd better get started," Aleksey replied. They divided up into teams – Trosclair went with Ennio, of course, and Darra grabbed A.J.'s hand and led him in the opposite direction. Aleksey resisted the impulse to call his daughter back and began searching the hillsides with Kaleb.

It was well-past sundown when Aleksey heard Darra calling out in an excited voice, "Dad! We found it!" Darra kept calling periodically, and Aleksey and Kaleb made their way steadily toward the sound. Trosclair and Ennio had already beaten them there when they finally came upon the hillside. The teens were standing in front of a set of large, maple double doors; they were covered in hanging grass and moss, but they were intact. To Aleksey's surprise, there was even an old oak tree on the hillside directly above them.

"Well, I'll be," Aleksey said. "Whoever cast the spell on these doors must have protected the oak tree, too, to serve as a sign for future generations."

"Well, since I found it, I get to kick the door down," Darra said. "Like a chi-fighter would."

"Of course," Aleksey said, gesturing to the doors. Darra crossed to them, lifted a booted foot, and slammed it into one of the doors. She hid the pain that shot up her leg and, straightening her blouse, turned back to face her father.

"You can do it if you want," she said casually, clearing the way for the half-elf. Aleksey suppressed his laughter and positioned himself in front of the door. He took a running start and slammed into the doors with his shoulder, but his effort was no more successful than Darra's had been.

"Stand back," Kaleb said. "This is a job for a mage."

"You think you can open it?" Aleksey asked.

"After the Commandant threw us in the dungeon, I realized I never wanted to be trapped behind a locked door, ever again," Kaleb said. "So I've been studying a new spell that's supposed to undo any lock."

"That's brilliant, Kaleb!" Darra said.

"I just hope it works," the mage said as he focused his concentration on the doors. "*Daw ni, daw vi toa*!" His eyes glowed amber as he gestured, and Aleksey heard the lock mechanism moving.

"I think it's working, Kay!" the half-elf said.

"You're handier than a Swiss Army knife!" A.J. said. The others looked at him blankly. "That's a type of knife that's really... handy." The doors slowly began to swing open – and from the other side came a threatening growl.

"Back up!" Aleksey commanded. "There's something alive inside!"

"After a thousand years?" Darra asked. "What could possibly live that long without food and water?"

"Something big, from the look of it," Aleksey said as he

peered at the silhouette approaching the entrance. "Weapons up!" Darra raised her crossbow, A.J. lifted his spear, and Ennio drew his sword as a pale, sickly-looking ogre emerged from the doors. He was fully eight feet tall, with only shreds of faded animal skins clothing him, and his own skin was a pale grey. He bellowed at the adventurers, but his ribs showed when he did, making him seem more weak than threatening.

"Gods," Darra said, lowering her weapon. "He looks like he's about to fall over." She took her waterskin off.

"Darra, what are you doing?" Aleksey asked as she took a few steps toward the beast with the waterskin held out before her. The dog started barking and growling.

"It's clearly thirsty," Darra said. The ogre suddenly reached out a hand and snatched the waterskin from the young woman, who squealed and jumped back just a little. The beast unplugged the skin and turned it over above its mouth, draining its contents. "See?" Darra said, after she regained her composure. "You're starving, too, aren't you, fella?" She dug a hand into her satchel and came out with a couple of plums, which she again held out to the ogre. The animal dropped the waterskin, which spilled out onto the ground. He took the plums from Darra slowly, holding her eye contact, and then he opened his mouth and threw both plums in at the same time. He swallowed both fruits whole in a single gulp. When he looked back at Darra, she could swear there were tears welling up in his eyes. Then he simply turned and leapt away. Within a few seconds, he had disappeared into the trees.

"Wow," Darra said. "That was close!"

"I don't understand," A.J. said. "If it was really trapped in there for a thousand years with no food or water, how did it survive?"

"Ogres are like dragons," Aleksey said.

"You mean they don't have souls?" the pilot asked, and Darra folded her arms over her chest and rolled her eyes.

"Ogres have souls," Aleksey said, ignoring his daughter. "They're just animalistic. But they're similar to dragons because it takes a sacred object to kill them."

"I guess virtual immortality doesn't guarantee a good life," Kaleb said. "Just a long one."

"That's for certain," Aleksey said. "And I would know. Now,

let's see what the ogre was guarding." The half-elf moved to the doorway and ducked his head inside. His eyes quickly adjusted to the darkness, and he saw there was a set of steps leading down into another chamber. Aleksey and the teens crept inside and down the stairs by the light of Kaleb's finger flame, which he'd learned to grow to about the size of a fist. When they reached the lower chamber, they stopped. Four open doorways stood before them. Above the first doorway was a symbol that resembled flames. The second doorway had a similar design that looked like a tornado, and the third and fourth had symbols resembling waves and a mountain.

"Which one do we take?" Darra asked.

"Let's see," Kaleb said as he tried to remember the second verse. "And through the doors you'll no doubt find a trouble of the monstrous kind," he sang. "Oops. I should've sung that part before we opened the doors."

"It's okay," Aleksey said. "Keep going."

"A trouble of the monstrous kind," Kaleb half-sang at a sped up tempo to find his place. "What lies below can rise above to summon her, the wisest of the oracles all known to man, if cross the maze your feet can land."

"It's a maze?" Trosclair asked.

"Uh-oh," Ennio said.

"What is it?" Darra asked.

"I'm amazing at working out mazes!" Trosclair said.

"Here we go," Ennio said under his breath.

"I know because, when I visit other castles and palaces, I always figure out their hedge mazes," Trosclair said. "Without a guide. I love them so much, I even have a few of the farmers around the city carve mazes into their corn fields before harvest every fall."

"It's true," Ennio said. "He's mad for mazes."

"How long will it take you?" A.J. asked.

"That depends on how big and how complex it is," Trosclair said. "It could take the better part of the evening, that's for sure."

"Then we'd better split up again," Aleksey said as he moved to the wall and removed an ancient torch from its cobweb-covered sconce. He held it above Kaleb's finger flame, and the dry, brittle cloth went up instantly. Still, it burned hot enough to catch the resin-soaked wood on fire. "Kaleb, you go with Ennio and Trosclair. Search the fire and air paths. Darra, A.J. and I will take the water and earth. And stay alert! We don't know what else could be down here." The mage nodded and crossed to Ennio.

"Well?" the soldier asked. "Which shall we try first?"

"Fire, definitely," Kaleb said. "It's my element. That should be lucky, right?"

"Let's hope," Ennio said as the three teens started through the doorway.

"The key to solving a really good maze is making a detailed map as you go," Trosclair said, as he withdrew one of the sealed envelopes Milian had sent with him. Next he pulled out a pencil and drew a straight line on the back of the envelope to indicate the corridor they were in. When they reached the end, the corridor split into two paths. Above one was a picture of the sun; above the other, moons and stars.

"Day or night?" Ennio asked.

"Day, I guess," Kaleb said. They followed their chosen path, which twisted and turned, and Trosclair marked it all down. "So..." the mage began, before he said quickly, "Never mind."

"What?" Ennio asked.

"Can I ask you two a personal question?" Kaleb asked.

"Sure," Ennio said.

"How personal?" Trosclair asked, but he was smiling.

"I just wondered when you first knew," Kaleb said.

"Knew what?" Ennio asked.

"That you might be, you know – queer," Kaleb said.

"Oh. I've sort of always known," Trosclair said. "In fact, I remember going to the dictionary when I was about nine and looking up the word 'queer' just to see if it meant what I thought it meant."

"Wow," Kaleb said, before turning to Ennio. "What about you?"

"I honestly couldn't say," Ennio replied. "I guess I didn't know for sure until we first kissed. And that was almost a year and a half ago, so I was about your age."

"I see," Kaleb said.

"Why do you ask?" Trosclair asked.

"Oh, uh... it's my—my girlfriend," the mage said. "Or my ex-girlfriend. She thinks she might like girls as well as boys."

"Well, I hope you were supportive of her," Trosclair said.

"It can be very difficult to come to terms with at first." The trio turned a corner and came upon a dead end.

"Oh, yeah," Kaleb said, waving one hand dismissively. "No, I was very supportive, for sure."

"Good," Trosclair said as they turned around and headed back down the corridor. When they made it back to the original path, they took the 'night' passage, and Trosclair kept mapping their progress. They finally came upon a round chamber with three doors, marked with depictions of the heads of an eagle, a bear and a lion.

"It's your turn to pick," Ennio said to the prince.

"Bear," Trosclair said. "Definitely."

"I just hope we don't have to face the animal we chose or something like that," Kaleb said as they started down the passageway.

"That's not a real possibility, is it?" Trosclair asked.

"With the ancients, you never know," Kaleb said.

"Is there anything about it in your song?" Ennio asked.

"I don't think so," Kaleb said. "The next verse is just a rhyme for the children to chant along to."

"Well, how's it go?" Ennio asked.

"The lightning in the dark struck the king with its spark," Kaleb said. "The hunter drew his bow and hit the target on the mark. The virgin took her bath in the water in the brook. The giant showed his wrath to the daughter of the crook."

"Great," Trosclair said. "I can already feel that getting stuck in my head."

"So who was the first person you told?" Kaleb asked. "That you were queer."

"I guess technically it was my cousin, Frederick," Trosclair said. "Although my nanny, the Lord Advisor, and a whole roomful of strangers sort of found out at the same time."

"That must have been humiliating," Kaleb said.

"Actually, it was very liberating," Trosclair replied. "They were all very supportive."

"Is your ex-girlfriend considering telling people?" Ennio asked.

"Oh, no!" Kaleb said. "Definitely not! She's not ashamed or anything; she just doesn't think it's anyone else's business."

"Well, it's her decision to make," Trosclair said. "Although I know I'm a lot happier not having to hide my true self."

"Yeah," Kaleb said. "You're probably right." The trio rounded a curve and was met with another brick wall. "Gods damn it! Another dead end!"

"Hey, calm down," Trosclair said. "It's all part of the process." The prince drew an 'x' at the end of the line to indicate the end of the corridor, and they started back the way they'd come. When they got back to the chamber with the animal heads above the doors, Trosclair was struck with an idea.

"The king!" he said excitedly.

"What?" Ennio asked. "What king?"

"The lion!" Trosclair said. "He's the king of the jungle!"

"So?" Kaleb asked.

"The lightning in the dark struck the king with its spark," the prince repeated. "The first door we took had fire on it, and lightning is essentially a type of fire, according to the science books I've read. And we took the 'dark' path when we took the door with night above it. Now we're to take the path with the 'king' above it, and I'd wager my whole kingdom it will lead to a door that has something to do with a spark."

"That's brilliant!" Kaleb said.

"We can follow the clues in the rhyme directly to the oracle," Ennio said. "You're a genius!" The soldier kissed the prince on the lips, and Kaleb blushed and looked away.

Aleksey carried the torch, but the dog was leading the way. She was still mimicking the half-elf's emotions and attitude. She was excited but cautious, and she placed each paw down slowly and deliberately. When Aleksey stopped, she stopped, even if that meant freezing in place with one front paw lifted off the ground. After several minutes of this, Darra couldn't help herself, and she burst into laughter.

"What's so funny?" her father asked.

"The dog," Darra said. "She's just so much like you!"

"It is pretty cute," the pilot put in.

"She needs a name," Aleksey said, bending down to scratch the animal behind her ears.

"I know!" Darra said. "I just haven't thought of any that

really fit her, you know?"

"Tina," A.J. suggested.

"No," Darra said. "I'm not giving her a human name. That's too pedestrian."

"Desperado," the pilot said.

"That's a boy's name," Darra replied.

"You're putting far too much thought into it, honey," Aleksey said.

"But it's going to be her name for the rest of her life," Darra said. "I wanna get it right."

"How did you pick Darra's name?" A.J. asked.

"That was simple. It was my great-grandmother's," the half-elf answered. "It means 'little snowflake' in the old speak. I picked it because I knew any child of mine would grow up to be unique, and I wasn't wrong."

"Oh, Dad," Darra said, shaking her head. "I'm just like any other fifteen-year-old girl."

"Yeah," A.J. said, grinning. "Except you're a warrior, you spend a great deal of your time in the forest, and you could shoot the wings off a mosquito."

"Yeah," Darra said, smiling back at the pilot. "Except for that stuff."

"You forgot her intelligence and exceptionally kind heart," Aleksey said, stepping in between the teens and spoiling their moment.

"No," A.J. said. "I remembered."

The floor beneath Aleksey's feet shifted and sank a few inches. The half-elf's reflexes kicked in, and he leapt to another stone as the one below him fell out of the floor and crashed into the chamber below. Darra and A.J. backed away from the gaping hole left in the middle of the corridor, while the dog crept up to get a closer look.

"Unholy hells!" Aleksey said. "This place is falling apart."

"After a thousand years, that's no surprise," Darra said.

"Is it safe to go on?" A.J. asked.

"I'm not sure," Aleksey said. "We should spread our weight out, just in case." The teens separated, and then father, daughter, pilot and dog stepped carefully around the hole one by one as they resumed their search.

"So what is this Oracle like?" A.J. asked.

"I don't know much about that either," Aleksey said. "I know it's supposed to be the most powerful Oracle the ancients knew of, and that it's connected to distant realms. The ancients built this entire complex just to protect access to the artifact that will summon it."

"The song called the Oracle a 'her,'" Darra said. "So we know it's a woman."

"And is she immortal, like that ogre?" A.J. asked. "I mean, how do we even know she's still alive, after all this time?"

"We don't," Aleksey said.

"You just have to have a little faith," Darra said. The dog barked up at A.J. once as if to agree, and they walked on.

"Trixie," A.J. said, and Darra made a face and shook her head. Aleksey and the dog suddenly stopped, and the half-elf held out his hand forbiddingly.

"What is it, Dad?" Darra asked as the teens stopped a few feet behind him.

"There are skeletons up ahead," Aleksey said, peering at the slumped piles of bones lining both sides of the corridor. "Which probably means a booby trap of some kind."

"We should go back," A.J. said.

"This could be your best chance at ever seeing your family and friends again," Darra said. "Do you really want to give that up?"

"No," the pilot replied. "But it's not worth risking our lives."

"We're almost there," Darra said. "And besides, any trap set up in here is bound to be falling apart like the rest of this place."

"She's right," Aleksey said as he took off his pack. "But just to be sure..." He swung the pack and then released it, and it fell to the floor several feet ahead of them. The stone it landed on sank a fraction of an inch, and holes opened up in the walls on both sides of it, out of which jutted dozens of long, sharp wooden spikes.

"Jesus!" A.J. said.

"What?" Darra asked.

"It doesn't matter," A.J. said. "He's just someone Earth people sometimes say the name of when they're surprised or shocked."

"Hmph," Aleksey half-chuckled. "I can't believe your people named their home planet 'earth.' That would be like naming an ocean 'water.' Or if we named the dog 'dog.' Your people must lack creativity." The half-elf turned sideways and made his way through the narrow gap between the sharp ends of the spikes. He picked up his pack and looked back to the teens.

"Well?" he asked. "Are you coming, or not?"

"It'll be fine, I promise," Darra said to the pilot. She repeated her father's movements and made her way through the spikes, and when she looked back, A.J. was behind her. When they reached the other side, Aleksey was staring at the wall.

"You see something, Dad?" Darra asked.

"Maybe," he said, swiping his hand across the surface of the dusty wall to reveal writing. He kept wiping until the entire message came clear and then read aloud, "We came to see the Oracle. Got past the beast behind the door. But now my friends are dead and gone, their blood and guts spilled on the floor. So with their blood I write these words: Turn back before you meet the same! This maze is damned, and you are cursed to play a deathly game."

"Ew," Darra said. "Now I'm gonna have rhyming nightmares, like when I read those horror poems by L.T. Atkins."

"Why is everything here written in poems or songs, anyway?" A.J. asked as they continued walking.

"It was a necessity back in ancient times," Aleksey said. "Before the invention of the printing press, most people couldn't read, which left them vulnerable to exploitation from those elites who could. Important knowledge had to be passed down orally from generation to generation, and melodies and rhymes are easier to remember." They turned a corner and entered a large circular chamber. There were three doors inside, but unlike the ones they'd passed before, these doors were shut and had no identifiers above them. They also didn't have handles or any other visible way to open them. Next to each door was a thin slot with something sticking out of it.

"What are those?" Darra asked, as Aleksey walked to one of the slots to get a closer look.

"They look like playing cards, only bigger," Aleksey said, examining the dusty edge of the card. "This must be the 'deathly game' the message mentioned."

"So how do we play?" A.J. asked.

"I suppose we start by picking a card," Aleksey said.

"Although it could be another booby trap, so you and Darra ought to stand back." He grabbed the card next to the middle door.

"No," A.J. said, approaching the half-elf. "I should be the one to do it, just in case it is a trap."

"You're not exactly a warrior," Aleksey said. "Suppose this door has another ogre waiting behind it – a less friendly one than before. What would you do?"

"Scream, probably," A.J. said, and Aleksey smiled.

"Well, at least you're honest," the half-elf said.

"But you guys have been protecting me ever since I got here," A.J. said. "And we are looking for this oracle for me. Besides, I can't stand the thought of putting Darra in harm's way."

"Okay, you've convinced me," Aleksey said, stepping back a few paces and gesturing to the door. "It's all yours."

A.J. gripped the card with the tip of his fingers, took a deep breath, and pulled it out of its slot. The middle door suddenly flew up and open; at the same time, a door slammed down from out of the ceiling and into place in the corridor behind the adventurers.

"Great!" Darra said as she tested the new door. "Now we're stuck in here."

"I think we have a more immediate problem," A.J. said, as he looked upward into the doorway that had opened. It was a high shaft, and hanging from the ceiling was a large metal box. Aleksey could hear chains rattling as the box slowly eased toward the ground.

"What is it?" Aleksey asked.

"There's something coming down here," A.J. said. "A big metal box."

"The card," Aleksey said. "What's on it?" The pilot flipped it over and swallowed hard. He flashed the card at Aleksey. "Unholy hells!"

"Is that a demon?" Darra asked, coming closer. The image showed a horned, hoofed creature with shaggy grey fur and ferocious fangs and claws.

"It certainly looks like one," Aleksey said. "And I'd wager that's what's in the box."

"I—I don't want to fight that," A.J. said.

"Well, it's too late now," Aleksey said, as the bottom of the box came into view at the top of the doorway. The half-elf took off his pack and slid it to the floor. He drew his sword, and Darra took aim at the doorway with her crossbow. The pilot sat down his satchel and raised his spear. The box was sealed, but when it landed gently on the floor, the front side fell open - and Aleksey started to laugh. Darra gave him a quizzical look, and he pointed back to the box. "Go ahead," he said. "See for yourself!" The teens peered into the dark box and saw a pile of bones, including a horned, fanged skull. "I guess he wasn't immortal."

Suddenly there was a loud sound somewhere between a scrape and a groan. The stones underneath the box caved in, taking a good deal of the floor with it. The rest of the floor tilted and crashed down, and even Aleksey's half-elven reflexes couldn't keep him from tumbling down to the chamber below, along with his daughter, the pilot and the dog. He called Darra's name as they fell, but it was lost in the sound of the crash and the teens' screams. He landed on the floor on his hands and knees, picked up the torch, and swung his head around to find Darra. He saw that she had landed on the pilot, and both appeared unharmed. "The dog!" Aleksey cried. "Where is she?" The animal barked, and Aleksey saw her in the corner of the chamber. He exhaled a sigh of relief.

"Yeah, Dad, I'm fine," Darra said as she smiled down at A.J. "I'll, uh—I'll get off you now. You okay?" She rolled over onto the floor and stood up, then held out a hand to him.

"Yeah, I'm fine," A.J. said, taking her hand and standing. "Maybe a little bruised, but nothing's broken."

"I guess the weight of that box was too much for the floor," Aleksey said.

"Why is there no door in this chamber?" Darra asked, looking around at the brick walls.

"My guess is it's behind what used to be the floor," Aleksey said, as he took stock of their situation. "I think we'll have to go back up to get out. Stand back." The teens and dog backed away as directed. Aleksey jumped as high as he could, but his hands fell just short of the edge of the floor that remained intact above.

"It must be fourteen, fifteen feet," Darra said. "Even you can't jump that high, Dad."

"Still, it's very impressive," A.J. said. "You'd be great at basketball."

"I don't have time to wonder what that is," Aleksey said.

"So we're stuck?" Darra asked.

"We could always try the lift," Aleksey said, and Darra perked up.

"Okay!" she said excitedly.

"What's the lift?" A.J. asked.

"Just watch," Darra instructed. She backed up against the wall, and Aleksey squatted down and laced his fingers together, palms open upward. Darra ran at Aleksey at full speed, and when she got to him, she stepped up onto his hands with one foot and pushed off his shoulders with her hands. At the same time, he lifted his hands and stood up. Darra spun around as she flew above the half-elf's head, squeezing her whole body, and the half-elf caught her shoes in his palms. She raised her arms as high as she could, but even standing on her father's hands, she could not reach the floor above. "I don't think it's gonna work, Dad."

"Alright then," Aleksey said. "On three. One... Two... Three!" He popped her feet into the air just a few inches, and she twisted again, skirts swirling as she fell in a bow-shaped position. Aleksey caught her at the back and the legs, cradling her gently, and let her back down on the floor.

"Wow!" A.J. said. "Where'd you learn how to do that?"

"Oh, we've been pulling that little trick ever since she was three years old," Aleksey said. "My little girl's balance is impeccable. She was going to be a dancer, you know."

"So what do we do now?" Darra asked.

"I'm a lot taller than you," A.J said to Darra, before turning to Aleksey. "I can't lift a whole person like you just did, but you could stand on my shoulders."

"It's worth a try," Darra said. "You'd have a better chance of getting past that door than me, too."

"Okay," Aleksey said. The pilot lunged, and Aleksey stepped onto his thigh. He held Darra's hands to balance himself as he climbed up onto the young man's shoulders, and then he stood up. When he extended his hands, he was still short of the edge – but another leap had him pulling himself up onto the floor on his first try. When he reached the top, he looked back down at the teens. "I'll be back with a rope or some vines or something. Just stay safe, and don't be scared."

"I'm not," Darra said.

"I was talking to the dog," her father said as he turned and walked away.

"That's it," Ennio said, pointing to a doorway with a masked man carrying bars of gold above it. "The crook. This should be the last passageway." Kaleb and Trosclair followed the soldier inside.

"So how long have you practiced magic?" Trosclair asked.

"Oh, about six months," Kaleb said. "My Tribe has a rule that you can't be taught magic until you turn fourteen. But I had a few magical episodes before that."

"What's a magical episode?" Ennio asked.

"Oh, you know, the usual," Kaleb said. "Accidental fires. Random telekinesis. The occasional prophetic dream."

"What did you dream about?" the prince asked.

"Nothing big," Kaleb said. "A woman in our tribe was pregnant, and I dreamt she'd have twins – two boys. And I was right. Another time I dreamt of a terrible thunderstorm. It hit our tribe not three days later. It took us months to rebuild all the structures we lost."

"That's amazing," Ennio said. "You could be very useful in service to the prince. Think about it, Trosc – you could know Commandant Burke's every move before he made them. We'd crush him on the battlefield."

"I don't think it works like that," Kaleb said. "At least not yet."

"Still, having a magical ally is an advantage we have over the Commandant," Ennio said. "I'm glad we met you."

"Yeah, you've really opened our eyes to some fantastic possibilities," Trosclair said.

"Thanks," Kaleb replied. "I'm glad we met, too. And you've opened my eyes, as well."

"About what?" the prince asked.

"Oh, uh – my girlfriend," Kaleb said. "*Bwah!*" The mage jumped back, pulling thick strands of spider webs off his shoulder. His finger flame flared with his agitation. A brown, fuzzy spider fully six inches across scurried over the web that remained in front of them, and Ennio drew his sword. He slashed once, cutting through both the web and the arachnid, which was killed instantly and fell to the floor.

"Gross," Trosclair said as they each stepped around the

remains.

"It's better than having it crawl all over you," Ennio said, finger-walking his hand across Trosclair's shoulder in imitation of a spider. "Besides, it could have been poisonous. You may not be on the throne - yet - but I still take my job very seriously."

"I can tell," Trosclair said as he grabbed Ennio's hand.

"Venomous," Kaleb mumbled, not looking at the young couple.

"What?" Ennio asked.

"Plants and foods are poisonous," Kaleb said. "Spiders and snakes are venomous."

"Oh," Ennio said. "That's just my lack of education making itself known again."

"Oh, no," Trosclair said. "You've had an education."

"The military academy doesn't exactly churn out scholars," Ennio said.

"But you've sat in on plenty of my lessons. You're just as smart as anybody else here... Except for me," Trosclair said sporting his best snooty expression and cocky smile.

"Yeah, I'm sorry I said that," Kaleb said. "I only know the difference because we live among the plants and animals of the forest. On other subjects, like art and science, I have less of an education than you."

"The Tribe doesn't have schools?" Trosclair asked.

"No, they do," Kaleb said. "But if you're a good student, you have to do a lot of self-teaching. Like how I'm learning magic." They reached the end of the corridor and found a set of stairs leading down. When they reached the bottom, they found a chamber with a set of musical instruments lined up on separate pillars against the far wall. There were rusty brass instruments, several drums, triangles, cymbals and mallets, fifes and flutes, and even a lute and a bagpipe.

"Is this what we're looking for?" Ennio asked.

"I think so," Kaleb said.

Darra and A.J. sat with their backs against the brick wall, playing with the dog. Darra was pretending to hold something above its head, and the dog was jumping up at her hand, its tail wagging from the stimulation.

"Gingerbread," A.J. said, and Darra made a confused face.

"For the dog."

"Oh," Darra said. "Better. But I'd rather not name her after food. We come across far too many things that might like to eat her, and I don't want to tempt fate."

"You're silly," A.J. said.

"I'm serious!" Darra said. "They say Fela, the goddess of fortune, casts your fate according to your name."

"I thought you didn't believe in the gods and all that religious stuff," A.J. said.

"I don't worship the gods," Darra said. "But somebody has to be answering Lilith's prayers. I can't wait until I have power like hers!" Darra stood up, hiked up her skirt, and kicked at the empty air. A.J. chuckled and stood up.

"You're already pretty powerful, in my opinion," A.J. said. "You could take me down in a heartbeat." Darra smiled and pointed an authoritative finger at his chest.

"And don't you forget it!" she said. There was a beat of silence as the teens looked at each other. "So, my Dad's gone..." Darra said.

"Yeah?" A.J. prompted.

"Wanna make out?" the young woman asked.

"Yes," A.J. said, nodding. "I would like that." The teens started kissing, and almost immediately, the dog started barking at them. They ignored it for a few seconds, and then Darra broke away.

"Sorry," she said to the pilot, before craning her head toward the dog at their feet. "What's the matter, girl?" The dog kept barking.

"I think she really does take after your father," A.J. said. "She doesn't seem to like seeing us kiss. I think he left her as your guardian in his place."

"Hey, I like that," Darra said. "Guardian. It's simple, strong, and it describes her well. Come here, Guardian!" The dog leapt up at Darra's leg. "I think she likes it, too."

"Did I do good, then?" A.J. asked. Darra moved her face back in front of the pilot's.

"Yes," she said. "You did very well." They kissed again, and A.J. casually leaned back against the wall – and it started to crumble behind him. The teens backed away as a large section of bricks fell out all at once, crumbling to the floor. When the dust cleared, the teens could see clearly into the next chamber, where Kaleb, Ennio and Trosclair were standing with their mouths open in surprise.

"Hey!" Trosclair said. "Cutting through the walls of a maze is cheating!"

Darra and A.J. stepped through the gaping hole and into the next chamber, and the dog jumped along after them.

"You made it all the way through?" Darra asked, and the prince nodded.

"Trosclair figured out the next verse of the song, and it led us here," Kaleb said.

"What's all this, then?" she asked, pointing to the musical instruments.

"It's the last part of the song," Kaleb said. He cleared his throat again and sang, "The choice is yours alone to make, which instrument you choose to take. Just pick the one that doesn't drain the lake. And for those souls both lost and true, we'll sing this final clue for you: Some say the angels play the harp with gifted hand, but this has always been the leader of our band."

"So we have to pick an instrument," Darra said.

"Any clue which one?" A.J. asked.

"The leader of the band," Trosclair repeated. "In a lot of arrangements, the highest instrument carries the melody. That would probably mean one of the horns."

"But most bands today focus on stringed instruments," Darra said. "That would mean the lute."

"Hang on," Ennio said. "This isn't just any band. See the straps on the drums? These are all instruments you can play while you march. This is a military band."

"Okay. Well, what instrument leads a military marching band?" Darra asked.

"Hmm," Ennio said, as he thought about it. "We time our march to the beat of the bass drum, so it kind of 'leads' us. And it's also the loudest of them. That would be my guess."

"That makes sense," Darra said. "Do you want to do the honors?" The soldier nodded and crossed to the instruments. He reached out and picked up the bass drum, and the pillar it was on rose up several inches. There was the sound of stone scraping against stone, followed by a rushing noise that filled the chamber.

“What is that?” Darra said as a hole opened up in the ceiling. A second later, gallons and gallons of water splashed down through the hole in a steady stream. At the same time, a heavy metal door slammed down in front of the stairs.

“Uh-oh,” Trosclair said. “I think we drained the lake!”

“Put it back!” A.J. said, and Ennio rushed to return the instrument to its pillar. The pilot moved over to the wall of instruments next to the soldier. Both teens tried to push down on the circular column, but it wouldn’t budge.

“Kaleb,” Darra said. “Please tell me you know a spell that can stop that!” The water was already well past the teens’ ankles and rising quickly - and that was with the spillover into the next chamber. The little dog was already forced to paddle to keep its head above the surface. Ennio bent down and scooped up the frightened animal, placing it high on the section of missing wall, and it shook itself off.

“I’m a fire mage, not a water-witch!” Kaleb said. “I can’t stop this!”

“Maybe if we pick the right one, it’ll stop,” A.J. said.

“Well, which one should we try next?” Darra asked. A.J. shrugged and then grabbed the lute. The pillar underneath it rose, and a second hole opened up in the ceiling. After another few moments, a second torrent of water was cascading into the chamber. The water rose at an incredible rate, soon coming up to Darra’s thighs.

“Great!” Darra said. “I don’t think we can afford any more guesses!”

“I don’t think we can afford not to guess!” A.J. said, as he returned the lute to its pillar.

“The bugle!” Trosclair screamed. “Try the bugle!” Ennio waded forward and grabbed the horn, and the pillar underneath it rose - but the ones bearing the lute and the bass drum sank back to their original positions. The holes in the ceiling closed, and the water slowed to twin trickles dripping down on the waist-high surface. The door in front of the stairs began to rise. Ennio crossed to Trosclair and gave him a hug that lifted the young prince off his feet.

“You really are a genius!” Ennio said, as he put Trosclair back down. “How did you know that was the one?”

"I remembered your letters from the military academy," Trosclair said. "You said you hated the bugle-player, because he always woke you up before dawn."

"So 'the leader of the band' meant the first instrument to play each day," Kaleb said, and Trosclair nodded. "That's devious!"

"Darra!" came Aleksey's worried voice from through the next chamber. "Are you okay?"

"I'm fine, Dad!" she called back. "We're all fine!"

"What about the dog?" the half-elf yelled back worriedly.

It was approaching midnight by the time they emerged from the complex. Aleksey carried the bugle, having cleaned it as best he could on the way back through the maze.

"So all that just for a bugle, huh?" A.J. asked.

"Not just any bugle," Aleksey said. "One blow on this is supposed to summon the Oracle, instantly." The half-elf moved the mouthpiece to his lips, but Darra put her hand on his shoulder.

"Wait," she said. "Trosclair's the one who saved us. He should get to do it." Aleksey offered the horn to the prince, but he took one look at the rusty mouthpiece and shook his head.

"No, thank you," the prince said. "You go ahead." Aleksey moved the horn back to his lips and blew, holding down a single valve. A loud, brassy note sounded out into the night. The adventurers waited several seconds, but nothing seemed to be happening.

"Well, I guess the Oracle isn't still alive, after all," A.J. said. "Or if she is, she isn't answering her phone."

"What's a phone?" Darra asked.

"It's a–" A.J. stopped mid-sentence as a strange white glow formed in the distance. It grew brighter, until the trees and hillside around them were lit up like daytime, and into the middle of this glow flashed a unicorn at full sprint. It was white, with a white mane and tail, and black spots on its hindquarters - and of course that glorious, golden horn sticking out of its forehead. It neared the adventurers and slowed down, until it came to a stop a few feet from them. "Holy crap! It's a unicorn," the pilot said.

"I thought they were extinct!" Kaleb said.

"It's beautiful," Darra said. She took a few tentative steps toward it, and the creature didn't shy away as she expected. She raised her hand and slowly moved it toward the animal's mane.

"Darra, no!" Kaleb said. "You can't touch a—" Darra's hand stroked the animal down the side of its neck. "—unicorn."

"What?" Darra asked, glancing over her shoulder at the mage. "Why not?" Kaleb glanced at Aleksey, who had an alarmed look in his eyes.

"Uh, never mind," Kaleb said. "I guess I was wrong. It's nothing."

"She likes it," Darra said. "Don't you, girl?" The unicorn's eyes glowed a royal blue, and the creature shimmered and shifted, until a human woman was standing in front of them. She looked about sixty, had long white hair that blended in with her robes, and wore a heavy gold crown low on her forehead.

"I'm fine with it," the woman said. "Although I wish you'd call me by my name, instead of 'girl.' I'm Gadera."

"Wow," Darra said, drawing back her hand. "I'm Darra."

"Yes," Gadera said. "I know."

"So you're the Oracle?" Aleksey asked.

"That is what they called me, in the olden days," Gadera said. "Although I have not been summoned to this realm in a long time."

"We wish to—"

"You wish to contact the outworlder's people on their flying ships, and direct them to this planet," Gadera said.

"Yeah, that's right," A.J. said.

"Can it be done?" Aleksey asked.

"The outworlder's people do not have magic," Gadera said. "If I am to make contact with them, it will have to be through their machines. And machines and magic, as a rule, do not mix."

"So it won't work?" A.J. asked.

"That depends on a number of factors," Gadera said. "But before we try that, I sense that there are others of you with questions. The prince, for example."

"Me?" Trosclair asked in a surprised tone.

"You wonder about the fate of your kingdom," Gadera said.

"Well, of course," the prince said. "I want to know if we'll be successful in taking back the throne."

"In time, you will rule again," Gadera said.

"Yes!" Ennio said, pumping his fist in the air. "I knew it!"

"How much time?" Trosclair asked.

"That depends on what you're willing to do to gain back what you've lost," Gadera said. "And what you're willing to give up."

"What do I need to give up?" Trosclair asked. "I've already lost my kingdom!"

"I'm sorry, princeling," Gadera said, reaching out to touch Trosclair on the shoulder. "But some questions must go unanswered, or we would all go mad." Trosclair frowned. "But the mage..." Gadera continued.

"Yes?" Kaleb responded.

"You wish to know if you will become a great sorcerer," Gadera said, and Kaleb nodded. "I can only say that you have a vast potential that will either lead to your glory or to your doom."

"My doom?" Kaleb repeated. "I don't want that. Is there any way I can make sure it leads to my – my glory instead?"

"All I can advise you to do is be true to yourself," Gadera said. "It may be the key to your magical ascension." The woman turned back to Darra. "And finally, Darra. You wanted to ask me if your father would keep his promise to let you train as a chi-fighter, but you were afraid it would hurt his feelings if he knew you doubted him."

"Darra," Aleksey said, the hurt evident in his voice. "You really think I wouldn't keep my word?"

"I didn't think you'd lie," she said. "It's just so expensive."

"Why do you think I took the job protecting the prince?" Aleksey asked.

"I thought it was out of a sense of civic duty," Trosclair mumbled.

"That's your tuition money, and I'll earn it just in time for your birthday," Aleksey said. "The prince is only a few weeks older than you."

"You're really gonna spend all that money to send me to the Warrior Women's Academy?" Darra asked, and Aleksey smiled and nodded.

"No, he isn't. That much I can say with certainty," Gadera said, and Darra's hopes crashed. "He's going to hire a private tutor, so you can train without leaving him."

"Gods!" Aleksey said. "That's the most brilliant idea I've ever heard! It'll likely cost a bit more, but it'll be well worth it. And your training will go so much faster with a private instructor."

"I don't know," Darra said. "Who would you even get to do the teaching?" Aleksey looked to Gadera questioningly.

"A retired warrior woman, of course," Gadera said.

"I have to say, I'd rather have you around than at some old academy," A.J. said.

"The outworlder - I mean, A.J. - is making sense, honey," Aleksey said.

"That's if you're still here this summer," Darra said to the pilot.

"Will I - be here this summer?" A.J asked the woman in white.

"Your future is more uncertain than any of the others here," Gadera said. "And this is a group bound to tempt fate repeatedly. I can say it will all come down to whether or not you get the message back to your people tonight."

"Well, maybe we should get started, then," A.J. said. "How is it gonna work?"

"Simply speak your message, and I will concentrate on the flying ships you have described," Gadera said. "I'll send my consciousness out into the universe and merge it with the device you use to capture sights and sounds and communicate with one another."

"The computer?" A.J. asked, and Gadera nodded.

"Thank you," she said. "It will help to know the name of it."

"Okay, then," A.J. said. "Here goes."

"Wait," Gadera said. "I have to be in my natural form for this. That's what the horn is for, after all."

"Oh," Darra said. "I thought it was for self-defense."

"Oh, sweet child," Gadera said. "It's for that, too." She stroked Darra's cheek, and then she shimmered and shifted again, until the unicorn was standing in front of them, staring at A.J.

"Okay," A.J. said. "I don't know where to begin, but if someone gets this message, my name is A.J. Brandt. This message is for Admiral Brandt, my aunt. First, I want you to know that I am alive, unharmed and safe - more or less. The anomaly transported our shuttle to a planet called Ona, in a star system I can't identify. It's habitable, and beyond that, there are people here. And elves, and dragons, and wizards. And everybody speaks English. I know, it probably sounds like I've gone crazy..." The pilot continued on, explaining more about the world he'd been cast into, as well as what had happened to Tarun. When he was finished, he told his aunt to tell his parents he loved them. "Okay," he said to the unicorn. "I'm done." The animal's eyes glowed blue again, and once more it took the form of the woman. "Well?" he prompted her. "Did it work?"

"I—" Gadera's face froze in fear, and she turned it toward the black sky. "There's something watching us. Something old, and powerful. I have to go!" She shifted back to her unicorn form and galloped away, her glow fading with her, until there was nothing left but darkness. Aleksey drew his sword, and Darra fished her crossbow out of her satchel and loaded it. The half-elf scanned the night all around them, but he couldn't see any danger.

"We should go, too!" Ennio said as he drew his sword.

"What could possibly frighten a unicorn like that?" Kaleb asked.

"I don't think I want to find out," A.J. said.

"Agreed," Aleksey said, and the adventurers hurried away into the moonlit night.

Kaleb got up before dawn the next morning and shook Aleksey awake. They'd made camp underneath the wide, flat branches of a *himari* tree. "Is something wrong, Kay?" Aleksey asked as he sat up and yawned.

"No," the mage whispered. "I was just hoping we could talk. In private." Aleksey stood and followed Kaleb as he walked away from the other teens. When the tribal lad was sure they wouldn't wake them, he turned to the half-elf. "Darra touched the unicorn last night," he said, as he pulled out his pipe. "Twice."

"So?" Aleksey said, affecting casualness, when his heart was suddenly pounding in his chest.

"So I've read about unicorns," Kaleb said, holding in a hit. He exhaled. "They never allow humans to touch them - unless the human is royalty."

"Is that what your books said?" Aleksey asked. "It must have been a myth."

"Darra's middle name is Esmerelda," Kaleb continued. "That's the name of the princess who disappeared fifteen years ago. Trosclair's sister. And as you pointed out, they're nearly the same age."

"Half the girls in the kingdom born that year were named after the missing princess," Aleksey said.

"The DuVerres royal family is known for their fire-colored hair," Kaleb said. "And I've known Darra long enough to remember before you started lightening her hair. Please don't lie to me anymore." The mage and the half-elf locked eyes for a tense moment. "Darra is really Princess Esmerelda, Trosclair's twin sister, isn't she?"

"Yes," Aleksey whispered.

"So the story about her mother entrusting her to you before she died in the Elven Wars," Kaleb said. "Was that all lies?"

"I've never lied to Darra," Aleksey said. "I've just never told her the full truth."

"Why not?" Kaleb said.

"It's complicated," Aleksey said. "There are forces – people in the world – who would want to harm Darra, if they knew who she truly was."

"But that doesn't explain why you haven't told her," Kaleb said.

"Darra's going through a – a rebellious phase," Aleksey said. "If I told her now, she'd be hurt, confused, probably angry."

"But Trosclair is her brother," Kaleb said. "And he thinks she's dead. It would change his whole world to know she was alive."

"That's why it was so fortunate that we were thrown together," Aleksey said. "Now they'll get a chance to know one another."

"But not as siblings," Kaleb said, before he took another drag off his pipe.

"Not yet," Aleksey said. "But someday."

"The longer you wait to tell her, the harder it will be for her to accept," Kaleb said. "You know that, right?"

"I'm counting on her blossoming maturity to ease the blow," Aleksey said. "And by that time, hopefully the prince will have his kingdom back, and he can devote all his resources to helping protect her."

"Who – or what – is after her?" Kaleb asked.

"An entity I'd rather not name," Aleksey said. "He rules on the Dread Continent, and he has vast resources at his command."

"Okay," the mage said. "I think that's most of my burning questions."

"Kaleb, you have to promise me you won't say anything to Darra - or the prince - about what you know," Aleksey said, holding the tribal lad's gaze for another long moment.

"Fine," Kaleb said. "But you owe me." The half-elf nodded. "And if she asks me directly, I won't lie to her."

"That's fair enough," Aleksey said.

Admiral Brandt was sleeping - dreaming of an old television series she'd loved in her youth, in fact. When the intercom in her room buzzed her awake, she was not pleased, but she sat up in bed anyway. "Hello?" she said sleepily.

"Admiral Brandt," came Gracie's voice. "It's me."

"Jesus, Gracie," the Admiral said, looking at a clock. "It's 4:30. Are you sleeping at all these days?"

"That doesn't matter," the young woman replied, excitement evident in her voice. "There's been a development - with A.J.! I knew you'd want to get up and come see for yourself."

Within four minutes, the captain was dressed and on the command deck. "Alright," she said to Gracie as she crossed to the young woman. "What is it?"

"Somehow he got a message onto the ship's mainframe," Gracie said, before turning to another crew member. "Play it back again." The crew member tapped her tablet a few times, and A.J.'s face suddenly appeared on the main video screen.

"Okay," he said. "I don't know where to begin, but if someone gets this message, my name is A.J. Brandt..."

"Thank god!" the Admiral said. "He's okay!" She hugged Gracie, who beamed back at her.

"It gets better," Gracie said. "Admiral, he did it. He made first contact."

"Start it over," Admiral Brandt said. "I don't want to miss a thing."

CHAPTER TEN
"CAPTIVE AUDIENCE"

Aleksey, the teens and Guardian walked down a bustling street with shops and businesses lining both sides. Carriages and other pedestrians passed on either side of the adventurers, and the smells from street vendors selling a range of foods mingled with the aromas of the legitimate restaurants they passed.

"Mm," Ennio said as they passed a vendor selling sausages.

"You hungry?" Trosclair asked.

"Starving, now that I've smelled it," Ennio said. "I could definitely go for a real meal. I think I've lost five pounds in just the last two weeks. Foraging from the forest is fine for a day or two, but I miss meat and potatoes. And bread."

"Me too," Trosclair said. The prince turned to Aleksey and the others. "What do you say? Shall we splurge on dinner?"

"We haven't got any money," Darra said.

"But I've got plenty," Trosclair said. "Consider it a down payment on your reward for helping me out."

"That's very kind of you," Aleksey said. Soon the prince, his bodyguard and Kaleb were eating sausages and buttered, spiced corn still on the cob, while Darra, Aleksey and A.J. had fried bread with chili beans, cheese and other toppings. Even Guardian got a strip of beef, grilled rare, which Aleksey tore apart and fed to her bit by bit.

"Would you like to try the sausage?" Ennio asked the pilot, offering him a slice.

"I would," A.J. said. "But I'm sort of trying to avoid meat."

"Really?" Darra asked. "You're becoming a vegetarian?"

"Maybe," A.J. said. "If I can stand it."

"I think that's a great decision," Darra said. "It's good for the body and spirit."

"Yeah, but I don't care about that," A.J. said. "I'm just doing it so my mouth is more kissable to other vegetarians." A.J. took Darra's hand and looked at her like he was going to kiss her.

"Hey!" Aleksey said. "I'm standing right here!"

"Sorry," the pilot said as he and Darra separated.

"Now, about your clothes," the half-elf said to Trosclair. "Now that we're safely out of your kingdom, you'll need to buy some new ones."

"Oh, I know!" Trosclair said. "I've been shuffling between the same two outfits ever since we left the palace. They're positively filthy!"

"That's not what I meant," Aleksey said. "You need to buy clothes that a peasant could afford. And we may want to dye that hair of yours."

"No!" Trosclair said, as if he'd suggested cutting off a toe.

"But it's so recognizable," Aleksey said. "You may as well be wearing a circlet on your forehead."

"Then I'll - I'll buy a cap," Trosclair said.

"That will work, too," Aleksey said. After a while, they came upon a little shop that sold fabrics and some premade clothes, and Aleksey pointed to a sign announcing a sale. "Here we go," Aleksey said.

"Oh, I—I think we can do better than this," Trosclair said, looking inside the shop windows and frowning. "Does this town have a *Shahla's*, by any chance?"

"Nope," Aleksey said. "But I'm sure you can find something that will do." The half-elf gently nudged the prince inside, and Ennio followed. Soon the prince emerged in his new outfit. He wore loose-fitting brown pants clearly meant for a larger man; they had to be rolled up at the bottom hems and cinched at the waist with a drawstring. His dark blue shirt fit him slightly better, but it was just as plain. Finally, he topped off the outfit with a hunting cap with side flaps that completely covered his fiery hair.

"Wow," Darra said, trying not to laugh. "You look like a

totally different person."

"But do I look poorer?" Trosclair asked.

"Definitely," Kaleb said.

"Okay, then," the prince said, and they continued on. Soon they were standing in front of a large inn and tavern. It was handsome but old, with chipping paint on the trimmings and a slightly overgrown lawn. A sign near the street proclaimed it to be another of Eliza Dell's establishments.

"The train for the coast doesn't leave until morning," Aleksey said as he led the way to the front door. "So we may as well spend the night in comfort." They entered the inn and the hostess, a short, middle-aged woman with a round face and glasses, smiled widely.

"Aleksey!" she said in a thick accent reminiscent of Eliza Dell herself. "And Darra!" She moved from behind the counter to give Darra a hug, then turned to the half-elf. "It's so good to see you! You haven't been through here in over a year! Are you meeting Ms. Dell here in secret again? Because the Lovers' Suite is vacant."

"Oh, no," Aleksey said. "We're just passing through. We'll only be staying the night."

"And we'll need two rooms," Trosclair said. Aleksey sent him a puzzled look, and the prince said, "Ennio and I could do with a little privacy."

"Ah," Aleksey said. "Very well, then. Two rooms, please, Eada. As for payment–"

"Oh, don't be silly, Aleksey!" Eada said. "Ms. Dell would have me out on the street if I charged you a single credit!"

"Thank you, Eada," the half-elf said, smiling.

"So where are you headed to this time?" Eada asked.

"The coast," Aleksey said. "A small village called Adaya's Hollow."

"Never heard of it," Eada said.

"Most people haven't," Aleksey said. "It's sort of off the beaten path."

"I'll just go get your rooms ready, then," she said. "Please, have a drink in the pub while you wait." Eada shuffled away.

"A pint does sound really good right about now," Ennio said, looking over at the doorway that led to the tavern.

"Ew," Trosclair said. "You and your ale! Give me a good

glass of wine any day."

"Does anybody want to join us?" Ennio asked.

"No, thanks," Kaleb said. "I want to get some studying in."

"Wow," Darra said. "You've had your nose in your spellbook all week. Any particular reason?"

"It's what Gadera said," Kaleb answered. "That my magic could lead to my doom. I'm really, really trying to avoid that."

"And I'm trying to look responsible in front of Darra's dad," A.J. said.

"You go. Enjoy yourselves," Aleksey said to the prince and the soldier, and the young couple moved toward the tavern.

"I can't believe you," Darra said to her father after they'd gone.

"Me?" he asked. "What did I do?"

"You're letting them drink alcohol," she said. "And you let them get their own room!"

"So?" her father prompted.

"So if I tried either of those things, you'd ground me until the moons started spinning backwards," Darra said.

"It's different," Aleksey said.

"Because they're boys?" Darra asked.

"Because they're not my children," Aleksey said. "Besides, one drink isn't going to do them any harm at their ages."

"But Trosclair and I are the same age!" Darra said.

"Do you want to try a drink, honey?" Aleksey asked in a drawn-out, tired voice, his eyebrows lifted.

"Yes!" she said.

"What do you want?" he asked.

"I don't know," she said. She turned to the pilot. "What's good?"

"Vodka and fruit juice, definitely," A.J. said, before looking to Aleksey. "Not that I drink a lot."

"I expect you to be up in the room within the half-hour," Aleksey said.

"Sure, no problem," Darra said, pulling A.J. away by the hand. "Come on, A.J. – before he changes his mind."

"And just the one glass!" the half-elf called after them, and Darra gave a thumbs up over her shoulder to show that she understood. She and the pilot joined the prince and his bodyguard at the bar, passing a billiards table and a dart board on the way.

"What are you drinking?" the old man behind the bar asked.

"Do you have vodka and orange juice?" A.J. asked.

"Can't get oranges in this kingdom in winter, son," the bartender said. "But I have brushberry-pomegranate juice."

"That sounds fine," the pilot said. "Two, please." The bartender left to make their drinks.

"So, Darra," Trosclair said. "Are you a gambling woman?"

"I never have been," she said. "Unless gambling with my life counts."

"Would you like to play a game of billiards?" the prince asked, and Darra nodded. The bartender came back with two fruit beverages in hand and sat them down on the counter. Darra took a sip of hers and made a face.

"You don't like it?" A.J. asked.

"I think my juice is spoiled," Darra said. "It tastes vile." The pilot took a tiny sip out of her glass.

"No, that's just how alcohol tastes," the pilot said.

"Gross. I'll be back," Darra said as she and the prince made their way to the empty game table. Darra sat her drink down and grabbed two cues off the rack on the wall, handing one to Trosclair. The prince sat down his own drink and leaned his stick against the table; next he began removing balls and placing them on the table inside the racking triangle.

"So what are we playing for?" he asked.

"Oh, gods. I don't have anything of value," she said.

"It doesn't have to be monetary," Trosclair said, leaning in conspiratorially. "We could play for secrets."

"I don't really have any secrets," Darra said, and Trosclair tilted his head disbelievingly. "I don't!"

"Fine," Trosclair said. "For every ball you sink, I'll give you five credits. But for every one I knock in, you have to answer a question."

"Deal," Darra said. She picked up a large metal coin and balanced it on her thumb and index finger. "Prince or pauper?" she asked.

"Prince, of course," he said, and Darra flipped the coin. It landed on the table with the image of a man in rags face-up.

"Sorry, Trosc," Darra said. She moved the coin off the table, and Trosclair removed the rack from around the balls. Darra lined up the cue ball with the top ball of the triangular formation, then took aim with her cue. She slid it between her fingers a few times, testing the glide, and then rammed the cue ball with it. The white ball rolled forward and broke up the other balls with a quick succession of cracking noises, and the multi-colored balls scattered around the table. One almost went into a corner pocket, but it came to a stop just before the gentle slope that would guide it into the hole. Trosclair took stock of the placement of the balls, chose the one near the hole and lined up his cue. He took the shot, and the ball clacked into the pocket.

"Alright!" Trosclair said. "That's one question you have to answer - truthfully!"

"I will, I promise," Darra said.

"Okay, let's see," Trosclair said, lining up another shot. "We'll start with an easy one. What is your biggest fear?"

"I don't know," Darra said. "When I was little, I was always afraid of getting lost - in the woods, or in public. Does that count?" Trosclair took his shot, and another ball fell in one of the side pockets.

"I guess," Trosclair said. "Although kid fears aren't the same as adult fears."

"What are you afraid of?" Darra asked.

"It used to be the boogeyman," Trosclair said. He took another shot, but the ball he aimed for missed the hole and bounced off the table wall. "Now I'm more afraid of losing my kingdom."

"But the oracle said you'd rule again," Darra said.

"In time," Trosclair said. "Those were her exact words."

"Well, here's to making that time as short as possible," Darra said. Trosclair clinked his wine goblet against her raised glass.

"You get another," Darra said, as she lined up another shot.

"Okay, but this one's gonna be tougher," the prince warned.

"That's fine," Darra replied.

"A.J.," Trosclair said as Darra slid her cue back. "Do you love him?" Darra scraped the cue along the top of the felt-covered table, nicking the white ball and moving it just a few inches. When Trosclair made eye contact with her, she was blushing.

"I—I..." she stammered. "I can't answer that."

"That's not how the game is played," Trosclair said. "You have to."

"I care about him, a lot," she said. "And he is so handsome!"

"But is it love?" the prince pushed.

"I... think it could be," Darra said. "Someday. We're trying not to rush things. You better not tell anybody I said so, though."

"You have my word," Trosclair said. They played the rest of the game, and Darra wound up answering questions about everything from her favorite books to her travels around the continent. In the end, Trosclair felt he knew her a lot better, and Darra came away with thirty-five credits and a light buzz. She ran up to the room her father and Kaleb were in and asked for permission to go back to the clothiers for a new dress; Aleksey acquiesced, with the caveat that she be back before sundown. She set out for the store with her boyfriend, the prince and the soldier in tow.

In a temple dedicated to the old gods in the Free City, Lilith was hard at work kneading dough. She had spent every day of the last two weeks waking up before dawn to help the temple prepare meals for the homeless. She worked until sunset, stopping only for a few minutes in the middle of each day to eat something herself and to pray. As a volunteer, she was given menial tasks like peeling potatoes and carrots, baking breads, and taking out the trash. But for some reason, her mind had always cleared when concentrating on everyday tasks like these, allowing for some of her deepest realizations.

The first thing she realized was that deep down, she feared Aleksey might be right about killing, and the karmic toll it could take upon a person. In hindsight, she regretted attacking Darra and Aleksey, of course, but she was also plagued by the near-death of the orc she'd stabbed. Even the beating that she'd given the Commandant's torturous underling, Bidzil, haunted her; she didn't know if she'd left him dying or merely maimed on the palace lawn, but the image of his bloody, bruised and swollen face kept her awake some nights. So she started talking to her god. Not out loud, like a madwoman would, but silently, inside her own mind. They had long, winding conversations about whether killing another sentient being was ever justifiable. Of course, she had to imagine his parts of the dialogue, but that was easy to do for a woman who had devoted her life to his teachings. She imagined him reminding her of the delicate balance between life and death, and of her part in maintaining it. She confessed to him her self-doubt and confusion, and he promised her a hopeful new beginning, though she couldn't imagine what form that would take.

The next thing she realized was that she was lonely. Her encounter with Aleksey in the palace dungeon had satisfied her at the time, but ultimately it served to remind her that she had no one in her life on whom she could truly rely. In her younger days, she'd told herself that was how she preferred it. But she was approaching sixty – the appearance of youth aside – and she wondered how her life would be different if she had a man she loved in it, or even a family. She assumed she could still have children, if she desired, and the possibility of it did not offend her as it once had.

At night, because she couldn't sleep, she trained. She practiced with her sword and lifted heavy weights to build muscle, and every evening around nine, she took a jog through one of the popular city parks. It was in the bad part of town, and she secretly hoped a mugger or other ruffian would jump in front of her path. So far, the closest she'd come to that was a pair of territorial ducks that chased her away from their pond.

After her runs, she spent a few hours reading. The book she was currently working her way through was a Pentonese treatise on karma that gave her fuel for her pretend conversations with Rebos. Around midnight, she would lie down, but it took hours to fall asleep with her racing thoughts. Only a few hours after that, she would rise again to start the whole process over.

Darra bought a purple dress and wore it out of the store. With her left-over money, she bought A.J. a clean shirt from the sale rack, but he decided to save it until after he had a chance to bathe. Trosclair bought Ennio a whole new outfit and apologized for not thinking of him earlier. Being taller and more muscular than Trosclair, the soldier fit the clothes well. "You look nice," Trosclair said as Ennio emerged from the store. They headed back toward Eliza Dell's as the sun hung low in the sky.

"I don't see why I can't just wash my uniform," Ennio said.

"There's no sense wasting your money on me."

"It's not that much," Trosclair said. "And it's not a waste. They're looking for you, too, potentially even in this kingdom. When we get on that train tomorrow, you should look like an ordinary citizen."

"I feel naked without my cape," Ennio said.

"I know you do," Trosclair said as he patted him sympathetically on the shoulder.

"What about you?" Darra asked. "Do you miss your crown?"

"Oh, I don't wear that day to day," Trosclair said. "It's just for ceremonial purposes. Or if I want to intimidate someone. Still, it's better than this thing." He scratched his scalp under his cap, and a curl of bright red hair flopped free.

"Your hair," Ennio said as he reached out and pushed the stray lock back under the prince's cap with his thumb. The prince smiled up at his boyfriend.

"Queers!" said a young man passing them in a group of half a dozen other youths, who laughed.

"What did you say?" Ennio asked angrily.

"I said you look like queers," the man said. "You're not, are you?"

"You ought to watch your damned mouth!" Ennio said. "You don't know who you're talking to!" The soldier started to move toward the man, but Trosclair and Darra held him back.

"I know there's six of us, and two of you," the man said.

"Three," A.J. said, moving to stand beside the prince.

"Make that four," Darra said.

"Hah!" the man said. "Did you hear that? The girl wants to fight, too."

"I'll wrassle with her, if that's what she wants," said another of the youths, and the rest laughed. Up ahead, a constable turned a corner onto the sidewalk.

"Come on, guys," Darra said, pulling A.J. and Ennio backwards down the street. "These jerks aren't worth getting in trouble." The man and his friends chuckled as they turned and walked away.

"Gods, I hate men like that!" Darra said. "It makes me wish I'd bought steel-toed boots." Trosclair gave her a puzzled look, and she mimed kicking someone. "Just once, right between the legs!"

"Ah," the prince said. "I'm gonna try to stay on your good side."

"Oh, you don't have to worry about that," Darra said. "You've been very kind. And that move is reserved for the worst of the worst, anyway."

"You mean you've actually practiced that?" A.J. asked.

"Sure," Darra said. "Dad says it's a man's most vulnerable area, and it would be foolish not to exploit it if the opportunity presents itself. In self-defense only, of course." The teens approached a crowd that had gathered around a carriage. Every so often, the crowd would erupt in laughter or applause, and it soon became clear they were watching a performance of some kind. A man and woman in fine clothing ahead of them were just leaving the crowd, so Darra asked, "Excuse me, Miss? Could you tell me what's happening over there?"

"Oh, it's fabulous!" the woman said. "I haven't laughed so hard in years!"

"They had me on the edge of my seat," the man said. "Not literally, of course, because I was standing. But it was magical, I tell you! Magical!"

"But what is it?" Trosclair asked.

"Actors!" the man said.

"An improvisational troupe!" the woman cried. "They're marvelous! You should stay for the show - it's free."

"We can't," Darra said. "I have to get back to my father."

"Oh, well - they have more shows, every hour until midnight," the woman said. "Maybe you can make one of those." The man and woman passed them and continued on.

"That sounds like fun," Trosclair said as the teens resumed their walk. "I'm a bit of a theatre buff."

"I'll have to get my dad's permission," Darra said. "But he's been in an incredible mood ever since we got Guardian, so that shouldn't be a problem."

The finely-dressed man and woman entered an alleyway, and a mustachioed man in his mid-thirties followed behind them. "Hey, you!" he called, and the man and woman turned to face him.

"Yes?" the finely-dressed man prompted.

"Give me all your credits and your pocketwatch," the man

with the mustache said, before turning to the woman. "And I want all your jewelry."

"Oh, sure!" the other man said, and he fished out his wallet and handed it over.

"Do you like improv?" the woman asked as she removed her diamond earrings. "There's a fabulous performance going on!"

Darra and the boys got back to Eliza Dell's and tromped up the stairs to their rooms. Trosclair and Darra agreed they should try to make the show at seven, and then the prince and Ennio went into their room. "Okay," Darra whispered. "When we ask my dad about going back out, let me do the talking."

"Why?" A.J. asked. "I think I'm growing on your dad. Slowly. Like ivy."

"But you don't know how to play him like I do," she said. She and the pilot entered the room, which had two full beds next to one another, as well as a couple of chairs and a small round table with a lantern burning on it. Kaleb was reading from his spellbook in one of the chairs, and Aleksey had stretched out on one of the beds with his eyes closed. Guardian lay at his feet, snoring softly.

"Hey, Daddy," she said. "I'm back." Aleksey opened his eyes.

"I see that," he said. "Did you find a nice dress?"

"Uh-huh," she said, turning from side to side to model it for him. "And I have enough left over to get Guardian a treat or a toy for the ride to the coast tomorrow."

"That's very sweet of you, dear," the half-elf said, closing his eyes again.

"Um, Daddy?" Darra asked, and her father's eyes snapped back open.

"Yes?"

"I was thinking I might take Guardian for a walk," Darra said.

"We've been walking for two weeks straight," Aleksey said. "I think Guardian just wants to rest."

"Oh, okay," Darra said. "Well, the thing is, we saw a theatre company performing in the streets on our way back, and the prince and I thought it would be fun to go watch a show."

"I don't know, Darra," Aleksey said. "It's after sundown.

You know I don't like you running around at night unsupervised."

"But I'll have Trosclair and Ennio and A.J. with me," Darra said. "We'll just go there and come right back. We won't get in any trouble, I promise."

"Hmm," Aleksey said as he mulled it over. "Okay."

"Thank you, Daddy!" Darra said.

"But tomorrow on the train, I want you to be prepared to compose a short essay on the strengths and weaknesses of the performance," Aleksey said. "With special attention paid to the archetypes and inherent themes."

"That's fine," Darra said.

Ennio brought up a large pot of warm water from the kitchen to wash in. Trosclair went first at the soldier's insistence, because he wanted the prince to have clean water for washing his blistered feet. They had healed somewhat since the last time he saw them, but the soldier was still glad they were switching to a more comfortable mode of transportation in the morning. "Do they still hurt?" he asked the prince as he removed the bandages Kaleb had wrapped around them.

"A little, at the end of the day," Trosclair said. He slid his feet into the pot, and Ennio started to gently clean them with a wash rag. "That feels good."

"Maybe we shouldn't go to the show," the soldier suggested.

"No!" Trosclair said. "I'm looking forward to it. It'll be nice to have a return to normalcy, even if it is for just an hour."

"Normal would be the luxury box at the Théatre Majestique," Ennio said. "I wouldn't expect such grand performances from street players, though, no matter how good the reviews are."

"You're probably right," Trosclair said. "But that's the great thing about improvisational comedy: When it's bad, you laugh almost as hard as when it's great."

A knock sounded through the door, and Ennio rose and answered it. Eada was standing in the hall, holding two thick green towels. "Here you go," she said, handing them over to the soldier. She glanced in the room and saw Trosclair with his cap off. "My goodness, child! Look at that hair! You look just like the prince of DuVerres! Has anyone ever told you that before?"

"Oh, uh - yeah," Trosclair said. "I hear that a lot."

"How do you know what the prince looks like?" Ennio asked. "I mean, living all the way in another kingdom."

"Oh, he's been all over our broadsheets," Eada said. "They say he's been deposed. Do you think you could be related to the royal family?" she asked the prince. "Maybe distantly?"

"Oh, I don't think so," Trosclair said. "I come from... simple folk."

"Oh, okay," she said. "You boys have a nice night, now." She turned and walked away, and Ennio closed the door.

"Wow!" he said as he crossed to the prince and placed the towels on the bed beside him. "That was close! You don't think she suspects, do you?"

"Even if she does - which I doubt - she doesn't seem like the type to go blabbing about it," Trosclair said. "Besides, we'll be gone by morning. And I'll keep my cap on tonight, so I won't get recognized."

"That cap," Ennio said, shaking his head.

"What?" Trosclair asked. "You don't like it?"

"It's growing on me, kiddo," Ennio said, putting his arm around Trosclair's waist. "Although now you look like the proverbial farmer's son, like in that dirty poem."

"And you're the warrior," Trosclair said, leaning in to kiss him.

Lilith's flat was a large, simple room with a small bed, a chair by the window, a large chest doubling as a table, and two pictures on opposite walls. One was an eclipse - Rebos, of course, moving across the sun; the other was a portrait of her parents. She kept the furniture and décor to a minimum because she moved around so much, and because she liked the open space it created. She was sitting on the floor cross-legged, her eyes closed, deep into a ritual trance that was supposed to bring guidance to True Believers.

She was dreaming of a great battle. She didn't know where or when this battle would take place, but somehow she knew she had aligned herself with a group of other virtual immortals. There was a dwarf war king of old, squat and muscular, with a gold crown atop his long, shaggy auburn hair and a double-sided axe. An elven woman in the ritual robes of a necromancer stood behind the king, her arms raised out toward the formless forces that Lilith knew surrounded them. To her right, there was a being Lilith couldn't identify who seemed composed entirely out of light; it was humanoid, but beyond that, she could discern nothing about it. Next was a madwoman who had chosen to fight stripped of her clothing and wearing a blindfold, a long leather whip in one hand and a shield in the other. And finally came a face she knew well; Aleksey smiled at her as he drew his sword.

The enemy that surrounded them moved forward to attack, and the immortals went to battle. The formless figures began to take shape, and Lilith identified them as a motley mix of different races and species. The madwoman lashed out with her whip, the end of which wrapped around the throat of an ogre leading the enemies' charge. She yanked, and the muscle-bound creature fell to its knees. The madwoman laughed and raised her shield just in time to deflect a couple of arrows aimed at her head. The figure made of light stepped forward and raised its arms, and a wave of energy flashed out, knocking the approaching forces to the ground. The dwarf king and the necromancer raced forward, fighting back to back, the former swinging his axe wide and low, and the latter jabbing a long, thin sword out at her enemies with deadly precision.

Lilith squared off against the enemy in front of her, a furry, fanged wolf-man and a dread nymph with black, soulless eyes squinted into a predatory gaze. She raised her swords as the monsters charged at her, spinning in between the two with her blades out. She slashed the wolfman across his stomach, but the dread nymph lurched back, receiving only a minor cut to one palm. The wolfman fell to his knees, his guts spilling out, and Aleksey was suddenly at the assassin's side.

"Lilith, what did you do?" he asked, shaking his head. Lilith looked back at the wolfman, but in his place was the carcass of a dead female wolf, her stomach slashed open. A litter of pups milled around the body, whimpering and whining. "Are you gonna kill them, too?" the half-elf asked. Lilith looked around, confused and frightened. The battle was over. In fact, they were in a whole new location – a street in a city in Vilmos, by the looks of it. The half-elf was still at her side, but the other immortals and the enemies they'd been facing were nowhere to be seen. Suddenly Aleksey doubled over in pain. Lilith knew he'd been stabbed, but there was no one else around, so she had no idea who had done the stabbing.

Lilith opened her eyes, the dreamy fog of her trance fully lifted, and smiled.

Darra and A.J. strolled through the streets hand in hand, Trosclair and Ennio beside them. "I have to admit, I'm jealous," Trosclair said, and Darra cocked her head curiously. "You get to hold your boyfriend's hand in public. Ennio and I can't even look at each other without almost getting assaulted."

"Yeah, but as a man, you have way more rights than I have, under the law," Darra replied, and the prince wagged his head from side to side ambivalently as he considered it.

"I could've taken those guys," Ennio said.

"We, you mean," A.J. said, and Darra smiled up at the pilot.

"You know how sexy I find it that you stood up for our friends, right?" she asked.

"I didn't, no," A.J. said. "But I'm glad you mentioned it." They passed a homeless man sitting on the curb with his hand held out.

"Spare a credit?" the man asked.

"I'm sorry," Darra said. "I don't have any money."

"Ennio, give him some money," Trosclair said, and the soldier fished two credits out of the pouch at his belt. "He needs more than that for a decent meal." Ennio fished out three more credits and gave it all to the man.

"Gods bless you!" the man said, and the teens continued on.

"That was kind of you," Darra said. "I hated to lie to him, but the money I have left is for a treat for Guardian."

"You're gonna spoil that dog," A.J. said.

"That's the idea, yeah," Darra said. "She deserves it, after the life she used to have. People who mistreat animals are just as bad as those who abuse women or hate queer people, in my opinion."

"I agree," A.J. said. "In fact, on my home planet, even the animals have rights under the law."

"You're kidding!" Darra said.

"No, seriously," A.J. said. "You can get in big trouble if you harm an animal."

"But your people still eat meat," Darra said. "That's a

contradiction."

"Ah, why did you have to say meat?" A.J. asked. "Now I'm craving a cheeseburger."

"What's that?" Ennio asked.

"Oh, no," the pilot said. "I can't just describe it to you. I'll have to make it for you sometime. And I'll make you a veggie burger."

"Okay," Darra said. "Maybe when we get to the Elven Isles, you can teach my uncle Acasius how to cook it. He loves learning the cuisines of new cultures."

"It's a date!" A.J. said.

"Oh gods!' Darra said. "I just realized that's what this is: our first real date."

"It's a double-date, technically," Trosclair said.

"If you had told me two months ago that I'd have a boyfriend and be friends with a prince, I would have thought you were smoking Kaleb's herb," she said. "But it all feels so natural now - almost like we were all meant to find one another." They arrived at the street with the performers and approached the edge of the crowd. There were three people standing in front of a large carriage, two men and a woman.

"The waiter took the royal order swift," the narrator at the side of the scene said. One of the actors played a frazzled waiter, scribbling on a pad, while the other affected a posture and expression denoting superiority and aloofness. "And left to serve the Queen her pie forthwith." The waiter spun on his heel and scurried away a few steps, mimed picking up a pie, and crossed back to the queen. "But since the Queen had no more sweets decreed, she looked upon a pie baked full of seed." The Queen made a shocked and outraged face, and the audience laughed.

"Oh gods," Darra said. "They improv in iambic pentameter?"

"How clever!" Trosclair said.

"The Queen had also been the first to say, 'Throw all the leafy greens and beans away!'" the narrator said, and the Queen wagged her finger at the crowd. "And so her salad bowl was filled with hay!" The waiter handed an imaginary bowl to the Queen, who took a dainty bite with a pretend utensil and then sputtered and spit all over the street. The crowd laughed and applauded. "But worst of all was that dessert served last, a pudding made from puss and scabs and grass," the narrator said. The waiter handed another bowl to the Queen, who took one horrified look down at it and began to swoon. "And so it was that after this repast, the Queen and all her court began a fast." The Queen cinched her stomach with her hands and sucked in her cheeks, and the waiter lifted his hand over his forehead, as if he might faint. "But too long on a diet makes a man consider taking matters in his hands." The waiter struck a thoughtful pose with his hand on his chin – and then reached out to the Queen and began strangling her. The crowd roared with surprise and delight. The actors froze in place, then turned to the crowd and took a couple of quick bows. The music in the background, a gentle lute solo coming from behind the carriage, stopped, and it was the first time Darra had noticed the music at all, so subtly had it been played throughout the scene. "All right, let's give a big hand for our players," the narrator said, and the crowd obeyed. "That was 'Queen on a strange diet,' and I think they did a great job!"

"There's no way that was all made up on the spot," Ennio said. "I think they rehearse ahead of time and plant people in the audience to provide the suggestions."

Two more players came up, and the narrator said, "All right, we're gonna need some new ideas. First, I need a profession." The crowd started yelling out different types of jobs. "I heard tax collector." One of the actors scrunched up her eyes and mouth in a miserly expression and mimed carrying a heavy bag. "Next, what are some different types of smells?" The crowd started yelling their answers.

"Body odor!" Ennio yelled, and Trosclair gave him a surprised look.

"Okay," the narrator said, chuckling a bit. "I heard sandalwood and body odor, so we're gonna go with those. Now finally, I'm gonna need an emotion or feeling."

"Inquisitive!" Darra yelled, but the narrator went with 'confused.' The show lasted about forty-five minutes, with the four actors taking turns but the same narrator throughout. Trosclair remarked on how talented the man was, and Darra agreed. The performance kept the teens enthralled as promised, and after it was over and the crowd started to disperse, they couldn't stop talking about it excitedly.

"I've slept with men of strength and height and girth, but never with a man of noble birth!" Trosclair said. "That was the best line."

"No, it was, 'With a saddle and a hose, milady.'" Darra said, and Ennio laughed.

The mustachioed man approached them and said, "Give me all your money."

"Here you go," Darra said, fishing her few credits out of her pocket.

"I'm broke," A.J. said.

"He carries the purse," Trosclair said, pointing to Ennio.

"Sorry," the soldier said, as he fumbled with the pouch around his belt. He finally loosened its strings and handed it over to the mustachioed man, who took a look inside and whistled. "There must be three hundred credits in here. Hey, Dacy!"

Another man wearing a bright red shirt approached. "Yeah?" he prompted.

"These kids are loaded!" the man with the mustache said.

"Really?" Dacy asked. "They don't look like it."

"They were carrying over three hundred credits," the other man replied.

"Well, well," Dacy said. "Looks like we have some good candidates for a ransom. Come on, kids!" Dacy started toward the back of the carriage, and the teens fell in line behind him.

Lilith entered the foyer of *The Laughing Stocks* and found Ani at her hostess' podium. "You!" the young woman said to the assassin. "Get out of here! We don't cater to your kind!"

"What kind is that?" Lilith asked. "True Believers?"

"No, the kind who try to kill my friends," Ani said. "Now go! I don't want to have to call my brother over here."

"Look, I can tell you don't like me," Lilith said.

"What gave me away?" Ani asked sweetly.

"But I've come here for a reason," Lilith continued. "Your friends are in trouble."

"What are you talking about?" Ani asked.

"I had a – a vision of things to come," Lilith said.

"Yeah, right," Ani said. "And I'm a four-winged fairy!"

"It's true," Lilith said. "Someone is going to try to kill the half-elf and his daughter. Tonight."

"And you came to me because...?" Ani prompted.

"I've prayed on it, and my god has shown me a way to save them. But I'm going to need a little help," Lilith said. "You were the only person I could think of."

"Where are they?" Ani asked.

"A little city in Vilmos," Lilith said. "Not two hours from here, by train. I'll even buy your ticket."

"Can you afford three tickets?" Ani asked.

"Sure," Lilith said. "Who did you—"

"Borri!" Ani yelled into the tavern. "Get out here!" After a few seconds, a very tall, thick man appeared in the doorway. He was wearing a red and black plaid shirt, and pants held up by a pair of black suspenders. His black boots were enormous, as were his hands, and Lilith thought he must be part giant. He had to stoop to pass under the threshold, and Lilith could smell the ale lingering on his breath and his straw-blonde beard.

"Yeah?" he asked. "What is it?"

"This lady says Darra and Aleksey are in trouble," Ani said. "She wants our help."

"You believe her?" he asked, and Ani shrugged.

"I don't see what she'd get out of lying to us," she said.

"Aleksey saved my life once," Borri said to the assassin. "Whatever you need, I'll do it."

"Great," Lilith said. "First, I'll need you to get some cotton balls..."

Dacy and the mustachioed man brought the teens to the far side of the carriage, where the four players stood lined up against the side of the vehicle with limp postures, their expressions completely blank. A lantern hung from a hook off the side of the carriage, casting deep shadows on their faces. "I guess that means we're done with these ones?" the mustachioed man asked, and Dacy nodded.

"About time, too," Dacy said. "They're getting more warn out with very show. Bet they wouldn't make it through tomorrow."

"You heard him," the man with the mustache said. "Time to go!"

"Go where?" asked one of the cast members in a lifeless

voice.

"Anywhere!" Dacy answered. "Go home! Go to temple! Just get away from here, and forget you ever met us." The players began to wander away in different directions, and Dacy turned to the teens. "Line up for me, so we can get a good look at you." The teens obeyed, moving underneath the lantern. "Hm," Dacy said as he looked Ennio up and down. "He's got a soldier's haircut and stance. He'd be good for playing a warrior, a constable or other authority figure." Dacy moved on to Trosclair. "Fop," was all he said, before moving on to Darra. "Well now, aren't you a lovely little thing," he said. He put his hands on Darra's shoulders, and she frowned. "Aw, what's the face for, love?" Dacy asked. "Maybe we should go around the corner and get a little more friendly."

"You shouldn't... be touching her," A.J. said slowly, as if he was just realizing it.

"Are they coming out of it already?" the mustachioed man asked, and Dacy nodded again. He knocked on the carriage door and said, "Lyle!" A few seconds later, the door swung open. A man in fine clothing was sitting on the cushioned bench inside, lute in hand. He had dark hair and brown eyes, and around his neck he wore a large, triangular golden amulet with a green gem in its center. The gem glowed faintly as he idly strummed his lute. Two pretty young women sat on either side of him with fawning expressions, and the narrator sat on the bench opposite. "Lyle!" Dacy said, sweeping a hand at the teens. "We got some new players. They had money, so we thought they'd be good to ransom. But they're starting to come around."

"Very well," Lyle said, rising. "If you'll excuse me, ladies." He climbed out of the carriage and began plucking away at the lute, and the gem around his neck glowed brighter. The eyes of the teens glowed a bright green that matched the gem perfectly. "There. That should keep them in line for another hour or two."

"It's about time for another show," the narrator said as he emerged from the carriage. "How much have we made so far?"

"Just over three thousand," the man with the mustache said. "Plus a pile of jewels."

"Paltry!" Lyle said. "We need to move on to the bigger cities, where the real money is."

"Will the amulet work on the bigger crowds?" Dacy asked.

"The mage said it would work on anyone who could hear my music," Lyle said. "But if we start working bigger crowds, we'll need more men."

"I got three or four cousins looking for work," the mustachioed man said.

"Will they work as hard as you do?" Lyle asked.

"Sure," the man said.

"Then I don't want them anywhere near this operation," Lyle said, and Dacy and the narrator laughed. "Well, what are you waiting for? Go make us some more money." The narrator turned and left, and the teens followed him out in front of the crowd.

"Welcome, welcome, ladies and gentleman!" the narrator said as he took his place at the side. "We are *Instant Gratification*, and we are so happy to be here tonight! Aren't we happy, players?" The teens cheered, clapped and whistled energetically. "Now, we need a couple of things from you guys. Who has a funny name for a book?" The crowd erupted with catchphrases and puns. "Okay, I heard '*The Knight and Shining Armoire*,' so we'll use that. So one of our actors is writing a book with that title." Trosclair stepped forward, pulled an imaginary pencil from the air, and made scribbling strokes on an invisible piece of paper. "Now I need a type of woman."

"Whore!"

"Nun!"

"Wet nurse!"

"Teacher!"

"Okay, I heard 'teacher,'" the narrator said. Darra stepped forward, pushed an imaginary pair of glasses up her nose and began writing in the air as if on a blackboard. "The muse had struck the author late at night..." Trosclair stretched and yawned, then resumed scribbling. "A bell rang out and gave the man a fright." The prince "heard" the bell and put his hand over his heart. "He opened up the door and saw the sight of someone he once knew bathed in moonlight." Darra spun around dramatically to face Trosclair, whose jaw dropped with recognition.

"Miss Prim, I said, to she who'd taught me speech," Trosclair said, to the audience's delight and the narrator's shock. "Come in and tell of what you do beseech."

"I came to ask that when you write your book, you think of

those the world has long forsook," Darra said. Now the narrator was really losing it, but to his credit, he remained visibly calm.

"On whose behalf do you now think to speak?" Trosclair asked. "The poor, the blind, the lost, or just the weak?"

"For all of these my heart and soul does ache," Darra said. "But far worse is the fate of those who bake."

"The baker is the richest man in town," Trosclair said. "For him you'd have me lay my quill now down?"

"To bake and earn fair pay is only just," Darra said. "But I meant those who bake and also dust."

"The cleaner earns a very decent wage," the prince replied. "To him you think I should devote a page?"

"Not him, but one to whom he turns in need whenever strikes the urge in him to breed," Darra said.

"But husbandry pays even more than books," Trosclair said. "So I say no! Cast off your dirty looks!"

"I did not mean the man who breeds the horse."

"Then who? Speak to me of your worry's source."

"I meant the women of the world, of course," Darra said.

"A woman's proper place is in the home," Trosclair said. "I'll not allow them to invade my tome."

"I taught you how to read and how to write," Darra said. "Does that not prove to you we are as bright?"

"I do suppose some have a certain wit," Trosclair said. "Though I would rather see them sew and knit." The teens continued bantering back and forth about women and men and the various roles they were expected to play in society. When the scene was over, the narrator added a couple of lines, but they were lost in the sound of ecstatic applause. Darra and Trosclair bowed and stepped back in line with A.J. and Ennio. The narrator took new suggestions, and this time Ennio and A.J. stepped forward. They gave it their all, miming everything the narrator described, but neither of them attempted dialogue like the prince and Darra had. They did a few more scenes, switching up partners each time, and Darra and Trosclair shined in every scene they were in. Soon they were standing behind the carriage again, lined up with lifeless expressions on their faces, waiting for their next directions.

Aleksey woke from his catnapping around nine. "Did Darra

come back yet?" he asked as he rubbed the sleep from his eyes.

"Nope," Kaleb said.

"She should've been back an hour ago," Aleksey said, sitting up. "Come on, Kay – we should find them before it gets too late." The mage put his spellbook down and followed the half-elf out of the room.

The narrator and Lyle were arguing inside the carriage. "I didn't do anything different, I swear!" the narrator said. "I just introduced them and gave them the prompts like all the others, and they ran with it!"

"They're not supposed to be able to think clearly, let alone rhyme – in iambic pentameter!" Lyle said. "Are you sure you didn't give them an order to speak? Maybe it was the power of the amulet."

"I didn't tell them to say a word!" the narrator said. "But it sure did make my job easier. And the audience loved them!" Lyle climbed out of the carriage, and the narrator followed him.

"One thing I hated – this hat!" Lyle said, yanking Trosclair's cap off his head. When the prince's red and gold curls came into view, a look of recognition crept over Lyle's face.

"It's time for another show," the narrator said.

"Screw the show!" Lyle said.

"But the crowd's already gathered," the narrator said.

"So tell them something – a lie, anything," Lyle said. "Just send them away."

"Why?" the narrator asked.

"You don't recognize him?" Lyle asked. "Even with the hair?" The narrator took a long look at the prince, and then his lips twisted into a smile.

"It can't be!" he said. "He's dressed like a peasant!"

"Look at those shoes," Lyle said, indicating Trosclair's fine leather loafers. "No peasant can afford those."

"Even if it is him, who's gonna pay his ransom?" the narrator asked. "He doesn't have family."

"I read there's a military man in control of the prince's palace, making a move for the throne," Lyle said. "I bet he'd pay a lot to have the prince delivered to his doorstep."

"So we're going to DuVerres?" the narrator asked, and Lyle

nodded.

"Looks like it," Lyle said.

"I'd wait 'til summer," Aleksey said as he lunged at Lyle and punched him, sending him to the ground. "It's more expensive, but everything's in bloom." The narrator backed up a few paces and then turned to run – but Kaleb was standing in his path, a fireball floating above his palm. "Darra!"

The young woman raised her head and asked in a loopy voice, "Yes?"

"Run!" Aleksey said.

"Where to?" Darra asked lifelessly.

"What did you do to my daughter?" Aleksey asked the narrator, grabbing him by the shirt collar.

"N-nothing," the narrator stammered. "I swear!" Aleksey shook the man violently. "It was him!" the man said, pointing to Lyle, who was crawling toward his lute, which was propped up against the carriage.

"Shut up, you fool!" Lyle said. "He'll kill us both!"

"I'd like nothing more," Aleksey said, but he released the narrator. "And there was a time I would have done just that. But I follow a different path now." Aleksey sucker-punched the narrator, who cried out and fell to the ground. The man with the mustache came up behind Aleksey and caught his arms around his waist in a bear hug, but the half-elf easily broke out of the hold and spun to face him. The man drew his sword, and Aleksey did the same. A few people from the crowd ventured a look behind the carriage as they began exchanging thrusts and parries.

"What's going on back here?" one of the men asked.

"They're fighting! Call the constable!" said a woman.

"That won't be necessary!" Lyle said, as he stood up with his lute. He strummed it and picked out a quick chord progression, and the gem in his amulet glowed again. The eyes of everyone who heard the sound flashed green. "They were just playing around. Weren't you?"

"Yes," Aleksey said, releasing his grip on his sword, which clattered to the street below. Kaleb's flame extinguished as the narrator stood back up.

"Get these idiots out there and give the people a damn show, but make it quick," Lyle instructed. "I want to be out of here within the hour." The narrator nodded his understanding and led the teens and the half-elf out in front of the crowd.

"They won't all fit in the carriage with us," the man with the mustache said.

"We only need the prince," Lyle said. "We'll kill the others and dump the bodies in the lake on our way out of town."

"Okay," the narrator said to the crowd, trying to ignore his aching jaw. "We're about to head out for the evening." The audience booed and grunted disappointedly, and from behind the carriage, Lyle started gently playing his lute. "But we are going to do one more skit for you before we go." The audience cheered. "First, I need someone to suggest a setting."

"Tavern!"

"Apothecary shop!"

"Farm!"

"Okay, we'll go with that," the narrator said. "So we're on a farm." The teens and the half-elf began miming various types of farm chores: Kaleb and A.J. shoved imaginary pitchforks into a pile of hay, Aleksey and Ennio hoed the street, Trosclair watered a row of invisible vegetables, and Darra squatted to milk a cow that wasn't there. "Now I need a type of wild animal..." The audience yelled out their suggestions, and the narrator went on to set up a scene in which a moose wandered onto the farm. Trosclair delivered a funny monologue about the trampling of his rutabagas, after which Darra delivered her own describing the moment the moose and her cow locked eyes – and instantly fell in love. The audience loved them both, and finding himself once again unable to top the teens' rhyming skills, the narrator ended the scene. The teens and the half-elf took a bow and then stepped back in a line against the carriage.

The crowd applauded and began to disperse, and when it had thinned to only a few people, Ani and Borri stood side by side in front of the carriage. Ani wore a heavy cloak, and Borri had his massive arms crossed over his broad chest. The mustachioed man approached them and said, "Give me all your money." Borri laughed.

"What'd he say?" Ani asked in a voice that was slightly louder than usual.

"I think he said he wants our money," Borri said. The man with the mustache backed up several feet.

"Lyle!" the man yelled. "We got a problem out here!" A few seconds later, Lyle turned the corner of the carriage with his lute in his hand. "They're not doing what I tell 'em!"

Lyle started plucking away on his lute, and his amulet glowed. He watched Ani and Borri's eyes as he played, but they didn't light up with enchantment as he expected. "Something's wrong," Lyle said. "They aren't responding!"

The mustachioed man drew his sword. "I'll get a response out of them," he said as he approached Ani.

"You want me to take care of him?" Borri asked.

"Nah," Ani replied. She drew a large crossbow out from under her cloak and pointed it at the man's face. He dropped his sword. "I got it covered."

"Now you, with the lute," Borri said. "Put it down and bring me that amulet."

"I'm afraid I can't do that," Lyle said, before turning to the teens and the half-elf. "Kill them!" Aleksey and the teens moved forward and formed a half-circle around Ani and Borri.

"Aleksey!" Borri said. "I don't want to fight you!"

"Me either!" Ani said as Darra and Kaleb stalked closer to her. Aleksey lunged at Borri. The half-elf's movements were slower than normal, and he wasn't using with his full half-elven strength, or even Borri would have succumbed to the onslaught. Darra grabbed the crossbow and yanked it from Ani's hands as Borri wrapped his arms around Aleksey in a headlock.

"I think he's fighting it!" Borri said as Ani backed away from Kaleb and Darra.

Dacy came back from a nearby alley with a handful of credits and a lady's purse, which he nearly dropped when he saw the fight in front of the carriage. "We got a problem, boss?" The pilot and Ennio moved to either side of Borri. They each grabbed an arm and pulled him off of Aleksey.

"Nothing we can't handle," Lyle said.

"I wouldn't be too sure of that," Lilith said as she popped up from behind the carriage, scimitars in both hands. She slammed the hilt of one of her blades into the side of Dacy's head, and he fell to the ground. Lyle backed up and raised his lute. He strummed a few chords, fumbling on the last one.

"Sorry," she said. "But that little trick won't work on me."

Lilith slashed, and the lute splintered and fell to the street. She raised her sword.

"Stop!" Lyle yelled. "If you kill me, with my dying breath, I'll make sure your friends do the same to each other!"

"Then I guess I'll have to cut out your throat," Lilith said, but she hesitated.

"Kill each other!" Lyle commanded. "Kill everybody!" Borri managed to shake off A.J. and Ennio, and he backed up a few steps to stand beside his sister once more. The pilot swung at Borri and grazed his chin, but the larger man returned the blow, sending A.J. to his knees. Aleksey and Ennio drew their swords. The half-elf stalked toward Borri again, and the soldier turned his sights on the prince. Darra raised the crossbow and pointed it at her father, but Kaleb tackled her before she could fire.

Every instinct inside Lilith told her to swing her sword and take off Lyle's head; but her higher reasoning worried about the guilt she would feel after taking another human life. She made a split decision, reached out and snatched the amulet. Yanking it from around his neck, she threw it onto the street and brought both her swords down on it at the same time. The gem inside the amulet shattered with a flash of bright green energy.

The teens and Aleksey instantly came back to their senses. Ennio stopped a swing of his sword just before it sliced Trosclair open. His mouth fell slack at what he had almost done, and he dropped his weapon. Aleksey sheathed his sword and held out a hand to Borri, who had fallen onto the street. The large man took the half-elf's offered hand and pulled himself back to his feet. Darra rolled off Kaleb, whom she had pinned in a brief wrestling match, and they both stood back up.

Ani and Borri turned the men over to the constabulary a little while later. They kept their story simple: The men had tried to rob them after a performance. When Lyle started ranting about the prince of DuVerres, the constables merely thought him mad, and they hauled the men off to jail in their own carriage - which Aleksey had already cleared of valuables. He filled a sack with the men's haul. Ennio searched through the bag full of credits, gold and jewels and pulled out his pouch, reattaching it to his belt.

"What are we going to do with the rest of this?" A.J. asked.

"It'll take fully half to buy our tickets to the coast," Aleksey said. "And I guess we get to keep the rest."

"I don't know, Dad," Darra said. "Somehow that doesn't sound right."

"It is all stolen property," Kaleb agreed.

"But we steal all the time," Aleksey said.

"Yeah, but not from innocent citizens," Darra said.

"Well, there's no way to return it all," Aleksey said. "What would you propose we do with it?"

"Hm," Darra said as she thought about it.

"I have an idea," A.J. said. He led the group a couple of blocks away, until he found the homeless man from earlier. "A small fortune like that could really change his life."

"I think that's a great idea," Aleksey said as he counted out roughly half the credits from the bag. He put them in his pocket and handed the bag full of valuables to A.J., who walked over and offered it to the man.

"What is it?" the man asked. "Food?"

"No," A.J. said. "But you can buy plenty of food with it." The man looked inside the bag, and his face lit up.

"Bless you!" he said excitedly. "Gods bless you!" The pilot smiled at the man and returned to his group, who started toward Eliza Dell's. Darra took the pilot's hand.

"You just keep getting sexier by the minute," Darra said.

"Really?" the pilot asked.

"What can I say?" Darra said as she gazed up at him. "I like a man with a kind heart, who's not afraid to show it." Aleksey walked up beside Lilith.

"Thank you for saving us," the half-elf said. "We were completely under his spell."

"Where did he get the amulet, anyway?" Lilith asked.

"I'm not sure," Aleksey said. "A sorcerer, obviously. Everywhere we go these days, there seems to be a mage with some nefarious scheme in the works."

"Will you need help to face them?" Lilith asked.

"Possibly, eventually," Aleksey said. "Although I don't know who we would even be fighting. Are you offering your services? Because I think technically your debt to us is fulfilled."

"You're right," Lilith said. "I'm no longer required to save your life... I'm just so used to the idea by now, it's become second nature."

"Speaking of your nature," Aleksey said. "I noticed you didn't kill anybody back there. And you had plenty of opportunity."

"I could have done this by myself, you know," Lilith said. "Taken out the men one by one. My god offered me that path."

"But you chose to take a different one," Aleksey said. "You asked for help, and nobody had to die. But you still saved our lives. You're a hero. How does it feel?"

"Calm," Lilith said. "Like I wasn't just fighting a little while ago."

"That's sounds like a good thing," Aleksey said.

"But I'm also still... unsatisfied," the assassin said.

"What do you mean?" the half-elf asked. "You can't tell me you actually miss killing."

"Not the action of it," Lilith said. "Nor its gruesomeness. But I long for the... completeness of it. I made enemies tonight who will live to see another day – and that brings with it an inherent threat."

"I know you're not saying you're afraid of those men," Aleksey said. "You could best them blindfolded." Lilith remembered her dream battle, and the madwoman who fought with her eyes covered.

"It's not just them," Lilith said. "I face some pretty tough opponents on a regular basis. What happens if I let the wrong one live, and he kills someone? Or kills me?"

"I think your survival instincts are strong enough to see you through," Aleksey answered. "We're headed to Adaya's Hollow next, and from there we'll cross to the Elven Isles. Will you be coming with us?"

"I don't think that's a good idea," Lilith said. "I have a lot more work to do back at the temple."

"You're really going to walk away from a hundred-thousand-credit payday?" Aleksey asked.

"I have money," Lilith said. "That's never been why I do what I do."

"Then why?" he asked.

"My friend, I've been asking myself that same question," she said.

Lilith said her goodbyes to Aleksey, Darra and the others

and left to catch a midnight train back to the Free City. Ani and Borri followed Aleksey and the teens back to Eliza Dell's and up to their room. Guardian woke and greeted them with a few excited barks. "Oh my goodness!" Ani said upon seeing the animal. "When did you get a dog?" She crossed to the bed and sat down next to Guardian so she could pet her, and Darra sat on the bed on the opposite side of the dog.

"We've only had her a couple weeks," Darra said. "Her name is Guardian."

"Actually, it's fortunate you came to our aid tonight," Aleksey said. "I was hoping you could take Guardian home with you and look after her until we get back from the Elven Isles."

"Why can't we take her with us?" Darra asked.

"It's my brother," Aleksey said. "He's allergic. He'd never allow her in his house." The half-elf faced Ani again. "It would only be for a few weeks. And I'd pay you a small stipend when we get back."

"Is she housebroken?" Ani asked.

"I trained her myself," Aleksey said proudly.

"Okay," Ani said. "But your tab is getting higher and higher."

"Ani," Borri drawled reproachfully. "You worry too much about money. These people are practically family."

"I'll be able to pay it off in full when we get back," Aleksey said. "I promise."

"I can't believe how good you two were at coming up with all those rhymes," A.J. said to Darra and Trosclair.

"Yeah," Kaleb said. "What was that all about?"

"It just comes naturally to me," the prince said. "I have the Poet's Curse. But I was really shocked that you kept up with me, Darra. No one's ever been able to do that before."

"I have an affinity for poetry, too," she said. "I guess the spell just brought it to the surface."

"It's not too late to change your mind about warrior training, sweetie," Aleksey said. "You could become a great actor instead."

"No, thank you!" Darra said. "I could never stand all that attention."

"You get used to it," Trosclair said.

"Maybe *you* do," Darra replied. "Besides, everyone knows

actors are all very flakey people, even without being ensorcelled."

"What I can't get over is how powerless it felt," Ennio said. "I almost killed you tonight. I knew I was doing it, but I couldn't stop myself."

"None of us could," Trosclair said. "Don't blame yourself."

"I don't," Ennio said. "I blame those men." The soldier looked to Aleksey. "You should have let me kill them."

"Son, when you have a lot of men's blood on your hands, it doesn't wash off too easy," Borri said. "Believe me, I know."

"And I'm not eager for my boyfriend to become a murderer, either," Trosclair said. "I like you just the way you are."

"Lucky me," Ennio said as he moved in to kiss the prince.

"Hey," Darra said as their kiss drew on. "Take it to your room, boys."

"Or stay," Ani said as she gazed at the young couple. Darra gave her a quizzical look. "What? I've never seen two boys kiss before."

Ani and Borri got their own room, and early the next morning, they accompanied the adventurers to the train depot. The innkeeper siblings' train arrived first, and Aleksey said goodbye to them - and to Guardian. He projected a mental image of the dog leaving on the train with Ani and her brother, and Guardian whimpered. "It's just for a little while," Aleksey said in a soothing voice. "And when we get back, we'll have enough money to get a real house, with a yard for you to play in." He projected those images into the dog's mind as well, and Guardian's mood seemed to brighten. Darra hugged Ani and Borri and kissed Guardian on the forehead, and the siblings boarded the train, the dog following obediently along behind them.

"I thought the Lord Advisor wasn't going to pay you until this summer," Darra said. "Where are we going to get enough money for a house?"

"Have you ever known me to make a promise I can't keep?" the half-elf asked. "The DragonSword - I plan to give it to the elven king. And I expect he will be very generous with his gold in return."

"But it's broken," Darra said. "What would he want with it?"

"It still has great value to the elves, trust me," Aleksey said. Darra shrugged. A.J. pointed out a vendor selling some sort of breakfast at the other end of the platform, and at Ennio's suggestion, the prince offered to buy everyone's meal.

"Get me something while you're over there?" Kaleb asked Darra. "I'm gonna stay here with your dad to watch our stuff."

"Me too, please," A.J. said. "I'm gonna head to the restroom."

"Sure," Darra said, and she led Trosclair and Ennio over to the vendor. A.J. darted behind the partition that led to the men's room.

"Man, that was close last night," Kaleb said when the others had gone.

"I know," Aleksey said. "We very nearly killed one another."

"No, I meant with Trosclair and Darra," the tribal lad said. "When they started talking about the Poet's Curse, I thought for sure they'd figure out they were brother and sister. And Trosclair's royal blood almost got him ransomed and our throats slit. So I see what you meant the other night, about the people who would want to harm Darra if they knew she was a princess."

On the other side of the partition directly behind them, A.J. stood frozen, a look of shock on his face. "Princess?" he whispered as he stared across the platform at Darra and her brother.

CHAPTER ELEVEN
"LITTLE EARTHQUAKES"

The adventurers took the train to the coast, and after a half a day's walk, they entered a foggy seaside cemetery scattered with gravestones, statues and small mausoleums stretching as far as they could see. A small flock of *kathari*, a type of carrion bird twice the size of a crow but with colorful plumage and a curved beak reminiscent of a vulture, circled just to the left of them. The smell of decaying flesh hit Aleksey's nose. He recognized the scent as vaguely mammalian, but it was too badly decomposed to determine the exact species.

"Well," the half-elf said, breathing through his mouth. "We're here."

"A cemetery?" Trosclair asked.

"Yes," Aleksey said.

"It's huge!" A.J. said. "How far does it go?"

"It stretches several miles," Aleksey said.

"The beach seems like a weird place to bury your dead," Kaleb said.

"Here in Ordway, there's a tradition of burying the dead on the land they died on, if at all possible," Aleksey said.

"You mean all these people died right here?" Trosclair asked.

"Yes," Aleksey said. "During one of the final battles of the Elven Wars."

"And this is Adaya's Hollow?" Ennio asked.

"No, of course not," Darra said.

. "Then where is it?" Ennio asked, looking up and down the beach in both directions.

"You're standing on it," Darra said. "Or over it."

"Oh, I get it," Kaleb said. "It's an underground city!"

"It's more of a village than a city," Darra said as they continued walking. "And it's integrated."

"Integrated?" Trosclair asked. "What does that mean?'

"It means multiple races live here together," Aleksey said. "Like in the olden days."

"What types of races?" the prince asked warily.

"There are humans, of course," Aleksey answered. "But Dwarfs and mole-men also live here with them. Last time I came through, there was even a small clan of earth elementals."

"I—I've never met a non-human before," Trosclair said.

"Will the prince be safe here?" Ennio asked.

"He'll be safer here than in a big city," Aleksey said. "Besides, it should only be for the one night. By tomorrow morning, I hope to be on the way across the channel to the Elven Isles on one of those beauties." The half-elf pointed to the shore and a long pier with several small to medium-sized steamboats tethered to it. The ships were clearly old, with chipping paint, rust and barnacles on their sides.

"Beauties, really?" Darra asked. "They look like they're held together with seaweed and wet sand."

"But they'll get us to where we want to go," Aleksey said. "And much faster than a sailboat." The half-elf led the teens down a steep incline, along the beach and just past the pier, where an arched metal door stood flush with the face of the sloping earth around it. Aleksey approached the door and slammed the knocker several times, then stood back. After several seconds, a slat opened low in the door, and a pair of eyes gazed out at them.

"Yeah?" the owner of the eyes said. "Who are you?"

"My name is Aleksey Fabian," the half-elf replied. "I'm here to speak with your council. They'll recognize my name."

"Wait here." The slat slammed shut.

"Was that a Dwarf," Trosclair asked, and Darra nodded. "He didn't seem too friendly."

"Oh, that's just how Dwarfs are," Darra said. "They're very

gruff. But most of them have big hearts, deep down." Aleksey heard the lock on the door turning, and soon it swung wide open. A group of men and women of various races stood on the other side.

"Aleksey!" one of the Dwarf women cried. She had close-cropped light brown hair and a stout figure. "It is so fortunate you're here! We need your help!"

"Well, hello to you, too, Kilea," the half-elf said as he led the teens inside. The entrance hall was a wide, square space with a high ceiling and square columns spaced evenly throughout to support it. There was a large orbital clock jutting off of one wall, spinning imperceptibly slowly.

"What are those?" A.J. asked, pointing to the large chunks of orange-glowing stones that were attached high on the walls at regular intervals, illuminating the room.

"Never seen a radiant rock before, I guess?" asked a woman in her mid-thirties.

"Nope," the pilot replied. "But I'm guessing they're magic?"

"There is a myth the mole-men tell their children, that the god of magic created them," the woman said. "But they actually occur naturally here. We mine them to supply our village with light and heat. I'm Gemma."

"A.J." the pilot said, shaking her hand. They entered another large room, and the teens and half-elf took seats along one side of a long, rectangular table. Kilea and Gemma took seats on the opposite side next to the other councilmembers. The first was a fur-covered, bespectacled mole-man in fine clothing that made him look ridiculous, in Trosclair's opinion; but the prince had enough diplomacy to keep this thought to himself. The final councilman was what Trosclair could only guess was an earth elemental. He wore loose shorts without a shirt or shoes, and parts of his skin seemed caked in mud or covered with stones - until Trosclair realized these features were actually a part of the man's body. The man caught the prince staring, and Trosclair's eyes darted away.

"Aleksey," the mole-man said, nodding his head in greeting. "It's so fortunate you've decided to visit. We have need of your services."

"Kilea mentioned that," Aleksey said. "What do you need?"

"Several village children have gone missing," the earth elemental said in a raspy voice that startled Trosclair. "Your tracking skills could help us find them."

"Of course I'll help," Aleksey said. "How many kids are missing?"

"Three," Gemma said. "My son, Kilea's granddaughter, and Ademek, one of the earth clan children."

"When and where did they go missing?" Aleksey asked.

"We're not sure about my son," Gemma said. "He went out with his friends two days ago, but he never made it home that evening."

"Did his friends see or notice anything that might be of use to us?" the half-elf asked.

"No," Gemma said. "They said he left for home on the same path he took every night."

"My granddaughter was next," Kilea said. "She was playing in one of the common areas and left to go to the restroom. That was yesterday."

"And this morning, Ademek didn't show up for his lessons," the earth elemental said. "We can't find him anywhere."

"Hm," Aleksey said. "It sounds like kidnappings. Is there anyone you would suspect, off the top of your heads?"

"It's clearly one of the mole-men!" said a dwarf man standing at the end of the table. "None of their kids have gone missing!"

"That doesn't prove anything," said a mole-woman. "If anybody should be suspect, it's the earth clan. They're the new ones among us." The room was suddenly filled with the sound of bickering as people continued accusing one another.

"I don't think integration is going so well," Ennio whispered into Trosclair's ear. The mole-man councilman banged a gavel on the table with his wide, polydactyl forepaw.

"Citizens!" the mole-man said in a booming voice, and the room quieted. "Throwing these accusations at one another is not going to get our children back any sooner. We need to remain calm and civil."

"Easy for you to say," a woman mumbled, and the councilman shot her a quelling look over the rims of his glasses.

"If they're disappearing from inside the village, it stands to reason they may be being held here, too," Aleksey said.

"That is our hope and our assumption," Kilea said.

"Have you considered that it might be an attack on this council?" Aleksey asked. "Someone who's dissatisfied with the way you're running things?"

"When it was just my son and Kilea's granddaughter missing, that's what we thought was going on," Gemma said.

"But Ademek is only very distantly related to me," the earth elemental said. "And I have three children of my own they could have targeted."

"Okay, so there's no clear motive," Aleksey said. "Do you have something of Ademek's? Dirty clothing, or something with his scent? If he disappeared this morning, there's a chance I can still follow it."

"Really?" Gemma asked. "You could do that?"

"Possibly," Aleksey replied. "These stuffy halls of yours are perfect for preserving odors."

"Well, let's not waste a minute, then," the mole-man councilman said. He nodded to a mole-woman Trosclair supposed might be his wife, mother, sister or daughter, so difficult was it to discern even an approximate age of the furry creatures. The mole-woman left the room.

"I'm going to go see about getting a room set up for our guests," Gemma said as she left the table and headed out the door.

"We'll start from the last place he was known to be," Aleksey said as he rose from his seat.

"I want to help," Darra said, standing.

"Absolutely not," her father replied.

"But Dad, its children," Darra said.

"That's exactly why you'll be staying with Kilea," Aleksey said, placing a hand on Darra's shoulder. "Someone is taking children. I'm not about to let my own get mixed up in it."

"But you might need help," Darra said.

"Your Dad's right, Darra," A.J. said. "It's too dangerous." Darra frowned up at the pilot.

"Thank you, A.J.," Aleksey said.

"But Darra's got a point," A.J. said. "You should take someone along with you - and I can't just sit around while I know kids are in danger."

"You're a kid," the half-elf said.

"I'm eighteen," A.J. said. "My people consider that the age

adulthood starts."

The half-elf looked the pilot in the eye for a moment. "Fine. You can come along." Darra's frown deepened, but she didn't make any more protests. Suddenly the room lurched, as if it had been picked up at one end by a giant. There was a steady shaking for several seconds during which everyone in the room froze.

"Earthquake!" someone yelled in the silence. A crack formed running down the smooth stone surface of one of the walls. Then, just as abruptly as it had started, the shaking stopped.

"Check the upper levels for damage," the mole-man councilman told the earth elemental. "I'll take the lower levels."

"Do you get earthquakes a lot here?" Ennio asked.

"Oh, no," Kilea said as her fellow councilmembers left the room. "It's the missing earth clan boy. He's causing them."

"Like how the Tribe's water-witch stopped the rains?" A.J. asked Kaleb.

"It's similar," Kaleb said. "A mage who practices elemental magic can connect to Ona at a deep level, if they become very accomplished. But elemental people are actually composed out of the earth, air, water or fire. They're born with a strong psychic connection to those elements. These earthquakes probably mean the earth clan boy is terrified." Kilea led Darra, Kaleb, Trosclair and Ennio out of the room.

The mole-woman came back in a few minutes later with a pillow, which she handed to Aleksey without comment. The half-elf sniffed the item until he had the scent of the missing boy memorized. Gemma returned and led Aleksey and A.J. to the rooms Ademek's family called home, and Aleksey was able to pick up the elemental boy's distinctive smell. The trail led Aleksey to a stairwell. "Where does this lead?" he asked Gemma.

"Down to the lowest levels of the village," she said. "The floors we use for gardening, mining the radiant rocks, and of course the lowest level is the stream all of our water is pumped up from."

"The earth clan boy definitely came this way," Aleksey said. "Tell your people to form a search party. And bring weapons, just in case."

"We will - we have," Gemma said. "We've searched every nook and cranny. And we have a lot of those down here. I'll go get them to search again, but... could you go ahead and follow the trail, in the meantime? I don't like to think about what could be happening to my son and the other two."

"Of course," Aleksey said, and the woman departed. Aleksey and the pilot continued down the stairwell. The trail led to a level four flights down. When Aleksey and A.J. opened the door to the massive chamber, they had to shield their eyes, so bright was the light spilling out. They entered to find a series of garden plots between the columns. Lush, leafy greens and vegetables, some of which A.J. could not identify, grew to various heights in these plots. There were even grape vines dangling off of wooden trellises that ran along the rows of one plot. The plants' light and warmth were supplied entirely by the radiant rocks, which in this chamber were embedded into the stone walls and ceiling.

"So..." A.J. said.

"Yes?" Aleksey prompted.

"I actually had an ulterior motive in tagging along with you," the pilot said.

"And what was that?" the half-elf asked as they crossed the chamber.

"We need to talk - about Darra," A.J. said.

"Okay," the half-elf replied. "What about her?"

"I know the secret that you're keeping from her," A.J. said. "I know she's a princess, and Trosclair's sister." Aleksey's jaw dropped.

"I've kept this secret for fifteen years!" Aleksey said, bringing his hands to the sides of his head. "And now everyone is suddenly figuring it all out?"

"I didn't figure anything out," the pilot said. "I overheard you and Kaleb talking about it at the train station."

"You haven't said anything to Darra, have you?" Aleksey asked.

"No," A.J. said, and Aleksey exhaled with relief. "But I will, if you don't."

"Unholy hells!" the half-elf cursed. "Is that a threat?"

"Think of it more as a choice," A.J. said. "You can tell Darra yourself - the way she should find out - or I can do it for you, and you'll have to risk her hating you for lying to her."

"You don't know what you're doing!" Aleksey said. "Darra's situation is... complicated."

"So make it simple for me," A.J. said.

"There are people who would come after Darra, if they knew who she truly was," Aleksey said.

"I've seen you fight," the pilot said. "Are you telling me these people could beat you?"

"Easily," the half-elf said. "And they would take Darra away and do terrible things to her."

"Okay," A.J. said. "But that doesn't explain why Darra herself can't know."

"You've seen the dangers we face on a regular basis," Aleksey said. "Just in the last month, we've had our minds completely overtaken with magic - twice. Keeping Darra unaware of her... predicament prevents the possibility that it will become a liability for her, like it is for Trosclair."

"Are you sure that's what it really is?" A.J. pressed. "Or are you just scared?"

"Scared?" Aleksey repeated. "Of what?"

"You're afraid that if Darra knew the truth, she'd hate you, maybe even run away," A.J. said. "And the thought of this terrifies you so much that you're actually in danger of making it come true."

"How dare you!" Aleksey said. "You may think you know my daughter–"

"I do know her!" A.J. said. "But don't make this about me! I didn't have anything to do with the lies you've told her all her life."

"To protect her!" Aleksey said. "You make it sound like I'm some wicked stepfather, keeping Darra in the dark to hurt her, when the opposite is true. If she - or her brother - knew the truth about their parents, and how they died, they'd be devastated." The half-elf led the pilot into a narrow corridor.

"What happened that's so horrible it can't even be talked about?" the pilot asked.

"They sold her, alright!" Aleksey said, and A.J.'s face twisted in confusion.

"What do you mean?" he asked.

"Darra's parents were fighting a war - the last of the Elven Wars, to be exact, which were aimed at scaring the last of the elves from the continent." Aleksey answered. "I'll spare you the historical details, but the humans were losing the war. Darra's father sought help from an... entity who rules on the Dread Continent."

"I don't know what that is," A.J. said.

"It's an evil place that nothing but monsters and madmen call home," Aleksey said. "It doesn't really matter. The point is, Darra's father made a deal with a demon - literally. In exchange for his help winning the war, Darra's father promised to give the demon his first-born daughter."

"That's awful," A.J. said. "But how did you come to claim her?"

"When Darra's mother found out about the deal, she left her husband and fled into the woods," Aleksey said. "She was caught by Ramla and the Tribe. She told them about the pact with the demon, and they agreed to hide her until the baby was born. But as you know, Darra and Trosclair were twins, and the pregnancy was a difficult one. Darra's mother eventually left the Tribe to return to the palace, where her physicians could attend to her. The babies came, and Darra's father reneged on his promise, unable to bear the thought of parting with her. He summoned his army to defend her, but the forces of the Dread Continent swarmed the palace and cut a bloody path through the soldiers. Darra's father was killed, and her mother mortally wounded. With her last breaths, she begged me to take Darra away and protect her. And that's exactly what I've done ever since."

"You were at the palace when it happened?" A.J. asked, and Aleksey nodded. "Wow. That's... a lot to think about. But I don't think it changes anything fundamentally."

"So you're still going to tell Darra?" Aleksey asked.

"The truth will eventually come out," A.J. said. "It always does. And you won't have the luxury then of framing the story in your words, from your viewpoint."

"I had always planned on telling her on her thirteenth birthday," Aleksey said. "But she was still such a little girl then. And now there just - never seems to be the right opportunity."

"You should—" The pilot's words were lost in a crash of stones that fell from the corridor's ceiling as another earthquake rocked the village. The half-elf pushed A.J. out of the path of the falling stones, which fell between him and the pilot, followed by a good deal of displaced earth, until he could no longer see the young man.

"A.J.?" he called. "Are you okay?" A couple of loud coughs

answered him from the other side of the debris.

"I'm fine," the pilot said as he looked down the corridor. He couldn't see an exit. "I think I'm trapped back here, though."

"I'll go get the others, and we'll dig you out," Aleksey said. "Just stay put." The half-elf dashed back the way they'd come.

"Don't have much choice about that," A.J. said to himself.

Aleksey made it back up to the top level and found Kilea, his daughter and the other teens in the room set up for them just outside the entrance hall. He explained what had happened to the pilot, and Darra stood up with her crossbow in her hand.

"Okay, now there's no way I'm not coming with you," she said.

"Honey–"

"It's A.J., Dad!" was all she said, and somehow that settled the argument.

"I'm coming, too," Kaleb said.

"Should we join them, Ennio?" Trosclair asked.

"I don't think that's a good idea," Ennio said. "This place nearly collapsed with that last earthquake. I want to keep you as close to those exit doors as possible."

"There are other exits, through some of the mausoleums," Kilea said. "For emergencies."

"I think it's best if you stay here, too," Aleksey said. "We still don't know who's taking these kids, so I'd rather not present them with a royal target." The half-elf looked at Trosclair when he said these words, but A.J. couldn't help but feel he was actually making a point about Darra.

"I just want to be useful," Trosclair said.

"We're about to have an emergency meeting in the Great Hall," Kilea said, looking to the prince. "I expect it might devolve into a shouting match, as it almost did earlier. We could use someone impartial - someone with an air of authority - to mediate for us."

"That sounds like a brilliant way to help," Aleksey said.

"Okay," Trosclair said. "I'll do it."

"Dad!" Darra said from the doorway. "Come on! We're wasting time." Aleksey obeyed, and soon he was leading Kaleb and Darra down the stairwell and through the garden chamber. "See, this is why I should've been allowed to come with you in the first place," Darra said. "It would've saved time on me coming to the rescue."

"Very funny, honey," Aleksey said.

"I'm serious!" she said. "You always end up needing me in the end."

"I think you have that backwards," Aleksey said.

"I saved you from Ennio, when the Commandant and he cornered you," Darra said. "And I would have saved you from those men who kidnapped Talia, except they'd already moved on."

"Would have, sweetie," Aleksey said. "Would have. Meanwhile, I saved you from Lilith, the succubus – I freed Talia, who saved all of you."

"From the story I heard, that was Guardian!" Darra said. "And I got us past Trosclair the first time we met him."

"Barely!" Aleksey said. "My point is, I'll always be there to step in when you need—"

"Do not say 'when I need saving!'" Darra said.

"When you need a helping hand, as we all do from time to time," Aleksey said.

"But you have to admit that I've come a long way from washing your shirts," Darra said. "I've been tested in battle. I'm a real warrior now, like you."

"And what were you before?" Aleksey asked. "My apprentice?"

"No," Darra said. "I'm pretty sure apprentices get paid a stipend."

"You get your allowance," Aleksey said. "Usually. Sorry about that. You'll be getting back pay for the last few weeks." Darra smiled.

"I know you're good for it, Dad," Darra said.

"Do I get an allowance?" Kaleb asked.

"I don't know," Aleksey said. "Do you?"

"I do the same chores Darra does," Kaleb said.

"If I gave one to you, I'd have to give one to the outworlder, the prince and the soldier, too," Aleksey said as they entered the corridor.

"Trosclair has money," Kaleb said. "And Ennio has no real need for it. But I do need spell ingredients, the occasional scroll or leaflet, and I could use a new toothbrush and socks."

"Those sound like reasonable requests," Aleksey said.

"And it might not be a bad idea to start giving A.J. some money now and then, too," Kaleb said. "I know he wants to buy Darra a gift."

"Oh, really?" Darra asked. "What kind of gift?"

"He didn't say," the mage said. "He was just feeling homesick, and when I asked him about it, he mentioned a midwinter tradition of gift-giving among his people."

"Darra doesn't need anyone giving her gifts but me," Aleksey said.

"I strongly disagree," his daughter said.

"Gifts from boys come with expectations," the half-elf said.

"A.J.'s not like that," Darra said.

"Uh, guys," Kaleb said, pointing to the pile of rocks and dirt ahead of them. "Is this it?"

"Yes," Aleksey said as they closed in. He noticed the pile had been partially cleared and now only blocked the bottom half of the corridor.

"A.J.?" Darra called, but no answer came back.

"Did he clear this himself?" Kaleb asked as he picked up A.J.'s spear from the floor.

"Yeah," Darra said. "Maybe he climbed over it and found his way back upstairs."

"I don't think so," Aleksey said. "I smell blood in the air. A.J.'s blood."

"Can you follow his scent?" Darra asked worriedly, and her father nodded and led them back down the corridor.

Trosclair and Ennio followed Kilea to the Great Hall, a room of gigantic proportions - literally, as the ceilings were high enough to comfortably fit a giant inside. It consisted of a flat, circular stage and dozens of rows of stone bleachers surrounding it. The bleachers were filled to capacity, and the crowd was noisy and restless. A table and four chairs had been placed on the stage; the mole-man and earth clan councilmen were already in two of the chairs. Kilea took the third and gestured for Trosclair to take the fourth. "Ennio needs a chair," Trosclair said.

"Actually, I prefer to stand," Ennio said, moving behind Trosclair and placing his hand casually on the back of his chair. It was a familiar position and a visual reminder of the prince's stature, for the benefit of both the prince and the villagers watching him with curious and expectant expressions.

"Citizens," the mole-man councilman said, banging his gavel on the table again. The hall quieted to a low buzz of scattered whispers. "You all know why we're here. Our children are missing. First, I want to thank those of you who have volunteered to do another sweep with us. We are going to find these kids today, I'm sure of it."

"Do we know who took them?" someone shouted.

"No, we're still working on that," the mole-man answered.

"Will you be checking door to door?" someone else yelled.

"If it comes to it," the mole-man said. "But first I want to do another sweep of the lower levels."

"What are you doing to prevent any more kids from going missing?" asked an elderly dwarf woman in the plainest brown burlap dress Trosclair had ever seen.

"We've called up the reserve constabulary," the earth elemental rasped. "They're patrolling all the common areas and the borders of the residential levels. If your kids stick close to home, they should be safe."

"But what about when they go to lessons and back? Or to eat?" someone asked.

"I'm not sending my kid to lessons with some psycho mole-man on the loose!" said another.

"You don't know it's a mole-man," one of the mole-women shot back. "You're just being racist!"

"It's the earth clan endangering us all!" a Dwarf man said. "They'll bring the whole village down around us! We never should have let them live with us!"

"Citizens, I–"

"And who put you in charge, anyway?" a bald man asked the mole-man councilman. "There's supposed to be a human on the council to speak for us!"

"Gemma is coordinating the search effort," the mole-man councilman replied.

"And we have asked a human to sit in for her," Kilea said, gesturing to Trosclair.

"Yeah," someone yelled. "Let's hear what the prince has to

say!"

Trosclair cleared his throat as all eyes turned to him. "Um, I—We first want to say, thank you," he said. "Your people's hospitality - especially in light of the direness of your circumstances - has astonished us. And second, I would encourage all of you to remember the reason you chose to live in this community in the first place: To find strength in your diversity."

"It used to be safe here!" someone yelled.

"And it will be again," Trosclair said. "But you mustn't turn on one another before that can happen."

"What about the half-elf?" an earth clan woman asked. "Did he find Ademek?"

"He's still working on tracking down the person or people behind this," Kilea said.

"May we ask if there's been any other unusual activity, besides the earthquakes?" Trosclair asked. The hall was set abuzz with whispered observations and suspicions.

"A dozen chickens came up slaughtered a few days ago," the earth elemental councilman said. "You think it could be related?"

"Possibly," Trosclair said. "Anything else?" A woman stood up nervously in the third row of the bleachers.

"Your Grace?" she asked in a voice that trembled.

"Yes?" the prince prompted.

"I'm one of the teachers here," the woman said. "I was Ademek's teacher, and Gemma's son was also in my class a few years ago. I wanted to point out that they were both considered some of my best students."

"What about your granddaughter?" Trosclair asked Kilea. "Is she bright?"

"As the morning sun!" Kilea said.

"What do you think this means?" the mole-man councilman asked.

"Maybe the kidnapper was a bad student, and he's jealous of the kids he's taking," Ennio suggested.

"Hm," Trosclair said. "It could be. Or it could be someone who wants to see the entire village suffer, long-term, by losing those minds with the most potential." Suddenly a mole-woman ran onto the stage, flailing her arms wildly.

"My baby!" she screamed. "Somebody took my baby!"

When they got back to the gardens, Aleksey, Darra and Kaleb crossed to a new door and entered another passageway that led through a series of smaller rooms the villagers used for various chores and storage. They passed a room full of spinning wheels and looms, another with chairs in stacks to the ceiling spread from wall to wall, and several rooms with barrels of wine and food or shelves of clay pottery filled with what Aleksey could smell were some very strong spices. Kaleb was shocked at how clean everything in the village was; there wasn't a cobweb or dust bunny in sight, even down here in rooms the villagers rarely used.

"Can you tell anything about the person who took him?" Darra asked her father.

"No," he said. "There is another scent mixed with his, but it's very faint. And vaguely familiar."

"You've smelled it before?" she asked.

"Maybe," Aleksey replied. "But I can't remember where or when." They came upon an empty room, and they would have passed it by, had Darra not spied something out of the corner of her eye.

"Wait," she said, ducking inside the room. Her father and the mage followed her. One of the walls was covered in mystical symbols - written in blood.

"Dad, please tell me that's not A.J.'s blood," Darra said.

"It's not fresh enough to be his," Aleksey said, wiping a finger against the dry discoloration. "This blood is days old."

"Thank the gods!" Darra said.

"I wouldn't go thanking them yet," Aleksey said. "That just means it's probably one of the children's." Darra turned to stare at the symbols, and the largest was a triangular shape that she recognized.

"Hey!" she said. "I've seen that before."

"The bloody writing on the wall?" Aleksey asked. "Gods, I wish that were a metaphor."

"It's the same design as Lyle's amulet," Darra said, tracing it with her finger.

"Unholy hells!" Aleksey said. "I think you're right!" He turned to Kaleb proudly. "My girl is very smart. She gets that from me, you know."

"I just have a keen sense of fashion," Darra said.

"Lyle and his men were on their way to jail not two days ago," Kaleb said. "It can't be them."

"No," Aleksey said. "I suspect it's the mystery mage who seems to have been following us."

"The same one who kidnapped Talia?" Darra asked, and her father nodded.

"But the kids started disappearing days before we got here," Kaleb said. "And it was the same with Talia. I don't think we're being followed – I think we're doing the following."

"The Oracle did say there was someone – or something – powerful watching us," Aleksey said. "I assumed she meant someone literally watching us from the forest at that moment. But if it was a mage, he could be monitoring our conversations anytime and anywhere to stay ahead of our movements."

"And then he – or she – sets up a trap or a dangerous situation for us in each location," Kaleb said. "It would explain a lot. But why are they doing it?"

"I have enemies in the world, unfortunately," Aleksey said.

"You think it could be that Vilmosi sorcerer you stole the Chalice of Impossibilities from?" Darra asked. "He vowed revenge on you."

"That's one theory," Aleksey said. "But I also angered a whole coven of dread witches during the Elven Wars. One or all of them may have finally decided to track me down."

"Maybe if we figure out what they're up to, it will reveal a clue about who they are," Darra said. "Kay, do you have any idea what these symbols mean?"

"No," Kaleb answered. "I'm not allowed to study dread magic, remember?" The mage fixed the half-elf with a pointed look.

"Are you suggesting it's my fault you're not better educated in the evil arts?" Aleksey asked.

"I only want to study it so I know how to defend against it," Kaleb said. "It's not like I'd start sacrificing small animals."

"Good, because I couldn't be your friend if you did that," Darra said.

"We'll discuss it later," Aleksey said, and the mage smiled. They left the room and continued following the trail of the pilot's scent. It led them to another stairwell, which they took to the bottom level of the village. It was a vast natural cavern with the promised stream flowing through it. Radiant rocks had been scattered throughout to provide some light, but they were placed at ground level and cast distorted shadows on the walls as they passed. Stalagmites rose up from the floor sporadically, and the ceiling was just as craggy. The footfalls of the adventurers echoed as they walked alongside the stream, and far up ahead, Darra could just make out the dying rays of the sun outside what appeared to be a natural exit high on the cavern wall. There was a rustle of movement overhead, and they turned their faces skyward to see a colony of large bats fall from the ceiling into flight, heading toward the sunlit exit.

"Ew," Darra said. "I hate bats!"

"They won't bother us," Aleksey said.

"I wish they would," Darra said. "I'd kill them all."

"I thought you didn't like people hurting animals," Kaleb said. "Or is that just the furry, cute ones?"

"Bats killed Buttercup!" Darra said angrily. "Swarmed him and drank his blood, until his heart just – gave out."

"Gods," Kaleb said. "I'm sorry."

"It was my own fault," Darra said. "I spent the last of my money on clothes and shoes that month. If I'd spent it on feed for Buttercup instead, she would have been safe in the barn, instead of grazing in the pasture."

"Grazing is healthier for herd animals," Aleksey said. "There's no way you could have known what was going to happen."

"Still, if you'd like a pair of shoes and matching vest made out of bat-leather, just say the word," she said, pointing her crossbow up at the largest of the several bats who had remained attached to the ceiling. They heard a groan coming from around a bend up ahead and raced toward the sound. Darra cleared it first and saw A.J. lying face-down near the wall. She raced over to him and knelt down beside him. Kaleb and her father followed suit.

"A.J.?" Darra asked, but there was no response.

"Was he hit on the head or something?" Kaleb asked.

"Or something," Aleksey said as he rolled the pilot over to reveal two small puncture wounds on his throat oozing blood. "Gods, I know what this is now. And where I've smelled that other scent. We need to get him out of here, now!"

"What is it, Dad?" Darra asked as the pilot groaned again.

Suddenly one of the bats fell from the ceiling, flipping upright as it glided down unnaturally slowly in front of them. Its features - its very bones and skin - shifted as it took on a humanoid form in elaborate, archaic clothing. When the figure's shiny black shoes touched the cavern floor, there was no sound, as if he had the weight of a feather. He spun to face the adventurers, and they took in the pale, marble-like skin, the haunting, mesmeric eyes, and the protruding fangs of a very old vampire.

"Darra, Kaleb - take the outworlder and go!" Aleksey said.

"I don't think he can walk yet," Kaleb said.

"Then leave him," Aleksey said.

"Dad!" Darra protested. "I'm not—"

"Darra, listen to me!" Aleksey snapped. "Go!"

"No, please," the vampire said. "Stay. We haven't even been properly introduced yet. I'm Lucio." Darra turned to her father, keeping her crossbow trained on the vampire.

"I don't want to leave him," Darra said.

"I'll bring him up with me in just a minute, I promise," Aleksey said. "Now please, go!" Darra nodded, and Kaleb sat A.J.'s spear down beside him. Then the teens headed back the way they'd come.

"So," Lucio said. "Aleksey. I can't believe you're alive and well after all these years."

"I'd say the same about you," Aleksey said. "But we both know you haven't been alive for a very long time."

"True enough," Lucio said, taking a step toward the half-elf, who backed up an equal measure and drew his sword. "Ah, come now. Can't two old friends talk without it resorting to violence?" A.J. managed to pull himself upright against the cavern wall.

"We were never friends," Aleksey said.

"I guess you're right," said the vampire. "But we were allied together - even if it was for a short time. May I speak freely? Or do you intend to stab me with that thing?"

"I intend to cut your head off with it," Aleksey said. "Like I should have long ago."

"Then I'll be brief," Lucio said. "I like the girl. She's spunky. Darra, did you say her name was?"

"Say it again, and I'll cut your tongue out and shove it up

your—"

"Now, now!" Lucio said. "There's no need for explicit language. Though I do appreciate the gruesomeness of the image."

"So are you the one who's been setting up all these traps for us?" Aleksey asked.

"I can't say I know what you're talking about," Lucio said. "I'm here on a paying job."

"You're still working for him?" Aleksey asked, and the vampire nodded.

"Of course," Lucio said. "You don't get to just walk away from his service. Well, I guess you did, didn't you? But most people are not so fortunate."

"So he's the one who sent you?" Aleksey asked.

"Sadly, no," Lucio said. "Your little fake-death scenario convinced him well enough, and he stopped looking for you years ago. No, I'm here on more of what the young people would call a freelance gig. But if I'd known it was you I was entrapping, I would have planned something more elaborate than snatching your friend over there." Aleksey looked to the pilot, who was trying - and failing - to stand, using the wall to balance himself. "His blood had a strange flavor to it I've never tasted before. It was hard to pry myself away from him. But I needed him alive."

"For what?" Aleksey asked.

"You'll see!" the vampire said, as he lunged at the half-elf. Aleksey swung at him, but Lucio was just as fast as him, and the vampire pulled his head out of the way at the last second. The vampire swung a leg up and kicked Aleksey in the face. The half-elf fell back a few feet, shook his head to clear it, and charged at Lucio again. He swung his sword in an arc aimed at the vampire's neck, but the demon crouched and punched Aleksey in the stomach, knocking the breath out of him. Aleksey doubled over, and the vampire slammed his knee up into the half-elf's face. Aleksey staggered back, blood trickling from his mouth. "Mm. Smells delicious. I've always wanted to taste the blood of a half-elf. Especially yours."

"And I've always wanted a suit of armor that flies through the air," Aleksey said. "But I could never answer the riddles of the gorgon who guards it." He set his jaw and attacked the vampire again, and this time he scored a slash through the creature's puffy white sleeve, opening a gash on his arm. Lucio loosed a high-pitched shriek that sent the rest of the bats on the ceiling scattering.

"You bastard!" Lucio screamed. "Just for that, I'm going to take my time killing the little girl. And when she dies, I'll give her my blood to resurrect her as my slave for all eternity!"

"You don't have a lot of eternity left," Aleksey said as he closed the distance between himself and the vampire. He brought his sword down on Lucio again, a swing directly over his head that even the vampire could not avoid. Instead, he caught the blade in his hands. The weapon sliced into his palms to the bones, and the thick, dark blood of the vampire dripped to the ground as he held Aleksey off. Summoning all his strength, Lucio twisted the sword from Aleksey's grasp and hurled the weapon into the stream next to them.

"You're losing a lot of blood," Aleksey said. "And isn't that the source of your power?"

"But you've lost your weapon," Lucio said. "You've no way to kill me now."

"Try me," Aleksey said. "I'm very resourceful." The vampire lurched at Aleksey again, his bloody hands tipped with sharp claws with which he intended to tear out the half-elf's throat. Aleksey dropped to the ground and swung his leg, knocking the vampire from his feet. The creature splashed back into the shallows of the stream.

"Now you've really done it!" Lucio said angrily. "These shoes are over three hundred years old, and now they're ruined!" Aleksey tackled the vampire, and as soon as they splashed down into the stream, he realized his mistake. The vampire and he fought for dominance in the water, which only ran about four or five feet deep - but that was plenty of depth to deprive Aleksey of air, which the vampire didn't need to breathe. Every time Aleksey managed to wriggle from Lucio's grasp and come up for a breath, the vampire would shove him back down under the water. It wasn't the most efficient way to drown him, but it was taking the fight out of the half-elf. Finally the vampire got a solid hold on him and held him beneath the surface.

"Any last words?" the demon asked. "Oh, that's right. I've finally found a way to shut you up, for once! I should have tried this years ago—*aagh*!" The vampire shrieked again as the pilot drove his spear deep into the creature's shoulder from behind. Lucio spun around and pulled the weapon out of his back with a slurping sound. Aleksey splashed up out of the water and scrambled back to the edge of the stream to retrieve his sword and stand beside the pilot. The vampire's skin and skeleton began to shift again, until the bat was hovering just above the water. Aleksey stabbed at it, but the creature flew up and away, through the opening in the cavern wall and out into the night.

"Are you okay?" A.J. asked as he waded into the stream to retrieve his spear.

"I'll be fine," Aleksey said. "We should get back upstairs."

"What about the missing kids?" the pilot asked.

"We'll keep looking - after we warn the villagers about what they're facing," Aleksey answered, and they started toward the stairs.

Aleksey and A.J. got back to the upper level and found Gemma, Kilea and the other councilmembers in their meeting chamber. The pilot left to go find Darra, and Aleksey told the council who and what they were facing. "I want to prepare you for the reality of this situation," Aleksey said.

"Gemma, when you send out the next search parties, make sure they have the appropriate weapons with them," the mole-man councilman said. He looked to Aleksey over the rim of his glasses. "Stakes, swords, and fire, am I right?" The half-elf nodded.

"But it will take more than the usual weapons to kill this vampire," Aleksey said. "He's very old, very powerful - and he is as soulless and evil as any creature I've ever met. I cannot overstate the danger your children are in."

"Merciful gods," Kilea said. "You have to go back down and keep searching, please! My granddaughter is only eight! That's far too young to die."

"That's the good news," Aleksey said. "It appears the vampire may be keeping the kids alive, for now - although he appears to have some dread magic ritual in the works."

"Do you think you can defeat him?" Gemma asked.

"If I can track him down again," Aleksey said. "We should send search parties out into the cemetery, too. He's probably out there somewhere healing, and he won't try to sneak back in until closer to dawn."

"We'll cover all the exits and entrances," the earth clan councilman said. "There are only so many ways in and out of this village."

"I'll organize that," Gemma said. "That way I can coordinate it with the search effort."

"Great. Thank you," Aleksey said.

Aleksey tried to retrace Ademek's trail, but the scent had cleared. The search parties scoured the village high and low, literally, working in shifts throughout the night and into the next morning. Darra was worried when her father didn't come into their room all through the night. When they met him for breakfast in one of the dining halls, he looked haggard.

"Any luck, Dad?" Darra asked as she took a seat on the bench next to her father. He shook his head. The pilot sat down on Darra's other side, while Kaleb, Trosclair and Ennio sat across from them. The hall was full, and everyone sat expectantly with clean dishes and silverware arranged before them. A couple of different people moved along the tables, pushing carts loaded with pots of steaming food that they served up by the ladleful as they went along.

"Mm," A.J. said. "That smells delicious!"

"Oh boy, are you gonna be disappointed," Darra said.

"Why?" A.J. asked. "Is it not good?"

"I don't really know," Darra said as a matronly woman came by with her cart. "I'll just have the potatoes, please."

"You're not on a diet, are you, lass?" the woman asked. "Because you're already too thin!"

"No, I just don't eat meat," Darra said.

"Nor do I," Aleksey said, and Darra looked to the pilot at her side.

"I think I might cheat, and have a little meat this morning," A.J. said. "Just because I lost so much blood yesterday, I need to build my strength back up. You won't think less of me, will you?" Darra shook her head.

"Nope," she said. "You can eat all the meat here you want. Just don't expect me to kiss you until you've brushed your teeth."

"It's that gross to you?" he asked, and she nodded. "I'll just have the potatoes, too, then."

"That's a wise choice," Darra said as the woman served up

the pilot's portion and looked across the table at Kaleb.

"What about you, son?" she asked.

"Oh, I love meat!" the young mage said.

"Good!" the woman said. "Did you want the red, or the white?"

"Um, I'll take the red, I guess," Kaleb said. The woman scooped into her pot and came out with a spoonful of gooey, gelatinous meat that she plopped down onto Kaleb's dish. He looked at the strange meat with a lack of comprehension. "This doesn't look like beef." He moved the meat around with his fork, as Trosclair leaned over to examine it more closely.

"Beef?" the woman asked. "And just where do you think we'd keep the cows down here, son?" she asked. "No, that there is baked and spiced earthworm. We harvest them ourselves. Well, the mole-men do; but we wash them and cook them - to perfection, I might add!"

Trosclair jerked his head back from Kaleb's dish and covered his mouth with his hands. "I think I'm gonna be sick!" he mumbled, leaning away from the table.

"Go ahead, try it!" the woman urged, and Kaleb speared a chunk with his fork. He lifted it to his lips, but he couldn't bring himself to take the bite.

"I'm sorry," he said. "I can't eat this."

"That's okay," the woman said as she scooped up from another pot. "Would you rather try the grub?" She wagged the ladle in front of Kaleb's face, and he followed it back and forth with his eyes open wide.

"No, thank you," he said, swallowing hard. "I'll just have the potatoes."

"Told you," Darra said as the woman shrugged and served the other teens.

The rest of the day was spent with more searches, punctuated by the occasional localized earthquake. Gemma arranged parties of five or more people, to assure strength in numbers, and divided the levels of the village among them. They searched all day and well into the early hours of the next morning, working in shifts. After their fifth sweep of the lowest levels of the village, Gemma, Aleksey and the rest of their search party returned to the entrance hall. Aleksey noticed Gemma looking at the orbital clock.

"Are you worried?" he asked.

"What?" she asked.

"About your son," Aleksey clarified. "I see you watching the clock. Are you worried that he's been in the vampire's hands for so long?"

"You read my mind," Gemma said.

"We'll get him back, I promise," Aleksey said, and Gemma smiled at him politely. "You should get some sleep."

"Oh, I couldn't sleep if I tried," Gemma said. "Too anxious. What about you?"

"I'm good for a few more hours," the half-elf said. "I'd like to do a sweep of the upper levels now. But first I need to go check in on my daughter. I'll be right back."

"I'll be here," Gemma said as Aleksey walked away. He came back a few minutes later with Darra, A.J. and Kaleb trailing along behind him. "You're bringing them along?"

"They wanted to help," Aleksey said. "And I feel better with my daughter in my sights, anyway."

"Okay, then," Gemma said. "Let's get started."

They searched the upper levels chamber to chamber for the next few hours. Finding nothing, they came back to the entrance hall, where the mole-man councilman and Kilea had risen early to meet them.

"It's a half-hour until dawn," the mole-man said, looking to the orbital clock. "Are the exits covered?"

"All but one mausoleum," Gemma said. She turned to the half-elf. "I thought we could guard that one ourselves. Once I get some men to back us up, of course."

"Sounds good," Aleksey said, and Gemma left the hall. The half-elf turned to Kilea. "Maybe you should wait here."

"If you're taking the children, you've got room for an old person, too," the Dwarf woman replied as she lit the oily rags of a torch ablaze with a candle. Aleksey acquiesced, and soon Gemma returned with two village men.

"Be careful," the mole-man said as Gemma led Aleksey, Kilea, the teens and the men away.

"So you know this vampire?" Darra asked her father.

"Yes," Aleksey said. "His name is Lucio."

"How?" she asked.

"I took a job, a long time ago, that brought me into contact with him," Aleksey said.

"Oh," Darra said. "What kind of job?"

"I was hired to procure a package," Aleksey said. "Lucio was part of a team sent as muscle, to distract the people I was stealing from."

"You worked with a vampire?" Kaleb asked.

"And you say I'm naïve for being friends with a dragon," Darra said.

"I never said you were naïve, honey," Aleksey said. "And I didn't know when I took the job that I'd be working with him."

A few seconds passed by. "So what was it?"

"What was what?" Aleksey asked.

"The package that you stole," Darra said. "What was it?"

The half-elf tried to hide his rising panic. "It was... something precious," he said. Another earthquake shook the village. By now, everyone had grown used to them, and they quickly surveyed their surroundings for damage and continued on. They arrived at the stairs that led up to the mausoleum exit, and Aleksey cocked his head.

"You smell something, Dad?" Darra asked.

"It's the earth clan boy," the half-elf answered. "He's been through here. Very recently."

"The vampire must have taken him outside through the mausoleum," Gemma said.

"Then we should hurry," Aleksey said, heading for the stairs. "If we can catch up to them before the sun rises, they'll probably lead us to the children." The teens followed Aleksey up the stairs, followed by Kilea, Gemma and the village men. Aleksey opened the door to the mausoleum, and the adventurers stepped inside. It was completely dark.

"Kaleb?" Aleksey prompted, and the mage said a word in the old speak and summoned a ball of fire. With the new light, they could make out the far wall, which had been smeared with more blood and covered with those same symbols. There was also a bloody pentagram drawn across the wide-open floor. They also saw the iridescent eyes of the vampire standing over by the exit; he had the earth clan boy by the throat, and the other children were bound and gagged at the various points of the pentagram. Even the mole-man child, which was no older than a toddler, was bound at his paws, to keep him from crawling away.

"Joslyn!" Kilea cried as she saw her granddaughter. She started to cross to her, but Lucio held up his free hand.

"I'd stay right where you are," the vampire said. "Or I'll snap this child's neck."

"He'll do it, Kilea," Aleksey said. "Stay back."

"I'm glad you brought the girl with you again," Lucio said. "You've saved me the trouble of procuring her myself." Darra aimed her crossbow at Lucio's chest.

"I don't know," Darra said. "I think I might still be able to cause you a little trouble."

"Doubtful," Lucio said.

"You're playing a losing game, Lucio," Aleksey said. "There are eight of us, and one of you. You may be strong, but even you can't take on odds like that."

"Actually," Gemma said as she closed the door to the stairs behind her. "Make that four to five." The woman smiled, and the tiny fangs of a newborn vampire slowly protruded out of her mouth. The two village men beside her also popped fangs out of their mouths.

"Merciful gods!" Kilea said, backing away from her fellow councilwoman.

"And specifically, that's four vampires against a frail old dwarf woman, three kids, and a half-elf who barely survived his encounter with just one of us," Gemma said.

"Why are you doing this, Gemma?" Kilea asked. "It's your own son, for the sake of the heavens!"

"There's no use trying to talk sense to her," Aleksey said. "The woman you knew is dead. This creature is nothing more than a shell, controlled by the demon that spawned her."

"He's quite right," Lucio said. "Now, I was about to destroy this village once and for all." Lucio dragged Ademek a few steps over to a point on the pentagram and threw him down on the floor. The two vampires beside Gemma moved forward, and each grabbed Aleksey by an arm. They walked him over to the final point in the symbol on the floor and held him there. "It's funny. We needed a fifth race to sacrifice to complete the ritual. I thought the outworlder might do, but his blood was fully human, if terribly exotic. If you hadn't been so eager to help, half-elf, everyone here would be safe. Instead, you're about to die, and they're about to go to hell – literally, as this village will be sucked into one of the dreadworlds."

"That sounds like a pretty diabolical plan," Aleksey said. "But you forgot about one thing."

"And what's that?" Lucio asked.

"Sunrise!" Aleksey yelled at the top of his lungs. The mausoleum door swung open wide, and Ennio rushed in, sword in hand, followed by the two other councilmembers. More villagers stood outside, weapons and torches raised high. But what really shocked Lucio, Gemma and the other vampires was the light that streamed in through the open door. The sky was brightening, and the sun was about to peek over the horizon.

"The sun!" Gemma shrieked, darting into the shadows. "But it's not supposed to rise for another twenty minutes!"

"That would be my boyfriend's handiwork," Ennio said. "He had the brilliant thought to wind the orbital clock back, to disorient you."

"You knew what she was?" Kilea asked Aleksey, and the half-elf nodded. "Why didn't you warn me?"

"There was no opportunity," Aleksey said. "Gemma's been watching my every move ever since I got here. That was my first clue she had fallen under the vampire's control." He turned to Gemma. "Now, about those odds you were so sure of a minute ago. We'll give you a choice. You can face the angry mob of villagers, or you can flee, and never return to this village again. I'd say you have a good two minutes before the sun actually crests, and you go up like so much kindling."

"Bastard half-elf!" Lucio cried as he lunged at Aleksey. The half-elf shook the fledgling vampires on either side of him off in time to catch Lucio's wrists, and they were locked in a stalemate. "Kill them!" Lucio commanded the other vampires, and they moved forward to obey. Darra aimed her crossbow at one of them and fired, and the wooden bolt flew into his chest with a thud. His mouth fell open, and after a moment, he disintegrated in front of her. Kaleb hurled his fireball at the other vampire, but the demon ducked, and the flaming sphere sailed against the wall and dissipated. The vampire reached out and grabbed the mage by the collar of his robes, drawing him forward to tear his throat out with his fangs. A.J. punched the demon, and the vampire let Kaleb go as he turned to the pilot. A.J. raised his spear defensively. Gemma stalked toward Kilea, who waved her torch in front of her from side to side.

"Stay back!" the dwarf said. "I don't want to hurt you, Gemma!"

"I don't think there's any real chance of that," Gemma said. She reached out and grabbed the torch just below the flames. It singed her hand, but she managed to yank the wooden shaft from Kilea's grasp.

"When I kill your girl, I'll make you watch," Lucio said between clenched teeth. Aleksey kicked the vampire in the stomach, and the demon doubled over. The vampire growled and flew forward, wrapping his arms around Aleksey's midsection and driving him up against the wall with all his might. He wrapped his claw-tipped fingers around Aleksey's throat and began to squeeze. Suddenly a sword jutted through the vampire's chest; when the creature fell, Ennio drew his weapon back and fixed Aleksey with a cocky smile. In no time, however, Lucio was back on his feet. He lunged at Ennio, but the soldier darted out of the way. The vampire caught his cape and pulled, ripping the fabric around the gold rings that secured the accessory to the shoulder of his tunic. Lucio rushed for the door. The earth elemental councilman jumped in front of him, but the vampire pushed him aside easily. "This isn't over, half-elf!" he called behind him as he made it to the doorway. His body shifted and reformed as the giant bat, and he flew off over the tops of the villager's heads, the soldier's cape clutched in the claws of his feet.

The other vampire man ran out after him, and the villagers parted and made way for him. He sprinted through the cemetery in vain, his skin already smoldering from the first rays of sunlight. Within a few moments, he had disintegrated.

The mole-man councilman stabbed his sword into Gemma's shoulder, and she cried out in pain. The mole-man brought his sword up to Gemma's throat. "Not here!" Kilea cried. "Not in front of her boy!" The earth elemental and the mole-man took Gemma by the arms and led her out of the mausoleum. A few seconds later, they heard a terrible, high-pitched shriek, and Kilea scrambled to close the door as the children began to sob.

Back at the entrance hall a little later, Darra watched with misty eyes as Gemma's son was led away by his father. "That poor boy," she said. "What a terrible way to lose a parent."

"Yes," Aleksey agreed. "He'll likely be traumatized." The half-elf looked to the mole-man councilman. "They all will be. You'll need someone to work with them every day to help them process their pain and grief."

"I'll see to it," the mole-man said. "But you did save them, Aleksey. How can we repay you? We owe you everything."

"I wouldn't ask for everything," Aleksey said. "Just a loan – of one your boats."

"That shouldn't be a problem," the earth clan councilman said. "Do you plan to travel the coast? Or do some deep-sea fishing?"

"Actually, we're headed to the Elven Isles to visit my family," the half-elf said. "But I'll return your vessel within a week or two, I promise."

"You have proven you are a man who keeps his word," Kilea said. "Will you need anything else for your journey?"

"Just a little food," Aleksey said.

"Vegetables!" Kaleb said. "Not worms!"

"We'll take a quick walk and pick out the right ship for your needs," the mole-man said, gesturing to the exit. The guard at the door began opening it.

"I'm gonna take a look at the boats with your Dad," A.J. said. "I might be able to help helm it."

"Okay," Darra said as the pilot followed the half-elf and mole-man out the door.

"That vampire," A.J. said as they walked onto the pier. "He wanted to hurt Darra especially, didn't he?"

"Yes," Aleksey said. "And he meant what he said, about it not being over."

"What do you mean?" the pilot asked. "You think he'll follow us to the Elven Isles?"

"No," Aleksey said. "But he works for the demon I told you

about earlier – the one from the Dread Continent. And that demon believes Darra is his possession by rights. When he finds out she and I are still alive, he won't rest until I am dead and Darra is his slave."

"What are you gonna do?" A.J. asked.

"Keep moving," Aleksey said. "Stay on the edges of society. Maybe even change our identities."

"Will that work?" A.J. asked.

"It's our best shot," Aleksey said. "There are also a few items I could try to gather – items of legendary power that might offer us some protection. But that will have to wait until the prince is safe in the elven king's court."

"Is there anything I can do?" the pilot asked.

"Keep training with your spear," the half-elf said. "You never know when it will come in handy. And..."

"Yes?"

"If you could reconsider, and not say anything about all of this to Darra, it might very well keep her out of future danger," Aleksey said. "I hope this experience has taught you that." Aleksey met and held the pilot's gaze as they reached the end of the pier.

"That's the one you want!" the mole-man councilman said, pointing to a steamship tethered to one of the pier's posts. It was smaller than some of the other boats, but it could easily fit twenty or thirty sleeping men on its deck. It had a small cabin whose floor fell below the water level, and a steering column on a raised platform in front of that. A larger lower-level engine room at the back of the ship was filled with bins of coal. The ship was also cleaner and newer looking than the other boats, and it had the one feature Aleksey really cared about: a small wooden rowboat that attached to the stern for loading, unloading, and emergencies.

"Sea Fairy," Aleksey read from the ship's stern. He glanced up at the bow and saw a tiny wooden fairy figurehead, her wand raised to point directly ahead of the vessel. "I think she'll do."

"You'll wait out the storm here, of course," the mole-man said, pointing to the dark clouds that were gathering over the sea.

"Of course," Aleksey said.

The half-elf and the pilot returned to the entrance hall. "So?" Darra prompted. "Did you pick out one that won't sink?"

"Please don't even joke about that, honey," Aleksey said.

"Sorry, Dad," she said. The half-elf and the teens returned to their room, where they found Trosclair pacing the floor. "Well?" he asked. "Did it work?"

"Like an enchanted charm!" Ennio said as he crossed to the prince and gave him a big hug that lifted the young man off his feet. "You're beginning to make a habit out of saving us all, you know."

"But I didn't do anything!" Trosclair said. "I just hid in here like a coward!"

"It was the smart thing to do," Aleksey said as he stretched out on his bedroll on the floor. "Lucio is very old, which makes him strong."

"Please!" Ennio said. "I could have taken him!"

"Maybe," Aleksey conceded. "But only because he was weakened from mixing his blood with the vampires he created. If he'd been at full strength, I'm not sure even I could have held him off for long. But Ennio is right. Without your plan for the clock, those kids might still be missing, and we might all be dead."

"Yeah, you'd make a half-decent adventurer, Trosc," Darra said.

"Thank you, but no thank you," the prince said. "You can keep your vampires and your ogres and your death mazes. Is it always like this for you?"

"We've always faced dangers – that's just a part of Dad's job – but it's definitely gotten more intense for us over the last few months," Darra replied.

"Well, hopefully whoever has been plaguing us won't have a reach that extends to the elven kingdom," Aleksey said with his eyes closed. "Now please, if you're going to continue being loud teenagers, take it elsewhere. This room is for sleeping."

The teens obeyed and left the half-elf to catch up on his rest. Kaleb found a quiet corner in the entrance hall and sat down to study his spellbook. Trosclair and Ennio were lured to the dining hall by Kilea's promise that they would be rewarded with eggs.

"That's chicken eggs, right?" Trosclair asked. "Not, like, beetle eggs or something?" Kilea laughed as she led the teens away.

"I'm tired of being cooped up in here," Darra said as she led A.J. to the dwarf guard posted by the main doors. "Can we get out?"

"You're not leaving already, are you, young miss?" the dwarf asked.

"No," Darra said. "We just want to take a walk in the fresh air and sunlight."

"I can let you out," the dwarf man said as he began cranking a wheel with a handle that unlocked the door. "But you'll have a hard time finding the sun. A storm's blowing in off the water." He opened the door and pointed out at the dark clouds in the sky. "You have maybe forty-five minutes before it starts raining – hard, if those mean clouds live up to their looks."

"That's plenty of time," she said, taking the pilot's hand and leading him out onto the sandy, rocky shore. They strolled along the beach parallel to the water.

"Thank you, for backing my Dad up today," she said. "Sorry it almost got you killed. Again."

"It wasn't your fault," A.J. said. "I'm the one who should be thanking your father. The way he came to my defense against Lucio was... insane!"

"About that," Darra asked. "I can't help feeling there's more to my dad's story than what he's telling me." A cold breeze picked up, and the pilot shivered. "Did he say anything about it?"

A.J. face froze for a split-second before he said, "Uh, no. He didn't mention anything."

"Are you sure?" she pressed.

"Yeah," the pilot said. "I'm sure." Darra smiled, but something about the momentary hesitation she'd witnessed made her suspect A.J. might be lying. She put the thought out of her mind, telling herself she was being paranoid, and felt the first few drops of rain on her head and shoulders.

CHAPTER TWELVE
"BROTHER'S KEEPER"

The teens and the half-elf took the *Sea Fairy* up the coast the next day. A.J. helmed the vessel, having been given a brief lesson by the mole-man councilman back at Adaya's Hollow. He felt good being back behind the controls of a ship, even if this one was literally centuries behind the technology of the ones he was used to piloting. Kaleb and Ennio took turns shoveling coal into the steam engine, keeping the boat moving at a steady pace. Darra and Trosclair had retreated to the cabin, and Aleksey was at the ship's stern, his head held out over the water. He gripped the railing so hard his knuckles had turned white, and his face was also paler than normal. Every once in a while, when they would hit an especially large wave, the boat would lurch into the air several feet, and Aleksey would dry heave, having long ago given up the entire contents of his stomach. When they'd gone about sixty miles, they passed some large boulders jutting out along the shoreline.

"Now head due east," Aleksey managed to yell to A.J., and the pilot turned the wheel until the boat was headed into the open ocean.

"Gods, your dad does not look good," Trosclair said a few hours later as he peered out of the cabin at the half-elf, who was still hunched over the rail.

"He'll be fine, once we're on land again," Darra said. "He just really hates being on the water because of his mom."

"What about her?" the prince asked.

"She was lost at sea, years ago," Darra said. "Dad doesn't talk about her much. But I know she was an explorer, with her own boat and crew and everything."

"So that's where your family's adventurous streak comes from," Trosclair said.

"I guess," Darra said. "I just wish I could have met her."

"It must be awful not to have a mother or a grandmother," the prince said.

"It was hard to pick up a few things at first, with no other women to learn from," Darra said.

"Like what?"

"Like, I didn't know how to shave, so I had to teach myself," Darra said. "I went through a lot of tiny bandages until I got the hang of it. And I didn't try on make-up until last year. But I have some wonderful girlfriends who make up the difference, like Ani - so I feel like I have a big family, even though I'm technically an only child. Does that make sense?"

"Yes," Trosclair said. "I was surrounded by people growing up in the palace, too. But it still got lonely from time to time."

"Land, ho!" A.J. yelled from the deck. Darra and Trosclair got up and exited the cabin. A thin strip of green stretched along the horizon in front of them.

"Is that it?" Trosclair said. "Are we here?"

Aleksey made his way to the bow, careful to keep his hands on the rail at all times to keep his balance. "That's it," he said. "That's Majidah, the largest of the Elven Isles. That's where we'll find my brother, and the elven court." They got close enough to make out the individual trees, and A.J. cut off the propeller so that the boat glided gently toward the beach. It came to rest about thirty feet from shore, in warm tropical waters about fifteen feet deep, and Ennio dropped the anchor. They loaded into the rowboat with their bags, and A.J. and Ennio took the oars and paddled them toward the shore. When they were halfway between the boat and the beach, a party of elves on horseback emerged from the trees and lined up on the white sands. They wore the armor and carried weapons.

"I think they were expecting us," Kaleb said.

"Should we turn around?" A.J. asked.

"No, it's fine," Aleksey said. "That's just the greeting party." They beached the rowboat and climbed out of it, then dragged it fully onto the sand. Aleksey approached an elf who sat on his horse with his arms folded across his chest, a frown on his face and no weapon in sight.

"Aleksey," he said, nodding once.

"Acasius," Aleksey said, returning the nod.

"I see you've come by steamship," Acasius said. "Did you steal it?"

"No!" Aleksey said. "My stealing days are behind me. For the most part."

"Yes, until the next time you want something you can't afford," Acasius said. "Isn't that how it works?"

"Pretty much," the half-elf replied. Acasius turned to Darra. "Darra! It's wonderful to see you, my girl."

"Hi, Uncle Acasius," Darra said, approaching the elf, who leaned down from his steed to hug her. "How's Gavriella?"

"She's well," Acasius answered.

"How did you know we were coming?" Darra asked.

"That would be thanks to Qiana," Acasius said, gesturing to a dark-skinned elf woman.

"Hello, Aleksey," Qiana said. "It's been a long time."

"Qiana, you're looking as lovely as ever," Aleksey said.

"And you look - sick, actually," the elf woman said, smiling. "I dreamed of your arrival days ago. I just didn't foresee that you'd be bringing so many human children along with you."

"I thought the elves no longer practiced magic," Kaleb said.

"We don't," Acasius said. "But Qiana was an accomplished sorceress for over a thousand years, before the Cataclysm."

"Wow," Kaleb said.

"The magics linger in me still, which is why I sometimes have the dreams," Qiana said. "I suppose I always will, as long as I live. But I refrain from casting any actual spells."

"That must take an awful lot of self-control," Kaleb said.

"You have no idea," the elf woman said with a friendly smile directed at the tribal lad. "Now I spend my days at court, advising King Laban."

"So what brings you back home?" Acasius asked his brother.

"We've come to introduce the prince to the king," Aleksey said, hiding his amusement at his brother's shock.

"Prince?" the elf asked as he took in the human children.

"Prince Trosclair, of the kingdom of DuVerres," Ennio said, and Trosclair stepped forward and offered Acasius his hand.

"Well, I'm – I'm sure the king will be thrilled to host a royal entourage," Acasius said. "And Gavriella may faint from sheer excitement."

"I've also brought this," Aleksey said, opening up his pack for his brother's inspection.

"Is that what I think it is?" Acasius asked, his eyes going wide, and Aleksey nodded.

A short while later they sat in the drawing room of Acasius' home, a comfortable chamber with three couches, beige with black leather accents, arranged in a semi-circle around a low square black table. There were photographs and paintings on the walls, and a short but long bookshelf backed into one corner. The fragments of the DragonSword were laid out on the table before Acasius, who was scrutinizing them.

"Only you could find a DragonSword," Acasius said, and Aleksey smiled. "And break it within a day." Aleksey's smile disappeared.

"That wasn't my fault!" he said. "The outworlder did that on his arrival."

"Hm," Acasius said. "That does make some sense."

"How so?" A.J. asked.

"The legend of the DragonSwords said no force on Ona could destroy one," Acasius said. "But you're not a force from our world."

"Well, that's a fine distinction!" Aleksey said.

"Still, the king will likely want to pay you handsomely for bringing this to us," Acasius said. "Even in spite of the apology you still owe him." Acasius lifted his eyebrows at his brother.

"Why would the king want to pay for this?" Darra asked. "It's in pieces."

"The metal still has great value to us," Acasius said. "It's an extremely rare alloy, the mix for which was lost before the oldest elves today had even been born. It has powerful mystical properties embedded into its very essence."

"What kind of properties?" Kaleb asked.

"They say it can cut through some magic or spells," Acasius

answered. "And the gems on the hilt have various magical uses. They say the gems were gifts from the gods to the elves. You don't have the other missing gems, do you?"

"No," Aleksey said. "They were missing from the sword when I procured it."

"Procured?" Acasius repeated. "So you stole it?"

"From some very bad men," Aleksey said, holding up a finger in rebuttal.

"No matter - that you stole it," Acasius said. "The missing gems are a shame. Arol's gift was said to render any elf who held the sword invincible." He pointed to the indentation of the missing gem in the center of the hilt and then flipped it over to show the similar indentation on the other side. "And this one could imbue an elf with a great strength derived from Ona herself."

"So you want the sword for the gems?" Darra asked.

"No," Acasius said. "With the sword broken, it would take a mage to activate the remaining gems' powers. But the metal is still precious, for if it pierces the heart of a dread creature, it will instantly banish it to a dreadworld befitting its soulless, evil nature."

"Like the succubus?" A.J. asked, and Aleksey nodded.

"Or the dread forces that regularly attack our shores," Acasius said.

"I thought you said this place was safe," Ennio said to Aleksey. "You didn't mention anything about attacks from dread creatures!"

"The city is safe," Acasius said. "They only attack our coasts, and they never get more than a mile or two inland. There are few dread creatures who can match an elf's skill in battle. But they are hard to kill, and sometimes our patrols are outnumbered. We lose soldiers every year. This gift will save lives, Aleksey."

"I know," the half-elf replied. "But I'm only gifting you half of it. We need the rest for ourselves."

"I'll have to make sure the smiths stretch the metal as far as they can, then," Acasius said.

"Who will you get to do the work?" Aleksey asked.

"The king will want his own people in charge of something this important," Acasius replied as an elf woman with auburn hair pulled up in a bun came in with a tray of steaming mugs. "In fact, I should get this to him right away."

"Darra!" the woman cried as she placed the tray on the table before the adventurers. She moved in to give Darra a lingering hug. "I haven't seen you since you were this tall!" She held her hand up to her stomach. "Human children grow up so fast! Leks, you must bring her to visit more often from now on!"

"I will, Gavi," the half-elf said as he picked up a mug of what he could smell was a spiced, creamy chocolate beverage.

"And I heard there was a prince among you?" Gavriella prompted, and introductions were made all around as drinks were distributed.

"Dearest, I'm going to make a quick trip to the castle," Acasius said, and Gavriella nodded.

"I'll come with you," Aleksey said as he began placing the fragments of the sword back in his pack. "That way you can't steal all my glory."

"I want to see the castle," Darra said.

"Oh, you will, child!" Gavriella said. "Didn't my husband tell you? You all will, tonight. The king has announced a ball in honor of your visit."

"Oh, wow," Darra said. "I've never been to a ball before. That sounds like so much fun!"

"Of course, we'll need to get you all some clothes more fitting for a formal occasion," Gavriella said, and Darra beamed.

"I suppose I don't need to keep wearing this peasant's costume while I'm here," Trosclair said, pulling the waist of his oversized pants out for emphasis.

"I guess that means we're going shopping?" Darra asked, and Gavriella nodded.

A couple of hours later, Gavriella led the teens through the crowded city streets. The elves they passed openly stared at them, but there was no hostility in the looks, merely curiosity. More than a few vendors leapt out in front of the humans, eager to try their sales pitch on the teen tourists, but Gavriella kept them moving along until they reached a section of town that was clearly more affluent than the neighborhoods they'd crossed to get there. The elves here wore finer clothing, with jewels on proud display against their throats or hanging from their earlobes. The carriages that lined the street were newer and bigger, with drivers in sharp black uniforms and top hats. The stores themselves sold finer merchandise, from clothiers and a jeweler's shop to an art gallery and a furniture outlet. Gavriella led Darra up to the doors of a fancy women's boutique.

"Darra, wait a moment," Trosclair said before turning to Ennio. "How much money do we have left?"

"We're almost out of credits," Ennio said.

"The merchants here don't take continental credits anyway, child," Gavriella said.

"But we have several thousand worth in gold bars," Ennio finished, pulling out one of the long slim rectangles.

"Splendid!" Gavriella said. "Gold spends universally. You should have no trouble finding appropriate outfits over there, while Darra and I try on a few gowns." Trosclair took the gold bar from Ennio and tried to hand it to Darra.

"What's that for?" she asked.

"For your new gown and shoes," Trosclair said.

"Oh, no!" Gavriella cried. "I'm buying Darra's things. After all, I never get to give you any birthday presents."

"That's too kind, Aunt Gavi," Darra said, and the women entered the boutique, while the young men continued on to a mixed-gender clothing shop a little further down the street. Gavriella called a greeting to one of the saleswomen, who smiled, waved - and then almost spilled her coffee, when she caught sight of Darra's rounded ears. The elf woman put down her drink and came over to introduce herself.

"Faline, this is my niece, Darra," Gavriella said, and they shook hands. "There's to be a ball tonight at the castle to honor her visit, and we need something that will make her look splendid. She's to be presented alongside royalty."

"Oh, wow," Faline said. "Who's the royal?"

"Prince Trosclair of DuVerres," Darra answered.

"Is he your beau?" Faline asked.

"No, no," Darra said. "Nothing like that. We're just friends. And I'm sort of helping Dad with providing the prince's security."

"Darra here is a warrior in training," Gavriella said, putting a proud arm around her niece's shoulder. "Although tonight, she needs to look like a proper young lady."

"I have the perfect dress for you!' Faline said. She rushed to the back of the store, where long formal dresses, including some bridal gowns and funereal garb, were hanging from a tall rack. She picked out a green gown with a multi-colored bodice and a thick, lacy yellow collar and brought it back for the women's inspection.

"Very lovely," Gavriella said.

"It's made from the finest silks, so it will last a long time," Faline said. "And all the color will bring out your eyes."

"I'll try it," Darra said, taking the dress from Faline, who pointed out the dressing room. Darra went inside and started changing into the gown. Gavriella picked out a dress and casually draped it over herself, examining it in one of the shop's many mirrors.

"So, Darra," she said. "My husband mentioned that you're travelling with an outworlder. However did that come about?"

"He crashed his flying ship through a dragon's portal to another world," Darra said over the door. "I just happened to be there to see it."

"That's fascinating," Gavriella said. "You lead such an exciting life, yet you face it so calmly. You're very much like your grandmother in that respect."

"Oh, really?" Darra asked.

"Mm-hmm," Gavriella said. "I know you're not related to Sylanna by blood, but something of her spirit must have passed down to you through your father."

"I've never shared a family trait with anyone before," Darra said. "Unless you count Dad's stubbornness." Darra stepped out in the gown. "What do you think?" she asked, twisting a little to show the way the dress hung off her athletic body.

"Beautiful!" Gavriella said. "Now we just need to find some shoes to match it. Are you comfortable in heels?"

"Sure," Darra said. "If they're not too high." Gavriella bought the dress, which Faline folded expertly and put in a brown paper bag. The women went to a cobbler's next, and by the time they had picked out Darra's new heels, the young men had returned with their own purchases. Trosclair had already changed into his new outfit, a smart velvet jacket with matching pants and shiny black boots. He wore a long, dark brown cloak with thick white fur around the shoulders and collar.

"Well," Gavriella said. "Now you look like a prince!"

"Thank you," Trosclair said.

"Did you get something to wear?" Darra asked A.J.

"Just another clean shirt," the pilot said, and Darra frowned.

"We're supposed to look our best tonight," she said.

"Oh, I tried to get him into something finer," Trosclair said. "But Ennio set a bad example by insisting he wear his uniform tonight."

"I did get a new cape, though," Ennio said. "It really completes the look."

"I can go back, if you really want me to wear something else," A.J. said. "I just thought if I looked like a peasant, it would help Trosclair stand out more. He's the one who needs to make a good impression with the king, not me."

"And speaking of standing out," Gavriella said as they came up to the jeweler's shop. The awning of the little store had the words "The Wild Youth" scrawled across it in red paint that had dribbled down in several places from each letter.

"What's that?" Kaleb asked, pointing to the graffiti.

"Oh, that's just someone's idea of a prank," Gavriella said. "We've had a problem with some of our younger generations forming street gangs, like The Wild Youth."

"Are they dangerous?" Ennio asked.

"Oh, not really," Gavriella said. "They commit petty crimes and vandalisms, just to act out their frustration with the elders. They'll all grow out of it someday, just like your father did."

"Dad was in a street gang?" Darra asked.

"No, but he was quite the youthful offender," Gavriella said. "The king knew his name by the time he'd turned thirty - which, for a half-elf, is about the equivalent of a human twelve-year-old." Gavriella led the teens inside the jeweler's.

"I can't let you buy me any jewelry, Aunt Gavi," Darra said. "You've already been too generous."

"Oh, I was going to loan you something of your grandmother's to wear tonight, anyway," the elf woman said. "I actually brought us here for the last accessory our young prince needs to set the right tone for his visit." She crossed to a glass case with several tiaras, circlets and crowns, and gestured to them. "See any that you like?" Trosclair picked out a thick silver circlet, Ennio paid for it in gold, and Gavriella and the teens left the shop and started back toward her house.

King Laban had not been available to receive Acasius and Aleksey, but they'd left the DragonSword with his most trusted blacksmith, giving the woman all their suggestions for its reworking. She'd promised to treat it with the care it deserved and to allow only her most senior smiths to help in the re-forging.

The brothers were on the way back to Acasius' house, which was in the good neighborhood next to the castle. Two and three story houses lined the streets, some with marble columns supporting balconies or picket fences to keep a dog in, and all with perfectly manicured, lush green lawns. More than a few children were outside playing. One little elven girl ran smack into Aleksey. She backed up with her hands clasped behind her back, fear in her large brown eyes.

"Sorry, mister," she said, before running off again.

"Don't worry about it," Aleksey called after her. The brothers resumed their walk.

"She stole your purse," Acasius observed.

"I know," Aleksey said. "But I only had three credits and a piece of hard candy in there, anyway."

"You should have stopped her," Acasius said.

"I didn't want to embarrass her," Aleksey said. "You saw her clothes. Her family obviously needs the money."

"If we allow children to act immorally, they eventually become immoral adults," Acasius said. He lifted his eyebrows again.

"Are you accusing me of lacking morals?" Aleksey asked.

"Of course not," Acasius said. "The word 'lacking' would imply you missed having them."

"I have honor as great as any knight," Aleksey said. "I follow a code. I don't harm other creatures unless I have to—"

"But you put yourself in a position to have to do just that all the time, don't you?" his brother asked. "And you're still stealing things."

"If I wasn't, you wouldn't have just presented the king with a solution to his dread monster dilemma," Aleksey said. "You can thank me at your convenience."

"Thank you?" Acasius asked. "Have you forgotten the time you almost got me fired, stealing the king's carriage? Or any of the other times I had to bail you out? The constabularies still tease me about my delinquent little brother."

"Oh, and gods forbid your precious reputation should suffer in the slightest!" Aleksey said. "Acasius, the great and wise!"

"Don't mock me!" Acasius said. "You're just mad because I have a decent reputation, and a good-paying job, and all you've ever been known for is acting out."

"I've changed, ever since Darra came into my life," Aleksey said. "You just refuse to see it."

"Then what about the last time you came here?" Acasius asked. "The king honored you with a dinner invitation, and you didn't even bother to show up! I was mortified! I'm surprised the king decided to throw this little ball for you – which you had better be at, by the way."

"I will be, I promise," Aleksey said. "And last time, there were extenuating circumstances. Darra and I had to make a quick exit."

"It's always something with you, Leks," Acasius said.

"I'm sorry for the way I left," Aleksey said. "Truly."

"Really?" Acasius asked, and Aleksey nodded. "Then perhaps you wouldn't mind doing me a little favor? To show your contrition." One side of Aleksey's mouth lifted in an unsure half-smile as his brother told him what he had planned, and what he needed from him.

When they got back to Acasius' house, Gavriella insisted that Aleksey and the teens get dressed for the ball a little early. Then she led the half-elf and the teens out onto her back lawn, where a large white gazebo with a blue awning and curtains stood. An elven woman with curly brown hair was hunched over in front of a camera on a tripod, her head ducked beneath the cloth hood of the apparatus as she framed the gazebo.

"I'd like a picture of all of you, for my scrapbook," Gavriella said. Aleksey and the teens moved to the steps of the gazebo, and Gavriella started arranging them in two lines. She moved Ennio, Aleksey and A.J., who were the tallest among them, behind Trosclair, Darra and Kaleb. "Leks, tuck your hair behind your ears; you don't have to hide them here." Aleksey did as he was told, and then he placed a hand on Darra's shoulder. "Hold on one second," Gavriella said as she ducked back inside the house. A few moments later, she returned with Darra's crossbow and A.J.'s spear. "To show you're a warrior," she said to Darra as she handed the weapons over. "Now, is there any way we can show that you're a mage?" she asked Kaleb.

"Hm," he said as he considered it. "Actually, I have been working on a pretty neat trick. If you want to see it."

"I'd be delighted," Gavriella said.

"You might want to step back a little," the young mage said as he pushed the loose sleeves of his robe back from his wrists. Gavriella took a few steps back. Kaleb gestured and said the word for 'fire' in the old speak, and a fist-sized fireball burst into existence above his palm.

"Fabulous!" Gavriella cried.

"That isn't even the best part," Kaleb said. He gestured twice more, and two more fireballs appeared alongside the first. They floated lazily above his hand in a circle, like a tiny triple star system rotating about. Then he moved his other hand underneath one of the flaming spheres, and it suddenly leapt into the air, sailing above his head. A split-second later, all three of the fireballs were in motion. Kaleb juggled them with his hands open wide, palms upward, and Gavriella began to applaud.

"This will make such a fantastic picture!" Gavriella said.

"Wait!" Ennio said. "Before you take it..." The soldier threw his arm around Trosclair's shoulder and moved to give him a peck on his cheek.

"What was that for?" Trosclair asked with a smile.

"I just want to take a picture where we aren't hiding who we are, for once," Ennio said. "I hope I'm not gonna ruin your picture."

"No, no," Gavriella said, waving away the soldier's concern. "It'll be even better this way." Darra glanced up at A.J., and the pilot was looking at her with the same love-struck expression with which the soldier fixed the prince.

"Uh, guys, if we're gonna take this, we better do it quick," Kaleb said. His fireballs had started to swerve and veer, and he had to wrangle them back onto their circular path with wildly flailing arms. Gavriella signaled to the photographer, who lit a strip of magnesium wire attached to a reflector, and bright white light flooded over the half-elf and the teens. Gray, opaque fumes rose up into the air, and Aleksey had to struggle not to sneeze. They all tried to remain as still as possible, the only movement being Kaleb's arms and fireballs. After about forty-five seconds, one of the flaming spheres got away from the mage and flew to his left. It hit a swath of cloth hanging from the awning, and the fabric went up instantly.

"Oh, gods!" Kaleb said. "*Ercha*!" The fire extinguished, and Kaleb began swatting at the cloth, knocking loose some of the charred fibers. "I'm so sorry!"

"It's okay," Gavriella said. "We can take another one."

The photographer extinguished the magnesium and said, "Actually, I think the picture's going to come out fine, Gavi."

"Oh, wonderful!" Gavriella said. "Now, we should probably get going. The king appreciates punctuality."

They took a carriage the short distance to the castle, both to make the right impression with Trosclair's arrival and to spare their feet walking in new shoes. They were let out right in front of the gates, which the guards opened immediately upon their recognition of Acasius. The castle was not as tall or as spread out as Trosclair's palace, but it was certainly elegant. It was made of gray stone and concrete, and was laid out in a roughly square plan, with a guard tower up front built into the great wall that surrounded the keep. Behind that was the front lawn, which two gardeners were presently tending to with a rake and a scythe. A large fountain spewed water into the sky, catching the sunlight to create a rainbow in the courtyard. Then came the castle itself, a three-story structure with several spires that rose to twice that height.

Acasius led them across the courtyard, up the front steps past two more guards, and through the castle doors. An equerry met them in the foyer, bowing profusely to Trosclair, and led them to the ornately gilded ballroom. The equerry asked for the prince's full name and epithets, and Ennio was impressed when the elf repeated it back perfectly in his announcement of their arrival. All elven eyes turned to them as they made their way into the chamber.

"Acasius!" the elven king called across the room, raising one hand high. He was as old-looking as any elf Darra had ever seen, with long white hair underneath his heavily jeweled gold crown. Like all elves, he had no facial hair, and the lines and sagging skin of his face were clearly visible. Still, for someone approaching two thousand years of age, he had a vitality that could not be ignored. "Get over here, my boy!"

"Would you like to dance?" A.J. asked Darra.

"I'd love to!" she said, and she led the pilot onto the dance floor by the hand.

Qiana approached them and gave Aleksey a quick hug and kiss on the cheek, and then turned to Kaleb. "You wear the red robes of a fire mage," she said, and he nodded. "How long have you been in the practice?"

"Not very long," he said. "I'm not very accomplished yet."

"Well, I'd still like the chance to discuss some things with you, if you're up for it," Qiana said. "It's been ages since I had another person schooled in mystical theory to speak with." She offered Kaleb her arm.

"I'd like that," Kaleb said, taking her arm in his hand and following her out of the room.

"So, Aleksey," King Laban said as the half-elf, his brother and sister-in-law, and Trosclair and Ennio formed a half-circle around him. "It's been a while."

"It has, Your Grace," Aleksey said, bowing to the king.

"I never got a chance to say farewell to you the last time you were here," the king said.

"Yes, about that - I truly am sorry," Aleksey said. "Darra fell ill, and I was eager to get her back home and into bed."

"Oh, that makes sense," the king said sympathetically, and Acasius rolled his eyes and shook his head behind the old elf's back. "And you must be Prince Trosclair, future king of DuVerres." The old elf held out his hand, and Trosclair shook it, marveling at the strength in the elf's grip.

"I'm very pleased to make your acquaintance," the prince said.

"The honor is all mine, I assure you," King Laban said. "I knew your parents, you know."

"Really?" Trosclair asked.

"We were even cordial, before the last Elven War started back up," the king said. "I do hope your visit means a new era of cooperation and friendship between our people is possible."

"I wish for the same thing," Trosclair said.

"Aleksey, the DragonSword is a gift beyond measure," the

king said, turning back to the half-elf. "And the prospect of an alliance with the most powerful kingdom on the continent is equally as precious to me. What would you ask of me, as your reward?"

"Actually, we do have need of a few things," Aleksey said. "A military man has deposed the prince. He needs a safe place to stay until he turns sixteen this summer, when he'll be able to raise his own forces to take back the throne."

"We would be honored to have you as our guest, for as long as you would like," the king said to the prince, who nodded and smiled gratefully. "What else?"

"I've already given your smith the details of what I need out of the DragonSword," Aleksey said. "But we'll also need gold, to feed and pay the troops he's going to call up. And if you could spare any warriors, an elven century or two could mean the difference between a prolonged civil war and a virtually bloodless transition of power."

"Hm," King Laban said as he considered it. "Gold will not be a problem. But I'll have to think carefully about sending troops back to the continent. Not every ruler is as open to peaceful coexistence with the elves as you are, young prince, and I will not be led into another war."

"I understand," Trosclair said.

"How long do you plan to stay with us?" the king asked the half-elf.

"Just until the work on the sword is done," Aleksey said.

"Then I'll have my answer by the time you leave," the king said as a waiter brought around flutes of champagne on a silver tray.

Qiana led Kaleb to her personal chambers, two medium-sized rooms in the west wing of the castle. One was a library full of scrolls, spellbooks and scholarly texts on various mystic subjects; the other was her bedchamber, which Kaleb could see through the open door. It was decorated in shades of lilac and lavender, except for the carpet, which was the skin of a large jungle cat.

"Are there any magical topics on which you'd consider yourself an expert?" Qiana asked as Kaleb perused her bookshelves.

"Oh, no," Kaleb said. "I'm just a novice. But my gram says I have a lot power for someone just starting out."

"Yes," Qiana said, reaching a hand out to place on the tribal lad's chest. "I could sense that the very first moment I saw you. It's one of the reasons I'm so drawn to you."

"You're... drawn to me?" Kaleb asked as Qiana moved in closer to him.

"Oh, yes," Qiana said. "I felt the potential of your power the moment you stepped onto our shores, and it's been driving me mad with lust ever since."

"Lust?" Kaleb repeated breathlessly as the elf woman moved her face toward his. They kissed, but then Kaleb pulled back abruptly. "You're... not a demon, are you?"

"No, I'm just an elf," she said, a puzzled expression on her face.

"Okay, good," he said, and she kissed him again. This time she pulled back.

"You know that I'm old enough to be your ancestor," she said as she pulled the belt of his robes loose. "And that this can never be more than a bit of fun for us, don't you? I wouldn't want to lead you on."

"You're not," he said. Qiana took the young mage by the hand and led him into her bedroom, closing the door behind them.

Back in the ballroom, Darra was leading A.J. in a slow dance. The pilot's arms were around her waist, and she had hers resting on his broad shoulders as they swayed to the gentle music of the orchestra. Darra was aware that the elves around her were still looking at them, although now they were polite enough to keep it to lingering glances. She kept her focus on A.J.'s handsome face, rugged with a few days' growth of beard.

"They're staring," Darra whispered with a smile stretched deliberately across her lips.

"They're just curious," A.J. said. "Or jealous of me."

"When everybody turned to look at us, I almost ran back out the door," she said. "I don't know how Trosclair stands all the attention he gets."

"You don't think you'd get used to it, eventually?" A.J. asked.

"Maybe," Darra said. "The same way you get used to a limp, or a chronic ailment."

"That's good," A.J. said.

"What's good?" Darra asked.

"Oh, uh, nothing," the pilot said a little too quickly for Darra's comfort. "It's just good that you know yourself so well." Darra had the feeling he'd had another meaning entirely, but she couldn't imagine what it could be. She consciously kept herself from frowning, and they kept dancing long into the night.

The next day, Aleksey woke Kaleb, A.J. and Ennio up early. They gathered in Acasius' dining room, where the chef served them more of his hot, spiced chocolate drink, as well as apple slices that had been peeled, battered, fried and sprinkled with cinnamon and confectioners' sugar. Aleksey and his brother took turns telling the young men about the adventure they had in mind for them. It boiled down to Acasius' desire for an egg.

The elf explained that he was up for a possible promotion to head chef at the castle, and he wanted to present the king with his favorite dish - scrambled and herbed griffin's egg. In days of old, the elves had enjoyed them regularly, as they kept flocks of griffins they trained to ride into battle. Since they had forsworn magic, however, they had no way to capture the creatures from the wild to ensure the health of their domesticated stock, and their flocks had dwindled to a few small groups kept in the zoo and special nature preserves just outside the city. It was far too important to keep all the viable eggs with the animals to potentially hatch, and the king had not had his favorite meal in over four centuries.

"But there are flocks of wild griffins that still nest up on the bluffs near the beach," Acasius said. "And they have literally hundreds of eggs that will not get fertilized, because it's winter."

"So why don't the elves go and collect them?" A.J. asked.

"We used to, and they were sold at outrageous prices when we were successful," Acasius said. "But too often, our people were mortally wounded in the attempt to harvest them."

"I don't like the sound of that," A.J. said. "Why would we have any better luck than the elves?"

"Because you have me," Kaleb said. "And I have magic."

"You know a spell that could subdue a griffin?" Ennio asked.

"No, but I have a couple of other useful tricks that might

help us," Kaleb said.

"And you have Aleksey," Acasius said. "A half-elf."

"Doesn't that mean you're, like, half as strong as a full elf?" A.J. asked. "I thought you got your strength from your elven side."

"He does, in a way," Acasius answered before Aleksey could. "Do you know what a liger is?" The pilot nodded. "The offspring of a tigress and a male lion, the liger is a unique creature. It's bigger and stronger than either of its parents, with a blend of their other traits. A half-elf is a lot like that. An elf is twice is strong and agile as a human, but a half-elf is twice as strong as that, and faster, too. And their senses and coordination rival full-blooded elves when they summon their concentration. Aleksey should have no trouble getting me what I want."

"So why are we going?" Ennio asked a little later as they made their way to the beachside bluffs. "I should've stayed at the prince's side."

"Trosclair will be fine with Darra and my brother," Aleksey said. "And I really want to impress the king, so I needed the extra hands."

"Darra will be mad we didn't wake her up for this," A.J. said.

"Oh, she seldom wakes angry when I let her sleep in," Aleksey said. "Besides, it will give her a chance to get to know Trosclair better."

"That'll be good for both of them," A.J. said, and Kaleb's jaw dropped.

"Wait a second, does he know?" Kaleb asked Aleksey, and the half-elf nodded.

"Know what?" Ennio asked.

"Nothing," Aleksey said. "I just think it's good for them to get closer."

"They're already friends," Ennio said. "But you said it like it was really important." The soldier stared down the half-elf. "Look, I may not have a real education, but I know when something's being kept from me. So what is it?"

"Gods, me and my big mouth!" Aleksey said. "Fine, I'll tell you, too – if you swear me an oath to never repeat it to anyone."

"I swear it," Ennio said.

"On your love for the prince?" Aleksey asked, and Ennio nodded solemnly. Aleksey proceeded to tell the soldier the story of how he came to be Darra's father. As Ennio listened, his mouth fell agape. By the time the half-elf finished telling his tale and answering all of the soldier's questions, they were up on the bluffs, looking down on the elven city on one side and the vast ocean on the other.

"You have to tell them!" the soldier said. "Trosclair thinks his sister is dead!"

"I will - when the time is right," Aleksey said. "Maybe after their birthdays this summer, when Trosclair has taken his kingdom back."

"Why would you wait so long?" Ennio asked.

"Shh!" Aleksey said as they rounded a bend and a hatching nest came into view. There were hundreds of eggs scattered across the bluff in clusters which rested on round beds of dried grasses and leaves. Several sleeping griffins were curled up between the nests. Aleksey turned back to Ennio.

"If I tell them now, it will likely bring the wrath of the demon I've been hiding my daughter from all these years down on us all," Aleksey whispered. "Waiting until there's a whole kingdom to defend Darra is the smartest thing we can do."

"I'm not comfortable lying to my prince," Ennio said.

"Are you comfortable burying him?" Aleksey asked. "Or his sister? Because that's what it might come to if we told them before they were properly protected."

"But–" A shriek from one of the griffins silenced the soldier, and they all ducked back behind the bend and out of the creature's line of sight. After a few moments of silence, Aleksey poked his head back out and saw that the griffin had only shifted its position, stretching its front talons out ahead of it before closing its eyes once more.

"Okay, Kaleb," Aleksey whispered as he distributed a large cloth sack to each of the young men. "You're up." The mage pushed up his sleeves and gestured, then whispered the words for "feather" and "foot" in the old speak. His eyes glowed amber, and the others waited expectantly for something to happen.

"Did it not work?" A.J. asked after a few silent moments.

"No, I think it did," Kaleb said. He lifted his foot and brought it down on a twig, which snapped in half without a sound.

"What did you do?" Ennio asked.

"It's a spell I've used for hunting before," Kaleb said. "It'll mute any noise we make as we move among them."

"But won't they smell us?" A.J. asked.

"No," Aleksey said. "They have very poor olfactory senses." The half-elf crept out from the bend and made his way to the closest pile of eggs. He looked back to see the teens following along the same path. When they got to the pile, they started loading eggs into their sacks. Each one was about the size of a pineapple and weighed between six and eight pounds, with a light periwinkle-to-flint gray shell that was obviously much thicker than a chicken's egg. After a few minutes, their sacks were all full, and they backed away from the almost-empty nest. When they were safely around the bend again, Aleksey thanked the teens for a job well done, and they headed back down the slope toward the city.

Darra woke to find her father and boyfriend gone. Acasius had gone to work at the palace, and Gavriella was painting in a studio at the back of the house. She found Trosclair in the drawing room, reading from the only book Milian had packed for him, a biographical text about the explorer who discovered the Dread Continent.

"Good book?" she asked as she plopped down beside him on one of the sofas.

"It's alright," Trosclair said, lowering the tome. "It's a little dry. I'm already halfway through it, and I still don't have a clear image of the subject in my mind. You know, who he really was."

"So put it down and come outside with me," Darra said. "I saw a target set up on the back lawn. I could teach you how to shoot a crossbow."

"That would be useful to know," Trosclair said. "But Ennio says I should stick to knives."

"That works, too. You can practice throwing them at the target," Darra said. Trosclair folded the corner of the page he was on to mark his place and put the book down. Darra fetched her crossbow and bolts, and the prince rummaged through Kaleb's bag until he found the mage's throwing knives.

"Kaleb told me I could borrow them if I wanted, when he saw Ennio training me last week," the prince said to answer Darra's lifted brows.

"Okay," she said. "Come on." She led him out to the back

lawn, where a round, multi-colored target was indeed set up in front of the fence surrounding the yard. Darra gestured to it. "Well, show me what you can do."

"Oh, no!" Trosclair demurred. "I'm still learning. You go first."

"Would you like to place a little wager on our performances?" Darra asked.

"Let's just play for answers, like we did last time," Trosclair said. "You're much better trained than I am, so you'd just be robbing me blind if we played for money."

"Okay," Darra said. "So every time I get a bull's-eye, I'll answer one of your questions. And the same for you."

"I think it should count if I hit the target at all," Trosclair said.

"We'll compromise," Darra said. "If you hit the two inner circles, I'll answer your question. Deal?"

"Deal," he said. Darra lifted her crossbow, looked down the shaft of the arrow to aim it, and squeezed the trigger. Her bolt sailed through the air and thudded into the red inner circle of the target just left of its exact center. Trosclair applauded, but Darra frowned slightly.

"Hm," she said. "I guess I didn't adjust for the wind correctly. That should have been dead on."

"But you hit the bull's-eye," he said. "So what's your question?"

"What was it like, the first time you were with Ennio?" she asked.

"Oh gods," Trosclair said. "Are you asking for the full graphic details?"

"No!" Darra said. "Just - how did it make you feel?" Trosclair thought about it for a second.

"Alive," he said. "That's the best word for it. It was exciting, sure, and a little confusing. But the thing I remember most is that it made me feel like I'd only ever been half-alive, up until that moment."

"Wow," Darra said.

"So I take it you and A.J. haven't done it yet?" Trosclair asked, but Darra shook her head.

"Uh-uh-uh," she said, wagging her finger. "Not until you hit the target." Trosclair raised one of the throwing knives by the blade, moved his arm in imitation of a release a couple of times to line up his shot, and then hurled the weapon. It hit the target but bounced off onto the grass.

"That should count," Trosclair said. "It hit in the second circle."

"But it didn't stick," Darra said. "If it had been an attacker, it would have glanced off of him without slowing him down."

"So I'll give you an easy one, then," Trosclair said. "What did your parents do for a living?"

"I thought you wanted to know if A.J. and I had done it," she said.

"Oh, you told me everything I needed to know about that with your reddening complexion," Trosclair said. "You're still a virgin, I'd bet my life on it."

"Well, you'd win that bet," Darra said, blushing just a little. "And as for my parents, Dad says my mother ran a large household, and that my father was an amateur poet. That's where I get my knack for rhyming from."

"That's funny," Trosclair said. "My dad was something of a poet, too. All the DuVerreses are."

"Really?" Darra asked, and the prince nodded.

"Where were they from?" Trosclair asked.

"DuVerres. The capital city," Darra said as a random thought occurred to her. "Your sister," Darra said. "She had red and golden blonde hair like you, didn't she?"

"You didn't take a shot," Trosclair said. Darra lifted her crossbow and squeezed the trigger with hardly a glance at the target, but she knew she'd hit the inner circle again.

"So your sister," she prompted.

"Yes, I imagine she would have the family hair, if she were still alive," he said.

"What else do you know about her?" she asked.

"Just that she had blue eyes, like me," Trosclair said. "And Mrs. Applebaum - that was our nanny - she says Esmerelda had a strawberry-shaped birthmark on her left shoulder. She actually still holds out hope that we'll find her alive someday, but I don't kid myself that that's a real possibility."

"Will you excuse me for a minute?" Darra asked. "I need to

use the restroom."

"Of course," Trosclair said as Darra hurried back inside the house. The prince hurled his remaining knife, and it stuck in the yellow second circle of the target. He pumped his fist in triumph.

Darra entered the bathroom and closed the door behind her, twisting the lock to make sure no one would accidentally disturb her. She crossed to the mirror and slowly pulled down the collar of her dress to expose her left shoulder, revealing the strawberry-shaped patch of slightly darker skin that had always marked it.

Aleksey and his teenage companions made it back into the city just after noon. A.J. could tell they were in a poorer neighborhood because of the heavy graffiti, as well as the metal bars that covered all the windows. Children still played in the street here, but their clothes were stained and tattered, and the lawns they dashed around on were unkempt and overgrown with clovers, dandelions and purple devil's trumpets. Almost all the houses and occasional small shops needed new coats of paint, and the street itself was rougher, having been paved with gravel centuries ago.

"I was wondering," Kaleb said to Aleksey. "What do you think of Qiana?"

"She's wonderful," Aleksey said. "A bit distracted, sometimes, by the pull of magic still lingering in her. But as lovely an elf woman as I've ever known. Why do you ask?"

"Oh, no reason," Kaleb said, but Aleksey noticed his cheeks flushing.

"Gods," the half-elf said. "She's gotten to you already, hasn't she?"

"That depends on your meaning," the tribal lad replied, not making eye contact.

"Last night at the castle?" Aleksey asked, and Kaleb nodded. The half-elf laughed.

"What's so funny?" Kaleb asked.

"It's just so very like Qiana," Aleksey said. "She's always had a penchant for making boys into men."

"I was already a man," Kaleb said. "All she made me was very happy."

"Oh, I'm quite sure of that," Aleksey said.

"Wait, how would you know?" the tribal lad asked, and Aleksey merely smiled. They turned a corner and saw a long line of elves in ragged clothes stretching down the sidewalk and around the next block. Each of them carried a bowl or cup. At the front of the line, an elven woman was serving up stew from the steps of a small temple, one scoop at a time. An elf next to her, so androgynously beautiful that their gender was not immediately obvious, tore pieces of bread from loaves and handed it to the other elves as they exited the line.

"Jesus," A.J. said. "Are they all homeless?"

"Many of them. They live in tents in the poorer districts of the city," Aleksey said. "The king provides the temples with enough food to keep them alive, but they still suffer from ill health, incidents of violence, and extremes in temperature and weather."

"Why doesn't he provide some kind of housing for them?" Kaleb asked. "In my Tribe, that's a right everyone is guaranteed from birth."

"His view is that they could move out of the city if they desired," Aleksey said. "He even set up an incentive program granting those who wished to do so a plot of land to farm. But he didn't account for the chronic mental illnesses that plague a lot of these elves. And most of the others have lived their whole lives here and wouldn't know how to farm anyway."

An elven boy who looked about the size of a human of six or seven years pointed at Aleksey and the teens as they passed. "Mommy, look at their ears!" the child said.

"Shh!" his mother said, putting a finger over her lips. "It's not polite to stare, dear."

"Are you warriors?" the child asked, seeing their weapons, and Aleksey smiled.

"Something like that," he said. He lifted an egg from his sack and offered it to the child's mother.

"What's that for?" she asked.

"You can sell it," Aleksey said. She reached out her scrawny arms and took the egg from him.

"Thank you," she said, and Aleksey nodded. He and the teens kept moving down the street, and the line of hungry elves behind them shrank until it disappeared from view completely.

"So how long have you known?" Ennio asked A.J. "About

Darra and Trosclair."

"About a week," A.J. said. "I overheard Aleksey and Kaleb talking about it."

"And I figured it out myself," Kaleb said. "After Darra touched the unicorn."

"Listen, Aleksey, I know I swore you an oath," Ennio said. "But I don't think I can lie to Trosclair's face. Not believably, anyway."

"Don't lie," Aleksey advised. "Just – don't say anything."

"What if he mentions his sister?" the soldier asked.

"Find an excuse to turn away from him, or leave the room for a bit," Aleksey said.

"Are you really gonna coach him on how to cover this up?" A.J. asked. "Instead of just telling Darra and Trosclair the truth?"

"I thought you agreed with me that it was in Darra's best interest to wait," Aleksey said.

"That was before everybody else knew," A.J. said. "Now it just feels like we're ganging up on them."

"He's right," Ennio said. "It's not fair that they're the last to know."

"No, 'fair' would have been Darra growing up in the palace, with her brother and parents," Aleksey said. "So 'fair' is really not a possibility at this point. But there is a possibility we can spare them future pain - and possible death - if we keep this amongst ourselves."

"What about the pain Trosc is in right now?" Ennio asked. "He thinks I'm literally all he has left in this world."

"Can't you continue being that for him, just for a little while longer?" Aleksey asked. "You're his bodyguard, and I know you're good with a sword. But do you really think you could protect him from an army of dread monsters, if it came to it, with just our help?"

"No," Ennio said. "But we could keep hiding or stay on the move."

"We've been doing both of those things, and somehow someone has still been able to predict our every movement," Aleksey said.

"You think it could be the demon that's after Darra?" Kaleb asked. "You said he had vast resources."

"No," Aleksey said. "Lucio told me it wasn't him."

"And you'd really trust the word of a vampire?" Ennio asked.

"Not even a little," Aleksey said. "But I have faith in his arrogance. He was gloating when he said it, confident he was about to kill me."

"Uh, guys," Kaleb said as he stared at the road ahead of them. "I think we have a problem." Aleksey and the pilot turned and saw a group of four youthful-looking elves lining up in the street in front of their path. They wore mostly black, with a single red accent piece somewhere on their person, and they all had heavy leather jackets with "WY" embroidered on the chests. The men on the ends had swords; in between them stood a woman with plum-colored hair and a spiked chain mace and another man with a bow, his arrow already nocked. They struck poses clearly meant to intimidate.

"Hey, there," the elf with the sword on the left called.

"Good afternoon," Aleksey said with as much friendliness as he could muster.

"We don't get a lot of humans around here," the elf woman said. "What's your business in the city?"

"We've just come to see the sights," Aleksey said.

"Are you rich?" the elf on the left asked. Aleksey chuckled.

"No," he said. "Not even remotely."

"That's too bad," the elf with the bow said. "Because there's a tax on human tourists."

"And I assume you're going to tell me you're the tax collectors?" Aleksey asked.

"That's right," the elf with the bow said.

"Well, I'm afraid we haven't got any money," the half-elf said.

"We'll take whatever's in those bags, then," the elf woman said. "We're not picky."

"I can't let you do that," Aleksey said, placing his sack gently on the ground. The teens did the same. "These are a gift."

"I like gifts," the elf woman said as she took a step toward them. Aleksey and Ennio drew their swords, A.J. readied his spear, and Kaleb pushed back his sleeves.

"Fine!" the elf with the bow said, drawing back his arrow. He let it loose at the same time Kaleb brought up his hand in a strange gesture and yelled, "*Feles eya dal*!" His eyes glowed amber, and the arrow came to an abrupt halt in midair - about three inches from A.J.'s chest.

"Jesus!" the pilot yelled as Ennio and Aleksey rushed toward the elves. "Thanks, Kaleb!" The mage nodded as the elf with the bow nocked another arrow and the elf woman at his side ran forward, swinging her weapon at the pilot, who backed up just in time to avoid being hit.

Aleksey charged the elf at the far left, and Ennio took on the one at the right. The half-elf swung his sword with such strength that it slid down the blade of his opponent's weapon, casting off sparks. When their hilts met, the half-elf slammed his head forward into his opponent's face. The elf cried out in pain and backed away, blood gushing from a nose that had clearly been broken.

Ennio's battle was also going well for him. He knew he wasn't as strong as the elf he faced, so he avoided a stalemate at all costs, keeping his sword dancing around the elf so quickly, and with such precise thrusts, that soon the elf had small bloody slashes on each of his arms, as well as one across his chest. Ennio laughed, and the elf took the opportunity to tackle him, knocking the sword from his hand. They rolled around on the ground, struggling for a dominant position.

The elf woman swung her chain mace at A.J. again, and the pilot raised his spear defensively in front of him with both hands. The spiked ball of the elf woman's weapon slammed down on the wooden shaft of A.J.'s own, and it splintered in his hands. He raised the bladed end like a knife and backed up a pace. The elf woman smiled. "What's the matter, cutie?" she asked. "Can't handle a real woman?"

"Stay back!" the pilot said. "I don't want to hurt you!"

"Well, I still wanna hurt you!" she said, lunging and swinging her weapon again. It would have connected with his skull, had Aleksey not thrown his sword in the way at the last second.

Kaleb stopped another arrow, this one aimed at himself, and the elf with the bow threw it down in frustration. He pulled another arrow from his quiver and stalked toward Kaleb. The mage backed up until his leg brushed up against one of the sacks of griffin's eggs. He bent down and quickly pulled one out, and just as the elf with the arrow was about to jab it down into his back, Kaleb twisted and slammed the egg into the man's face with all his strength. There was a loud crunching sound as the egg cracked, shattering like a porcelain vase, its gooey insides smearing the elf's face so that he had to close his eyes.

The elf wrestling with Ennio pinned the soldier's arms beneath his legs as he sat on his chest. He raised his sword above Ennio's head, but before he could bring it down on him, Kaleb kicked the elf in the back of his skull. The mage tried to wrest the sword from the elf's hand, but his grip was too strong. The elf did have to lift up to keep ahold of the hilt, though, and one of Ennio's arms came free. He struck the elf in the stomach as hard as he could, and Kaleb succeeded in pulling the sword from the elf's hand. The tribal lad brought the weapon to the throat of the elf, who raised his hands in surrender. "Yield!" he said. "I yield!"

The elf with egg on his face wiped his eyes clean enough to open them and promptly turned and ran away. The elf woman backed up next to the elf with the broken nose as their remaining companion slowly stood up off of Ennio. "Now," Aleksey said. "Shall we finish this, or have you learned your lesson?"

"Spare us the lecture!" the elf woman said, lifting her pinky and index finger in a gesture the elves considered obscene as the trio ducked into an alleyway.

"Come on," Aleksey said as he sheathed his sword and picked up his sack of eggs. "They could come back with friends. I don't want to be here for that." The teens picked up their sacks and continued on behind the half-elf. They got back to Acasius' house a short while later and brought the eggs to him in his large kitchen.

"Good gods!" the chef exclaimed on seeing the teens unload their haul. "How many did you get?"

"Over two dozen," Aleksey said.

"With that many, I can feed the whole court!" Acasius said. "It will be a meal people talk about for the next century! Thank you, Aleksey."

"It was no problem," Aleksey said.

"Except when the street gang tried to kill us and take them," A.J. said.

"Yes, except for that," Aleksey said.

"Well, I can say this will definitely impress the king," Acasius said. "He might even offer you a seasonal position collecting them for him."

"I hope not," Aleksey said. "I'd hate to have to turn him down."

"Why would you do that?" Acasius asked.

"Harvesting eggs is not exactly the kind of work I ordinarily do," Aleksey said.

"Oh, I see," Acasius said. "Working a boring normal job like mine would threaten your freewheeling criminal lifestyle."

"I never said what you do is boring," Aleksey said. "That must be your own opinion coming to the surface."

"I love what I do," Acasius said. "I make people's lives richer."

"One elf's life, to be specific - and he's already the richest elf there ever was!" Aleksey said.

"See?" Acasius asked. "You do look down on my work." The brothers continued squabbling as the teens stepped quietly from the room. They entered the drawing room, where Trosclair was reading through the titles on the bookshelf.

"Hey," he said as he turned sideways to accept a hug from Ennio. "How did it go?"

"Fine," Ennio said. Trosclair noticed his knee, which he'd scraped during his scuffling.

"What's that from?" the prince asked.

"Some thugs tried to steal our eggs on the way back here," Ennio said. "But we taught them not to mess with humans just because we seem weaker."

"Where's Darra?" A.J. asked.

"She's laying down in one of the guest rooms," Trosclair said. "She said she wasn't feeling well."

"Maybe I should go see if she wants me to brew up one of Gram's remedies," Kaleb suggested.

"You could ask," Trosclair said. "But she said she just wanted to be left alone."

"Oh," Kaleb said. "I'll let her sleep, then, and check on her a little later."

Several hours later, as the sun was beginning to set, Darra emerged from the guest room and strode through the house, a determined expression fixed on her face. She passed the drawing room and glanced inside, but seeing only Kaleb and Gavriella inside, she kept moving. She went to the back doors, and through the window she saw her father and A.J., sitting inside the gazebo. She went outside and crossed the lawn toward them.

"Honey," Aleksey said upon seeing her. "Are you feeling better?"

"Not exactly," Darra said. "Dad, we need to talk."

"Okay," her father said, frowning slightly at her serious tone. "What about?"

"My parents," Darra said. "Who were they, really?" Aleksey's face froze.

"I should let you two talk," A.J. said, but Darra held up a hand to his chest to stop him.

"No, please," she said. "Stay. I have some questions for you, too." The pilot swallowed hard and nodded. "But first, I want an answer from you, Dad. Who were my parents?" The half-elf thought his heart might burst. He considered repeating what he'd told her before, but the look in her eyes told him she already knew the truth.

"Your dad was the late King Halian," he finally said, looking down at the ground. "And your mother was his wife, Queen Noelani."

"So it's true," Darra said. "Trosclair is my brother."

"Yes," Aleksey said.

"How could you keep that from me?" Darra asked.

"Darra, I can explain," her father said.

"You better start, then!" she said.

"Maybe we should go inside," Aleksey suggested.

"No, damn it!" Darra said. "Just tell me."

"I took a job, just days before you were born," Aleksey said. "I was hired to pick up and deliver a package. Unbeknownst to me, you were that package."

"The king and queen - my parents - were killed the same night princess Esmerelda - gods, is that my real name?" she asked, losing her train of thought.

"Yes," Aleksey said.

"They were killed the same night I disappeared," Darra said.

"Yes," Aleksey said again.

"Well?" Darra prompted. "Did you do it?"

"Gods, no!" Aleksey said. "I swear it, honey! All I did that night was remove you from harm's way."

"Then who did kill them?" she asked.

"A dread monster by the name of Olwydd killed your father," Aleksey said. "He died trying to protect you."

"And my mother?"

"She was mortally wounded by the vampire, Lucio."

"Did she really give me to you?" Darra asked.

"Yes," Aleksey said. "With her last strength, she put you in my arms and asked me to protect you. And that's what I've always tried to do."

"Why didn't you take Trosclair, too?" Darra asked.

"They weren't interested in him," Aleksey said. "I knew he'd be safest raised in the palace."

"But we're twins!" Darra said. "That's supposed to mean something – a life of shared experiences and a special bond. Now we're practically strangers."

"It's not too late to develop that relationship," Aleksey said. "I'm sure Trosclair will be thrilled to know the truth."

"Speaking of truth," Darra said, turning to A.J. "Did you know about all this, when I asked you about Lucio the other day?"

"Yes," A.J. said. "Darra, I wanted to tell you, but—"

"But my dad convinced you not to, right?" she asked, and the pilot nodded.

"It's true, honey," Aleksey said. "I demanded he keep the secret. But we always had your own good in mind."

"But you're supposed to be on my side, no matter what," Darra said to A.J. "I mean, you're my boyfriend, for the sake of the heavens. Or you were."

"Were?" A.J. repeated, his heart breaking.

"I can't date someone who could lie to my face about something so important," Darra said. She turned to leave.

"Darra?" Aleksey called after her. "Honey, can we please talk about this some more?"

"It's just gonna make me more angry," Darra said over her shoulder.

"Do you think you can ever forgive me?" Aleksey asked in a plaintive voice.

"I just... need time," Darra said. "To process everything."

She went back inside the house as Ennio was coming out.

"Is she okay?" he asked. "She looks upset."

"She knows," A.J. said. "Aleksey just told her."

"Oh," Ennio said. "That's actually good. Because I sort of already told Trosclair."

"How did he take it?" A.J. asked.

"He... has a lot of questions," the soldier said.

"That's to be expected," Aleksey said.

Darra went back into the guest bedroom and locked the door. She went to her satchel and began rummaging through it, until she drew out a heart-shaped necklace on a silver chain. She slipped the necklace on, turned around - and almost screamed. Volos was standing not two feet away.

"You came," she said after she'd regained her composure. "Just like you said you would."

"Of course," he said. "Are you in some sort of trouble? Or did you need something?"

"No," Darra said. "I just want to get away from here."

"Then I'd be happy to be provide your escort," Volos said, extending his hand. Darra grabbed her satchel, took Volos' hand and stepped closer to him. Volos snapped his fingers, and they faded away together.

CHAPTER THIRTEEN
"MIGHTIER THAN THE SWORD"

The next morning, Acasius cracked open one of the eggs and transferred its gooey insides into a large skillet. The chef's kitchen had a big black metal stove with a wide firebox beneath several slatted burners and a flue that ran into the wall and up out of the roof. The elf took several pieces of half-charred wood out of the stove's firebox and struck a match to light the remaining kindling. Soon small flames were burning away beneath the skillet, and most of the smoke was caught in the flue and directed outside. Acasius took a large spoon from a drawer and began scraping it along the bottom and sides of the skillet as Aleksey entered the room.

"There's tea in the kettle," the elf said. Aleksey drew a mug from the cupboard and filled it with the steaming light brown liquid.

"I couldn't sleep," Aleksey said, blowing on the rim of his mug. "I just kept thinking about how mad Darra is at me."

"I warned you," Acasius said.

"Oh, here we go," Aleksey said, rolling his eyes and setting down his mug.

"I told you that you were too young to have a child of your own," Acasius said. "This is what happens when babies have babies."

"I am not a baby!" his brother replied. "And Darra is mad because I kept the truth from her, not because I'm relatively young."

"A more mature elf would have realized that was the wrong thing to do from the beginning," Acasius said.

"Well, I'm only a half-elf," Aleksey replied, shrugging. A.J.

entered the kitchen.

"Good morning," Acasius said as he grabbed a shaker full of pre-mixed herbs and began sprinkling the eggs with one hand while continuing to stir the lumpy mass with the other.

"Hey," A.J. said as he pulled out a chair at the table and sunk down into it.

"Tea?" Aleksey asked, and the pilot nodded.

"Please," he said. Aleksey retrieved another mug, filled it, and handed it over. "Thank you."

"So why are you up so early?" Acasius asked.

"It's hard for me to sleep past sunrise," A.J. said. "And I was worried about Darra."

"That makes two of us," Aleksey said.

"Do you think she hates me now?" A.J. asked.

"Not as much as she hates me," Aleksey said. "I'm sorry I put you in the middle of this when I asked you to keep my secret."

"She doesn't hate either of you," Acasius said. "She's just going through something. But she will get over it eventually."

"I hope you're right," Aleksey said, lowering his face into his hands miserably.

"And to help her get back into good spirits..." Acasius said as he removed the skillet from the flames. "I'm making her the best breakfast she's ever tasted. A meal fit for the royalty she really is. And I'll let you deliver it to her."

"Thank you, brother," Aleksey said, and they smiled at one another. A little while later, Acasius had assembled a beautiful platter. The entrée was the egg dish, which had been buttered, salted and covered with melted white cheese. The sides were a scoop of *dalsom* - a piquant vegetable paste with a consistency similar to hummus - and a warm, soft pumpkin roll cut in two, with one half covered in a red berry compote and the other in green apple jam. The elf put the platter on a tray with a mug of tea, some utensils and a napkin, and then he handed all of it over to Aleksey.

"Can I go with you?" A.J. asked. "I never got a chance to apologize to her last night."

"Sure," the half-elf said, and the pilot stood and followed him out of the room. They got to Darra's room, and Aleksey nodded to the door. "Can you knock for me?" he whispered, and the pilot rapped on the door a few times. There was no answer, so he knocked again, louder this time; still there was no response. "Darra, honey?" Aleksey called out. "Are you awake?" He waited a few seconds, then handed the tray to the pilot. "Darra!" he cried even louder. "Sweetie, say something! You're scaring me!" Acasius and Gavriella came down the hall as Aleksey tried the knob, but the door was locked. "Do you have a key?" Aleksey asked, and Acasius shook his head. "Then I'm sorry, and I'll pay you back."

"For what?" his brother asked. Aleksey slammed into the door with his shoulder. The frame splintered and the door fell open.

"She's gone!" Aleksey said as he entered the room.

"Did she crawl out the window?" A.J. asked, moving over to examine it.

"You think she ran away?" Gavriella asked.

"No," Aleksey said. "There's another scent in here. One I recognize. Darra didn't run away. Not by herself, anyway. Somebody took her. And I think I know where they went."

Darra was still in bed. She'd had a restless night and woke early, but she kept her eyes closed, tossing and turning for what felt like hours. It was a large, comfortable feather bed, with silk sheets and pillows so soft it felt like her head was resting on a giant marshmallow. There was a fireplace in the wall opposite the bed, but the fire had died out sometime in the night. Darra's face and ears were cold, but her body was warm underneath two thick velvet blankets, and this was incentive enough to stay where she was. She wished the fire was still going - and suddenly she heard soft crackling. She snapped up and stared over at the fireplace with her mouth agape. Flames roared in the firebox, burning away at logs that had been magically replenished.

Darra threw back the covers and slipped on her boots, glad that she had slept in her clothes. She left the room and strode down the long torch-lit hallway until she came to a sizeable chamber that served as the kitchen. It had a stove and oven on one wall, a long stretch of cabinets below a marble countertop along another, and a third with large twin wash basins, each with its own pump and faucet, as well as a door to the dining hall. Behind Darra was a cooling pantry, with ice brought up daily from the castle's cellar. The man who brought the ice up every morning, Tarun, stood at the stove, tending to a pan of thick strips of sizzling bacon with a fork. He glanced up at Darra and smiled.

"You're awake," he said. "You hungry? I'm making breakfast."

"No, thanks," Darra said. "I don't eat meat. This castle - it's not like, haunted or something, is it?"

Tarun laughed. "I don't think so," he said. "Unless we're the ones haunting it. Why do you ask?"

"I was just lying in bed, wishing the fire was still going, and then it was," Darra said. "And I know it had gone completely out hours before."

"That's just one of the perks of living with a dragon," A.J. said. "This place runs on his magic. Some of the spells can sense your needs and desires, and others use command words. Watch." Tarun looked up at one of two torches in the chamber and said, "*Ercha.*" The torch snuffed out, as if a gust of wind had suddenly blown up - but the air was perfectly still. It was also heavy with the smell of the frying pork, which turned Darra's stomach just a little.

"Wow," she said.

"It gets even cooler," Tarun said. "Literally. The cellar where we make the ice is kept at a constant freezing temperature."

"I haven't been below the castle's main floors," she said. "Except when we first came through the tunnels."

"Oh, you wouldn't want to go down there," Tarun said. "Besides the ice chamber, there's just a wine cellar and an old, unused dungeon. And there're lots of spiders. Best to stay up here, where it's warm and protected."

"Protected?" Darra asked.

"Volos says there are things in the tunnels beneath the castle that I wouldn't want to run into," Tarun said. "To keep those things out, all the doors to the castle have a charm over the threshold. If someone - or something - uninvited tries to pass under it, Volos will know. And to keep nosy hikers from discovering us, the castle's exterior features are spelled to blend into the mountain."

"I always wondered how it could sit so close to Morning's Peak and never be noticed," Darra said.

"But the best feature is the plumbing," Tarun continued. "There are two bathing pools and three shower rooms, all fed by hot springs that Volos redirected to flow up into the mountain.

That's where we get the hot water for the tap, too." He nodded to one of the washing basins. "Volos even has flushing toilets, something I thought I'd never see again."

"Most of our cities have upgraded to modern plumbing," Darra said.

"Yeah, but your idea of 'modern' and my idea of 'modern' are two very different things," Tarun said. "I—I only saw parts of a couple of cities. I spent most of my time in the forest, before Volos brought me back here."

"I remember," Darra said as Volos entered. He wore loose gray cotton pants and a robe that hung open, revealing his muscular stomach and chest.

"Darra," he said, closing his robe and cinching its belt. "I didn't think you'd be up so early. Did you sleep well?"

"Fine," she lied, not wanting to upset her host.

"Why is it so dark in here, Tarun?" Volos asked. "I need light to fully appreciate the beauty of my guest."

Tarun looked at the unlit torch and said, "*Verres.*" The flame sprang back into existence.

"*Verres,*" Volos repeated. "The old speak word for fire. And your name - your real name - is DuVerres, meaning 'of fire.' For your family's famous hair, of course. I'd like to see you grow it out to its natural color someday." Volos put a hand up to her hair and stroked down its length.

"I hadn't even thought about my last name," Darra said, looking away from him demurely. "I just know I don't feel like an Esmerelda."

"You can keep your name, then," Volos said. "The important thing is that you now know who you truly are."

"Actually, it feels like the opposite of that is true," Darra said. "I'm questioning everything. My very name, my father's intentions, what I want to do with my life - it's all so overwhelming suddenly, when I thought I had it all figured out."

"You no longer wish to be a warrior?" Volos asked.

"No, I still want to train as a chi-fighter," Darra said. "But then what? Do I live at the palace - assuming Trosclair can win it back - and marry some noble? Or should I stay with my Dad? I'm practically all he has in the world."

"There is a third option," Volos said. "You could stay here

with me." Darra flushed crimson.

"I—I appreciate you bringing me here, and letting me stay while I figure things out," Darra said. "But I don't think I should be making any long-term plans while everything's still up in the air."

"I understand," Volos said. "Just remember that the option is there for you."

"I will," Darra said.

"So what are we doing today, friends?" Tarun asked. "Painting? Sculpting? Maybe just a hike?"

"Actually, I did think we'd take a little walk later on," Volos said. "Into town."

"What for?" Darra asked.

"I thought we might spend a little of the obscene amount of gold I've collected over my long life," Volos said, grinning. "Or a lot of it."

"I'm always up for some shopping," Darra said, returning his smile. "But you have to let me make dinner for you tonight to show my gratitude. I'm not the best cook, but my uncle is a chef, and he's taught me a few dishes that usually turn out pretty decent."

"I'd love that," Volos said as Tarun served him a plate of bacon.

Aleksey, his brother and the teens met King Laban in the castle's armory. Racks and racks of weapons lined the walls and shelves, but the king led them to the back of the chamber. A special rack of shiny new weapons greeted the adventurers. There were thirty swords, ten each in three types: basket-hilted broadswords, traditional claymores with cross hilts of forward-sloping quillons, and short-swords used primarily as a secondary weapon and for parrying an opponent's attacks. There were also twenty throwing spears with metal shafts and an equal number of longer thrusting spears. For the mounted troops, there were dozens of horseman's picks with slightly curved spikes, slender-tipped halberds, and various other polearms. Thirty knives suitable for throwing or close combat were arranged in pairs with matching jewels on the hilts. Stacked next to this rack of war blades were dozens of quivers with twenty-five bolts or arrows in each of them.

"You got all this from one sword?" A.J. asked. "I mean, it was a big sword, don't get me wrong; but this is enough for a small army."

"Those were my very words, when my smith showed me what she and her team had accomplished," the king said. "The trick was in the design. Only the tips and edges of these weapons are made from the DragonSword, but that should be enough to kill any dread creatures or other soulless monsters that threaten our Isles."

"We'll only need to take a small fraction of this with us," Aleksey said.

"Please," the king said, gesturing to the weapons. "Take your pick."

Aleksey and the teens stepped forward and began trying out the heft of the weapons. A.J. picked up one of the throwing spears. "Geez," he said. "This thing weighs almost nothing!" Ennio pulled out a broadsword, but Aleksey went for the claymore. Kaleb picked out a pair of knives with yellow sapphires at the bottoms of the hilts. Trosclair picked up his own pair of knives with pinkish orange garnets.

"What are those for?" Ennio asked. "You can't possibly think you're coming with us?"

"Of course I am!" Trosclair said. "I've had enough of hiding."

"It's too dangerous," Ennio said. "You should stay here where it's safe."

"Ennio," Trosclair said. "She's my sister!"

"I know," the soldier replied. "And I promise we'll bring her back."

"You should listen to him," Aleksey said. "Facing the dragon is going to be the most difficult thing any of us has ever done. I can't guarantee that I can protect you and save my daughter."

"A dragon! Gods, you do lead an exciting life, Aleksey!" King Laban said.

"Right now, I'm wishing it was a lot more boring," the half-elf replied.

"I've never had any real family," Trosclair said, returning Aleksey's attention to him. "I'm not going to let other people fight to save her, when that's my responsibility – as both her brother and her prince."

"Well spoken," the king said. "You sound like you'll make a fine king someday."

"Speaking of that day," Trosclair said. "You said you'd have an answer for us, about whether you can help me retake my kingdom."

"Yes, well," the king said, looking slightly flustered. "I have given it a great deal of thought. And I do wish to support you in your effort. Having you on the throne would be the best thing for all our people."

"That's wonderful!" Aleksey said. "Would you be willing to send some troops with us now, to help rescue my daughter?"

"Unfortunately, no. I can't do that," the king said. "We lost too many of my people the last time we crossed over to the continent."

"I guess that means we're on our own," A.J. said.

"Not entirely," said Qiana from the doorway. She was holding a pair of books and a scroll.

"We do mean to help you," King Laban said as the elf woman entered the chamber. "With gold, and with knowledge."

"Qiana," Kaleb said. "I was hoping I'd see you before we left."

"Kaleb," she said with a smile. She crossed over to the tribal lad and kissed him quickly on both cheeks, and Acasius and the king exchanged amused looks.

"Are those spellbooks?" the young mage asked.

"No," Qiana said, handing over the books. "But they're treatises on the construction of spells. I brought you the volumes that deal with gem magic and portals to other realms. You should be able to synthesize the knowledge in them to craft an entirely new spell."

"That's amazing, Qiana," he said. "And the scroll?"

"It's a powerful incantation that we elves used when we went hunting dragons in the old days," she said. "I'm sure it will be useful to you."

"If I can learn it in time," Kaleb said.

"You've got until early morning tomorrow, Kay," Aleksey said. "We won't reach Morning's Peak until then."

"Morning's Peak?" Qiana asked. "You aren't facing the dragon called Volos, are you?"

"Yes," Aleksey said. "How did you know? Have you faced him before?"

"No," Qiana said. "But I've read about him. He's known to be manipulative, possessive, obsessive – and very powerful."

"Sounds like Darra's in more trouble than I thought," A.J. said.

"Is there anything you know about him that might be of use to us?" Aleksey asked. "A weakness of his we could exploit, or something like that?"

"Unfortunately, no," Qiana said. "The few people who have survived encounters with him didn't mention anything like that. But I can get you a map."

"Of what?" Aleksey asked.

"His lair," Qiana said. "And a route through the tunnels beneath it that leads into the lower levels of the Unseen Castle itself."

"Is that what it's called?" Kaleb asked, and Qiana nodded.

"The entrances are spelled, so you'll need to override his magic with your own," the elf woman said, and Kaleb nodded.

"Could you bring me any books or scrolls you have relating to the dragon?" Aleksey asked. "I'd like to know everything there is to know about him before I meet him in battle."

"Of course," Qiana said. She left, and the adventurers continued discussing the weapons with the king. Aleksey marveled at the craftsmanship of his sword, while Ennio split his time between A.J. and Trosclair, giving them both tips on the basics of wielding their new weapons. Kaleb was already skimming through the book on conjuring portals.

"Oh!" the king said, suddenly remembering something. "I have one more gift for you." The elven monarch crossed to a small chest on one of the shelves, opened it up, and pulled out a small purse. He brought it over to Aleksey and put it in the half-elf's hand with a smile.

"What's this?" Aleksey asked.

"The gems from the hilt of the DragonSword," the king replied. "There's still strong magic embedded in them – gifts from the gods."

"So I've heard," Aleksey said. "Thank you." Qiana came back with the promised map and another scroll, this one with the head of a dragon drawn across its top. The king and the elf woman saw them out to the front gates, where a four-horse carriage waited for them. Behind the carriage was another cart pulled by two more steeds. It was packed tight with crates of coal. Kaleb and Aleksey hugged Qiana goodbye, and the king signaled to one of his footmen. The elf stepped forward with a leather bag, the flap of which he opened to reveal stacks of gleaming gold bars. Aleksey thanked the king again and handed one of the gold bars to his brother. "For your door," he said, and Acasius nodded. The brothers hesitated but eventually moved in to hug one another, which was just a bit awkward for both of them. Then the adventurers climbed into the carriage, escorted by two of the king's guard. The first was an elf man who took a seat next to the driver, and the other was an elf woman who followed them inside the vehicle. Both guards were armed with bows and quivers of arrows forged from the DragonSword. Aleksey heard the driver call to the horses, and they pulled away from the gates.

Kaleb continued reading from his texts as the carriage rolled along toward the coast. Aleksey studied the map of the Unseen Castle, and A.J. stared out the window, deep in thought. On the cushioned bench across from them, the elven guard sat with her head leaned back and her eyes closed. Ennio sat in the middle, holding Trosclair's hand.

"What if we're too late?" the prince whispered to his boyfriend. "Or what if she and the dragon went somewhere other than this castle we're headed to?"

"We're not gonna be too late," Ennio said. "And if they're not at the castle, we'll find them some other way. Magic, maybe."

"It's just, if I lose her – before we've really gotten a chance to know each other – it'll prove Commandant Burke right," Trosclair said, and Ennio cocked his head in confusion. "Any prince who can't protect his own sister isn't fit to rule."

"I've never known anyone in my life more prepared to handle guiding a whole kingdom," Ennio said. "And I'm not just saying that because I love you, or because you were born to the position. And we will protect Darra." The soldier kissed the prince tenderly on his forehead.

"Ho!" Aleksey heard the driver call, and the carriage slowed to a crawl.

"We're here," A.J. said. "I can see our boat."

"Maera!" the guard up front called, and the elf woman's eyes snapped open. "We've got trouble!" The carriage came to a complete stop, and Maera climbed out of the vehicle first, bow in hand, followed by the half-elf and the teens. The other guard jumped down from the driver's seat and pointed at the *Sea Fairy*. It was still anchored in the shallows, but six bulky figures milled about on the deck. Four more figures stood on the deck of a smaller but newer looking steamship anchored a little further out. They were clad in skins and furs, with necklaces threaded with small bones, talons and fangs. Their skin was dirty, their beards were shaggy, and to a man their eyes were dull and black where there should have been color. One of the men spotted them and shouted to the others, who all turned to get a look at the adventurers and their escort.

"Who are they?" A.J. asked.

"Dread warriors!" Maera said, and she spat on the ground in disgust.

"Maera hates the dread forces," the other guard said. "She takes any opportunity to come to the coast so she can face them."

"Why do you hate them?" A.J. asked.

"Because they're evil and soulless," she answered.

"But they look like men," Kaleb said. "Bad men, sure, but just men."

"They used to be. But I wasn't speaking figuratively," Maera said. "To become a dread warrior, a man trades his soul to a demon."

"Why would anyone do that?" Trosclair asked.

"It makes them part demon," Aleksey said. "Stronger, and tougher to kill."

"You've faced them before?" Trosclair asked, and Aleksey nodded.

"I lived on this island for half my life," he said. "I've helped ward off more than a few incursions."

"Well, it looks like you're about to get a chance to do it again," the male elf said. Aleksey looked back to the *Sea Fairy*; the half dozen dread warriors had disembarked from the steamship into a rowboat headed for the shore. Maera nocked her bow and took aim.

"Wait!" her companion said, holding up a hand. "These arrows are too precious to lose firing at them on the water. Wait until they've reached the shore, so we can recover them after we kill them."

"Good idea," Maera said.

"You're sure that's the way this is gonna go?" Trosclair asked. "You can take them all?"

"We can take them," Ennio said as he drew his new broadsword. Already the grip felt comfortable in his hand, even familiar somehow, so finely shaped were the contours of the finger grooves on the hilt. Aleksey followed his lead and unsheathed his claymore.

"You and the prince should stay back," Aleksey said to A.J. "We can take six of them by ourselves." The pilot nodded.

"Stay beside him," Ennio said, grasping A.J.'s forearm for emphasis.

"I will," A.J. said.

"Kaleb, you cover our backs," Aleksey said, and the mage nodded.

The dread warriors' boat scraped into the shallows, and they jumped out and splashed down into the knee-high waves. They grunted and growled as they slogged toward the beach. Maera and the other guard took aim, and as soon the men's feet touched the sandy shore, they released their arrows. The first arrow struck the shoulder of one of the attackers, and the dread warrior cried out in pain and fell to his knees. Maera's arrow, however, struck right where she intended - in the middle of the chest of the largest of the men. He screamed as the arrow pierced his heart, and he began to disintegrate. Within a few seconds, he was just tiny specs of disappearing organic matter swirling away on the wind. Maera smiled as she and the other guard each nocked another arrow.

The four dread warriors still standing rushed forward, and Aleksey and Ennio ran ahead to meet them. Another pair of arrows zipped through the air at the soulless men. This time one of them was struck in the eye socket and fell; the other sunk deep into a dread warrior's thigh. The half-elf and soldier used the distraction to lunge at the remaining two men.

"Go for the heart or take off their heads!" Aleksey yelled at the soldier beside him. "It's the only way to kill them!" The dread warrior in front of Aleksey caught his thrust with the blade of his own falchion. Aleksey tilted his head. "You're stronger than you look," he said. The half-elf gripped the hilt of his sword with his free hand, and with his full strength, he managed to twist the falchion from the warrior's hand. "But so am I!" Aleksey swung his claymore with both hands, slicing it through the warrior's thick neck, and the body disintegrated as it fell to the ground. Just behind the warrior was the first of his companions to have fallen. He'd pulled the arrow from his shoulder, and although he had the use of only one arm, in it he held a bardiche that Aleksey found rather intimidating.

Ennio was locked in a fierce duel with his chosen opponent, who wielded a rapier with cunning. The dread warrior was smaller than his companions, but he was quicker, too. Every thrust and slash from Ennio brought a parry or countermove from him, and it was beginning to frustrate the soldier.

"Want a little help?" Kaleb asked as he popped up just behind Ennio. The young mage didn't wait for an answer, instead raising his hands and flashing a short sequence of gestures, followed by the words "*Kiris tun chal*!" The dread warrior's weapon transmuted from steel to pine wood from its tip down to its hilt, and the wicked man's black eyes widened with fear. Ennio slashed again, and the wooden sword was no match for the elven metal. The wooden sword broke in two in the dread warrior's hand, and the soulless man began to back up. Ennio lunged forward and stabbed the warrior in the chest, and he disintegrated like his larger companion before him.

Kaleb started to celebrate, but one of the warriors lunged at him and caught him by the collar. He was limping, half of an arrow shaft still sticking out from his leg, but he was sturdy enough to lift Kaleb off his feet with one hand and sling him several yards away onto the ground. Ennio brought his sword up as the warrior lifted a long, two-handed flail with a cylindrical spiked head.

Suddenly a loud scraping noise caught their attention, and all eyes turned toward the water. The dread warriors had rammed their steamship up into the shallows, beaching it. They leapt from the boat and waded to shore. Two of them didn't have weapons, but they all bore malicious expressions. Even the warrior with the arrow in his eye stood back up, grabbed ahold of the shaft sticking out of his head, and yanked it out. His eyeball and a good deal of connective tissue came along with it, and he wailed so horrifically that a flock of nearby seabirds launched into the air, squawking agitatedly. The dread warrior threw down the arrow and huffed his rage, and he and his reinforcements charged forward.

The elf man took out one of the new arrivals with a shot through the heart, but Maera's target swerved and turned sideways at the last moment. Her arrow scraped along his chest and nicked his neck, but no real damage was done. He kept moving forward, as did his companions, and soon Maera and the other guard were each fighting one of the newly arrived warriors bare handed, while the third stomped toward A.J. and Trosclair.

Aleksey was still trying to get an advantage on the warrior with the bardiche. He knew he was stronger than his opponent, but the length of the poleaxe gave the warrior's swings better leverage. Aleksey had been ducking or backing up steadily to avoid the wide arc of the curved blade, but suddenly the warrior swung the blade in a low arc. Aleksey's half-elf reflexes kicked in, and he jumped straight into the air, lifting his knees almost to his chest. The warrior's weapon sailed below his feet. When Aleksey landed, he spun and kicked the warrior in the head, then drove his sword through the man's chest. The warrior disintegrated - but his companion with the missing eye was standing not far behind him, ready to take up the fight.

"Unholy hells!" Aleksey cursed. "How many of you do I have to kill?"

"Our forces are infinite!" the dread warrior said as he charged at Aleksey, his sword swinging wildly.

Ennio and Kaleb had backed away from the man with the flail to stay out of reach of the swaths it cut through the air. The soldier grew tired of the retreating and stood his ground, and when the flail flew at him next, he swung his sword directly at it. The blade caught the flail on the head and cut into it a couple of inches. Ennio pulled, but the blade of his weapon was firmly lodged in between the spikes of the flail. Realizing that he couldn't get his weapon free, Ennio instead pulled on it, jerking the warrior forward unexpectedly. Ennio punched the man as hard as he could. The warrior just grinned, revealing his yellow, rotting teeth, which had been filed into sharp points. He backhanded Ennio, and the blow sent the soldier to the ground. The dread warrior stood over him. He yanked Ennio's sword from his flail and then raised his weapon above his head - as the tip of a knife pushed through his chest. The man's black eyes had just enough time to go wide as he disintegrated. Kaleb wiped the blade of the knife on the sleeve of his robe out of habit even though it had come out clean, and then he held out a hand to help Ennio to his feet.

A dread warrior with a flanged mace approached the prince and the pilot, who exchanged a quick worried look. The warrior brought the mace down in arc aimed at A.J.'s head, but the pilot raised his spear horizontally in both hands and blocked the blow. He was shocked at the warrior's strength, as well as at the fact that the lightweight metal of his shaft was able to withstand the strike. Trosclair threw a knife at the man, but it sailed harmlessly past his head, and the dread warrior laughed at him. "That's a nice crown, boy!" the man said. "I'll try it on after I kill you!" Ennio's broadsword slashed down the warrior's arm from behind, and the soulless man cried out and dropped the mace.

"I don't think you're going to do either of those things," the soldier said as he pointed his sword at the dread warrior's heart. "Hold him!" Ennio commanded, and A.J. and Kaleb each took one of the man's arms. The warrior struggled, but the young men managed to hold him still as Ennio drove his sword through his chest. The teens looked from one to the other, smiling, and then turned around just in time to see Aleksey deliver a killing blow to the warrior with the missing eye. Maera and the other guard had also subdued their enemies, and they had them flat on the ground, face-down, with arrows held against their backs. Aleksey and the teens approached them.

"Do you want me to finish it?" Aleksey asked.

"No," Maera said. "We always try to keep a few alive, to bring back to the castle for interrogations. There are some ropes in the bin beneath the bench in the carriage, if one of you wouldn't mind going to get them for us."

"On it," A.J. said as he turned and ran toward the vehicle.

Darra, Volos and Tarun were on their way back from Morning's Peak, each carrying paper shopping bags or other items they had purchased. They had been to *Shalah's*, a cobbler, a jeweler, and a tanner who crafted fine leathers in various forms. They also made a pass through an open air market with dozens of booths hawking everything from orbital clocks and other small apparatuses to foodstuffs and trinkets depicting the gods. Volos had insisted on buying literally everything Darra tried on at each shop. Now she carried two bags stuffed with skirts, pants, and blouses, another with two pairs of shoes with short, sensible heels she could run or fight in, and a final bag containing a round straw hat with glossy, preserved flowers and a lightweight, wooden carving of a tiny songbird attached to the wide brim. Darra thought the hat was a bit garish, but Volos insisted she buy it to protect her fair skin from the sun. She also wore a long coat in a princess cut - another of Volos' firm suggestions - made from bumpy, dark grayish-green alligator skins. It had been the most expensive item at the tanner's, having been imported from Vilmos. Volos carried a phonograph under one arm and several wax disc records in the other, a format Darra had never seen before. Trailing behind them a few feet, Tarun carried a sack with a pair of knee-high boots Darra had fancied, as well as two bags full of the ingredients the young woman needed to make dinner.

"You should have let me buy you some jewelry," Volos said.

"You've already spent enough on me for one day," Darra replied. "And besides, if I want jewels, I can always go rummaging through your treasure chamber."

"I've almost got it all cleared out," Tarun said.

"So that's what you spend your days doing," Darra said, glancing over her shoulder at the young man. "Clearing rocks off of piles and piles of gold?"

"And moving the gold up into the castle," Tarun said.

"It doesn't get boring?" Darra asked.

"It beats wandering around the forest, waiting to get eaten," Tarun said with a shrug.

"The jewels at the castle have all been worn by other women," Volos said, commanding Darra's attention again. "You deserve something crafted just for you. Maybe I'll commission a tiara."

"That's sweet," Darra said. "But I think I'd feel silly in it. And I'm supposed to be hiding out, remember? A crown would draw a lot of attention."

"There's no need to hide anymore, with me as your protector," Volos said. "And attention is something you should get used to."

"Why?" Darra asked. "Trosclair is the one who's going to be king. I'm just his sister."

"A princess is more than a relative of the king," Volos said. "She is a symbol of her kingdom's prosperity, and a role model for the young girls who look up to her. The example she sets with her life will guide her people through theirs."

"Oh," Darra said. "I hadn't thought about any of that. I'm still trying to get used to the idea of it all. I suppose it won't be fully real to me until Trosclair takes back the throne this summer."

"You don't have to wait, you know," Volos said.

"What do you mean?" Darra asked.

"The cities of men no longer use magic," Volos said. "This makes them vulnerable. If you asked it of me, I could easily storm the palace, kill the usurper, and restore your brother - and you - to your rightful positions."

"You could really do that?" Darra asked.

"I believe so," Volos said.

"You'd have to kill a lot of men," Darra said. "I wouldn't ask that of you."

"Lesser men die all the time," Volos said. "That's just the way war works. Don't rush to answer yet; give it some consideration before you decide."

"Okay," Darra said. "But if I let a dragon fight my battles for me, the people of DuVerres would likely think I was a witch and cast me out - or worse."

"Oh, Darra," Volos said, raising a hand to cup her chin. "I'd never let you suffer like that."

The *Sea Fairy* sped across the channel with A.J. again at the helm. Ennio had resumed his position in the engine room, and Aleksey and Kaleb were in the cabin. The mage sat at the small table, studying his new texts. The half-elf had stretched out on the sofa with a bucket beneath his sagging head. With all his companions thus occupied, Trosclair had chosen to sit down in the middle of the deck and watch the waves go by. He spotted a flock of shorebirds overhead and knew they were close to reaching the continent, so he got up and ducked inside the engine room. "We're almost there," he said.

"That's good," Ennio said as he wiped sweat from his brow

with the back of his hand. "I'll be glad to get out of here."

"You should've let me take a shift," the prince said. "I can shovel coal as well as any other person. And I want to find ways to help, since I'm obviously not going to be able to do anything with these." He gestured to the knives secured to his belt.

"You'll get better," Ennio said. "You've certainly got the cunning required to wield them. You just need to build muscle memory."

"But I made a fool of myself in the fight against those dread warriors," Trosclair said.

"Nobody expects you to become a warrior overnight," the soldier said as he moved in and put his hands on Trosclair's arms. "Besides, that's what you have me for."

"Everyone hold on to something!" A.J. yelled over his shoulder. The ship ran into a larger-than-average swell, and its bow jolted skyward several feet. The pilot had to grip the helm to keep from flying backwards. Kaleb almost tipped over in his chair, and Aleksey cursed as his bucket spilled its revolting contents across the cabin floor. Ennio grabbed ahold of one of the coal bins, which were secured to the deck, but Trosclair lost his footing and stumbled forward - straight toward the furnace. The soldier threw his arm out and caught the prince just in time to stop him from getting badly burned. Trosclair smiled up at Ennio gratefully, and the soldier silently thanked the gods that his boyfriend was so light.

Darra spent the early evening in the castle's kitchen, preparing the meal she'd promised Volos. She chopped vegetables and herbs and simmered them to perfection to create a stew. Next, she assembled a thick, sweet, milky pudding and carefully and artistically arranged a selection of fruits on top of it. (Acasius had stressed the importance of presentation in preparing foods, and she was careful to apply his teaching to this meal.) After the pudding was placed in the cooling pantry to set, she mixed, kneaded, rolled out and cut dough into square buns that rose quickly in the warmth of the room. Placing them in the oven, she started on the entrée - sliced, battered and fried *emonigondi*, a type of vegetable with a consistency similar to eggplant, but with a spicy, zesty kick to it.

When she was finished, she wandered the halls, looking for Tarun and Volos. She found the former first; he was in a lower level of the castle, in the chamber into which he had been transferring the dragon's gold and other valuables. She tried not to let the massive amount of gold, silver and jewels stun her the way it first had, but having Volos' wealth neatly arranged and laid out around this chamber somehow made it seem like even more wealth than it had appeared to be when in loose piles.

"Hey," she said by way of greeting. The former pilot smiled and placed the box of gold bars he was carrying neatly on top of a stack of similar boxes. "Dinner's ready."

"Oh," he said. "That's so kind of you. But I already ate."

"Really?" she asked, minor disappointment evident in her voice. "I didn't see you come in the kitchen."

"I, uh, have a few snacks squirreled away in my room," Tarun said. "I guess I forgot that you were cooking, and I filled up on them. Sorry."

"No, no," she said, waving away his apology. "It's fine. But you can still join us, and maybe take a nibble here or there, if my food entices you. Which it should, if I measured everything correctly. My uncle says the secret to good cooking is accurate measuring."

"I think Tarun just wants to finish up his work here and get to bed," Volos said, appearing behind Darra in the corridor. "Unless you've changed your mind?"

"Oh, uh, nope," Tarun said. "I'm still trying to get to bed early."

"Why?" Darra asked. "It's not like you have anywhere to be in the morning."

"I'm just tired," Tarun said, his eyes glancing at and away from Volos almost imperceptibly quickly.

"Okay, then," Darra said, fighting off a slight frown. "We'll save some for you to try tomorrow."

"I'd like that," Tarun said.

"Darra, my dear, you are too kind," Volos said. "Come, let's enjoy your feast before it gets cold." Volos held out his arm, and Darra placed her hand inside his elbow as he guided her back up the stairs to the dining hall. She'd already arranged the table for three at one end. Volos took his seat at the head of the table, and she excused herself to go retrieve the entrée, which she'd left warming on top of the oven. When she got back, she placed the covered platter down in the center of the table and picked up a ladle.

"Stew?" she asked, and Volos smiled and nodded his head in the affirmative. "My uncle calls this 'Twelve Whispers,' because the exact recipe is a closely guarded family secret."

"It smells lovely," Volos said. "As do you."

Darra blushed a little as she served up the stew to her host. Next, she offered him a bun, which she had spread with butter and drizzled with honey after taking it out of the oven. Volos accepted the bread with another wide - and oddly intense - smile. Finally, she removed the lid from the platter to reveal the *emonigondi* - and Volos' smile disappeared.

"What's this?" he asked.

"Emonigondi, battered and fried," she answered.

"Is there no meat?" Volos asked.

"Oh, I - I didn't make any," Darra said. "I don't really know how. My dad and I are vegetarians."

Volos thought for a few moments before he replied. "Darra, I appreciate the effort you've made tonight. I truly do. But I must have meat. It's... kind of a dragon thing."

"I - I didn't think," Darra said. "I'm sorry."

"It's fine," Volos said. "I'll make myself a steak after I've enjoyed the rest of this beautiful meal."

"You don't have to - if you're just eating it to be nice," Darra said as she sat down to Volos' left.

"Nonsense!" Volos said. "I just consider myself lucky that you cooked for me at all. I... once had a lover - many, many years ago - and her culinary skills were unrivaled. I've missed having a woman's touch in my life, both in the kitchen and in... other places."

Darra blushed again, deeper this time. She cleared her throat. "What happened to her?"

"She died," Volos said matter-of-factly. "And I was unable to prevent it. I consider it my greatest failing in life."

"I'm sure you did everything you could," Darra said, placing her hand on top of Volos' own. The dragon clasped her hand and leaned in as if to kiss Darra, but she pulled her hand away and leaned back into her chair.

"I'm sorry," Volos said. "I know you don't want to rush into anything romantic. I'm just so drawn to you, it's hard to restrain myself sometimes."

"Don't worry about it," Darra said as casually as she could manage. "Let's just enjoy the food and conversation."

"As you wish," the dragon said. He raised his glass in a toast. "To good food, good conversation, and good friends - which I hope we are now becoming." Darra raised her own glass and clinked it against Volos', smiling amiably - but she hoped not flirtatiously - back at her host.

Aleksey and the teens had boarded a train at the coast, departing in Middlestead only long enough to pick up Guardian and recruit Ani for their mission. Aleksey had really been hoping Borri would be available, but he'd been out hunting, as usual, and Ani had insisted on accompanying them in his place. Now, back on a train and with only a few hours to go until they reached Morning's Peak, the group was assembled in one of the two sleeping compartments to which they'd laid claim. It was cramped and stuffy with six people and a dog inside of it, but they required privacy to go over the details of their plan. Aleksey familiarized them with the layout of the Unseen Castle, and then he began formulating the specific steps he imagined would be necessary to face and defeat the dragon. It all centered around the incantation Qiana had given Kaleb, as well as the new spell the young mage had been working on since leaving the Elven Isles.

"Do you think you're up to it?" Aleksey asked, after Kaleb explained in detail what he hoped his spell would do.

"Honestly?" he said. "I'm not sure. Even attempting this spell will likely deplete my mystical energies for days, possibly even weeks. So my first time casting it will be in the moment."

"You've always come through when it really mattered, Kay," Aleksey said. "I'm sure this will be no different."

"I hope so," Kaleb said.

"Before I met you, I thought - I'd been taught - that magic was dangerous, evil even," Trosclair said to the tribal lad. "But you've shown me the importance and power of the magic in this world. I trust you, and I have faith that you'll be able to get the job done. I can't thank you enough for helping me save my sister."

Kaleb's mood lightened a little at the prince's kind words. "She's like a sister to me, too," he said.

"Then I guess that makes us all like family," Trosclair said, and they continued plotting their rescue attempt.

Later that night, after Darra had lain in bed awake for several hours, she got up and pulled on her boots. She pulled out her crossbow and slung her quiver around her shoulder. Then she made her way through the dark halls and stairwells of the castle until she reached its lowest level. She entered a large central chamber with four doors, one on each wall. Just as Tarun had said, there was an ice chamber that was magically kept at freezing temperatures; when she walked by this door, her breath became visible in front of her face. Next she came upon the door to the wine cellar, which had a cask and bottle carved into it. But being a novice drinker, she passed by it without exhibiting any interest. She made her way to the third door and, after a moment's hesitation during which she considered what might be behind it, she swung it open wide. It led to another set of stairs, the bottom of which she could not see in the darkness. She closed this door and moved on to the final one. It was obvious from the wooden beam locking this door in place from the outside that it led to the room whose mention had piqued her curiosity and prompted her to leave her bed in search of it: the dungeon. Darra started to lift the beam to open the door, but a noise behind her made her spin, her crossbow aimed ahead of her. Tarun was standing a few feet away from her, a horrified expression on his face.

"What are you doing down here?" he asked in a harsh whisper. "You're supposed to be in bed."

"I couldn't sleep," Darra said, lowering her weapon. "What about you? I thought you were going to bed early, yourself."

"I... remembered something," Tarun said. "Something I need to take care of."

Darra crossed her arms disbelievingly. "I think you're lying."

"Lying?" Tarun asked with a scoff. "What would I - Why would I lie to you?"

"Because Volos asked you to keep an eye on me, and keep me from coming down here," Darra said. Tarun couldn't hide his shock at the accuracy of her guess.

"That's - that's—"

"The truth," Darra stated flatly. "I can see it written all over your face." Tarun took a few steps forward and grabbed Darra by the arm.

"It isn't safe down here," he said. "You need to get back to your room, before he finds out." Darra shook off Tarun's hand.

"What's in the dungeon?" Darra asked.

"Nothing!" Tarun said a little too emphatically. "I already told you, it hasn't been used in years."

Darra moved back to the dungeon door. "Then I guess it won't matter if I look inside," she said as she lifted the wooden beam.

"No!" Tarun cried. He moved to try to stop her, but he was too late. The door creaked open as Darra tossed the beam aside. It clattered to the floor with a wooden echo. And from inside the dungeon, Darra heard a soft, pain-filled moan. "Darra, I'm begging you: Do not go in there! If you do, he'll know, and I won't be able to protect you."

"I don't need your protection," she said, lifting her crossbow for emphasis. Darra entered the dungeon and rushed over to the slumped form of a man sitting with his back to the wall. His face and shirt were covered in blood, both dried and fresh, and his eyes were half-closed, glossy and distant. "Are you alright?" she asked. The man opened his mouth and a strange, guttural sound came out of it–along with more blood, gushing forth from gums that had not a single tooth protruding from them, although some broken roots remained. He quickly closed his mouth again. "Good gods," Darra whispered. "Did Volos do this to you?" The man simply nodded. "Why?" The man pointed to the opposite wall, where a single long, sharp dragon's tooth lay on the floor. Darra took it all in, and then she held out her hand to the man. "Come on," she said. "I'll show you the way out." She helped the man to his feet and then led him out of the dungeon. Tarun had disappeared. She led the man to the door with the stairs and ushered him down them. He seemed hesitant, gesturing for her to come along with him. "I can't," she said. "I've got unfinished business here." The man nodded his understanding, turned, and began descending the stairs into the darkness. Darra shut the door and turned around just in time to see Volos and Tarun enter the central chamber.

"Darra," Volos said. "You shouldn't have come down here." The dragon noticed the open dungeon door, and his brows furrowed angrily. "You let him out."

"Of course I did!" Darra said. "You've tortured him enough!"

"I only did to him what he had done to me," Volos said. "There's an ancient saying one of my ancestors picked up in a distant realm. It goes something like, 'An eye for an eye, a tooth for a tooth.' It speaks to the necessity of revenge."

"My dad was right: you are a monster," Darra said. "A soulless, evil monster."

"I may not have a soul, but I do not consider myself a monster," Volos said. "And you don't either. I've shown you how I treat my friends."

"That means nothing when you treat other people like - like so much meat to carve up!"

"Hmph," Volos said. "I'd hoped you'd be more open-minded than that."

"Open-minded?" Darra practically shouted. "You tortured him! And you clearly enjoyed it!"

"I'm a dragon," Volos said. "It's in my nature. It's in yours, too; you just repress it."

"That's not true," Darra said. "I could never–"

"I grow weary..." Volos said in a booming voice that silenced the young woman. "Of trying to explain myself to a silly mortal girl!"

"So I guess you're over your little crush on me?" Darra asked in a sarcastic tone reminiscent of her father.

"On the contrary," Volos said. "I don't think I'll ever be 'over' you. Metaphorically speaking." The dragon made a strange face, twisting his head up toward the ceiling. "Tarun - someone is outside the front gate of the castle."

"How is that possible?" Tarun asked. "I thought it was hidden."

"There are some who have seen this castle and lived to tell the tale," Volos said. "Go. Take care of it. It is extremely important that Darra and I are not disturbed for the next few hours."

"Yes," Tarun said. "Of course." The former pilot took one last look at Darra, an apologetic expression on his face, and then he left to follow the dragon's orders.

"If you think you can keep me here without a fight, you're wrong," Darra said, raising her crossbow.

"I don't think it," Volos said. "I know it." The dragon's dark brown eyes suddenly began to glow crimson, and he commanded softly, "Drop it." Darra obeyed, and her crossbow fell to the floor. She stared down at her weapon in disbelief. "I'd hoped I could make you love me without resorting to magic," the dragon said. "But I kind of always knew it would come to this eventually."

"I'll never love you," Darra said. "You disgust me."

"I have found that love, while a pleasant experience, is not necessary for the duty you will perform me," the dragon said.

"And what's that?" Darra asked.

"You have the honor of being the woman who shall bear my children," he said. Darra's face set in a stern look of defiance. "Even if the thought disgusts you, as you say it does. Your mind may resist me, but your body will obey my commands."

"What about my body?" Aleksey growled as he tackled Volos from behind.

Tarun reached the courtyard that sat behind the front gate of the castle. It was a small, lovely garden and orchard, filled to overflowing with fruiting trees and shrubs, plots of various vegetables, flowers in every brilliant color, and vines and ivies clinging to the rock walls that enclosed it. Tarun rushed along the path through its center to the gate, which was hewn from metal and wood but was spelled to blend into the rocky surface of the mountain when viewed from the outside. And yet, in spite of this, Tarun could hear a soft knocking coming from the other side.

"Who's there?" he called out. When he received no answer, he scanned around the garden and spotted a shovel. Taking it up as a weapon, he placed his hand on the lever that would open the gate, took a deep breath to calm himself, and pulled downward. The gate began to slowly open, and Tarun raised his shovel over his shoulder and behind his head, like a baseball player readying his bat for a swing. But when the gate opened, the former pilot saw only the mountainside. "Come on out!' Tarun yelled. "I know you're still there!"

Suddenly Ani stepped into view from the left of the gate, a crossbow pointed at Tarun. He swung his shovel at her weapon, but Ani backed up a pace, and the shovel struck the gate. She aimed and squeezed the trigger, and a bolt fired at the former pilot. He dropped his shovel as he lurched sideways, and the bolt sailed past him. Ani grabbed another bolt from her quiver, but Tarun stalked toward her angrily and pulled the weapon from her hands before she could reload it. He threw it aside and continued toward the young woman, who was slowly backing away from him. "Whoever you are, you shouldn't have come here," Tarun said. "I don't want to hurt you, but–" A large rock slammed down on Tarun's head from behind, and the former pilot slumped to the ground.

Trosclair tossed the rock aside and knelt down beside Tarun's body. He held a finger out in front of the former pilot's nose and mouth. "He's breathing," Trosclair said, relieved the blow had not been lethal. "I thought for sure he was dead when you fired at him."

"I may not be as good a shot as Darra, but I can aim," Ani said. "I missed him on purpose."

"That's good," Trosclair said. "A.J. wouldn't have liked it if we'd killed his best friend."

"Right now, I'm more concerned about my best friend than his, to be honest," the young woman replied.

"I agree with that sentiment wholeheartedly," Trosclair said. "Which is why I'm going into the castle."

"But that's not the plan!" Ani said. "We're supposed to wait here and guard our exit while they face the dragon."

"I only agreed to that plan so Ennio wouldn't argue with me," Trosclair said. "I can't just stay here while my sister and my boyfriend are in mortal danger."

Ani thought about it for a split-second, then said, "Go. I'll keep the gate open." Trosclair nodded his thanks and dashed toward the steps that led into the castle.

Aleksey and Volos rolled around on the dirty chamber floor. The half-elf marveled at the dragon's strength; he'd rarely battled another humanoid creature with enough raw physical power to match his own. And while Aleksey allowed his fury to fuel every swing of his fists, the dragon seemed oddly in control of his emotions – if indeed he felt any – while he returned the blows.

Ennio and Kaleb rushed out of the door through which Darra had led the toothless man. The soldier rushed at Volos with his sword drawn, while Kaleb rolled up his sleeves and began gesturing and reciting the incantation Qiana had gifted him. Volos had Aleksey pinned to the floor; just as Ennio was closing in to stab his sword through the dragon's back, Volos stood and turned to face the soldier. Volos caught the blade of Ennio's sword in his hand, and he let out a scream of both pain and surprise as the blade sliced into his palm.

"That hurt!" Volos screamed, a look of confusion on his face; yet he still held tight to the soldier's weapon. "The DragonSword," he said, realization taking over his features. "You've re-forged it. No matter. You'll all be dead in an instant." Volos' eyes began to glow crimson, and he said simply, "Stop breathing." But Volos was shocked a second time when the soldier kept drawing air into his lungs. "Die!" Volos growled, but Ennio still stood, unaffected, and he finally pulled his sword from the dragon's grasp. It was then that the dragon saw Kaleb's own eyes, which were glowing amber, and recognized the gesture the young mage was making with an outstretched hand.

"So," the dragon snarled. "You've brought a mage along to block my magic. That must be how you got in without my noticing. Very well. There's more than one way to kill humans, and to tell the truth, I prefer doing it the old-fashioned way." Ennio thrust his sword at Volos' chest, but the dragon was swift enough to avoid the blow. He charged into Ennio and threw the soldier against the wall with all his force, and then he crossed toward Kaleb. A crossbow bolt whizzed through the air just in front of Volos' nose, and the dragon turned to find Darra ready with another bolt loaded and aimed at his heart.

"You missed," he said.

"That was just to get your attention," Darra replied. "The next one goes through your heart."

"By all means, give it your best shot," Volos taunted, ripping open his shirt to reveal the taut muscles of his chest. Darra fired again, and the bolt hit Volos directly over his heart - and bounced off his skin without leaving so much as a scratch. "I'm afraid your own weapons are not up to the task of killing a dragon, little lamb."

"Nobody calls her that but me," Aleksey said as he pulled a quiver of crossbow bolts from his shoulder and threw it at Darra's feet. "These should do the trick, honey." Darra stooped to pick up the quiver as her father lunged at Volos again. The dragon used the half-elf's momentum against him and swung him wildly at Kaleb. The mage faltered on the gesture which controlled his spell, and Volos felt his mystical energies surge back through his body. He stepped toward Darra and kicked the quiver of bolts across the chamber floor, and then he lifted her off her feet by her throat. She grabbed onto his wrists and pulled herself up enough to keep from being strangled, kicking and struggling against his impossible strength. His form began to shift and change, taking on aspects of his dragon body. Scales, sharp talons and fangs replaced smooth flesh, fingers and teeth. But there the transformation ended. "I wish I could take my true form. I'd eat your father and friends in front of you, then have my way with you as you wept for their loss. As it is, I'll just have to content myself with burning them alive, and letting you inhale their ashes."

The dragon drew in a long, deep breath – but before he could release his fiery exhalation, the door to the ice chamber flew open, and A.J. jumped out, clad head to toe in his pilot's uniform. The dragon dropped Darra and turned toward the pilot, spewing a thick spear of flames at him. But the fire did not slow A.J. down; he crossed to the dragon and slammed his fist into Volos' ribs. The large pink gem, twin of the one which had brought him to this world, fell out of the pilot's hand. It bumped against Volos's stomach as it fell, and immediately, otherworldly swaths of pink and purple energy began swirling around it. Soon a new portal was opened up beside the dragon. Kaleb said a few words in the old speak, gesturing wildly, and the portal began to pull Volos into it. The dragon fought with all his strength, but within a few seconds, he had disappeared into the portal.

"Are you alright?" Aleksey asked as he crossed to his daughter. "Did he hurt you?"

"He didn't get a chance," Darra said. "You showed up just in time. Just like I knew you would." She smiled lovingly at her father as A.J. removed his helmet.

"I'm just glad my suit is fireproof," the pilot said. "So I could actually help."

"Ennio!" Trosclair cried out from the stairs. He rushed over to his boyfriend, whom Kaleb was helping back to his feet. "Is it over?" the prince asked, and Ennio shook his head in the affirmative.

"Thank the gods," Ennio said. "We wouldn't have lasted much longer against him, even with Kaleb holding back his magic."

"Once again, you've saved us all, Kaleb," Darra said. "Thank you."

"You'd have done the same for me, if the situation were reversed," Kaleb said.

Suddenly talons appeared at the edges of the still-swirling portal – not the small talons of Volos' hybrid form, but the large talons that meant he had taken on his full natural form. The head of the dragon popped back through the portal, and the group fell back. The dragon's black eyes glowed crimson again, and a pulse of concussive energy spread out, knocking Aleksey and the young men off of their feet. Darra alone was unaffected by the magical assault.

"I may not... have much longer... in this realm," Volos said, the effort to hold himself in the middle of the portal clearly exhausting him. "But I can still... take you with me!" The dragon stretched his massive arm through the portal and swiped at Darra. She barely avoided the talons.

Trosclair had landed near the quiver of bolts made from the DragonSword, and he stood and called out his sister's name. She turned in time to see him throw the quiver through the air toward her – and disappear behind a spear of flames. She heard her brother's agonized wail as she caught the quiver.

"Trosc!" Darra yelled. "You shouldn't have done that!" she said, staring into Volos' eyes, as she quickly loaded a bolt.

"I told you once: Where I am now, there are no people," Volos said. "To bring you with me, I'll gladly exhaust my mystical energies and remain trapped here forever." He swiped his talons at her again, but she moved against the far wall to stay out of his reach. The move brought the dragon's torso partially through the portal, and Darra took aim again.

"Oh, Volos," she said, her voice sweetly mocking. "I'd never let you suffer like that." She fired, and the bolt flew into the flesh of the dragon's chest. Volos' eyes went wide, and he began to disintegrate. Within a few seconds, he was gone.

A few hours later, the adventurers were gathered in the courtyard of the castle as the sun rose over the mountains. "This place is amazing," Kaleb said. "I can literally feel the magic that runs through the castle." He bent down and plucked a plump, ripe strawberry. "Even the garden is mystically replenished," he said, and the others watched in amazement as the stem he'd plucked the strawberry from grew a new fruit within just a few seconds. Kaleb bit into the strawberry and smiled. "We could eat out of here forever, and never have to replant a single crop."

"Wait until you get a load of the bathrooms," Darra said. "That reminds me: Where is Tarun?"

"He's not here," A.J. said.

"That's my fault," Ani said. "I was watching him closely, I swear! Then I went to get Guardian, and when we got back, Tarun was just... gone."

"We'll follow his tracks in the morning," Aleksey said. "Right now, I think we all need a rest."

"I know I do," Trosclair said, lifting a bandaged arm and wincing at the effort.

"Don't try to move it yet," Ennio said. "It'll just make it worse."

"I'm sorry I couldn't heal you," Kaleb said. "My mystical energy is exhausted from the spell I cast on the gem to open the portal. But I should be at full strength again once I get some sleep. And more food. Can you manage until tomorrow?"

"I guess I'll have to," Trosclair said. "The salve you put on it really did help numb the pain, though. I just don't want it to scar... That probably sounds really vain, doesn't it?"

"Not at all," Darra said. "A king needs to look healthy, or his people will worry."

"I'm not a king yet," Trosclair said. "Although the gold in this castle will certainly go a long way toward buying me an army to take back the throne."

"And to that end, this castle will make a fine headquarters for us to plan your next moves," Aleksey said. "And it's everything I promised Guardian as well." The dog barked once, as if in recognition of her name, as she chased a large blue butterfly through the paths of the courtyard.

"It feels a little weird, killing Volos and then taking over his home," Darra said.

"Spoils of war, honey," Aleksey said. "You earned the right to live here, fair and square. Although you should have told me your plan before you left with Volos."

"I couldn't," Darra said. "I knew he'd been the one watching us – or watching me – and I couldn't take the chance that he'd know if I let you in on the plan."

"That's very clever," A.J. said.

"My girl is something of a genius, in case you hadn't realized," Aleksey said. "And there's enough gold to find a smaller house, if that's what you really want, sweetie."

"You better not!" Ani said. "I've already picked out my room."

"Your room?" Darra asked. "You mean you intend to stay with us?"

"Mm, I'll probably split my time between the inn and here," Ani said. "If you can pay me my lifetime's salary as your lady-in-waiting in advance, of course."

"Easy enough," Aleksey said with a smile.

A little while later, Aleksey and Kaleb had retreated to the kitchen to prepare breakfast. Ennio, Trosclair and Ani had taken it upon themselves to explore the castle more fully. Darra stayed in the courtyard, relaxing on a bench under a green apple tree. A.J. approached her cautiously.

"May I sit down?" he asked.

"Of course," she said, scooting over to make room for him.

"I never got the chance to apologize," the pilot said. "For keeping the truth from you."

"Thank you," Darra said. "It means a lot to hear you say that."

"Friends?" A.J. asked, holding his hand out.

"Friends," Darra agreed, giving his hand a firm shake. "I do realize what you did back there, you know."

"What do you mean?"

"You gave up your chance at getting back to your world to open that portal," Darra said. "How did you find the gem, anyway?"

"Kaleb did a spell to locate it," A.J. said. "It was with the rest of Volos' treasure. Once I had it, I waited in the ice chamber for your father and the others."

"Gods!" Darra exclaimed. "I forgot to mention – there's a man in the tunnels below the castle. I sent him down there just before the others showed up. He's probably lost, and he was hurt. We should find him – before something else in the tunnels does."

"Sounds like another adventure," A.J. said, standing. "I'm in." He offered his hand. Darra accepted it and hauled herself up, and the two set off to find the toothless man together.

Inside the *Morningstar*, chaos had erupted. Admiral Brandt had been woken as soon as the anomaly began to activate again, as per her orders, and she'd made it to the bridge in under a minute, still in her pajamas.

"Diagnostic?" she prompted.

"It seems to be at full strength, just like it was when it swallowed the shuttle," Gracie said excitedly.

"The vibrational frequency is slightly deviated from the initial readings," Myra said. "But I concur: the anomaly seems to be ready to execute its portal functionality."

"Admiral, do we have orders to move in?" the pilot asked. Admiral Brandt thought for a moment, looking to Myra and Gracie for guidance. When both women gave a subtle nod of their heads, the admiral smiled. "Full speed ahead!" she commanded, and the pilot and other bridge crew burst into activity.

The *Morningstar* sailed toward the anomaly and disappeared within its bright celestial energies.

EPILOGUE

Lucio's ship ran aground on the shores of the Dread Continent - albeit the wrong side of the continent, in terms of where the vampire was headed. He'd boarded the vessel in the dead of the night and made a feast out of its crew, so the vampire had been left to his own to navigate the violent waters of the open ocean - by night, of course, using the stars to discern the proper route. His navigational skills had become rusty, however, in the centuries that he'd lived in the Kingdoms of Man. He'd suffered months of being lost at sea, all alone, with nothing to feed on. He'd become so desperate for sustenance, he even considered draining a dolphin when he'd encountered a pod of the creatures, but the animals were too swift to submerge and avoid his attacks.

The vampire slogged onto shore and made straight for the lighthouse that had guided him inland. There was a small cottage beside the towering structure. He gathered some dry sticks and, rubbing them together at a speed only a vampire could have managed, he produced a flame. He then used that flame to set the cottage on fire, careful to leave the front door untouched by the blaze. When the family that lived inside emerged into the night, he set upon the man, his wife, and their two sons with an appetite that ensured their swift and painful deaths.

He knew the Dread Lord would be angry that he had killed the caretakers of the lighthouse. But Lucio also knew he would be rewarded, when he presented his master with the soldier's cloak, which he'd carried with him all this way. It was, after all, the key to finding the half-elf and his daughter.

Made in the USA
San Bernardino, CA
06 September 2019